GREAT
WEIRD TALES

14 Stories by Lovecraft, Blackwood, Machen and Others

Edited and with an Introduction
by S. T. Joshi

DOVER PUBLICATIONS, INC.
Mineola, New York

DOVER HORROR CLASSICS
GENERAL EDITOR: S. T. JOSHI

Bibliographical Note

Great Weird Tales: 14 Stories by Lovecraft, Blackwood, Machen and Others, first published by Dover Publications, Inc., in 1999, is a new selection of fourteen stories reprinted from standard editions.

Library of Congress Cataloging-in-Publication Data

Great weird tales : 14 stories by Lovecraft, Blackwood, Machen and others / edited and with an introduction by S. T. Joshi.
  p.   cm. — (Dover horror classics)
  Includes bibliographical references (p.   ).
  ISBN 0-486-40436-6 (pbk.)
  1. Horror tales, American. 2. Horror tales, English.   I. Joshi, S. T., 1958–   . II. Series.
PS648.H6G73   1999
813'.087308—dc21   98–35750
                                                                     CIP

Manufactured in the United States of America
Dover Publications, Inc., 31 East 2nd Street, Mineola, N.Y. 11501

Contents

Introduction

The "Golden Age" of Anglo-American weird fiction—roughly the period between 1880 and 1940—saw not merely a tremendous outpouring of work from many hands, including several writers not primarily known for the weird, but also the development of a variety of subgenres that display the full breadth and richness of this literary mode.

Edgar Allan Poe (1809–1849) will always remain the grandfather of the field, and his pioneering work in advancing the weird tale beyond the stale conventions of the Gothic novel gives him a place of eternal honor in this realm. Realizing that terror and mystery work best in short compass, and that psychological realism must be the foundation for a tale, however *outré* its actual events, Poe united an intensely morbid vision with a style of deliberately tortured artificiality to produce his imperishable masterpieces. In Ireland, Joseph Sheridan LeFanu (1814–1873) both displayed the continuing vigor of a reconstituted Gothicism in such a gripping novel as *Uncle Silas* (1864) and advanced the psychological acuity of Poe with "Green Tea," "Carmilla," and other shorter works.

These and other writers set the stage for a tremendous burst of superb weird writing in the last two decades of the nineteenth century. In many ways this recrudescence owed its existence precisely to the fact that weird fiction as such was not a well-defined genre; indeed, we designate much of this work as weird only by a kind of retrospective co-option.

Writers of all types engaged in the most widely utilized subset of weird fiction, that of supernatural horror. In this mode, the supernatural phenomena are presented as such, with little explanation as to their origin or manifestation. Although there is frequently an emphasis on the characters' emotional responses to the phenomena, such tales can nonetheless not be referred to as instances of psychological horror, for there is really no question that the supernatural has come into play (as there is, for example, in many of Poe's tales as well as in that prototype of ambiguity, Henry James's *The Turn of the Screw* [1898]). The American architect Ralph Adams Cram (1863–1942) might be thought a highly unlikely individual to produce a weird masterpiece, but his fabulously rare collection *Black Spirits and White* (1895) contains several gems, none better than that triumph of atmosphere, "The Dead Valley." The Scottish writer William Sharp (1855–1905) maintained a kind of literary split personality, writing sober critical works and poetry under his own name while producing wild tales and fantasies under the female pseudonym Fiona Macleod. "The Sin-Eater" draws upon that ancient Celtic bit of folklore, the sin-eater—the person who, by eating a cake left upon a corpse, takes away that corpse's sins so that the deceased's soul can ascend to Heaven. Many will recall the superb dramatization of this story on "Rod Serling's Night Gallery."

William Hope Hodgson (1877–1918) is a figure of importance in the field for being one of the first to write actual horror novels. *The House on the Borderland* (1908) is a potent short novel, while *The Night Land* (1912), although hampered by flaws in diction, is of astounding imaginative scope in its account of the pitiful remnants of the human race in the far future. Of his short stories, "The Voice in the Night" is perhaps the most celebrated, and a good example of Hodgson's specialization in horrors from the sea. He had himself served as a sailor in his youth, and his untimely death in World War I cut short a career of great promise.

Poe, as mentioned, had already pioneered the tale of psychological horror in such works as "The Tell-Tale Heart" and "The Black Cat." In these stories there is ambiguity retained to the end as to whether the supernatural comes into play or is merely an illusion engendered by a disturbed mentality. Other stories fall into a class of non-supernatural horror, where from the beginning there is no question of the naturalness of all the recorded events. Some critics—

most notably H. P. Lovecraft, who remains a towering figure both as a fictionist and as a theoretician in the field—have denied that such works belong within the realm of the weird at all; but such a categorical assertion must be tempered by a more flexible outlook. It is true that tales of this type tread perilously close to the suspense or mystery story; and it is also true that the mundane fear of murder or torture is very different from the transcendental fear of witnessing some appalling violation of natural law, as in supernatural fiction; but to deny such works—ranging from Poe's "A Cask of Amontillado" to Robert Bloch's *Psycho* (1959) and Thomas Harris's *The Silence of the Lambs* (1988)—a place in weird fiction would seem, at the very least, uncharitable.

Ambrose Bierce (1842–1914?) clearly followed Poe in emphasizing the terrors of an aberrant consciousness, and many of his best tales are wholly non-supernatural. Even his famous narratives of the Civil War can legitimately be incorporated within the domain of the weird for their grippingly intense portrayal of psychological terror. *Tales of Soldiers and Civilians* (1891), as finally arranged in his *Collected Works* (1909–12), does not contain a single supernatural story, these all being relegated to *Can Such Things Be?* (1893). But that latter volume in its original edition contained works of varying types, including such a piece of macabre humor as "My Favorite Murder." The whole of Bierce's writing—fiction, essays, journalism, poetry—is driven by a satiric vision bordering on misanthropy, and his four tales of "The Parenticide Club" (of which "My Favorite Murder" is the first) carry outrage to conventional morals about as far as it is possible to carry it.

Bierce's friend W. C. Morrow (1853–1923) produced a somewhat more orthodox, but scarcely less compelling, tale of non-supernatural horror in "His Unconquerable Enemy," a potent vignette from his rare collection, *The Ape, the Idiot and Other People* (1897), which is perhaps best known for its inclusion of the proto-science-fiction story "The Monster Maker."

Weird fiction at its best transcends the chilling emotion of horror and attains something akin to religious awe. Horror, disgust, and repulsion dampen the spirit; awe raises it to a kind of mystic union with the universe. Two of the towering figures in classic weird fiction—Algernon Blackwood (1869–1951) and Arthur Machen (1863–1947)—sought in their best work to achieve that sense of awe, and in many cases did achieve it. Machen's "The Inmost Light" (in which a scientific experiment aims at nothing less than the extraction of a human soul) and Blackwood's "The Man Whom the Trees Loved" (in which a man's spirit is ultimately absorbed by the trees surrounding his estate) are two of the most ethereal and intangible works one could ever read, and in themselves justify the very existence of weird fiction. Only in this mode can such delicate effects be attained; only by the abandonment of conventional realism of setting, character, and incident can such delicate emotional and imaginative sensations be evoked.

It is difficult to speak in small compass of the work of Machen and Blackwood. The former, a Welshman, wrote prodigally in every literary mode from short story to treatise; but the works by which he will be remembered are his tales and novels of horror—*The Three Impostors* (1895), *The House of Souls* (1906), *The Terror* (1917), and others—his exquisite novel, *The Hill of Dreams* (1907), and his three autobiographies. Blackwood also wrote voluminously, and concentrated more in the weird than Machen; indeed, the conjoined quality and quantity of his output may make him the greatest weird writer in literary history. One only need recite a few of his collections and novels—*The Listener and Other Stories* (1907), *John Silence—Physician Extraordinary* (1908), *The Centaur* (1911), *Incredible Adventures* (1914)—to suggest the breadth of his achievement.

The "fantasy" tale is perhaps the most nebulous of all the subsets of weird fiction. In the strictest sense, a fantasy involves the wholesale creation of an imagined realm that may or may not have any resemblance to the known world—such things as the Pegana of Lord Dunsany or the Middle-Earth of J. R. R. Tolkien. In a looser sense, however, fantasy refers to any fictional work where the bounds of realism are transgressed but where little effort is made—as in supernatural horror—to convince the reader of the actual existence of the unreal. Such works are frequently very close to fairy tales, parables, or allegories, but they can be no less powerful for all that. "The King's Messenger" by F. Marion Crawford (1854–1909)—a story curiously omitted from his posthumous collection of weird tales, *Wandering Ghosts* (1911)—features a delicacy of touch prototypical of fantasy, even where, as in this instance, the outcome is known far ahead of the conclusion. Crawford's two Arabian fantasies—*Zoroaster* (1885) and *Khaled* (1891)—exhibit a somewhat similar atmosphere.

Of the work of Lord Dunsany (1878–1957), it is similarly difficult to speak without lapsing into transports of ecstasy; for this Irish writer is unquestionably the most significant fantasy writer in all literature, not excluding Tolkien. The stupendous imagination revealed in his early tales—collected in *The Gods of Pegana* (1905), *Time and the Gods* (1906), *The Sword of Welleran* (1908), *A Dreamer's Tales* (1910), and other volumes—would itself be sufficient to give him a revered place in the field; but Dunsany went on to write a dozen novels, two score plays, and hundreds of stories, essays, and poems, all endowed with that ethereal touch of fantasy that seems to come naturally to the Irish. The fact that nearly the whole of his work is out of print is a tragedy of the first order.

M. P. Shiel (1865–1947) also wrote bountifully, but much more unevenly than Dunsany or Blackwood. Perhaps his greatest work is the novel *The Purple Cloud* (1901), the ultimate "last man on earth" story. Lovecraft referred to "Xélucha" as a "noxiously hideous fragment," and each term of that expression is fitting. This piece of morbidity has no other purpose than the evocation of bizarre images in the most tortured of prose-poetry, and as such, it admirably fulfills its intention.

Two tales by disciples of Lovecraft, Frank Belknap Long (1901–1994) and R. H. Barlow (1918–1951), complete the section of fantasy tales. "The Eye Above the Mantel" is a sonorous prose-poem written while Long was still a teenager, and demonstrates how much weird fiction relies upon verbal witchery for its effects. It is rather sad to note that Long rarely exceeded this early effort in all the novels and stories he subsequently wrote in his lengthy career. Barlow's "A Dim-Remembered Story" displays a mastery of diction and conception that is similarly impressive for a teenager. Although several of his other stories were clearly revised by Lovecraft, all the documentary evidence points to Barlow as the sole author of this brooding masterpiece, in spite of its dedication to Lovecraft. We shall never know what dark jewels Barlow might have written had he not cut short his life by suicide.

If, from one side, the weird tale comes close to the mystery or suspense story, from another side it finds itself cheek by jowl with the science fiction tale. Of course, science fiction as a distinct genre only came into existence around the 1920s, but it had a variety of precursors and predecessors. When a weird tale is based upon some scientific principle or some extrapolated advance of science, or when scientific justification for the weird phenomena is supplied, then it can be said to be a proto- or pseudo-science-fiction story. Fitz-James O'Brien (1828–1862), although writing decades earlier than most of the other writers in this volume, produced several tales of this sort. "What Was It?" anticipates by many years several later accounts of invisible monsters (Bierce's "The Damned Thing," Blackwood's "The Wendigo," Lovecraft's "The Dunwich Horror"). As for "The Diamond Lens," this compelling novelette shows how often beauty and terror can be linked, each enhancing the other. O'Brien's death in the Civil War cut short a career that might have rivalled Poe's or Bierce's.

It would be difficult to compile an anthology of "Golden Age" weird fiction without including the work of H. P. Lovecraft (1890–1937), who in many ways subsumed the best features of his predecessors while at the same time pointing the way to future development. Indeed, Lovecraft's central contribution was the fusion of conventional supernaturalism with the burgeoning field of science fiction, the result being an indefinable compound that we can designate only as a Lovecraftian tale. "Facts Concerning the Late Arthur Jermyn and His Family" (1921) is an early precursor of such later ventures as "The Call of Cthulhu," "The Colour Out of Space," *At the Mountains of Madness,* and "The Shadow Out of Time." Lovecraft's dominant achievement—not so much evident in "Arthur Jermyn," with its emphasis on anthropological horror, as in his later novelettes and short novels—was the transference of the locus of fear from the mundane world to the illimitable gulfs of space. His chosen term for this tendency—"cosmicism"—unites horror, repulsion, and awe into an inextricable amalgam.

The half-century that has followed the "Golden Age" of weird fiction has certainly seen its share of masters: Robert Aickman with his "strange stories"; Shirley Jackson, with her haunting tales and novels of emotionally disturbed personalities; Robert Bloch and his psychological thrillers; and the contemporary work of Stephen King, Peter Straub, Clive Barker, Anne Rice, T. E. D. Klein, Thomas Ligotti, Dennis Etchison, and—preeminently—Ramsey Campbell, who in his wondrous prolificity is challenging even Algernon Blackwood for supremacy in this realm. These writers form a worthy "Silver Age" to the titans they have succeeded, and their work would perhaps be the more compelling if they drew somewhat more upon the great legacy of weird writing than most

of them are now doing. Many readers and writers have a sadly trun-
cated memory and fail to take note of the tradition in which they
operate; but the rich legacy of weird fiction over the last century
and a half should not only provide welcome nourishment for future
generations of writers but untold pleasures for readers of the present and future. All that is required is that it be brought to their
attention.

S. T. JOSHI

New York City
July 1996

I. Tales of Supernatural Horror

The Dead Valley

Ralph Adams Cram

I have a friend, Olof Ehrensvärd, a Swede by birth, who yet, by reason of a strange and melancholy mischance of his early boyhood, has thrown his lot with that of the New World. It is a curious story of a headstrong boy and a proud and relentless family: the details do not matter here, but they are sufficient to weave a web of romance around the tall yellow-bearded man with the sad eyes and the voice that gives itself perfectly to plaintive little Swedish songs remembered out of childhood. In the winter evenings we play chess together, he and I, and after some close, fierce battle had been fought to a finish—usually with my own defeat—we fill our pipes again, and Ehrensvärd tells me stories of the far, half-remembered days in the fatherland, before he went to sea; stories that grow very strange and incredible as the night deepens and the fire falls together, but stories that, nevertheless, I fully believe.

One of them made a strong impression on me, so I set it down here, only regretting that I cannot reproduce the curiously perfect English and the delicate accent which to me increased the fascination of the tale. Yet, as best as I can remember it, here it is.

"I never told you how Nils and I went over the hills to Hallsberg, and how we found the Dead Valley, did I? Well, this is the way it happened. I must have been about twelve years old, and Nils Sjöberg, whose father's estate joined ours, was a few months younger. We were inseparable just at that time, and whatever we did, we did together.

"Once a week it was market day in Engelholm, and Nils and I

went always there to see the strange sights that the market gathered from all the surrounding country. One day we quite lost our hearts, for an old man from across the Elfborg had brought a little dog to sell, that seemed to us the most beautiful dog in all the world. He was a round, woolly puppy, so funny that Nils and I sat down on the ground and laughed at him, until he came and played with us in so jolly a way that we felt that there was only one thing really desirable in life, and that was the little dog of the old man from across the hills. But alas! we had not half money enough wherewith to buy him, so we were forced to beg the old man not to sell him before the next market day, promising that we would bring the money for him then. He gave us his word, and we ran home very fast and implored our mothers to give us money for the little dog.

"We got the money, but we could not wait for the next market day. Suppose the puppy should be sold! The thought frightened us so that we begged and implored that we might be allowed to go over the hills to Hallsberg where the old man lived, and get the little dog ourselves, and at last they told us we might go. By starting early in the morning we should reach Hallsberg by three o'clock, and it was arranged that we should stay there that night with Nils's aunt, and, leaving by noon the next day, be home again by sunset.

"Soon after sunrise we were on our way, after having received minute instructions as to just what we should do in all possible and impossible circumstances, and finally a repeated injunction that we should start for home at the same hour the next day, so that we might get safely back before nightfall.

"For us, it was magnificent sport, and we started off with our rifles, full of the sense of our very great importance: yet the journey was simple enough, along a good road, across the big hills we knew so well, for Nils and I had shot over half the territory this side of the dividing ridge of the Elfborg. Back of Engelholm lay a long valley, from which rose the low mountains, and we had to cross this, and then follow the road along the side of the hills for three or four miles, before a narrow path branched off to the left, leading up through the pass.

"Nothing occurred of interest on the way over, and we reached Hallsberg in due season, found to our inexpressible joy that the little dog was not sold, secured him, and so went to the house of Nils's aunt to spend the night.

"Why we did not leave early on the following day, I can't quite remember; at all events, I know we stopped at a shooting range just outside of the town, where most attractive pasteboard pigs were sliding slowly through painted foliage, serving so as beautiful marks. The result was that we did not get fairly started for home until afternoon, and as we found ourselves at last pushing up the side of the mountain with the sun dangerously near their summits, I think we were a little scared at the prospect of the examination and possible punishment that awaited us when we got home at midnight.

"Therefore we hurried as fast as possible up the mountain side, while the blue dusk closed in about us, and the light died in the purple sky. At first we had talked hilariously, and the little dog had leaped ahead of us with the utmost joy. Latterly, however, a curious oppression came on us; we did not speak or even whistle, while the dog fell behind, following us with hesitation in every muscle.

"We had passed through the foothills and the low spurs of the mountains, and were almost at the top of the main range, when life seemed to go out of everything, leaving the world dead, so suddenly silent the forest became, so stagnant the air. Instinctively we halted to listen.

"Perfect silence,—the crushing silence of deep forests at night; and more, for always, even in the most impenetrable fastnesses of the wooded mountains, is the multitudinous murmur of little lives, awakened by the darkness, exaggerated and intensified by the stillness of the air and the great dark: but here and now the silence seemed unbroken even by the turn of a leaf, the movement of a twig, the note of night bird or insect. I could hear the blood beat through my veins; and the crushing of the grass under our feet as we advanced with hesitating steps sounded like the falling of trees.

"And the air was stagnant,—dead. The atmosphere seemed to lie upon the body like the weight of sea on a diver who had ventured too far into its awful depths. What we usually call silence seems so only in relation to the din of ordinary experience. This was silence in the absolute, and it crushed the mind while it intensified the senses, bringing down the awful weight of inextinguishable fear.

"I know that Nils and I stared towards each other in abject terror, listening to our quick, heavy breathing, that sounded to our acute senses like the fitful rush of waters. And the poor little dog we were leading justified our terror. The black oppression seemed to crush him even as it did us. He lay close on the ground, moaning feebly, and dragging himself painfully and slowly closer to Nils's feet. I think this exhibition of utter animal fear was the last touch, and must inevitably have blasted our reason—mine anyway; but just then, as we stood quaking on the bounds of madness, came a sound, so awful, so ghastly, so horrible, that it seemed to rouse us from the dead spell that was on us.

"In the depth of the silence came a cry, beginning as a low, sorrowful moan, rising to a tremulous shriek, culminating in a yell that seemed to tear the night in sunder and rend the world as by a cataclysm. So fearful was it that I could not believe it had actual existence: it passed previous experience, the powers of belief, and for a moment I thought it the result of my own animal terror, an hallucination born of tottering reason.

"A glance at Nils dispelled this thought in a flash. In the pale light of the high stars he was the embodiment of all possible human fear, quaking with an ague, his jaw fallen, his tongue out, his eyes protruding like those of a hanged man. Without a word we fled, the panic of fear giving us strength, and together, the little dog caught close in Nils's arms, we sped down the side of the cursed mountains, —anywhere, goal was of no account: we had but one impulse—to get away from that place.

"So under the black trees and the far white stars that flashed through the still leaves overhead, we leaped down the mountain side, regardless of path or landmark, straight through the tangled underbrush, across mountain streams, through fens and copses, anywhere so only that our course was downward.

"How long we ran thus, I have no idea, but by and by the forest fell behind, and we found ourselves among the foothills, and fell exhausted on the dry short grass, panting like tired dogs.

"It was lighter here in the open, and presently we looked around to see where we were, and how we were to strike out in order to find the path that would lead home. We looked in vain for a familiar sign. Behind us rose the great wall of black forest on the flank of the mountain: before us lay the undulating mounds of low foothills, unbroken by trees or rocks, and beyond, only the fall of black sky bright with multitudinous stars that turned its velvet depth to a luminous gray.

"As I remember, we did not speak to each other once: the terror was too heavy on us for that, but by and by we rose simultaneously and started out across the hills.

"Still the same silence, the same dead, motionless air—air that was at once sultry and chilling: a heavy heat struck through with an icy chill that felt almost like the burning of frozen steel. Still carrying the helpless dog, Nils pressed on through the hills, and I followed close behind. At last, in front of us, rose a slope of moor touching the white stars. We climbed it wearily, reached the top, and found ourselves gazing down into a great, smooth valley, filled half way to the brim with—what?

"As far as the eye could see stretched a level plain of ashy white, faintly phosphorescent, a sea of velvet fog that lay like motionless water, or rather like a floor of alabaster, so dense did it appear, so seemingly capable of sustaining weight. If it were possible, I think that sea of dead white mist struck even greater terror into my soul than the heavy silence or the deadly cry—so ominous was it, so utterly unreal, so phantasmal, so impossible, as it lay there like a dead ocean under the steady stars. Yet through that mist *we must go!* there seemed no other way home, and, shattered with abject fear, mad with the one desire to get back, we started down the slope to where the sea of milky mist ceased, sharp and distinct around the stems of the rough grass.

"I put one foot into the ghostly fog. A chill as of death struck through me, stopping my heart, and I threw myself backward on the slope. At that instant came again the shriek, close, close, right in our ears, in ourselves, and far out across that damnable sea I saw the cold fog lift like a waterspout and toss itself high in writhing convolutions towards the sky. The stars began to grow dim as thick vapor swept across them, and in the growing dark I saw a great, watery moon lift itself slowly above the palpitating sea, vast and vague in the gathering mist.

"This was enough: we turned and fled along the margin of the white sea that throbbed now with fitful motion below us, rising, rising, slowly and steadily, driving us higher and higher up the side of the foothills.

"It was a race for life; that we knew. How we kept it up I cannot understand, but we did, and at last we saw the white sea fall behind us as we staggered up the end of the valley, and then down into a region that we knew, and so into the old path. The last thing I remember was hearing a strange voice, that of Nils, but horribly changed, stammer brokenly, 'The dog is dead!' and then the whole world turned around twice, slowly and resistlessly, and consciousness went out with a crash.

"It was some three weeks later, as I remember, that I awoke in my own room, and found my mother sitting beside the bed. I could not think very well at first, but as I slowly grew strong again, vague flashes of recollection began to come to me, and little by little the whole sequence of events of that awful night in the Dead Valley came back. All that I could gain from what was told me was that three weeks before I had been found in my own bed, raging sick, and that my illness grew fast into brain fever. I tried to speak of the dread things that had happened to me, but I saw at once that no one looked on them save as the hauntings of a dying frenzy, and so I closed my mouth and kept my own counsel.

"I must see Nils, however, and so I asked for him. My mother told me that he also had been ill with a strange fever, but that he was now quite well again. Presently they brought him in, and when we were alone I began to speak to him of the night on the mountain. I shall never forget the shock that struck me down on my pillow when the boy denied everything: denied having gone with me, ever having heard the cry, having seen the valley, or feeling the deadly chill of the ghostly fog. Nothing would shake his determined ignorance, and in spite of myself I was forced to admit that his denials came from no policy of concealment, but from blank oblivion.

"My weakened brain was in a turmoil. Was it all but the floating phantasm of delirium? Or had the horror of the real thing blotted Nils's mind into blankness so far as the events of the night in the Dead Valley were concerned? The latter explanation seemed the only one, else how to explain the sudden illness which in a night had struck us both down? I said nothing more, either to Nils or to my own people, but waited, with a growing determination that, once well again, I would find that valley if it really existed.

"It was some weeks before I was really well enough to go, but finally, late in September, I chose a bright, warm, still day, the last smile of the dying summer, and started early in the morning along the path that led to Hallsberg. I was sure I knew where the trail struck off to the right, down which we had come from the valley of dead water, for a great tree grew by the Hallsberg path at the point where, with a sense of salvation, we had found the home road. Presently I saw it to the right, a little distance ahead.

"I think the bright sunlight and the clear air had worked as a tonic to me, for by the time I came to the foot of the great pine, I had quite lost faith in the verity of the vision that haunted me, believing at last that it was indeed but the nightmare of madness. Nevertheless, I turned sharply to the right, at the base of the tree, into a narrow path that led through a dense thicket. As I did so I tripped over something. A swarm of flies sung into the air around me, and looking down I saw the matted fleece, with the poor little bones thrusting through, of the dog we had bought in Hallsberg.

"Then my courage went out with a puff, and I knew that it was all true, and that now I was frightened. Pride and the desire for adventure urged me on, however, and I pressed into the close thicket that barred my way. The path was hardly visible: merely the worn road of some small beasts, for, though it showed in the crisp grass, the bushes grew thick and hardly penetrable. The land rose slowly, and rising grew clearer, until at last I came out on a great slope of hill, unbroken by trees or shrubs, very like my memory of that rise of land we had topped in order that might find the dead valley and the icy fog. I looked at the sun; it was bright and clear, and all around insects were humming in the autumn air, and birds were darting to and fro. Surely there was no danger, not until after nightfall at least; so I began to whistle, and with a rush mounted the last crest of brown hill.

"There lay the Dead Valley! A great oval basin, almost as smooth and regular as though made by man. On all sides the grass crept over the brink of the encircling hills, dusty green on the crests, then fading into ashy brown, and so to a deadly white, this last color forming a thin ring, running in a long line around the slope. And then? Nothing. Bare, brown, hard earth, glittering with grains of alkali, but otherwise dead and barren. Not a tuft of grass, not a stick of brushwood, not even a stone, but only the vast expanse of beaten clay.

"In the midst of the basin, perhaps a mile and a half away, the level expanse was broken by a great dead tree, rising leafless and gaunt into the air. Without a moment's hesitation I started down into the valley and made for this goal. Every particle of fear seemed to have left me, and even the valley itself did not look so very terrifying. At all events, I was driven by an overwhelming curiosity, and there seemed to be but one thing in the world to do,—to get to that Tree! As I trudged along over the hard earth, I noticed that the multitudinous voices of birds and insects had died away. No bee or butterfly hovered through the air, no insects leaped or crept over the dull earth. The very air itself was stagnant.

"As I drew near the skeleton tree, I noticed the glint of sunlight

on a kind of white mound around its roots, and I wondered curiously. It was not until I had come close that I saw its nature.

"All around the roots and barkless trunk was heaped a wilderness
of little bones. Tiny skulls of rodents and of birds, thousands of
them, rising about the dead tree and streaming off for several yards
in all directions, until the dreadful pile ended in isolated skulls and
scattered skeletons. Here and there a larger bone appeared,—the
thigh of a sheep, the hoofs of a horse, and to one side, grinning
slowly, a human skull.

"I stood quite still, staring with all my eyes, when suddenly the
dense silence was broken by a faint, forlorn cry high over my head.
I looked up and saw a great falcon turning and sailing downward
just over the tree. In a moment more she fell motionless on the
bleaching bones.

"Horror struck me, and I rushed for home, my brain whirling, a
strange numbness growing in me. I ran steadily, on and on. At last
I glanced up. Where was the rise of the hill? I looked around wildly.
Close before me was the dead tree with its pile of bones. I had circled
it round and round, and the valley wall was still a mile and a half away.

"I stood there dazed and frozen. The sun was sinking, red and
dull, towards the line of hills. In the east the dark was growing fast.
Was there still time? *Time!* It was not *that* I wanted, it was *will!* My
feet seemed clogged as in a nightmare. I could hardly drag them
over the barren earth. And then I felt the slow chill creeping
through me. I looked down. Out of the earth a thin mist was rising,
collecting in little pools that grew ever larger until they joined here
and there, their currents swirling slowly like thin blue smoke. The
western hills halved the copper sun. When it was dark I should
hear that shriek again, and then I should die. I knew that, and with
every remaining atom of will I staggered towards the red west
through the writhing mist that crept clammily around my ankles,
retarding my steps.

"And as I fought my way off from the Tree, the horror grew, until
at last I thought I was going to die. The silence pursued me like
dumb ghosts, the still air held my breath, the hellish fog caught at
my feet like cold hands.

"But I won! though not a moment too soon. As I crawled on my
hands and knees up the brown slope, I heard, far away and high in
the air, the cry that already had almost bereft me of reason. It was
faint and vague, but unmistakable in its horrible intensity. I glanced

behind. The fog was dense and pallid, heaving undulously up the brown slope. The sky was gold under the setting sun, but below was the ashy gray of death. I stood for a moment on the brink of this sea of hell, and then leaped down the slope. The sunset opened before me, the night closed behind, and as I crawled home weak and tired, darkness shut down on the Dead Valley."

The Sin-Eater

Fiona Macleod

SIN.
Taste this bread, this substance; tell me
Is it bread or flesh?
                    [*The* SENSES *approach.*
                THE SMELL.
Its smell
Is the smell of bread.
                SIN.
Touch, come. Why tremble?
Say what's this thou touchest?
                THE TOUCH.
Bread.
                SIN.
Sight, declare what thou discernest
In this object.
                THE SIGHT.
Bread alone.
                CALDERON: *Los Encantos de la Culpa.*

A wet wind out of the south mazed and moaned through the sea-mist that hung over the Ross. In all the bays and creeks was a continuous weary lapping of water. There was no other sound anywhere.

Thus was it at daybreak; it was thus at noon; thus was it now in the darkening of the day. A confused thrusting and falling of sounds through the silence betokened the hour of the setting. Curlews wailed in the mist; on the seething limpet-covered rocks the skuas and terns screamed, or uttered hoarse rasping cries. Ever and again the prolonged note of the oystercatcher shrilled against the air, as an echo flying blindly along a blank wall of cliff. Out of weedy places, wherein the tide sobbed with long gurgling moans, came at intervals the barking of a seal.

Inland by the hamlet of Contullich, there is a reedy tarn called the Loch-a-chaoruinn.[1] By the shores of this mournful water a man moved. It was a slow, weary walk, that of the man, Neil Ross. He had come from Duninch, thirty miles to the eastward, and had not rested foot, nor eaten, nor had word of man or woman since his going west an hour after dawn.

At the bend of the loch nearest the clachan he came upon an old woman carrying peat. To his reiterated question as to where he was, and if the tarn were Feur-Lochan above Fionnaphort, that is, on the strait of Iona on the west side of the Ross of Mull, she did not at first make any answer. The rain trickled down her withered brown face, over which the thin grey locks hung limply. It was only in the deep-set eyes that the flame of life still glimmered, though that dimly.

The man had used the English when first he spoke, but as though mechanically. Supposing that he had not been understood, he repeated his question in the Gaelic.

After a minute's silence the old woman answered in the native tongue, but only to put a question in return.

"I am thinking it is a long time since you have been in Iona?"

The man stirred uneasily.

"And why is that, mother?" he asked, in a weak voice hoarse with damp and fatigue; "how is it you will be knowing that I have been in Iona at all?"

"Because I knew your kith and kin there, Neil Ross."

"I have not been hearing that name, mother, for many a long year. And as for the old face o' you, it is unbeknown to me."

"I was at the naming of you, for all that. Well do I remember the day that Silis Macallum gave you birth; and I was at the house on the croft of Ballyrona when Murtagh Ross, that was your father, laughed. It was an ill laughing, that."

"I am knowing it. The curse of God on him!"

---

[1] *Contullich* i.e., Ceann-nan-tulaich, "the end of the hillocks." *Loch-a-chaoruinn* means the loch of the rowan-trees.

"'T is not the first, nor the last, though the grass is on his head three years agone now."

"You that know who I am will be knowing that I have no kith or kin now on Iona?"

"Ay, they are all under grey stone or running wave. Donald your brother, and Murtagh your next brother, and little Silis, and your mother Silis herself and your two brothers of your father, Angus and Ian Macallum, and your father Murtagh Ross, and his lawful childless wife Dionaid, and his sister Anna, one and all they lie beneath the green wave or in the brown mould. It is said there is a curse upon all who live at Ballyrona. The owl builds now in the rafters, and it is the big sea-rat that runs across the fireless hearth."

"It is there I am going."

"The foolishness is on you, Neil Ross."

"Now it is that I am knowing who you are. It is old Sheen Macarthur I am speaking to."

"*Tha mise*—it is I."

"And you will be alone now, too, I am thinking, Sheen?"

"I am alone. God took my three boys at the one fishing ten years ago, and before there was moonrise in the blackness of my heart my man went. It was after the drowning of Anndra that my croft was taken from me. Then I crossed the Sound, and shared with my widow sister, Elsie McVurie, till *she* went; and then the two cows had to go; and I had no rent; and was old."

In the silence that followed, the rain dribbled from the sodden bracken and dripping loneroid. Big tears rolled slowly down the deep lines on the face of Sheen. Once there was a sob in her throat, but she put her shaking hand to it, and it was still.

Neil Ross shifted from foot to foot. The ooze in that marshy place squelched with each restless movement he made. Beyond them a plover wheeled a blurred splatch in the mist, crying its mournful cry over and over and over.

It was a pitiful thing to hear; ah, bitter loneliness, bitter patience of poor old women. That he knew well. But he was too weary, and his heart was nigh full of its own burthen. The words could not come to his lips. But at last he spoke.

"*Tha mo chridhe goirt*," he said with tears in his voice, as he put his hand on her bent shoulder; "my heart is sore."

She put up her old face against his.

"'*S tha e ruidhinn mo chridhe*," she whispered,—"it is touching my heart you are."

After that they walked on slowly through the dripping mist, each dumb and brooding deep.

"Where will you be staying this night?" asked Sheen suddenly, when they had traversed a wide boggy stretch of land; adding, as by an afterthought—"ah, it is asking you were if the tarn there were Feur-Lochan. No; it is Loch-a-chaoruinn, and the clachan that is near is Contullich."

"Which way?"

"Yonder; to the right."

"And you are not going there?"

"No. I am going to the steading of Andrew Blair. Maybe you are for knowing it? It is called Le-Baile-na-Chlais-nambuidheag."[2]

"I do not remember. But it is remembering a Blair I am. He was Adam the son of Adam the son of Robert. He and my father did many an ill deed together."

"Ay, to the Stones be it said. Sure, now, there was even till this weary day no man or woman who had a good word for Adam Blair."

"And why that—why till this day?"

"It is not yet the third hour since he went into the silence."

Neil Ross uttered a sound like a stifled curse. For a time he trudged wearily on.

"Then I am too late," he said at last, but as though speaking to himself. "I had hoped to see him face to face again, and curse him between the eyes. It was he who made Murtagh Ross break his troth to my mother, and marry that other woman, barren at that, God be praised! And they say ill of him, do they?"

"Ay, it is evil that is upon him. This crime and that, God knows: and the shadow of murder on his brow and in his eyes. Well, well, 'tis ill to be speaking of a man in corpse, and that near by. 'T is Himself only that knows, Neil Ross."

"Maybe ay, and maybe no. But where is it that I can be sleeping this night, Sheen Macarthur?"

"They will not be taking a stranger at the farm this night of the nights, I am thinking. There is no place else, for seven miles yet, when there is the clachan before you will be coming to

---

[2] The farm in the hollow of the yellow flowers.

Fionnaphort. There is the warm byre, Neil my man, or if you can bide by my peats you may rest and welcome, though there is no bed for you, and no food either save some of the porridge that is over."

"And that will do well enough for me, Sheen, and Himself bless you for it."

And so it was.

After old Sheen Macarthur had given the wayfarer food—poor food at that, but welcome to one nigh starved, and for the heart-some way it was given, and because of the thanks to God that was upon it before even spoon was lifted—she told him a lie. It was the good lie of tender love.

"Sure now, after all, Neil my man," she said, "it is sleeping at the farm I ought to be, for Maisie Macdonald, the wise-woman, will be sitting by the corpse, and there will be none to keep her company. It is there I must be going, and if I am weary, there is a good bed for me just beyond the dead-board, which I am not minding at all. So if it is tired you are sitting by the peats, lie down on my bed there, and have the sleep, and God be with you."

With that she went, and soundlessly, for Neil Ross was already asleep, where he sat on an upturned *claar* with his elbows on his knees and his flame-lit face in his hands.

The rain had ceased; but the mist still hung over the land, though in thin veils now, and these slowly drifting seaward. Sheen stepped wearily along the stony path that led from her bothy to the farm-house. She stood still once, the fear upon her, for she saw three or four blurred yellow gleams moving beyond her eastward along the dyke. She knew what they were,—the corpse-lights that on the night of death go between the bier and the place of burial. More than once she had seen them before the last hour, and by that token had known the end to be near.

Good Catholic that she was, she crossed herself and took heart. Then, muttering—

> "Crois nan naoi aingeal leam
> 'O mhullach mo chinn
> Gu craican mo bhonn,"[3]

she went on her way fearlessly.

---

[3] "The cross of the nine angels be about me,
From the top of my head
To the soles of my feet."

When she came to the White House she entered by the milk-shed that was between the byre and the kitchen. At the end of it was a paved place, with washing-tubs. At one of these stood a girl that served in the house; an ignorant lass called Jessie McFall, out of Oban. She was ignorant, indeed, not to know that to wash clothes with a newly dead body near by was an ill thing to do. Was it not a matter for the knowing that the corpse could hear, and might rise up in the night and clothe itself in a clean white shroud?

She was still speaking to the lassie when Maisie Macdonald, the deid-watcher, opened the door of the room behind the kitchen, to see who it was that was come. The two old women nodded silently. It was not till Sheen was in the closed room, midway in which some-thing covered with a sheet lay on a board, that any word was spoken.

"*Duit sìth mòr,* Beann Macdonald."

"And deep peace to you, too, Sheen; and to him that is there."

"*Och, ochone, mise 'n diugh;* 't is a dark hour this."

"Ay, it is bad. Will you have been hearing or seeing anything?"

"Well, as for that, I am thinking I saw lights moving betwixt here and the green place over there."

"The corpse-lights?"

"Well, it is calling them that they are."

"I *thought* they would be out. And I have been hearing the noise of the planks,—the cracking of the boards, you know, that will be used for the coffin to-morrow."

A long silence followed. The old women had seated themselves by the corpse, their cloaks over their heads. The room was fireless, and was lit only by a tall wax death-candle, kept against the hour of the going.

At last Sheen began swaying slowly to and fro, crooning low the while. "I would not be for doing that, Sheen Macarthur," said the deid-watcher, in a low voice, but meaningly; adding, after a moment's pause, *"the mice have all left the house."*

Sheen sat upright, a look half of terror, half of awe in her eyes.

"God save the sinful soul that is hiding," she whispered.

Well she knew what Maisie meant. If the soul of the dead be a lost soul it knows its doom. The house of death is the house of sanc-tuary. But before the dawn that follows the death-night the soul must go forth, whosoever or whatsoever wait for it in the homeless, shelterless plains of air around and beyond. If it be well with the soul, it need have no fear; if it be not ill with the soul, it may fare forth with surety; but if it be ill with the soul, ill will the going be.

Thus is it that the spirit of an evil man cannot stay and yet dare not go; and so it strives to hide itself in secret places anywhere, in dark channels and blind walls. And the wise creatures that live near man smell the terror, and flee. Maisie repeated the saying of Sheen; then, after a silence, added:—

"Adam Blair will not lie in his grave for a year and a day, because of the sins that are upon him. And it is knowing that, they are, here. He will be the Watcher of the Dead for a year and a day."

"Ay, sure, there will be dark prints in the dawn-dew over yonder."

Once more the old women relapsed into silence. Through the night there was a sighing sound. It was not the sea, which was too far off to be heard save in a day of storm. The wind it was, that was dragging itself across the sodden moors like a wounded thing, moaning and sighing.

Out of sheer weariness, Sheen twice rocked forward from her stool, heavy with sleep. At last Maisie led her over to the niche-bed opposite, and laid her down there, and waited till the deep furrows in the face relaxed somewhat, and the thin breath laboured slow across the fallen jaw.

"Poor old woman," she muttered, heedless of her own grey hairs and greyer years; "a bitter bad thing it is to be old, old and weary. 'T is the sorrow that; God keep the pain of it."

As for herself she did not sleep at all that night, but sat between the living and the dead, with her plaid shrouding her. Once, when Sheen gave a low, terrified scream in her sleep, she rose, and in a loud voice cried "*Sheeach-ad!* Away with you!" And with that she lifted the shroud from the dead man, and took the pennies off the eyelids, and lifted each lid; then, staring into these filmed wells, muttered an ancient incantation that would compel the soul of Adam Blair to leave the spirit of Sheen alone, and return to the cold corpse that was its coffin till the wood was ready.

The dawn came at last. Sheen slept, and Adam Blair slept a deeper sleep, and Maisie stared out of her wan weary eyes against the red and stormy flares of light that came into the sky.

When, an hour after sunrise, Sheen Macarthur reached her bothy, she found Neil Ross, heavy with slumber, upon her bed. The fire was not out, though no flame or spark was visible, but she stooped and blew at the heart of the peats till the redness came, and once it came it grew. Having done this, she kneeled and said a rune of the morning, and after that a prayer, and then a prayer for the poor man Neil. She could pray no more because of the tears. She rose and put the meal and water into the pot, for the porridge to be ready against his awaking. One of the hens that was there came and pecked at her ragged skirt. "Poor beastie," she said, "sure, that will just be the way I am pulling at the white robe of the Mother o' God. 'T is a bit meal for you, cluckie, and for me a healing hand upon my tears—O, och, ochone, the tears, the tears!"

It was not till the third hour after sunrise of that bleak day in the winter of the winters that Neil Ross stirred and arose. He ate in silence. Once he said that he smelt the snow coming out of the north. Sheen said no word at all.

After the porridge, he took his pipe, but there was no tobacco. All that Sheen had was the pipeful she kept against the gloom of the Sabbath. It was her one solace in the long weary week. She gave him this, and held a burning peat to his mouth, and hungered over the thin, rank smoke that curled upward.

It was within half an hour of noon that, after an absence, she returned.

"Not between you and me, Neil Ross," she began abruptly, "but just for the asking, and what is beyond. Is it any money you are having upon you?"

"No."

"Nothing?"

"Nothing."

"Then how will you be getting across to Iona? It is seven long miles to Fionnaphort, and bitter cold at that, and you will be needing food, and then the ferry, the ferry across the Sound, you know."

"Ay, I know."

"What would you do for a silver piece, Neil my man?"

"You have none to give me, Sheen Macarthur, and if you had, it would not be taking it I would."

"Would you kiss a dead man for a crown-piece,—a crown-piece of five good shillings?"

Neil Ross stared. Then he sprang to his feet.

"It is Adam Blair you are meaning, woman! God curse him in death now that he is no longer in life!"

Then, shaking and trembling, he sat down again, and brooded against the dull red glow of the peats.

But, when he rose, in the last quarter before noon, his face was white.

"The dead are dead, Sheen Macarthur. They can know or do nothing. I will do it. It is willed. Yes, I am going up to the house there. And now I am going from here. God Himself has my thanks to you, and my blessing too. They will come back to you. It is not forgetting you I will be. Good-bye."

"Good-bye, Neil, son of the woman that was my friend. A south wind to you! Go up by the farm. In the front of the house you will see what you will be seeing. Maisie Macdonald will be there. She will tell you what's for the telling. There is no harm in it, sure; sure, the dead are dead. It is praying for you I will be, Neil Ross. Peace to you!"

"And to you, Sheen."

And with that the man went.

When Neil Ross reached the byres of the farm in the wide hollow, he saw two figures standing as though awaiting him, but each separate and unseen of the other. In front of the house was a man he knew to be Andrew Blair; behind the milk-shed was a woman he guessed to be Maisie Macdonald.

It was the woman he came upon first.

"Are you the friend of Sheen Macarthur?" she asked in a whisper, as she beckoned him to the doorway.

"I am."

"I am knowing no names, or anything. And no one here will know you, I am thinking. So do the thing, and begone."

"There is no harm to it?"

"None."

"It will be a thing often done, is it not?"

"Ay, sure."

"And the evil does not abide?"

"No. The—the—person—the person takes them away, and—"

"Them?"

"For sure, man! Them—the sins of the corpse. He takes them away, and are you for thinking God would let the innocent suffer for the guilty? No—the person—the Sin-Eater, you know—takes them away on himself, and one by one the air of heaven washes them away till he, the Sin-Eater, is clean and whole as before."

"But if it is a man you hate—if it is a corpse that is the corpse of one who has been a curse and a foe—if—"

"*Sst!* Be still now with your foolishness. It is only an idle saying, I am thinking. Do it, and take the money, and go. It will be hell enough for Adam Blair, miser as he was, if he is for knowing that five good shillings of his money are to go to a passing tramp, because of an old ancient silly tale."

Neil Ross laughed low at that. It was for pleasure to him.

"Hush wi' ye! Andrew Blair is waiting round there. Say that I have sent you round, as I have neither bite nor bit to give."

Turning on his heel Neil walked slowly round to the front of the house. A tall man was there, gaunt and brown, with hairless face and lank brown hair, but with eyes cold and grey as the sea.

"Good day to you an' good faring. Will you be passing this way to anywhere?"

"Health to you. I am a stranger here. It is on my way to Iona I am. But I have the hunger upon me. There is not a brown bit in my pocket. I asked at the door there, near the byres. The woman told me she could give me nothing—not a penny even, worse luck,—nor, for that, a drink of warm milk. 'T is a sore land this."

"You have the Gaelic of the Isles. Is it from Iona you are?"

"It is from the Isles of the West I come."

"From Tiree?—from Coll?"

"No."

"From the Long Island—or from Uist—or maybe from Benbecula?"

"No."

"Oh well, sure it is no matter to me. But may I be asking your name?"

"Macallum."

"Do you know there is a death here, Macallum?"

"If I did n't, I would know it now, because of what lies yonder."

Mechanically, Andrew Blair looked round. As he knew, a rough bier was there, that was made of a dead-board laid upon three milking-stools. Beside it was a *claar*, a small tub to hold potatoes. On the bier was a corpse, covered with a canvas sheeting that looked like a sail.

"He was a worthy man, my father," began the son of the dead man, slowly; "but he had his faults, like all of us. I might even be saying that he had his sins, to the Stones be it said. You will be knowing, Macallum, what is thought among the folk—that a stranger, passing by, may take away the sins of the dead, and that too without any hurt whatever—any hurt whatever."

"Ay, sure."

"And you will be knowing what is done?"

"Ay."

"With the Bread—and the Water—"

"Ay."

"It is a small thing to do. It is a Christian thing. I would be doing it myself, and that gladly; but the—the—passer-by who—"

"It is talking of the Sin-Eater you are?"

"Yes, yes, for sure. The Sin-Eater as he is called—and a good Christian act it is, for all that the ministers and the priests make a frowning at it—the Sin-Eater must be a stranger. He must be a stranger, and should know nothing of the dead man, above all bear him no grudge."

At that, Neil Ross's eyes lightened for a moment.

"And why that?"

"Who knows? I have heard this, and I have heard that. If the Sin-Eater was hating the dead man he could take the sins and fling them into the sea and they would be changed into demons of the air that would harry the flying soul till Judgment-Day."

"And how would that thing be done?"

The man spake with flashing eyes and parted lips, the breath coming swift. Andrew Blair looked at him suspiciously, and hesitated, before in a cold voice he spoke again.

"That is all folly, I am thinking, Macallum. Maybe it is all folly, the whole of it. But see here, I have no time to be talking with you. If you will take the bread and the water you shall have a good meal if you want it, and—and—yes, look you, my man, I will be giving you a shilling too, for luck."

"I will have no meal in this house, Anndra Mhic Adam; nor will I do this thing unless you will be giving me two silver half-crowns. That is the sum I must have, or no other."

"Two half-crowns! Why, man, for one half-crown—"

"Then be eating the sins o' your father yourself, Andrew Blair! It is going I am."

"Stop, man! Stop, Macallum. See here: I will be giving you what you ask."

"So be it. Is the—are you ready?"

"Ay, come this way."

With that the two men turned, and moved slowly towards the bier.

In the doorway of the house stood a man and two women; farther in, a woman; and at the window to the left the serving-wench, Jessie McFall, and two men of the farm. Of those in the doorway, the man was Peter, the half-witted youngest brother of Andrew Blair; the taller and older woman was Catreen, the widow of Adam the second brother; and the thin slight woman, with staring eyes and drooping mouth, was Muireall, the wife of Andrew. The old woman, behind these, was Maisie Macdonald.

Andrew Blair stooped and took a saucer out of the *claar.* This he put upon the covered breast of the corpse. He stooped again, and brought forth a thick square piece of new-made bread. That also he placed upon the breast of the corpse. Then he stooped again, and with that he emptied a spoonful of salt alongside the bread.

"I must see the corpse," said Neil Ross, simply.

"It is not needful, Macallum."

"I must be seeing the corpse, I tell you,—and for that, too, the bread and the water should be on the naked breast."

"No, no, man, it—"

But here a voice, that of Maisie the wise-woman, came upon them, saying that the man was right, and that the eating of the sins should be done in that way and no other.

With an ill grace the son of the dead man drew back the sheeting. Beneath it the corpse was in a clean white shirt, a death-gown long ago prepared, that covered him from his neck to his feet, and left only the dusky, yellowish face exposed.

While Andrew Blair unfastened the shirt, and placed the saucer and the bread and the salt on the breast, the man beside him stood staring fixedly on the frozen features of the corpse. The new laird had to speak to him twice before he heard.

"I am ready. And you, now? What is it you are muttering over against the lips of the dead?"

"It is giving him a message I am. There is no harm in that, sure?"

"Keep to your own folk, Macallum. You are from the West you say, and we are from the North. There can be no messages between you and a Blair of Strathmore, no messages for *you* to be giving."

"He that lies here knows well the man to whom I am sending a message—" and at this response Andrew Blair scowled darkly. He would fain have sent the man about his business, but he feared he might get no other.

"It is thinking I am that you are not a Macallum at all. I know all of that name in Mull, Iona, Skye, and the near isles. What will the name of your naming be, and of your father, and of his place?"

Whether he really wanted an answer, or whether he sought only to divert the man from his procrastination, his question had a satisfactory result.

"Well, now, it's ready I am, Anndra Mhic Adam."

With that, Andrew Blair stooped once more, and from the *claar* brought a small jug of water. From this he filled the saucer.

"You know what to say and what to do, Macallum."

There was not one there who did not have a shortened breath because of the mystery that was now before them, and the fearfulness of it. Neil Ross drew himself up, erect, stiff, with white, drawn face. All who waited, save Andrew Blair, thought that the moving of his lips was because of the prayer that was slipping upon them, like the last lapsing of the ebb-tide. But Blair was watching him closely, and knew that it was no prayer which stole out against the blank air that was around the dead.

Slowly Neil Ross extended his right arm. He took a pinch of the salt and put it in the saucer, then took another pinch and sprinkled it upon the bread. His hand shook for a moment as he touched the saucer. But there was no shaking as he raised it towards his lips, or when he held it before him when he spoke.

"With this water that has salt in it, and has lain on thy corpse, O Adam Mhic Anndra Mhic Adam Mòr, I drink away all the evil that is upon thee"—there was throbbing silence while he paused—"and may it be upon me, and not upon thee, if with this water it cannot flow away."

Thereupon he raised the saucer and passed it thrice round the head of the corpse sunways, and having done this, lifted it to his lips and drank as much as his mouth would hold. Thereafter he poured the remnant over his left hand, and let it trickle to the ground. Then he took the piece of bread. Thrice, too, he passed it round the head of the corpse sunways.

He turned and looked at the man by his side, then at the others who watched him with beating hearts.

With a loud clear voice he took the sins.

"Thoir dhomh do ciontachd, O Adam Mhic Anndra Mhic Adam Mòr! Give me thy sins to take away from thee! Lo, now, as I stand here, I break this bread that has lain on thee in corpse, and I am

eating it, I am, and in that eating I take upon me the sins of thee, O man that was alive and is now white with the stillness!"

Thereupon Neil Ross broke the bread and ate of it, and took upon himself the sins of Adam Blair that was dead. It was a bitter swallowing, that. The remainder of the bread he crumbled in his hand, and threw it on the ground, and trod upon it. Andrew Blair gave a sigh of relief. His cold eyes lightened with malice.

"Be off with you, now, Macallum. We are wanting no tramps at the farm here, and perhaps you had better not be trying to get work this side Iona, for it is known as the Sin-Eater you will be, and that won't be for the helping, I am thinking! There: there are the two half-crowns for you—and may they bring you no harm, you that are *Scapegoat* now!"

The Sin-Eater turned at that, and stared like a hill-bull. *Scapegoat!* Ay, that's what he was. Sin-Eater, scapegoat! Was he not, too, another Judas, to have sold for silver that which was not for the selling? No, no, for sure Maisie Macdonald could tell him the rune that would serve for the easing of this burden. He would soon be quit of it.

Slowly he took the money, turned it over, and put it in his pocket.

"I am going, Andrew Blair," he said quietly; "I am going, now. I will not say to him that is there in the silence, *A chuid do Pharas da!*—nor will I say to you, *Gu'n gleidheadh Dia thu,*—nor will I say to this dwelling that is the home of thee and thine, *Gu'n beannaicheadh Dia an tigh!*"[4]

Here there was a pause. All listened. Andrew Blair shifted uneasily, the furtive eyes of him going this way and that like a ferret in the grass.

"But, Andrew Blair, I will say this; when you fare abroad, *Droch caoidh ort!* and when you go upon the water, *Gaoth gun direadh ort!* Ay, ay, Anndra Mhic Adam, *Dia ad aghaidh 's ad aodann—agus bas dunach ort! Dhonas 's dholas ort, agus leat-sa!*"[5]

---

[4] (1) *A chuid do Pharas da!* "His share of heaven be his." (2) *Gu'n gleidheadh Dia thu!* "May God preserve you." (3) *Gu'n beannaicheadh Dia an tigh!* "God's blessing on this house."

[5] (1) *Droch caoidh ort!* "May a fatal accident happen to you" (lit. "Bad moan on you"). (2) *Gaoth gun direadh ort!* "May you drift to your drowning" (lit. "Wind without direction on you"). (3) *Dia ad aghaidh, etc!* "God against thee and in thy face—and may a death of woe be yours. Evil and sorrow to thee and thine!"

The bitterness of these words was like snow in June upon all there. They stood amazed. None spoke. No one moved.

Neil Ross turned upon his heel, and with a bright light in his eyes walked away from the dead and the living. He went by the byres, whence he had come. Andrew Blair remained where he was, now glooming at the corpse, now biting his nails and staring at the damp sods at his feet.

When Neil reached the end of the milk-shed he saw Maisie Macdonald there, waiting.

"These were ill sayings of yours, Neil Ross," she said in a low voice, so that she might not be overheard from the house.

"So, it is knowing me you are."

"Sheen Macarthur told me."

"I have good cause."

"That is a true word. I know it."

"Tell me this thing. What is the rune that is said for the throwing into the sea of the sins of the dead? See here, Maisie Macdonald. There is no money of that man that I would carry a mile with me. Here it is. It is yours, if you will tell me that rune."

Maisie took the money hesitatingly. Then, stooping, she said slowly the few lines of the old, old rune.

"Will you be remembering that?"

"It is not forgetting it I will be, Maisie."

"Wait a moment. There is some warm milk here."

With that she went, and then, from within, beckoned to him to enter.

"There is no one here, Neil Ross. Drink the milk."

He drank: and while he did so she drew a leather pouch from some hidden place in her dress.

"And now I have this to give you."

She counted out ten pennies and two farthings.

"It is all the coppers I have. You are welcome to them. Take them, friend of my friend. They will give you the food you need, and the ferry across the Sound."

"I will do that, Maisie Macdonald, and thanks to you. It is not forgetting it I will be, nor you, good woman. And now, tell me: Is it safe that I am? He called me a 'scapegoat,' he, Andrew Blair! Can evil touch me between this and the sea?"

"You must go to the place where the evil was done to you and yours; and that, I know, is on the west side of Iona. Go, and God preserve you. But here, too, is a *sian* that will be for the safety."

Thereupon with swift mutterings she said this charm: an old, familiar *sian* against Sudden Harm:—

Sian a chuir Moire air Mac ort,
Sian ro' marbhadh, sian ro' lot ort,
Sian eadar a' chlioch 's a' ghlun,
Sian nan Tri ann an aon ort,
O mhullach do chinn gu bonn do chois ort:
Sian seachd eadar a h-aon ort,
Sian seachd eadar a dha ort,
Sian seachd eadar a tri ort,
Sian seachd eadar a ceithir ort,
Sian seachd eadar a coig ort,
Sian seachd eadar a sia ort,
Sian seachd paidir nan seach paidir dol deiseil ri diugh narach ort, ga
do ghleidheadh bho bheud 's bho mhi-thapadh!

Scarcely had she finished before she heard heavy steps approaching.

"Away with you," she whispered; repeating in a loud angry tone, "Away with you! Seachad! Seachad!"

And with that Neil Ross slipped from the milk-shed and crossed the yard, and was behind the byres, before Andrew Blair, with sullen mien and swift wild eyes, strode from the house.

It was with a grim smile on his face that Neil tramped down the wet heather till he reached the high road, and fared thence as through a marsh because of the rains there had been.

For the first mile he thought of the angry mind of the dead man, bitter at paying of the silver. For the second mile he thought of the evil that had been wrought for him and his. For the third mile he pondered over all that he had heard, and done, and taken upon him that day.

Then he sat down upon a broken granite-heap by the way, and brooded deep, till one hour went, and then another, and the third was upon him.

A man driving two calves came towards him out of the west. He did not hear or see. The man stopped, spoke again. Neil gave no answer. The drover shrugged his shoulders, hesitated, and walked slowly on, often looking back.

An hour later a shepherd came by the way he himself had tramped.

He was a tall, gaunt man with a squint. The small pale-blue eyes glittered out of a mass of red hair that almost covered his face. He stood still opposite Neil, and leaned on his *cromak.*

"*Latha math leat,*" he said at last, "I wish you good day."

Neil glanced at him, but did not speak.

"What is your name, for I seem to know you?"

But Neil had already forgotten him. The shepherd took out his snuff-mull, helped himself, and handed the mull to the lonely wayfarer. Neil mechanically helped himself.

"*Am bheil thu 'dol do Fhionphort?*" cried the shepherd again, "are you going to Fionnaphort?"

"*Tha mise 'dol a dh' I-challum-chille,*" Neil answered in a low, weary voice, and as a man adream, "I am on my way to Iona."

"I am thinking I know now who you are. You are the man Macallum."

Neil looked, but did not speak. His eyes dreamed against what the other could not see or know. The shepherd called angrily to his dogs to keep the sheep from straying; then, with a resentful air, turned to his victim.

"You are a silent man for sure, you are. I'm hoping it is not the curse upon you already."

"What curse?"

"Ah, *that* has brought the wind against the mist! I was thinking so!"

"What curse?"

"You are the man that was the Sin-Eater over there?"

"Ay."

"The man Macallum?"

"Ay."

"Strange it is, but three days ago I saw you in Tobermory, and heard you give your name as Neil Ross, to an Iona man that was there."

"Well?"

"Oh, sure, it is nothing to me. But they say the Sin-Eater should not be a man with a hidden lump in his pack."[6]

"Why?"

"For the dead know, and are content. There is no shaking off any sins, then: for that man."

"It is a lie."

---

[6] *i.e.* With a criminal secret, or an undiscovered crime.

"Maybe ay, and maybe no."

"Well, have you more to be saying to me? I am obliged to you for your company, but it is not needing it I am, though no offence."

"Och, man, there's no offence between you and me. Sure, there's Iona in me, too, for the father of my father married a woman that was the granddaughter of Tomais Macdonald, who was a fisherman there. No, no, it is rather warning you I would be."

"And for what?"

"Well, well, just because of that laugh I heard about."

"What laugh?"

"The laugh of Adam Blair that is dead."

Neil Ross stared, his eyes large and wild. He leaned a little forward. No word came from him. The look that was on his face was the question.

"Yes: it was this way. Sure, the telling of it is just as I heard it. After you ate the sins of Adam Blair, the people there brought out the coffin. When they were putting him into it, he was as stiff as a sheep dead in the snow,—and just like that, too, with his eyes wide open. Well, some one saw you trampling the heather down the slope that is in front of the house, and said, 'It is the Sin-Eater!' With that, Andrew Blair sneered, and said, 'Ay, 'tis the scapegoat he is!' Then, after a while, he went on: 'The Sin-Eater they call him; ay, just so; and a bitter good bargain it is, too, if all 's true that 's thought true!'—and with that he laughed, and then his wife that was behind him laughed, and then—"

"Well, what then?"

"Well, 'tis Himself that hears and knows if it is true! But this is the thing I was told: After that laughing there was a stillness, and a dread. For all there saw that the corpse had turned its head and was looking after you as you went down the heather. Then, Neil Ross, if that be your true name, Adam Blair that was dead put up his white face against the sky, and laughed."

At this, Ross sprang to his feet with a gasping sob.

"It is a lie, that thing," he cried, shaking his fist at the shepherd, "it is a lie."

"It is no lie. And by the same token, Andrew Blair shrank back white and shaking, and his woman had the swoon upon her, and who knows but the corpse might have come to life again had it not been for Maisie Macdonald, the deid-watcher, who clapped a handful of salt on his eyes, and tilted the coffin so that the bottom of it slid forward and so let the whole fall flat on the ground, with Adam Blair in it sideways, and as likely as not cursing and groaning as his wont was, for the hurt both to his old bones and his old ancient dignity."

Ross glared at the man as though the madness was upon him. Fear, and horror, and fierce rage, swung him now this way and now that.

"What will the name of you be, shepherd?" he stuttered huskily.

"It is Eachainn Gilleasbuig I am to ourselves, and the English of that for those who have no Gaelic is Hector Gillespie; and I am Eachainn mac Ian mac Alasdair, of Srathsheean, that is where Sutherland lies against Ross."

"Then take this thing, and that is, the curse of the Sin-Eater! And a bitter bad thing may it be upon you and yours!"

And with that Neil the Sin-Eater flung his hand up into the air, and then leaped past the shepherd, and a minute later was running through the frightened sheep, with his head low, and a white foam on his lips, and his eyes red with blood as a seal's that has the death-wound on it.

On the third day of the seventh month from that day, Aulay Macneill, coming into Balliemore of Iona from the west side of the island, said to old Ronald MacCormick, that was the father of his wife, that he had seen Neil Ross again, and that he was "absent"— for though he had spoken to him, Neil would not answer, but only gloomed at him from the wet weedy rock where he sat.

The going back of the man had loosed every tongue that was in Iona. When, too, it was known that he was wrought in some terrible way, if not actually mad, the islanders whispered that it was because of the sins of Adam Blair. Seldom or never now did they speak of him by his name, but, simply, "The Sin-Eater." The thing was not so rare as to cause this strangeness, nor did many (and perhaps none did) think that the sins of the dead ever might or could abide with the living who had merely done a good Christian, charitable thing. But there was a reason.

Not long after Neil Ross had come again to Iona, and had settled down in the ruined roofless house on the croft of Ballyrona, just like a fox or a wild-cat, as the saying was, he was given fishing-work to do by Aulay Macneill, who lived at Ard-an-teine, at the rocky north end of the *Màchar* or plain that is on the west Atlantic coast of the island.

One moonlit night, either the seventh or the ninth after the earthing of Adam Blair at his own place in the Ross, Aulay Macneill saw Neil Ross steal out of the shadow of Ballyrona and make for the sea. Macneill was there, by the rocks, mending a lobster-creel. He had gone there because of the sadness. Well, when he saw the Sin-Eater he watched.

Neil crept from rock to rock till he reached the last fang that churns the sea into yeast when the tide sucks the land, just opposite.

Then he called out something that Aulay Macneill could not catch. With that he springs up, and throws his arms above him.

"Then," says Aulay, when he tells the tale, "it was like a ghost he was. The moonshine was on his face like the curl o' a wave. White! there is no whiteness like that of the human face. It was whiter than the foam about the skerry it was, whiter than the moonshining, whiter than—well, as white as the painted letters on the black boards of the fishing-cobles. There he stood, for all that the sea was about him, the slip-slop waves leapin' wild, and the tide making too at that. He was shaking like a sail two points off the wind. It was then that all of a sudden he called in a womany screamin' voice:—

"'I am throwing the sins of Adam Blair into the midst of ye, white dogs o' the sea! Drown them, tear them, drag them away out into the black deeps! Ay, ay, ay, ye dancin' wild waves, this is the third time I am doing it; and now there is none left, no, not a sin, not a sin.

'O-hi, O-ri, dark tide o' the sea,
I am giving the sins of a dead man to thee!
By the Stones, by the Wind, by the Fire, by the Tree,
From the dead man's sins set me free, set me free!
Adam mhic Anndra mhic Adam and me,
Set us free! Set us free!'

"'Ay, sure, the Sin-Eater sang that over and over. And after the third singing he swung his arms and screamed,—

'And listen to me, black waters an' running tide,
That rune is the good rune told me by Maisie the wise,
And I am Neil, the son of Silis Macallum,
By the black-hearted evil man Murtagh Ross,
That was the friend of Adam Mac Anndra, God against him!'

"And with that he scrambled and fell into the sea. But, as I am Aulay Mac Luais and no other, he was up in a moment, an' swimmin' like a seal, and then over the rocks again, an' away back to that lonely roofless place once more, laughing wild at times, an' muttering an' whispering."

It was this tale of Aulay Macneill's that stood between Neil Ross and the islefolk. There was something behind all that, they whispered one to another.

So it was always the Sin-Eater he was called at last. None sought him. The few children who came upon him, now and again, fled at his approach, or at the very sight of him. Only Aulay Macneill saw him at times, and had word of him.

After a month had gone by, all knew that the Sin-Eater was wrought to madness, because of this awful thing; the burden of Adam Blair's sins would not go from him! Night and day he could hear them laughing low, it was said.

But it was the quiet madness. He went to and fro like a shadow in the grass, and almost as soundless as that, and as voiceless. More and more the name of him grew as a terror. There were few folk on that wild west coast of Iona, and these few avoided him when the word ran that he had knowledge of strange things, and converse, too, with the secrets of the sea.

One day Aulay Macneill, in his boat, but dumb with amaze and terror for him, saw him at high-tide swimming on a long rolling wave right into the hollow of the Spouting Cave. In the memory of man, no one had done this and escaped one of three things: a snatching away into oblivion, a strangled death, or madness. The islanders know that there swims into the cave at full tide a Mar-Tarbh, a dreadful creature of the sea that some call a kelpie; only it is not a kelpie, which is like a woman, but rather is a sea-bull, off-spring of the cattle that are never seen. Ill indeed for any sheep or goat, ay or even dog or child, if any happens to be leaning over the edge of the Spouting Cave when the Mar-Tarbh roars; for, of a surety, it will fall in and straightway be devoured.

With awe and trembling Aulay listened for the screaming of the doomed man. It was full tide, and the sea-beast would be there.

The minutes passed, and no sign. Only the hollow booming of the sea, as it moved like a baffled blind giant round the cavern-bases; only the rush and spray of the water flung up the narrow shaft high into the windy air above the cliff it penetrates.

At last he saw what looked like a mass of sea-weed swirled out on

the surge. It was the Sin-Eater. With a leap, Aulay was at his oars.
The boat swung through the sea. Just before Neil Ross was about
to sink for the second time, he caught him, and dragged him into
the boat.

But then, as ever after, nothing was to be got out of the Sin-Eater
save a single saying: *"Tha e lamhan fuar! Tha e lamhan fuar!"* "It
has a cold, cold hand!"

The telling of this and other tales left none free upon the island
to look upon the "scapegoat" save as one accursed.

It was in the third month that a new phase of his madness came
upon Neil Ross.

The horror of the sea and the passion for the sea came over him
at the same happening. Oftentimes he would race along the shore,
screaming wild names to it, now hot with hate and loathing, now as
the pleading of a man with the woman of his love. And strange
chants to it, too, were upon his lips. Old, old lines of forgotten
runes were overheard by Aulay Macneill, and not Aulay only,—
lines wherein the ancient sea-name of the island, *Ioua,* that was
given to it long before it was called Iona, or any other of the nine
names that are said to belong to it, occurred again and again.

The flowing tide it was that wrought him thus. At the ebb he
would wander across the weedy slabs or among the rocks, silent,
and more like a lost *duinshee* than a man.

Then again after three months a change in his madness came.
None knew what it was, though Aulay said that the man moaned
and moaned because of the awful burden he bore. No drowning
seas for the sins that could not be washed away, no grave for the live
sins that would be quick till the Day of the Judgment!

For weeks thereafter he disappeared. As to where he was, it is
not for the knowing.

Then at last came that third day of the seventh month when, as
I have said, Aulay Macneill told old Ronald MacCormick that he
had seen the Sin-Eater again.

It was only a half-truth that he told, though. For after he had
seen Neil Ross upon the rock, he had followed him when he rose
and wandered back to the roofless place which he haunted now as
of yore. Less wretched a shelter now it was, because of the summer
that was come, though a cold wet summer at that.

"Is that you, Neil Ross?" he had asked, as he peered into the
shadows among the ruins of the house.

"That's not my name," said the Sin-Eater; and he seemed as strange then and there, as though he were a castaway from a foreign ship.

"And what will it be then, you that are my friend, and sure knowing me as Aulay Mac Luais,—Aulay Macneill that never grudges you bit or sup?"

"*I am Judas.*"

"And at that word," says Aulay Macneill, when he tells the tale, "at that word the pulse in my heart was like a bat in a shut room. But after a bit I took up the talk.

"'Indeed,' I said, 'and I was not for knowing that. May I be so bold as to ask whose son, and of what place?'

"But all he said to me was, '*I am Judas.*'

"Well, I said, to comfort him, 'Sure, it's not such a bad name in itself, though I am knowing some which have a more homelike sound.' But no, it was no good.

"'I am Judas. And because I sold the Son of God for five pieces of silver—' But here I interrupted him and said, 'Sure now, Neil,— I mean, Judas,—it was eight times five.' Yet the simpleness of his sorrow prevailed, and I listened with the wet in my eyes.

"'I am Judas. And because I sold the Son of God for five silver shillings, He laid upon me all the nameless black sins of the world. And that is why I am bearing them till the Day of Days.'"

And this was the end of the Sin-Eater,—for I will not tell the long story of Aulay Macneill, that gets longer and longer every winter, but only the unchanging close of it.

I will tell it in the words of Aulay.

"A bitter wild day it was, that day I saw him to see him no more. It was late. The sea was red with the flamin' light that burned up the air betwixt Iona and all that is west of West. I was on the shore, looking at the sea. The big green waves came in like the chariots in the Holy Book. Well, it was on the black shoulder of one of them, just short of the ton o' foam that swept above it, that I saw a spar surgin' by.

"'What is that?' I said to myself. And the reason of my wondering was this. I saw that a smaller spar was swung across it. And while I was watching that thing another great billow came in with a roar, and hurled the double-spar back, and not so far from me but I might have gripped it. But who would have gripped that thing if he were for seeing what I saw?

"It is Himself knows that what I say is a true thing.

"On that spar was Neil Ross, the Sin-Eater. Naked he was as the day he was born. And he was lashed, too, ay, sure he was lashed to it by ropes round and round his legs and his waist and his left arm. It was the Cross he was on. I saw that thing with the fear upon me. Ah, poor drifting wreck that he was! *Judas on the Cross!* It was his *eric!*

"But even as I watched, shaking in my limbs, I saw that there was life in him still. The lips were moving, and his right arm was ever for swinging this way and that. 'Twas like an oar working him off a lee shore; ay, that was what I thought.

"Then all at once he caught sight of me. Well, he knew me, poor man, that has his share of heaven now, I am thinking!

"He waved, and called, but the hearing could not be, because of a big surge o' water that came tumbling down upon him. In the stroke of an oar he was swept close by the rocks where I was standing. In that flounderin', seethin' whirlpool I saw the white face of him for a moment, an', as he went out on the resurge like a hauled net, I heard these words fallin' against my ears:—

"'*An eirig m'anama!*—In ransom for my soul!'

"And with that I saw the double-spar turn over and slide down the back-sweep of a drowning big wave. Ay, sure, it went out to the deep sea swift enough then. It was in the big eddy that rushes between Skerry-Mòr and Skerry-Beag. I did not see it again, no, not for the quarter of an hour, I am thinking. Then I saw just the whirling top of it rising out of the flying yeast of a great black, blustering wave that was rushing northward before the current that is called the Black-Eddy.

"With that you have the end of Neil Ross: ay, sure, him that was called the Sin-Eater. And that is a true thing, and may God save us the sorrow of sorrows!

"And that is all."

The Voice in the Night

William Hope Hodgson

It was a dark, starless night. We were becalmed in the Northern Pacific. Our exact position I do not know; for the sun had been hidden during the course of a weary, breathless week by a thin haze which had seemed to float above us about the height of our mast-heads, at whiles descending and shrouding the surrounding sea.

With there being no wind, we had steadied the tiller, and I was the only man on deck. The crew, consisting of two men and a boy, were sleeping forrard in their den; while Will—my friend, and the master of our little craft—was aft in his bunk on the port side of the little cabin.

Suddenly, from out of the surrounding darkness, there came a hail:—

"Schooner, ahoy!"

The cry was so unexpected that I gave no immediate answer, because of my surprise.

It came again—a voice curiously throaty and inhuman, calling from somewhere upon the dark sea away on our port broadside:—

"Schooner, ahoy!"

"Hullo!" I sung out, having gathered my wits somewhat. "What are you? What do you want?"

"You need not be afraid," answered the queer voice, having probably noticed some trace of confusion in my tone. "I am only an old—man."

The pause sounded oddly; but it was only afterwards that it came back to me with any significance.

"Why don't you come alongside, then?" I queried somewhat snap-pishly; for I liked not his hinting at my having been a trifle shaken.

"I—I—can't. It wouldn't be safe. I——" The voice broke off confusedly, and there was silence.

"What do you mean?" I asked, growing more and more astonished. "Why not safe? Where are you?"

I listened for a moment; but there came no answer, and then a sudden indefinite suspicion of I knew not what coming to me, I stepped swiftly to the binnacle, and took out the lighted lamp. At the same time, I knocked on the deck with my heel to waken Will. Then I was back at the side, throwing the yellow funnel of light out into the silent immensity beyond our rail. As I did so, I heard a slight muffled cry, and then the sound of a splash, as though someone had dipped oars abruptly. Yet I cannot say that I saw anything with certainty; save, it seemed to me, that with the first flash of the light there had been something upon the waters where now there was nothing.

"Hullo there!" I called. "What foolery is this?"

Then I heard Will's voice from the direction of the after scuttle:—

"What's up, George?"

"Come here, Will!" I said.

"What is it?" he asked, coming across the deck.

I told him the queer thing which had happened. He put several questions; then, after a moment's silence, he raised his hands to his lips, and hailed:—

"Boat, ahoy!"

From a long distance away, there came back to us a faint reply, and my companion repeated his call. Presently, after a short period of silence, there grew on our hearing the muffled sound of oars; at which Will hailed again.

This time there was a reply:—

"Put away the light."

"I'm damned if I will," I muttered; but Will told me to do as the voice bade, and I shoved it down under the bulwarks.

"Come nearer," he said, and the oar-strokes continued. Then, when apparently some half-dozen fathoms distant, they again ceased.

"Come alongside," exclaimed Will. "There's nothing to be frightened of aboard here!"

"Promise that you will not show the light?"

"What's to do with you," I burst out, "that you're so infernally afraid of the light?"

"Because——" began the voice, and stopped short.

"Because what?" I asked, quickly.

Will put his hand on my shoulder.

"Shut up a minute, old man," he said, in a low voice. "Let me tackle him."

He leant more over the rail.

"See here, Mister," he said, "this is a pretty queer business, you coming upon us like this, right out in the middle of the blessed Pacific. How are we to know what sort of a hanky-panky trick you're up to? You say there's only one of you. How are we to know, unless we get a squint at you—eh? What's your objection to the light, anyway?"

As he finished, I heard the sound of the oars again, and then the voice came; but now from a greater distance, and sounding extremely hopeless and pathetic.

"I am sorry—sorry. I would not have troubled you, only I am hungry, and—so is she."

The voice died away, and the sound of the oars, dipping irregularly, was borne to us.

"Stop!" sung out Will. "I don't want to drive you away. Come back! We'll keep the light hidden, if you don't like it."

He turned to me:—

"It's a damned queer rig, this; but I think there's nothing to be afraid of?"

There was a question in his tone, and I replied:

"No, I think the poor devil's been wrecked around here, and gone crazy."

The sound of the oars drew nearer.

"Shove that lamp back in the binnacle," said Will; then he leaned over the rail, and listened. I replaced the lamp, and came back to his side. The dipping of the oars ceased some dozen yards distant.

"Won't you come alongside now?" asked Will in an even voice. "I have had the lamp put back in the binnacle."

"I—I cannot," replied the voice. "I dare not come nearer. I dare not even pay you for the—the provisions."

"That's all right," said Will, and hesitated. "You're welcome to as much grub as you can take——" Again he hesitated.

"You are very good," exclaimed the voice. "May God, who understands everything, reward you——" It broke off huskily.

"The—the lady?" said Will, abruptly. "Is she——"

"I have left her behind upon the island," came the voice.

"What island?" I cut in.

"I know not its name," returned the voice. "I would to God——!" it began, and checked itself as suddenly.

"Could we not send a boat for her?" asked Will at this point.

"No!" said the voice, with extraordinary emphasis. "My God! No!" There was a moment's pause; then it added in a tone which seemed a merited reproach:—

"It was because of our want I ventured—— Because her agony tortured me."

"I am a forgetful brute," exclaimed Will. "Just wait a minute, whoever you are, and I will bring you up something at once."

In a couple of minutes he was back again, and his arms were full of various edibles. He paused at the rail.

"Can't you come alongside for them?" he asked.

"No—I *dare not*," replied the voice, and it seemed to me that in its tones I detected a note of stifled craving—as though the owner hushed a mortal desire. It came to me then in a flash that the poor old creature out there in the darkness was *suffering* for actual need of that which Will held in his arms; and yet, because of some unintelligible dread, refraining from dashing to the side of our little schooner, and receiving it. And with the lightning-like conviction there came the knowledge that the Invisible was not mad; but sanely facing some intolerable horror.

"Damn it, Will!" I said, full of many feelings, over which predominated a vast sympathy. "Get a box. We must float off the stuff to him in it."

This we did, propelling it away from the vessel out into the darkness by means of a boathook. In a minute, a slight cry from the Invisible came to us, and we knew that he had secured the box.

A little later he called out a farewell to us, and so heart-full a blessing that, I am sure, we were the better for it. Then, without more ado, we heard the ply of oars across the darkness.

"Pretty soon off," remarked Will, with perhaps just a little sense of injury.

"Wait," I replied. "I think somehow he'll come back. He must have been badly needing that food."

"And the lady," said Will. For a moment he was silent; then he continued:—

"It's the queerest thing ever I've tumbled across since I've been fishing."

"Yes," I said, and fell to pondering. And so the time slipped away—an hour, another, and still Will stayed with me; for the queer adventure had knocked all desire for sleep out of him.

The third hour was three parts through when we heard again the sound of oars across the silent ocean.

"Listen!" said Will, a low note of excitement in his voice.

"He's coming, just as I thought," I muttered.

The dipping of the oars grew nearer, and I noted quietly that the strokes were firmer and longer. The food had been needed.

They came to a stop a little distance off the broadside, and the queer voice came again to us through the darkness.

"Schooner, ahoy!"

"That you?" asked Will.

"Yes," replied the voice. "I left you suddenly; but—but there was great need."

"The lady?" questioned Will.

"The—lady is grateful now on earth. She will be more grateful soon in—in heaven."

Will began to make some reply in a puzzled voice; but became confused, and broke off short. I said nothing. I was wondering at the pauses, and, apart from my wonder, I was full of a great sympathy.

The voice continued:—

"We—she and I, have talked, as we shared the result of God's tenderness and yours——"

Will interposed; but without coherence. And there came a gentle reproof:—

"I beg of you not to—to belittle your deed of Christian charity this night. Be sure that it has not escaped His notice." It stopped, and there was a full minute's silence. Then the voice came again:—

"We have spoken together upon that which—which has befallen us. We had thought to go out, without telling any of the terror which has come into our—lives. She is with me in believing that to-night's happenings are under a special ruling, and that it is God's wish that we should tell you all that we have suffered since—since——"

"Yes," said Will, softly.

"Since the sinking of the 'Albatross.'"

"Ah!" I exclaimed, involuntarily. "She left Newcastle for 'Frisco some six months ago, and hasn't been heard of since."

"Yes," answered the voice. "But some few degrees to the North of the line she was caught in a terrible storm, and dismasted. When the day came it was found that she was leaking badly, and, presently, it falling to a calm, the sailors took to the boats, leaving—leaving a young lady—my *fiancée*—and myself upon the wreck. We were below, gathering together a few of our belongings, when they left. They were entirely callous through fear, and when we came up upon the decks we saw them only as small shapes afar off upon the horizon. Yet we did not despair, but set to work and constructed a small raft. Upon this we put such few matters as it would hold, including a quantity of water and some ship's biscuit. Then, the vessel being very deep in the water, we got ourselves on to the raft and pushed off.

"It was later I observed that we seemed to be in the way of some tide or current, which bore us from the ship at an angle; so that in the course of three hours by my watch, her hull became invisible to our sight, her broken masts remaining in view for a somewhat longer period. Then, towards evening, it grew misty, and so through the night. The next day we were still encompassed by the mist, the weather remaining quiet. For four days we drifted through this strange haze, until, on the evening of the fourth day, there grew upon our ears the murmur of breakers at a distance. Gradually it became plainer, and, somewhat after midnight, it appeared to sound upon either hand at no very great space. The raft was raised upon a swell several times, and then we were in smooth water, and the noise of the breakers was behind.

"When the morning came, we found that we were in a sort of great lagoon; but of this we noticed little at the time; for close before us, through the enshrouding mist, loomed the hull of a large sailing vessel. With one accord we fell upon our knees and thanked God; for we thought that here was an end to our perils. We had much to learn. The raft drew near to the ship, and we shouted on them to take us aboard, but none answered. Presently the raft touched against the side of the vessel, and, seeing a rope hanging downwards, I seized it and began to climb. Yet I had much ado to make my way upwards, because of a kind of grey, lichenous fungus which had formed upon the rope, and which blotched the side of the ship, lividly. I reached the rail, and clambered over it on to the deck. Here, I saw that the decks were covered in great patches with the grey masses, some of them rising into nodules several feet in height; but at the time, I thought less of this matter than of the possibility of their being people aboard the ship. I shouted; but none answered. Then I went to the door below the poop deck. I opened it, and peered in. There was a great smell of staleness, so that I knew in a moment that nothing living was within, and with the knowledge I shut the door quickly, for I felt suddenly lonely. I went back to the side where I had scrambled up. My—my sweetheart was still sitting quietly upon the raft. Seeing me look down, she called up to know whether there were any aboard of the ship. I replied that the vessel had the appearance of having been long deserted; but that if she would wait a little, I would see whether there was anything in the shape of a ladder by which she could ascend to the deck. Then we would make a search through the vessel together. A little later, on the opposite side of the decks, I found a rope side-ladder. This I carried across, and a minute afterwards she was beside me.

"Together, we explored the cabins and apartments in the after part of the ship; but there were nowhere any signs of life. Here and there, within the cabins themselves, we came across odd patches of that queer fungus; but this, as my sweetheart said, could be cleansed away.

"In the end, having assured ourselves that the after portion of the vessel was empty, we picked our way to the bows, between the ugly grey nodules of that strange growth, and made a further search, which told us that there was indeed none aboard but ourselves.

"This being now beyond any doubt, we returned to the stern of the ship, and proceeded to make ourselves as comfortable as possible. Together, we cleared out and cleaned two of the cabins, and after that I made examination whether there was anything eatable in the ship. This I soon found was so, and thanked God in my heart for His goodness. In addition to this, I discovered the whereabout of the freshwater pump, and having fixed it, I found the water drinkable, though somewhat unpleasant to the taste.

"For several days we stayed aboard the ship without attempting to get to the shore. We were busily engaged in making the place habitable. Yet thus early we became aware that our lot was even less to be desired than might have been imagined; for though, as a first step, we scraped away the odd patches of growth that studded the floors and walls of the cabins and saloons; yet they returned almost to their original size within the space of twenty-four hours, which not only discouraged us, but gave us a feeling of actual fear.

Still, we would not admit ourselves beaten; but set to work afresh, and not only scraped away the fungus, but soaked the places where it had been with carbolic, a can-full of which I had found in the pantry. Yet, by the end of the week, the growth had returned in full strength, and, in addition, it had spread to other places, as though our touching it had allowed germs from it to travel elsewhere. On the seventh morning, my sweetheart woke to find a small patch of it growing on her pillow close to her face. At that she came to me so soon as she could get her garments upon her. I was in the galley at the time, lighting the fire for breakfast.

"'Come here, John,' she said, and led me aft. When I saw the thing upon her pillow I shuddered, and then and there we agreed to go right out of the ship and see whether we could not fare to make ourselves more comfortable ashore. Hurriedly, we gathered together our few belongings, and even among these, I found that the fungus had been at work, for one of her shawls had a little lump of it growing near one edge. I threw the whole thing over the side without saying anything to her.

"The raft was still alongside; but it was too clumsy to guide, and I lowered down a small boat that hung across the stern, and in this we made our way to the shore. Yet, as we drew near to it, I became gradually aware that here the vile fungus which had driven us from the ship was growing riot. In places it rose into horrible, fantastic mounds, which seemed almost to quiver as with a quiet life, when the wind blew across them. Here and there it took on the forms of vast fingers, and in others it just spread out flat and smooth and treacherous. In odd places it appeared as stunted trees, seeming extraordinarily kinked and gnarled, the whole quaking vilely at times.

"At first it seemed to us that there was no single portion of the surrounding shore which was not hidden beneath the masses of the hideous lichen; yet in this I found we were mistaken; for somewhat later, coasting along the shore at a little distance, we descried a smooth white patch of what appeared to be fine sand, and there we landed. It was not sand. What it was I do not know. All that I have observed is that upon it the fungus will not grow; while everywhere else, save where it wanders oddly path-wise amid the grey desolation of the lichen, there is nothing but that loathsome greyness.

"It is difficult to make you understand how cheered we were to find one place absolutely free from the growth, and here we deposited our belongings. Then we went back to the ship for such various things as it seemed to us we should need. In this way I managed to bring with me a sail, with which I constructed two small tents, which, though exceedingly rough, served the purposes for which they were intended. In these we lived and stored our various matters, and thus for a matter of some three weeks all went smoothly and without particular unhappiness. Indeed, I may say with some considerable sense of—pleasure; for—for we were together.

"It was on the thumb of her right hand that the growth first showed. It was only a small circular spot, much like a little grey mole. My God! how the fear leapt to my heart when she showed me the place. We cleansed it between us, washing it with carbolic and water. In the morning of the following day she showed her hand to me again. The grey warty thing had returned. For a little while we looked at one another in silence. Then, still wordless, we started again to remove it. In the midst of the operation, she spoke suddenly.

"'What's that on the side of your face, dear?' she said, and her voice was very anxious. I put my hand up to feel.

"'There! Under the hair by your ear—a little to the front a bit,' she told me. My finger rested upon the place, and then I knew.

"'Let us get your thumb done first,' I said. And she only submitted because she was afraid to touch me until it was cleansed. I finished washing and disinfecting her thumb, and then she turned to my face. After it was finished, we sat together and talked awhile of many things; for there had come into our lives a sudden very terrible thought. We were all at once afraid of something worse than death. We spoke of loading the boat with provisions and water, and making our way out on to the sea; yet we were helpless for many causes, and—and the growth had attacked us already. We decided to stay. God would do with us what was His will. We would wait.

"A month, two months, three months passed, and the places grew somewhat, and there had come others. Yet we fought so strenuously with the fear, that its headway was but slow, comparatively speaking.

"Occasionally, we ventured off to the ship for such stores as we needed. There we found that the fungus grew persistently, one of the nodules on the main deck presently becoming as high as my head.

"We had now given up all thought or hope of leaving the island. We had realised that it would be unallowable to go among healthy fellow-creatures, with the thing from which we were suffering.

"With this determination and knowledge in our minds, we knew that we should have to husband our food and water; for we did not know at that time but that we should possibly live for many years.

"This reminds me that I have told you that I am an old man. Judged by years this is not so. But—but——"

He broke off; then continued somewhat abruptly:—

"As I was saying, we knew that we should have to use care in the matter of food. But we had no idea then how little food there was left, of which to take care. It was a week later that I made the discovery that all the other bread tanks—which I had supposed full— were empty, and that (beyond odd tins of vegetables and meat, and some other matters) we had nothing on which to depend but the bread in the tank which I had already opened.

"After learning this, I bestirred myself to do what I could, and set to work at fishing in the lagoon; but with no success. At this, I was somewhat inclined to feel desperate, until the thought came to me to try outside the lagoon, in the open sea. Here, at times, I caught odd fish; but with such indifferent success, that they proved of but little help in keeping us from the hunger which threatened. It seemed to me that our death was likely to come by hunger, and not by the growth of the thing which had seized upon our bodies.

"We were in this state of mind when the fourth month wore out. Then I made a very horrible discovery. One morning, a little before midday, I came off from the ship with a portion of the biscuits which were left. In the mouth of her tent, I saw my sweetheart sitting, eating something.

"'What is it, my dear?' I called out as I leapt ashore. Yet, on hearing my voice, she seemed confused, and, turning, slyly threw something towards the edge of the little clearing. It fell short, and, a vague suspicion having arisen with me, I walked across and picked it up. It was a piece of the grey fungus.

"As I went to her with it in my hand, she turned deathly pale; then rosy red.

"I felt strangely dazed and frightened.

"'My dear! My dear!' I said, and could say no more. Yet at my words she broke down and cried bitterly. Gradually, as she calmed, I got from her the news that she had tried it the preceding day, and—and liked it. I got her to promise on her knees not to touch it again, however great our hunger. After she had promised, she told me that the desire for it had come suddenly, and that, until the moment of that desire, she had experienced nothing for it but the most extreme repulsion.

"Later in the day, feeling strangely restless, and much shaken with the thing which I had discovered, I made my way along one of the twisted paths—formed by the white, sand-like substance—which led among the fungoid growth. I had once before ventured along there; but not to any great distance. This time, being wrapped in perplexing thought, I went much further than hitherto. Suddenly, I was called to myself by a queer hoarse sound on my left. Turning quickly, I saw that there was movement among an extraordinarily shaped mass of fungus, close to my elbow. It was swaying uneasily, as though it possessed life of its own. Abruptly, as I stared, the thought came to me that the thing had a grotesque resemblance to the figure of a distorted human creature. Even as the fancy flashed into my brain, there was a slight, sickening noise of tearing, and I saw that one of the branch-like arms was detaching itself from the surrounding grey masses, and coming towards me. The head of the thing—a shapeless grey ball, inclined in my direction. I stood stupidly, and the vile arm of the thing brushed across my face. I gave out a frightened cry, and ran back a few paces. There was a sweetish taste upon my lips where it had touched me. I licked them, and was immediately filled with an inhuman desire. I turned and seized a mass of the fungus. Then more, and—more. I was insatiable. In the midst of devouring, the remembrance of the morning's discovery swept into my mazed brain. It was sent by God. I dashed the fragment I held, to the ground. Then, guiltily, I made my way back to the little encampment.

"I think she knew, by some marvellous intuition which love must have given, so soon as she set eyes on me. Her quiet sympathy made it easier for me, and I told her of my fall; yet omitted to mention the extraordinary thing which had gone before. For I would spare her all unnecessary terror. The ship in the lagoon had not been always empty.

"Thereafter, we kept from the abominable food. Yet, our punishment was upon us; for, day by day, with monstrous rapidity, the fungoid growth took hold of our poor bodies. Nothing we could do would check it materially, and so——and so——we, who had been human, became——Well, it matters less each day. Only——only we had been man and maid!

"A week ago we ate the last of the biscuit, and since that time I have caught three fish. I was out here fishing to-night when your schooner drifted upon me out of the mist. I hailed you. You know the rest, and may God out of His great heart bless you for your goodness to a—a couple of poor outcast souls."

There was the dip of an oar—another. Then the voice came again, and for the last time, sounding through the slight surrounding mist, ghostly and mournful:—

"God bless you! Good-bye!"

"Good-bye!" we shouted together, hoarsely, our hearts full of many emotions.

I glanced about me. I became aware that the dawn was upon us.

The sun flung a stray beam across the hidden sea; pierced the mist dully, and lit up the receding boat with a gloomy fire. Indistinctly, I saw something nodding between the oars. I thought of a sponge—a great, grey nodding sponge—— The oars continued to ply. They were grey—as was the boat—and my eyes searched a moment vainly for the conjunction of hand and oar. My gaze flashed back to the—head. It nodded forward as the oars went backward for the stroke. Then the oars were dipped, the boat shot out of the patch of light, and the—the thing went nodding into the mist.

II. Tales of Non-Supernatural Horror

His Unconquerable Enemy

W. C. Morrow

I was summoned from Calcutta to the heart of India to perform a difficult surgical operation on one of the women of a great rajah's household. I found the rajah a man of a noble character, but possessed, as I afterwards discovered, of a sense of cruelty purely Oriental and in contrast to the indolence of his disposition. He was so grateful for the success that attended my mission that he urged me to remain a guest at the palace as long as it might please me to stay, and I thankfully accepted the invitation.

One of the male servants early attracted my notice for his marvellous capacity of malice. His name was Neranya, and I am certain that there must have been a large proportion of Malay blood in his veins, for, unlike the Indians (from whom he differed also in complexion), he was extremely alert, active, nervous, and sensitive. A redeeming circumstance was his love for his master. Once his violent temper led him to the commission of an atrocious crime,—the fatal stabbing of a dwarf. In punishment for this the rajah ordered that Neranya's right arm (the offending one) be severed from his body. The sentence was executed in a bungling fashion by a stupid fellow armed with an axe, and I, being a surgeon, was compelled, in order to save Neranya's life, to perform an amputation of the stump, leaving not a vestige of the limb remaining.

After this he developed an augmented fiendishness. His love for the rajah was changed to hate, and in his mad anger he flung

46

discretion to the winds. Driven once to frenzy by the rajah's scornful treatment, he sprang upon the rajah with a knife, but, fortunately, was seized and disarmed. To his unspeakable dismay, the rajah sentenced him for this offence to suffer amputation of the remaining arm. It was done as in the former instance. This had the effect of putting a temporary curb on Neranya's spirit, or, rather, of changing the outward manifestations of his diabolism. Being armless, he was at first largely at the mercy of those who ministered to his needs,—a duty which I undertook to see was properly discharged, for I felt an interest in this strangely distorted nature. His sense of helplessness, combined with a damnable scheme for revenge which he had secretly formed, caused Neranya to change his fierce, impetuous, and unruly conduct into a smooth, quiet, insinuating bearing, which he carried so artfully as to deceive those with whom he was brought in contact, including the rajah himself.

Neranya, being exceedingly quick, intelligent, and dexterous, and having an unconquerable will, turned his attention to the cultivating of an enlarged usefulness of his legs, feet, and toes, with so excellent effect that in time he was able to perform wonderful feats with those members. Thus his capability, especially for destructive mischief, was considerably restored.

One morning the rajah's only son, a young man of an uncommonly amiable and noble disposition, was found dead in his bed. His murder was a most atrocious one, his body being mutilated in a shocking manner, but in my eyes the most significant of all the mutilations was the entire removal and disappearance of the young prince's arms.

The death of the young man nearly brought the rajah to the grave. It was not, therefore, until I had nursed him back to health that I began a systematic inquiry into the murder. I said nothing of my own discoveries and conclusions until after the rajah and his officers had failed and my work had been done; then I submitted to him a written report, making a close analysis of all the circumstances and closing by charging the crime to Neranya. The rajah, convinced by my proof and argument, at once ordered Neranya to be put to death, this to be accomplished slowly and with frightful tortures. The sentence was so cruel and revolting that it filled me with horror, and I implored that the wretch be shot. Finally, through a sense of gratitude to me, the rajah relaxed. When Neranya was charged with the crime he denied it, of course, but, seeing that the rajah was convinced, he threw aside all restraint, and, dancing, laughing, and shrieking in the most horrible manner, confessed his guilt, gloated over it, and reviled the rajah to his teeth,—this, knowing that some fearful death awaited him.

The rajah decided upon the details of the matter that night, and in the morning he informed me of his decision. It was that Neranya's life should be spared, but that both of his legs should be broken with hammers, and that then I should amputate the limbs at the trunk! Appended to this horrible sentence was a provision that the maimed wretch should be kept and tortured at regular intervals by such means as afterwards might be devised.

Sickened to the heart by the awful duty set out for me, I nevertheless performed it with success, and I care to say nothing more about that part of the tragedy. Neranya escaped death very narrowly and was a long time in recovering his wonted vitality. During all these weeks the rajah neither saw him nor made inquiries concerning him, but when, as in duty bound, I made official report that the man had recovered his strength, the rajah's eyes brightened, and he emerged with deadly activity from the stupor into which he so long had been plunged.

The rajah's palace was a noble structure, but it is necessary here to describe only the grand hall. It was an immense chamber, with a floor of polished, inlaid stone and a lofty, arched ceiling. A soft light stole into it through stained glass set in the roof and in high windows on one side. In the middle of the room was a rich fountain, which threw up a tall, slender column of water, with smaller and shorter jets grouped around it. Across one end of the hall, half-way to the ceiling, was a balcony, which communicated with the upper story of a wing, and from which a flight of stone stairs descended to the floor of the hall. During the hot summers this room was delightfully cool; it was the rajah's favorite lounging-place, and when the nights were hot he had his cot taken thither, and there he slept.

This hall was chosen for Neranya's permanent prison; here was he to stay so long as he might live, with never a glimpse of the shining world or the glorious heavens. To one of his nervous, discontented nature such confinement was worse than death. At the rajah's order there was constructed for him a small pen of open iron-work, circular, and about four feet in diameter, elevated on four slender iron posts, ten feet above the floor, and placed between the balcony and the fountain. Such was Neranya's prison.

The pen was about four feet in depth, and the pen-top was left open for the convenience of the servants whose duty it should be to care for him. These precautions for his safe confinement were taken at my suggestion, for, although the man was now deprived of all four of his limbs, I still feared that he might develop some extraordinary, unheard-of power for mischief. It was provided that the attendants should reach his cage by means of a movable ladder.

All these arrangements having been made and Neranya hoisted into his cage, the rajah emerged upon the balcony to see him for the first time since the last amputation. Neranya had been lying panting and helpless on the floor of his cage, but when his quick ear caught the sound of the rajah's footfall he squirmed about until he had brought the back of his head against the railing, elevating his eyes above his chest, and enabling him to peer through the open-work of the cage. Thus the two deadly enemies faced each other. The rajah's stern face paled at sight of the hideous, shapeless thing which met his gaze; but he soon recovered, and the old hard, cruel, sinister look returned. Neranya's black hair and beard had grown long, and they added to the natural ferocity of his aspect. His eyes blazed upon the rajah with a terrible light, his lips parted, and he gasped for breath; his face was ashen with rage and despair, and his thin, distended nostrils quivered.

The rajah folded his arms and gazed down from the balcony upon the frightful wreck that he had made. Oh, the dreadful pathos of that picture; the inhumanity of it; the deep and dismal tragedy of it! Who might look into the wild, despairing heart of the prisoner and see and understand the frightful turmoil there; the surging, choking passion; unbridled but impotent ferocity; frantic thirst for a vengeance that should be deeper than hell! Neranya gazed, his shapeless body heaving, his eyes aflame; and then, in a strong, clear voice, which rang throughout the great hall, with rapid speech he hurled at the rajah the most insulting defiance, the most awful curses. He cursed the womb that had conceived him, the food that should nourish him, the wealth that had brought him power; cursed him in the name of Buddha and all the wise men; cursed by the sun, the moon, and the stars; by the continents, mountains, oceans, and rivers; by all things living; cursed his head, his heart, his entrails; cursed in a whirlwind of unmentionable words; heaped unimaginable insults and contumely upon him; called him a knave, a beast, a fool, a liar, an infamous and unspeakable coward.

The rajah heard it all calmly, without the movement of a muscle, without the slightest change of countenance; and when the poor wretch had exhausted his strength and fallen helpless and silent to the floor, the rajah, with a grim, cold smile, turned and strode away.

The days passed. The rajah, not deterred by Neranya's curses often heaped upon him, spent even more time than formerly in the great hall, and slept there oftener at night; and finally Neranya wearied of cursing and defying him, and fell into a sullen silence. The man was a study for me, and I observed every change in his fleeting moods. Generally his condition was that of miserable despair, which he attempted bravely to conceal. Even the boon of suicide had been denied him, for when he would wriggle into an erect position the rail of his pen was a foot above his head, so that he could not clamber over and break his skull on the stone floor beneath; and when he had tried to starve himself the attendants forced food down his throat; so that he abandoned such attempts. At times his eyes would blaze and his breath would come in gasps, for imaginary vengeance was working within him; but steadily he became quieter and more tractable, and was pleasant and responsive when I would converse with him. Whatever might have been the tortures which the rajah had decided on, none as yet had been ordered; and although Neranya knew that they were in contemplation, he never referred to them or complained of his lot.

The awful climax of this situation was reached one night, and even after this lapse of years I cannot approach its description without a shudder.

It was a hot night, and the rajah had gone to sleep in the great hall, lying on a high cot placed on the main floor just underneath the edge of the balcony. I had been unable to sleep in my own apartment, and so I had stolen into the great hall through the heavily curtained entrance at the end farthest from the balcony. As I entered I heard a peculiar, soft sound above the patter of the fountain. Neranya's cage was partly concealed from my view by the spraying water, but I suspected that the unusual sound came from him. Stealing a little to one side, and crouching against the dark hangings of the wall, I could see him in the faint light which dimly illuminated the hall, and then I discovered that my surmise was correct—Neranya was quietly at work. Curious to learn more, and knowing that only mischief could have been inspiring him, I sank into a thick robe on the floor and watched him.

To my great astonishment Neranya was tearing off with his teeth the bag which served as his outer garment. He did it cautiously, casting sharp glances frequently at the rajah, who, sleeping soundly on his cot below, breathed heavily. After starting a strip with his teeth, Neranya, by the same means, would attach it to the railing of his cage and then wriggle away, much after the manner of a caterpillar's crawling, and this would cause the strip to be torn out the full length of his garment. He repeated this operation with incredible patience and skill until his entire garment had been torn into strips. Two or three of these he tied end to end with his teeth, lips, and tongue, tightening the knots by placing one end of the strip under his body and drawing the other taut with his teeth. In this way he made a line several feet long, one end of which he made fast to the rail with his mouth. It then began to dawn upon me that he was going to make an insane attempt—impossible of achievement without hands, feet, arms, or legs—to escape from his cage! For what purpose? The rajah was asleep in the hall—ah! I caught my breath. Oh, the desperate, insane thirst for revenge which could have unhinged so clear and firm a mind! Even though he should accomplish the impossible feat of climbing over the railing of his cage that he might fall to the floor below (for how could he slide down the rope?), he would be in all probability killed or stunned; and even if he should escape these dangers it would be impossible for him to clamber upon the cot without rousing the rajah, and impossible even though the rajah were dead! Amazed at the man's daring, and convinced that his sufferings and brooding had destroyed his reason, nevertheless I watched him with breathless interest.

With other strips tied together he made a short swing across one side of his cage. He caught the long line in his teeth at a point not far from the rail; then, wriggling with great effort to an upright position, his back braced against the rail, he put his chin over the swing and worked toward one end. He tightened the grasp of his chin on the swing, and with tremendous exertion, working the lower end of his spine against the railing, he began gradually to ascend the side of his cage. The labor was so great that he was compelled to pause at intervals, and his breathing was hard and painful; and even while thus resting he was in a position of terrible strain, and his pushing against the swing caused it to press hard against his windpipe and nearly strangle him.

After amazing effort he had elevated the lower end of his body until it protruded above the railing, the top of which was now across the lower end of his abdomen. Gradually he worked his body over, going backward, until there was sufficient excess of weight on the outer side of the rail; and then, with a quick lurch, he raised his head and shoulders and swung into a horizontal position on top of the rail. Of course, he would have fallen to the floor below had it not been for the line which he held in his teeth. With so great nicety had he estimated the distance between his mouth and the point where the rope was fastened to the rail, that the line tightened and checked him just as he reached the horizontal position on the rail. If one had told me beforehand that such a feat as I had just seen this man accomplish was possible, I should have thought him a fool.

Neranya was now balanced on his stomach across the top of the rail, and he eased his position by bending his spine and hanging down on either side as much as possible. Having rested thus for some minutes, he began cautiously to slide off backward, slowly paying out the line through his teeth, finding almost a fatal difficulty in passing the knots. Now, it is quite possible that the line would have escaped altogether from his teeth laterally when he would slightly relax his hold to let it slip, had it not been for a very ingenious plan to which he had resorted. This consisted in his having made a turn of the line around his neck before he attached the swing, thus securing a threefold control of the line,—one by his teeth, another by friction against his neck, and a third by his ability to compress it between his cheek and shoulder. It was quite evident now that the minutest details of a most elaborate plan had been carefully worked out by him before beginning the task, and that possibly weeks of difficult theoretical study had been consumed in the mental preparation. As I observed him I was reminded of certain hitherto unaccountable things which he had been doing for some weeks past—going through certain hitherto inexplicable motions, undoubtedly for the purpose of training his muscles for the immeasurably arduous labor which he was now performing.

A stupendous and seemingly impossible part of his task had been accomplished. Could he reach the floor in safety? Gradually he worked himself backward over the rail, in imminent danger of falling; but his nerve never wavered, and I could see a wonderful light in his eyes. With something of a lurch, his body fell against the outer side of the railing, to which he was hanging by his chin, the line still held firmly in his teeth. Slowly he slipped his chin from the rail, and then hung suspended by the line in his teeth. By almost imperceptible degrees, with infinite caution, he descended the line, and, finally, his unwieldy body rolled upon the floor, safe and unhurt!

What miracle would this superhuman monster next accomplish? I was quick and strong, and was ready and able to intercept any dangerous act; but not until danger appeared would I interfere with this extraordinary scene.

I must confess to astonishment upon having observed that Neranya, instead of proceeding directly toward the sleeping rajah, took quite another direction. Then it was only escape, after all, that the wretch contemplated, and not the murder of the rajah. But how could he escape? The only possible way to reach the outer air without great risk was by ascending the stairs to the balcony and leaving by the corridor which opened upon it, and thus fall into the hands of some British soldiers quartered thereabout, who might conceive the idea of hiding him; but surely it was impossible for Neranya to ascend that long flight of stairs! Nevertheless, he made directly for them, his method of progression this: He lay upon his back, with the lower end of his body toward the stairs; then bowed his spine upward, thus drawing his head and shoulders a little forward; straightened, and then pushed the lower end of his body forward a space equal to that through which he had drawn his head; repeating this again and again, each time, while bending his spine, preventing his head from slipping by pressing it against the floor. His progress was laborious and slow, but sensible; and, finally, he arrived at the foot of the stairs.

It was manifest that his insane purpose was to ascend them. The desire for freedom must have been strong within him! Wriggling to an upright position against the newel-post, he looked up at the great height which he had to climb and sighed; but there was no dimming of the light in his eyes. How could he accomplish the impossible task?

His solution of the problem was very simple, though daring and perilous as all the rest. While leaning against the newel-post he let himself fall diagonally upon the bottom step, where he lay partly hanging over, but safe, on his side. Turning upon his back, he wriggled forward along the step to the rail and raised himself to an upright position against it as he had against the newel-post, fell as before, and landed on the second step. In this manner, with inconceivable labor, he accomplished the ascent of the entire flight of stairs.

It being apparent to me that the rajah was not the object of

Neranya's movements, the anxiety which I had felt on that account was now entirely dissipated. The things which already he had accomplished were entirely beyond the nimblest imagination. The sympathy which I had always felt for the wretched man was now greatly quickened; and as infinitesimally small as I knew his chances for escape to be, I nevertheless hoped that he would succeed. Any assistance from me, however, was out of the question; and it never should be known that I had witnessed the escape.

Neranya was now upon the balcony, and I could dimly see him wriggling along toward the door which led out upon the balcony. Finally he stopped and wriggled to an upright position against the rail, which had wide openings between the balusters. His back was toward me, but he slowly turned and faced me and the hall. At that great distance I could not distinguish his features, but the slowness with which he had worked, even before he had fully accomplished the ascent of the stairs, was evidence all too eloquent of his extreme exhaustion. Nothing but a most desperate resolution could have sustained him thus far, but he had drawn upon the last remnant of his strength. He looked around the hall with a sweeping glance, and then down upon the rajah, who was sleeping immediately beneath him, over twenty feet below. He looked long and earnestly, sinking lower, and lower, and lower upon the rail. Suddenly, to my inconceivable astonishment and dismay, he toppled through and shot downward from his lofty height! I held my breath, expecting to see him crushed upon the stone floor beneath; but instead of that he fell full upon the rajah's breast, driving him through the cot to the floor. I sprang forward with a loud cry for help, and was instantly at the scene of the catastrophe. With indescribable horror I saw that Neranya's teeth were buried in the rajah's throat! I tore the wretch away, but the blood was pouring from the rajah's arteries, his chest was crushed in, and he was gasping in the agony of death. People came running in, terrified. I turned to Neranya. He lay upon his back, his face hideously smeared with blood. Murder, and not escape, had been his intentions from the beginning; and he had employed the only method by which there was ever a possibility of accomplishing it. I knelt beside him, and saw that he too was dying; his back had been broken by the fall. He smiled sweetly into my face, and a triumphant look of accomplished revenge sat upon his face even in death.

My Favorite Murder

Ambrose Bierce

Having murdered my mother under circumstances of singular atrocity, I was arrested and put upon my trial, which lasted seven years. In charging the jury, the judge of the Court of Acquittal remarked that it was one of the most ghastly crimes that he had ever been called upon to explain away.

At this, my attorney rose and said:

"May it please your Honor, crimes are ghastly or agreeable only by comparison. If you were familiar with the details of my client's previous murder of his uncle you would discern in his later offense (if offense it may be called) something in the nature of tender forbearance and filial consideration for the feelings of the victim. The appalling ferocity of the former assassination was indeed inconsistent with any hypothesis but that of guilt; and had it not been for the fact that the honorable judge before whom he was tried was the president of a life insurance company that took risks on hanging, and in which my client held a policy, it is hard to see how he could decently have been acquitted. If your Honor would like to hear about it for instruction and guidance of your Honor's mind, this unfortunate man, my client, will consent to give himself the pain of relating it under oath."

The district attorney said: "Your Honor, I object. Such a statement would be in the nature of evidence, and the testimony in this case is closed. The prisoner's statement should have been introduced three years ago, in the spring of 1881."

"In a statutory sense," said the judge, "you are right, and in the Court of Objections and Technicalities you would get a ruling in your favor. But not in a Court of Acquittal. The objection is overruled."

"I except," said the district attorney.

"You cannot do that," the judge said. "I must remind you that in order to take an exception you must first get this case transferred for a time to the Court of Exceptions on a formal motion duly supported by affidavits. A motion to that effect by your predecessor in office was denied by me during the first year of this trial. Mr. Clerk, swear the prisoner."

The customary oath having been administered, I made the following statement, which impressed the judge with so strong a sense of the comparative triviality of the offense for which I was on trial that he made no further search for mitigating circumstances, but simply instructed the jury to acquit, and I left the court, without a stain on my reputation:

"I was born in 1856 in Kalamakee, Mich., of honest and reputable parents, one of whom Heaven has mercifully spared to comfort me in my later years. In 1867 the family came to California and settled near Nigger Head, where my father opened a road agency and prospered beyond the dreams of avarice. He was a reticent, saturnine man then, though his increasing years have now somewhat relaxed the austerity of his disposition, and I believe that nothing but his memory of the sad event for which I am now on trial prevents him from manifesting a genuine hilarity.

"Four years after we had set up the road agency an itinerant preacher came along, and having no other way to pay for the night's lodging that we gave him, favored us with an exhortation of such power that, praise God, we were all converted to religion. My father at once sent for his brother, the Hon. William Ridley of Stockton, and on his arrival turned over the agency to him, charging him nothing for the franchise nor plant—the latter consisting of a Winchester rifle, a sawed-off shotgun, and an assortment of masks made out of flour sacks. The family then moved to Ghost Rock and opened a dance house. It was called 'The Saints' Rest Hurdy-Gurdy,' and the proceedings each night began with prayer. It was there that my now sainted mother, by her grace in the dance, acquired the *sobriquet* of 'The Bucking Walrus.'

"In the fall of '75 I had occasion to visit Coyote, on the road to Mahala, and took the stage at Ghost Rock. There were four other passengers. About three miles beyond Nigger Head, persons whom I identified as my Uncle William and his two sons held up the stage. Finding nothing in the express box, they went through the passengers. I acted a most honorable part in the affair, placing myself in line with the others, holding up my hands and permitting myself to be deprived of forty dollars and a gold watch. From my behavior no one could have suspected that I knew the gentlemen who gave the entertainment. A few days later, when I went to Nigger Head and asked for the return of my money and watch my uncle and cousins swore they knew nothing of the matter, and they affected a belief that my father and I had done the job ourselves in dishonest violation of commercial good faith. Uncle William even threatened to retaliate by starting an opposition dance house at Ghost Rock. As 'The Saints' Rest' had become rather unpopular, I saw that this would assuredly ruin it and prove a paying enterprise, so I told my uncle that I was willing to overlook the past if he would take me into the scheme and keep the partnership a secret from my father. This fair offer he rejected, and I then perceived that it would be better and more satisfactory if he were dead.

"My plans to that end were soon perfected, and communicating them to my dear parents I had the gratification of receiving their approval. My father said he was proud of me, and my mother promised that although her religion forbade her to assist in taking human life I should have the advantage of her prayers for my success. As a preliminary measure looking to my security in case of detection I made an application for membership in that powerful order, the Knights of Murder, and in due course was received as a member of the Ghost Rock commandery. On the day that my probation ended I was for the first time permitted to inspect the records of the order and learn who belonged to it—all the rites of initiation having been conducted in masks. Fancy my delight when, in looking over the roll of membership, I found the third name to be that of my uncle, who indeed was junior vice-chancellor of the order! Here was an opportunity exceeding my wildest dreams—to murder I could add insubordination and treachery. It was what my good mother would have called 'a special Providence.'

"At about this time something occurred which caused my cup of joy, already full, to overflow on all sides, a circular cataract of bliss. Three men, strangers in that locality, were arrested for the stage robbery in which I had lost my money and watch. They were brought to trial and, despite my efforts to clear them and fasten the guilt upon three of the most respectable and worthy citizens of Ghost Rock, convicted on the clearest proof. The murder would now be as wanton and reasonless as I could wish.

"One morning I shouldered my Winchester rifle, and going over to my uncle's house, near Nigger Head, asked my Aunt Mary, his wife, if he were at home, adding that I had come to kill him. My aunt replied with her peculiar smile that so many gentleman called on that errand and were afterward carried away without having performed it that I must excuse her for doubting my good faith in the matter. She said I did not look as if I would kill anybody, so, as a proof of good faith I leveled my rifle and wounded a Chinaman who happened to be passing the house. She said she knew whole families that could do a thing of that kind, but Bill Ridley was a horse of another color. She said, however, that I would find him over on the other side of the creek in the sheep lot; and she added that she hoped the best man would win.

"My Aunt Mary was one of the most fair-minded women that I have ever met.

"I found my uncle down on his knees engaged in skinning a sheep. Seeing that he had neither gun nor pistol handy I had not the heart to shoot him, so I approached him, greeted him pleasantly and struck him a powerful blow on the head with the butt of my rifle. I have a very good delivery and Uncle William lay down on his side, then rolled over on his back, spread out his fingers and shivered. Before he could recover the use of his limbs I seized the knife that he had been using and cut his hamstrings. You know, doubtless, that when you sever the *tendo Achillis* the patient has no further use of his leg; it is just the same as if he had no leg. Well, I parted them both, and when he revived he was at my service. As soon as he comprehended the situation, he said:

"'Samuel, you have got the drop on me and can afford to be generous. I have only one thing to ask of you, and that is that you carry me to the house and finish me in the bosom of my family.'

"I told him I thought that a pretty reasonable request and I would do so if he would let me put him into a wheat sack; he would be easier to carry that way and if we were seen by the neighbors *en route* it would cause less remark. He agreed to that, and going to the barn I got a sack. This, however, did not fit him; it was too short and much wider than he; so I bent his legs, forced his knees up against his breast and got him into it that way, tying the sack above his head. He was a heavy man and I had all that I could do to get him on my back, but I staggered along for some distance until I came to a swing that some of the children had suspended to the branch of an oak. Here I laid him down and sat upon him to rest, and the sight of the rope gave me a happy inspiration. In twenty minutes my uncle, still in the sack, swung free to the sport of the wind.

"I had taken down the rope, tied one end tightly about the mouth of the bag, thrown the other across the limb and hauled him up about five feet from the ground. Fastening the other end of the rope also about the mouth of the sack, I had the satisfaction to see my uncle converted into a large, fine pendulum. I must add that he was not himself entirely aware of the nature of the change that he had undergone in his relation to the exterior world, though in justice to a good man's memory I ought to say that I do not think he would in any case have wasted much of my time in vain remonstrance.

"Uncle William had a ram that was famous in all that region as a fighter. It was in a state of chronic constitutional indignation. Some deep disappointment in early life had soured its disposition and it had declared war upon the whole world. To say that it would butt anything accessible is but faintly to express the nature and scope of its military activity: the universe was its antagonist; its methods that of a projectile. It fought like the angels and devils, in mid-air, cleaving the atmosphere like a bird, describing a parabolic curve and descending upon its victim at just the exact angle of incidence to make the most of its velocity and weight. Its momentum, calculated in foot-tons, was something incredible. It had been seen to destroy a four year old bull by a single impact upon the animal's gnarly forehead. No stone wall had ever been known to resist its downward swoop; there were no trees tough enough to stay it; it would splinter them into matchwood and defile their leafy honors in the dust. This irascible and implacable brute—this incarnate thunderbolt—this monster of the upper deep, I had seen reposing in the shade of an adjacent tree, dreaming dreams of conquest and glory. It was with a view to summoning it forth to the field of honor that I suspended its master in the manner described.

"Having completed my preparations, I imparted to the avuncular pendulum a gentle oscillation, and retiring to cover behind a contiguous rock, lifted up my voice in a long rasping cry whose diminishing final note was drowned in a noise like that of a swearing cat, which

emanated from the sack. Instantly that formidable sheep was upon
its feet and had taken in the military situation at a glance. In a few
moments it had approached, stamping, to within fifty yards of the
swinging foeman, who, now retreating and anon advancing,
seemed to invite the fray. Suddenly I saw the beast's head drop
earthward as if depressed by the weight of its enormous horns;
then a dim, white, wavy streak of sheep prolonged itself from that
spot in a generally horizontal direction to within about four yards
of a point immediately beneath the enemy. There it struck sharply
upward, and before it had faded from my gaze at the place whence
it had set out I heard a horrid thump and a piercing scream, and
my poor uncle shot forward, with a slack rope higher than the limb
to which he was attached. Here the rope tautened with a jerk,
arresting his flight, and back he swung in a breathless curve to the
other end of his arc. The ram had fallen, a heap of indistinguishable
legs, wool and horns, but pulling itself together and dodging as its
antagonist swept downward it retired at random, alternately shaking
its head and stamping its fore-feet. When it had backed about the
same distance as that from which it had delivered the assault it paused
again, bowed its head as if in prayer for victory and again shot forward, dimly visible as before—a prolonging white streak with monstrous undulations, ending with a sharp ascension. Its course this
time was at a right angle to its former one, and its impatience so
great that it struck the enemy before he had nearly reached the
lowest point of his arc. In consequence he went flying round and
round in a horizontal circle whose radius was about equal to half
the length of the rope, which I forgot to say was nearly twenty feet
long. His shrieks, *crescendo* in approach and *diminuendo* in reces-
sion, made the rapidity of his revolution more obvious to the ear
than to the eye. He had evidently not yet been struck in a vital spot.
His posture in the sack and the distance from the ground at which
he hung compelled the ram to operate upon his lower extremities
and the end of his back. Like a plant that has struck its root into
some poisonous mineral, my poor uncle was dying slowly upward.

"After delivering its second blow the ram had not again retired.
The fever of battle burned hot in its heart; its brain was intoxicated with the wine of strife. Like a pugilist who in his rage forgets
his skill and fights ineffectively at half-arm's length, the angry beast
endeavored to reach its fleeting foe by awkward vertical leaps as he
passed overhead, sometimes, indeed, succeeding in striking him

feebly, but more frequently overthrown by its own misguided eagerness. But as the impetus was exhausted and the man's circles narrowed in scope and diminished in speed, bringing him nearer to the ground, these tactics produced better results, eliciting a superior quality of screams, which I greatly enjoyed.

"Suddenly, as if the bugles had sung truce, the ram suspended hostilities and walked away, thoughtfully wrinkling and smoothing its great aquiline nose, and occasionally cropping a bunch of grass and slowly munching it. It seemed to have tired of war's alarms and resolved to beat the sword into a plowshare and cultivate the arts of peace. Steadily it held its course away from the field of fame until it had gained a distance of nearly a quarter of a mile. There it stopped and stood with its rear to the foe, chewing its cud and apparently half asleep. I observed, however, an occasional slight turn of its head, as if its apathy were more affected than real.

"Meantime Uncle William's shrieks had abated with his motion, and nothing was heard from him but long, low moans, and at long intervals my name, uttered in pleading tones exceedingly grateful to my ear. Evidently the man had not the faintest notion of what was being done to him, and was inexpressibly terrified. When Death comes cloaked in mystery he is terrible indeed. Little by little my uncle's oscillations diminished, and finally he hung motionless. I went to him and was about to give him the *coup de grâce,* when I heard and felt a succession of smart shocks which shook the ground like a series of light earthquakes, and turning in the direction of the ram, saw a long cloud of dust approaching me with inconceivable rapidity and alarming effect! At a distance of some thirty yards away it stopped short, and from the near end of it rose into the air what I at first thought a great white bird. Its ascent was so smooth and easy and regular that I could not realize its extraordinary celerity, and was lost in admiration of its grace. To this day the impression remains that it was a slow, deliberate movement, the ram—for it was that animal—being upborne by some power other than its own impetus, and supported through the successive stages of its flight with tenderness and care. My eyes followed its progress through the air with unspeakable pleasure, all the greater by contrast with my former terror of its approach by land. Onward and upward the noble animal sailed, its head bent down almost between its knees, its fore-feet thrown back, its hinder legs trailing to rear like the legs of a soaring heron.

"At a height of forty or fifty feet, as fond recollection presents it to view, it attained its zenith and appeared to remain an instant stationary; then, tilting suddenly forward without altering the relative position of its parts, it shot downward on a steeper and steeper course with augmenting velocity, passed immediately above me with a noise like the rush of a cannon shot and struck my poor uncle almost squarely on the top of the head! So frightful was the impact that not only the man's neck was broken, but the rope too; and the body of the deceased, forced against the earth, was crushed to pulp beneath the awful front of that meteoric sheep! The concussion stopped all the clocks between Lone Hand and Dutch Dan's, and Professor Davidson, a distinguished authority in matters seismic, who happened to be in the vicinity, promptly explained that the vibrations were from north to southwest.

"Altogether, I cannot help thinking that in point of artistic atrocity my murder of Uncle William has seldom been excelled."

III. Tales of Awe

The Inmost Light

Arthur Machen

I

One evening in autumn, when the deformities of London were veiled in faint blue mist, and its vistas and far-reaching streets seemed splendid, Mr. Charles Salisbury was slowly pacing down Rupert Street, drawing nearer to his favourite restaurant by slow degrees. His eyes were downcast in study of the pavement, and thus it was that as he passed in at the narrow door a man who had come up from the lower end of the street jostled against him.

"I beg your pardon—wasn't looking where I was going. Why, it's Dyson!"

"Yes, quite so. How are you, Salisbury?"

"Quite well. But where have you been, Dyson? I don't think I can have seen you for the last five years?"

"No; I dare say not. You remember I was getting rather hard up when you came to my place at Charlotte Street?"

"Perfectly. I think I remember your telling me that you owed five weeks' rent, and that you had parted with your watch for a comparatively small sum."

"My dear Salisbury, your memory is admirable. Yes, I was hard up. But the curious thing is that soon after you saw me I became harder up. My financial state was described by a friend as 'stone broke.' I don't approve of slang, mind you, but such was my condition. But suppose we go in; there might be other people who would like to dine—it's human weakness, Salisbury."

"Certainly; come along. I was wondering as I walked down

63

whether the corner table were taken. It has a velvet back you know."

"I know the spot; it's vacant. Yes, as I was saying, I became even harder up."

"What did you do then?" asked Salisbury, disposing of his hat, and settling down in the corner of the seat, with a glance of fond anticipation at the menu.

"What did I do? Why, I sat down and reflected. I had a good classical education, and a positive distaste for business of any kind: that was the capital with which I faced the world. Do you know, I have heard people describe olives as nasty! What lamentable Philistinism! I have often thought, Salisbury, that I could write genuine poetry under the influence of olives and red wine. Let us have Chianti; it may not be very good, but the flasks are simply charming."

"It is pretty good here. We may as well have a big flask."

"Very good. I reflected, then, on my want of prospects, and I determined to embark in literature."

"Really; that was strange. You seem in pretty comfortable cir-cumstances, though."

"Though! What a satire upon a noble profession. I am afraid, Salisbury, you haven't a proper idea of the dignity of an artist. You see me sitting at my desk—or at least you can see me if you care to call—with pen and ink, and simple nothingness before me, and if you come again in a few hours you will (in all probability) find a creation!"

"Yes, quite so. I had an idea that literature was not remunerative."

"You are mistaken; its rewards are great. I may mention, by the way, that shortly after you saw me I succeeded to a small income. An uncle died, and proved unexpectedly generous."

"Ah, I see. That must have been convenient."

"It was pleasant—undeniably pleasant. I have always considered it in the light of an endowment of my researches. I told you I was a man of letters; it would, perhaps, be more correct to describe myself as a man of science."

"Dear me, Dyson, you have really changed very much in the last few years. I had a notion, don't you know, that you were a sort of idler about town, the kind of man one might meet on the north side of Piccadilly every day from May to July."

"Exactly. I was even then forming myself, though all uncon-sciously. You know my poor father could not afford to send me to the University. I used to grumble in my ignorance at not having completed my education. That was the folly of youth, Salisbury; my University was Piccadilly. There I began to study the great science which still occupies me."

"What science do you mean?"

"The science of the great city; the physiology of London; literally and metaphysically the greatest subject that the mind of man can conceive. What an admirable salmi this is; undoubtedly the final end of the pheasant. Yet I feel sometimes positively overwhelmed with the thought of the vastness and complexity of London. Paris a man may get to understand thoroughly with a reasonable amount of study; but London is always a mystery. In Paris you may say: 'Here live the actresses, here the Bohemians, and the *Ratés';* but it is different in London. You may point out a street, correctly enough, as the abode of washerwomen; but, in that second floor, a man may be studying Chaldee roots, and in the garret over the way a forgotten artist is dying by inches."

"I see you are Dyson, unchanged and unchangeable," said Salisbury, slowly sipping his Chianti. "I think you are misled by a too fervid imagination; the mystery of London exists only in your fancy. It seems to me a dull place enough. We seldom hear of a really artistic crime in London, whereas I believe Paris abounds in that sort of thing."

"Give me some more wine. Thanks. You are mistaken, my dear fellow, you are really mistaken. London has nothing to be ashamed of in the way of crime. Where we fail is for want of Homers, not Agamemnons. *Carent quia vate sacro,* you know."

"I recall the quotation. But I don't think I quite follow you."

"Well, in plain language, we have no good writers in London who make a specialty of that kind of thing. Our common reporter is a dull dog; every story that he has to tell is spoilt in the telling. His idea of horror and of what excites horror is so lamentably deficient. Nothing will content the fellow but blood, vulgar red blood, and when he can get it he lays it on thick, and considers that he has produced a telling article. It's a poor notion. And, by some curious fatality, it is the most commonplace and brutal murders which always attract the most attention and get written up the most. For instance, I dare say that you never heard of the Harlesden case?"

"No; no, I don't remember anything about it."

"Of course not. And yet the story is a curious one. I will tell it to you over our coffee. Harlesden, you know, or I expect you don't know, is quite on the out-quarters of London; something curiously different from your fine old crusted suburb like Norwood or Hampstead, different as each of these is from the other. Hampstead, I mean, is where you look for the head of your great China house with his three acres of land and pine-houses, though of late there is the artistic substratum; while Norwood is the home of the prosperous middle-class family who took the house 'because it was near the Palace,' and sickened of the Palace six months afterwards; but Harlesden is a place of no character. It's too new to have any character as yet. There are the rows of red houses and the rows of white houses and the bright green Venetians, and the blistering doorways, and the little backyards they call gardens, and a few feeble shops, and then, just as you think you're going to grasp the physiognomy of the settlement, it all melts away."

"How the dickens is that? The houses don't tumble down before one's eyes, I suppose!"

"Well, no, not exactly that. But Harlesden as an entity disappears. Your street turns into a quiet lane, and your staring houses into elm trees, and the back-gardens into green meadows. You pass instantly from town to country; there is no transition as in a small country town, no soft gradations of wider lawns and orchards, with houses gradually becoming less dense, but a dead stop. I believe the people who live there mostly go into the City. I have seen once or twice a laden bus bound thitherwards. But however that may be, I can't conceive a greater loneliness in a desert at midnight than there is there at midday. It is like a city of the dead; the streets are glaring and desolate, and as you pass it suddenly strikes you that this too is part of London. Well, a year or two ago there was a doctor living there; he had set up his brass plate and his red lamp at the very end of one of those shining streets, and from the back of the house, the fields stretched away to the north. I don't know what his reason was in settling down in such of an out-of-the-way place, perhaps Dr. Black, as we will call him, was a far-seeing man and looked ahead. His relations, so it appeared afterwards, had lost sight of him for many years and didn't even know he was a doctor, much less where he lived. However, there he was settled in Harlesden, with some fragments of a practice, and an uncommonly pretty wife. People used to see them walking out together in the summer evenings soon after they came to Harlesden, and, so far as could be observed, they seemed a very affectionate couple. These walks went on through the autumn, and then ceased, but, of course, as the days grew dark and the weather cold, the lanes near Harlesden might be expected to lose many of their attractions. All through the winter nobody saw anything of Mrs. Black, the doctor used to reply to his patients' inquiries that she was a 'little out of sorts, would be better, no doubt, in the spring.' But the spring came, and the summer, and no Mrs. Black appeared, and at last people began to rumour and talk amongst themselves, and all sorts of queer things were said at 'high teas,' which you may possibly have heard are the only form of entertainment known in such suburbs. Dr. Black began to surprise some very odd looks cast in his direction, and the practice, such as it was, fell off before his eyes. In short, when the neighbours whispered about the matter, they whispered that Mrs. Black was dead, and that the doctor had made away with her. But this wasn't the case; Mrs. Black was seen alive in June. It was a Sunday afternoon, one of those few exquisite days that an English climate offers, and half London had strayed out into the fields, north, south, east, and west to smell the scent of the white May, and to see if the wild roses were yet in blossom in the hedges. I had gone out myself early in the morning, and had had a long ramble, and somehow or other as I was steering homeward I found myself in this very Harlesden we have been talking about. To be exact, I had a glass of beer in the General Gordon, the most flourishing house in the neighbourhood, and as I was wandering rather aimlessly about, I saw an uncommonly tempting gap in a hedgerow, and resolved to explore the meadow beyond. Soft grass is very grateful to the feet after the infernal grit strewn on suburban sidewalks, and after walking about for some time I thought I should like to sit down on a bank and have a smoke. While I was getting out my pouch, I looked up in the direction of the houses, and as I looked I felt my breath caught back, and my teeth began to chatter, and the stick I had in one hand snapped in two with the grip I gave it. It was as if I had had an electric current down my spine, and yet for some moment of time which seemed long, but which must have been very short, I caught myself wondering what on earth was the matter. Then I knew what had made my very heart shudder and my bones grind together in an agony. As I glanced up I had looked straight towards the last house in the row before me, and in an upper window of that house I had seen for some short fraction of a second a face. It was the face of a woman, and yet it was not human. You and I, Salisbury, have heard in our time, as we sat in our seats in church in sober English fashion, of a lust that cannot be satiated and of a fire that is unquenchable, but few of us have any notion what these words mean. I hope you never may, for as I saw that face at the window, with the blue sky above me and the warm air playing in gusts about me, I knew I had looked into another world—looked through the window of a commonplace, brand-new house, and seen hell open before me. When the first shock was over, I thought once or twice that I should have fainted; my face streamed with a cold sweat, and my breath came and went in sobs, as if I had been half drowned. I managed to get up at last, and walk round to the street, and there I saw the name 'Dr. Black' on the post by the front gate. As fate or my luck would have it, the door opened and a man came down the steps as I passed by. I had no doubt it was the doctor himself. He was of a type rather common in London; long and thin, with a pasty face and a dull black moustache. He gave me a look as we passed each other on the pavement, and though it was merely the casual glance which one foot-passenger bestows on another, I felt convinced in my mind that here was an ugly customer to deal with. As you may imagine, I went my way a good deal puzzled and horrified too by what I had seen; for I had paid another visit to the General Gordon, and had got together a good deal of the common gossip of the place about the Blacks. I didn't mention the fact that I had seen a woman's face in the window; but I heard that Mrs. Black had been much admired for her beautiful golden hair, and round what had struck me with such a nameless terror, there was a mist of flowing yellow hair, as it was an aureole of glory round the visage of a satyr. The whole thing bothered me in an indescribable manner; and when I got home I tried my best to think of the impression I had received as an illusion, but it was no use. I knew very well I had seen what I have tried to describe to you, and I was morally certain that I had seen Mrs. Black. And then there was the gossip of the place, the suspicion of foul play, which I knew to be false, and my own conviction that there was some deadly mischief or other going on in that bright red house at the corner of Devon Road: how to construct a theory of a reasonable kind out of these two elements. In short, I found myself in a world of mystery; I puzzled my head over it and filled up my leisure moments by gathering together odd threads of speculation, but I never moved a step towards any real solution, and as the summer days went on the matter seemed to grow misty and indistinct, shadowing some vague terror, like a nightmare of last month. I suppose it would before long have faded into the background of my brain—I should not have forgotten it, for such a thing could never be forgotten—but one morning as I was looking over the paper my eye was caught by a heading over some two dozen lines of small type. The words I had seen were simply: 'The Harlesden Case,' and I knew what I was going to read. Mrs. Black was dead. Black had called in another medical man to certify as to cause of death, and something or other had aroused the strange doctor's suspicions and there had been an inquest and post-mortem. And the result? That, I will confess, did astonish me considerably; it was the triumph of the unexpected. The two doctors who made the autopsy were obliged to confess that they could not discover the faintest trace of any kind of foul play; their most exquisite tests and reagents failed to detect the presence of poison in the most infinitesimal quantity. Death, they found, had been caused by a somewhat obscure and scientifically interesting form of brain disease. The tissue of the brain and the molecules of the grey matter had undergone a most extraordinary series of changes; and the younger of the two doctors, who has some reputation, I believe, as a specialist in brain trouble, made some remarks in giving his evidence which struck me deeply at the time, though I did not then grasp their full significance. He said: 'At the commencement of the examination I was astonished to find appearances of a character entirely new to me, notwithstanding my somewhat large experience. I need not specify these appearances at present, it will be sufficient for me to state that as I proceeded in my task I could scarcely believe that the brain before me was that of a human being at all.' There was some surprise at this statement, as you may imagine, and the coroner asked the doctor if he meant to say that the brain resembled that of an animal. 'No,' he replied, 'I should not put it in that way. Some of the appearances I noticed seemed to point in that direction, but others, and these were the more surprising, indicated a nervous organization of a wholly different character from that either of man or the lower animals.' It was a curious thing to say, but of course the jury brought in a verdict of death from natural causes, and, so far as the public was concerned, the case came to an end. But after I had read what the doctor said I made up my

mind that I should like to know a good deal more, and I set to work
on what seemed likely to prove an interesting investigation. I had
really a good deal of trouble, but I was successful in a measure.
Though why—my dear fellow, I had no notion at the time. Are you
aware that we have been here nearly four hours? The waiters are
staring at us. Let's have the bill and be gone."

The two men went out in silence, and stood a moment in the
cool air, watching the hurrying traffic of Coventry Street pass
before them to the accompaniment of the ringing bells of hansoms
and the cries of the newsboys; the deep far murmur of London
surging up ever and again from beneath these louder noises.

"It is a strange case, isn't it?" said Dyson at length. "What do you
think of it?"

"My dear fellow, I haven't heard the end, so I will reserve my
opinion. When will you give me the sequel?"

"Come to my rooms some evening; say next Thursday. Here's the
address. Good-night; I want to get down to the Strand." Dyson
hailed a passing hansom, and Salisbury turned northward to walk
home to his lodgings.

II

Mr. Salisbury, as may have been gathered from the few remarks
which he had found it possible to introduce in the course of the
evening, was a young gentleman of a peculiarly solid form of intellect, coy and retiring before the mysterious and the uncommon,
with a constitutional dislike of paradox. During the restaurant dinner he had been forced to listen in almost absolute silence to a
strange tissue of improbabilities strung together with the ingenuity
of a born meddler in plots and mysteries, and it was with a feeling
of weariness that he crossed Shaftesbury Avenue, and dived into
the recesses of Soho, for his lodgings were in a modest neighbourhood to the north of Oxford Street. As he walked he speculated on
the probable fate of Dyson, relying on literature, unbefriended by
a thoughtful relative, and could not help concluding that so much
subtlety united to a too vivid imagination would in all likelihood
have been rewarded with a pair of sandwich-boards or a super's
banner. Absorbed in this train of thought, and admiring the perverse dexterity which could transmute the face of a sickly woman
and a case of brain disease into the crude elements of romance,

Salisbury strayed on through the dimly lighted streets, not noticing the gusty wind which drove sharply round corners and whirled the stray rubbish of the pavement into the air in eddies, while black clouds gathered over the sickly yellow moon. Even a stray drop or two of rain blown into his face did not rouse him from his meditations, and it was only when with a sudden rush the storm tore down upon the street that he began to consider the expediency of finding some shelter. The rain, driven by the wind, pelted down with the violence of a thunderstorm, dashing up from the stones and hissing through the air, and soon a perfect torrent of water coursed along the kennels and accumulated in pools over the choked-up drains. The few stray passengers who had been loafing rather than walking about the street had scuttered away, like frightened rabbits, to some invisible places of refuge, and though Salisbury whistled loud and long for a hansom, no hansom appeared. He looked about him, as if to discover how far he might be from the haven of Oxford Street, but strolling carelessly along, he had turned out of his way, and found himself in an unknown region, and one to all appearance devoid even of a public house where shelter could be bought for the modest sum of two pence. The street lamps were few and at long intervals, and burned behind grimy glasses with the sickly light of oil, and by this wavering glimmer Salisbury could make out the shadowy and vast old houses of which the street was composed. As he passed along, hurrying, and shrinking from the full sweep of the rain, he noticed the innumerable bell-handles, with names that seemed about to vanish of old age graven on brass plates beneath them, and here and there a richly carved penthouse overhung the door, blackening with the grime of fifty years. The storm seemed to grow more and more furious; he was wet through, and a new hat had become a ruin, and still Oxford Street seemed as far off as ever; it was with deep relief that the dripping man caught sight of a dark archway which seemed to promise shelter from the rain if not from the wind. Salisbury took up his position in the driest corner and looked about him; he was standing in a kind of passage contrived under part of a house, and behind him stretched a narrow footway leading between blank walls to regions unknown,. He had stood there for some time, vainly endeavouring to rid himself of some of his superfluous moisture, and listening for the passing wheel of a hansom, when his attention was aroused by a loud noise coming from the direction of the passage behind, and growing louder as it drew nearer. In a couple of minutes he could make out the shrill, raucous voice of a woman, threatening and renouncing and making the very stones echo with her accents, while now and then a man grumbled and expostulated. Though to all appearance devoid of romance, Salisbury had some relish for street rows, and was, indeed, somewhat of an amateur in the more amusing phases of drunkenness; he therefore composed himself to listen and observe with something of the air of a subscriber to grand opera. To his annoyance, however, the tempest seemed suddenly to be composed, and he could hear nothing but the impatient steps of the woman and the slow lurch of the man as they came towards him. Keeping back in the shadow of the wall, he could see the two drawing nearer; the man was evidently drunk, and had much ado to avoid frequent collision with the wall as he tacked across from one side to the other, like some bark beating up against a wind. The woman was looking straight in front of her, with tears streaming from her blazing eyes, but suddenly as they went by the flame blazed up again, and she burst forth into a torrent of abuse, facing round upon her companion.

"You low rascal, you mean, contemptible cur," she went on, after an incoherent storm of curses, "you think I'm to work and slave for you always, I suppose, while you're after that Green Street girl and drinking every penny you've got? But you're mistaken, Sam—indeed, I'll bear it no longer. Damn you, you dirty thief, I've done with you and your master too, so you can go your own errands, and I only hope they'll get you into trouble."

The woman tore at the bosom of her dress, and taking something out that looked like paper, crumpled it up and flung it away. It fell at Salisbury's feet. She ran out and disappeared in the darkness, while the man lurched slowly into the street, grumbling indistinctly to himself in a perplexed tone of voice. Salisbury looked out after him, and saw him maundering along the pavement, halting now and then and swaying indecisively, and then starting off at some fresh tangent. The sky had cleared, and white fleecy clouds were fleeting across the moon, high in the heaven. The light came and went by turns, as the clouds passed by, and, turning round as the clear, white rays shone into the passage, Salisbury saw the little ball of crumpled paper which the woman had cast down. Oddly curious to know what it might contain, he picked it up and put it in his pocket, and set out afresh on his journey.

III

Salisbury was a man of habit. When he got home, drenched to the skin, his clothes hanging lank about him, and a ghastly dew besmearing his hat, his only thought was of his health, of which he took studious care. So, after changing his clothes and encasing himself in a warm dressing-gown, he proceeded to prepare a sudorific in the shape of hot gin and water, warming the latter over one of those spirit-lamps which mitigate the austerities of the modern hermit's life. By the time this preparation had been exhibited, and Salisbury's disturbed feelings had been soothed by a pipe of tobacco, he was able to get into bed in a happy state of vacancy, without a thought of his adventure in the dark archway, or of the weird fancies with which Dyson had seasoned his dinner. It was the same at breakfast the next morning, for Salisbury made a point of not thinking of any thing until that meal was over; but when the cup and saucer were cleared away, and the morning pipe was lit, he remembered the little ball of paper, and began fumbling in the pockets of his wet coat. He did not remember into which pocket he had put it, and as he dived now into one and now into another, he experienced a strange feeling of apprehension lest it should not be there at all, though he could not for the life of him have explained the importance he attached to what was in all probability mere rubbish. But he sighed with relief when his fingers touched the crumpled surface in an inside pocket, and he drew it out gently and laid it on the little desk by his easy chair with as much care as if it had been some rare jewel. Salisbury sat smoking and staring at his find for a few minutes, an odd temptation to throw the thing in the fire and have done with it struggling with as odd a speculation as to its possible contents, and as to the reason why the infuriated woman should have flung a bit of paper from her with such vehemence. As might be expected, it was the latter feeling that conquered in the end, and yet it was with something like repugnance that he at last took the paper and unrolled it, and laid it out before him. It was a piece of common dirty paper, to all appearance torn out of a cheap exercise book, and in the middle were a few lines written in a queer cramped hand. Salisbury bent his head and stared eagerly at it for a moment, drawing a long breath, and then fell back in his chair gazing blankly before him, till at last with a sudden revulsion he burst into a peal of laughter, so long and loud and uproarious that

the landlady's baby in the floor below awoke from sleep and echoed
his mirth with hideous yells. But he laughed again and again, and
took the paper up to read a second time what seemed such meaningless nonsense.

"Q. has had to go and see his friends in Paris," it began. "Traverse
Handel S. 'Once around the grass, and twice around the lass, and
thrice around the maple-tree.'"

Salisbury took up the paper and crumpled it as the angry woman
had done, and aimed it at the fire. He did not throw it there, however, but tossed it carelessly into the well of the desk, and laughed
again. The sheer folly of the thing offended him, and he was
ashamed of his own eager speculation, as one who pores over the
high-sounding announcements in the agony column of the daily
paper, and finds nothing but advertisement and triviality. He
walked to the window, and stared out at the languid morning life of
his quarter; the maids in slatternly print dresses washing door-
steps, the fish-monger and the butcher on their rounds, and the
tradesmen standing at the doors of their small shops, drooping for
lack of trade and excitement. In the distance a blue haze gave some
grandeur to the prospect, but the view as a whole was depressing,
and would only have interested a student of the life of London, who
finds something rare and choice in its every aspect. Salisbury
turned away in disgust, and settled himself in the easy chair, uphol-
stered in a bright shade of green, and decked with yellow gimp,
which was the pride and attraction of the apartments. Here he
composed himself to his morning's occupation—the perusal of a
novel that deal with sport and love in a manner that suggested the
collaboration of a stud-groom and a ladies' college. In an ordinary
way, however, Salisbury would have been carried on by the interest
of the story up to lunch time, but this morning he fidgeted in and
out of his chair, took the book up and laid it down again, and swore
at last to himself and at himself in mere irritation. In point of fact
the jingle of the paper found in the archway had "got into his head,"
and do what he would he could not help muttering over and over,
"Once around the grass, and twice around the lass, and thrice
around the maple-tree." It became a positive pain, like the foolish
burden of a music-hall song, everlastingly quoted, and sung at all
hours of the day and night, and treasured by the street boys as an
unfailing resource for six months together. He went out into the
streets, and tried to forget his enemy in the jostling of the crowds

and the roar and clatter of the traffic, but presently he would find himself stealing quietly aside, and pacing some deserted byway, vainly puzzling his brains, and trying to fix some meaning to phrases that were meaningless. It was a positive relief when Thursday came, and he remembered that he had made an appointment to go and see Dyson; the flimsy reveries of the self-styled man of letters appeared entertaining when compared with this ceaseless iteration, this maze of thought from which there seemed no possibility of escape. Dyson's abode was in one of the quietest of the quiet streets that lead down from the Strand to the river, and when Salisbury passed from the narrow stairway into his friend's room, he saw that the uncle had been beneficent indeed. The floor glowed and flamed with all the colours of the East; it was, as Dyson pompously remarked, "a sunset in a dream," and the lamplight, the twilight of London streets, was shut out with strangely worked curtains, glittering here and there with threads of gold. In the shelves of an oak armoire stood jars and plates of old French china, and the black and white of etchings not to be found in the Haymarket or in Bond Street, stood out against the splendour of a Japanese paper. Salisbury sat down on the settle by the hearth, and sniffed the mingled fumes of incense and tobacco, wondering and dumb before all this splendour after the green rep and the oleographs, the gilt-framed mirror, and the lustres of his own apartment.

"I am glad you have come," said Dyson. "Comfortable little room, isn't it? But you don't look very well, Salisbury. Nothing disagreed with you, has it?"

"No; but I have been a good deal bothered for the last few days. The fact is I had an odd kind of—of—adventure, I suppose I may call it, that night I saw you, and it has worried me a good deal. And the provoking part of it is that it's the merest nonsense—but, however, I will tell you all about it, by and by. You were going to let me have the rest of that odd story you began at the restaurant."

"Yes. But I am afraid, Salisbury, you are incorrigible. You are a slave to what you call matter of fact. You know perfectly well that in your heart you think the oddness in that case is of my making, and that it is all as plain as the police reports. However, as I have begun, I will go on. But first we will have something to drink, and you may as well light your pipe."

Dyson went up to the oak cupboard, and drew from its depths a rotund bottle and two little glasses, quaintly gilded.

"It's Benedictine," he said. "You'll have some, won't you?"

Salisbury assented, and the two men sat sipping and smoking reflectively for some minutes before Dyson began.

"Let me see," he said at last, "we were at the inquest, weren't we? No, we had done with that. Ah, I remember. I was telling you that on the whole I had been successful in my inquiries, investigation, or whatever you like to call it, into the matter. Wasn't that where I left off?"

"Yes, that was it. To be precise, I think, 'though' was the last word you said on the matter."

"Exactly. I have been thinking it all over since the other night, and I have come to the conclusion that the 'though' is a very big 'though' indeed. Not to put too fine a point on it, I have had to confess that what I found out, or thought I found out, amounts in reality to nothing. I am as far away from the heart of the case as ever. However, I may as well tell you what I do know. You may remember my saying that I was impressed a good deal by some remarks of one of the doctors who gave evidence at the inquest. Well, I determined that my first step must be to try if I could get something more definite and intelligible out of that doctor. Somehow or other I managed to get an introduction to the man, and he gave me an appointment to come and see him. He turned out to be a pleasant, genial fellow; rather young and not in the least like the typical medical man, and he began the conference by offering me whisky and cigars. I didn't think it worth while to beat about the bush, so I began by saying that part of his evidence at the Harlesden inquest struck me as very peculiar, and I gave him the printed report, with the sentences in question underlined. He just glanced at the slip, and gave me a queer look. 'It struck you as peculiar, did it?' said he. 'Well, you must remember that the Harlesden case was very peculiar. In fact, I think I may safely say that in some features it was unique—quite unique.' 'Quite so,' I replied, 'and that's exactly why it interests me, and why I want to know more about it. And I thought that if anybody could give me any information it would be you. What is your opinion of the matter?'

"It was a pretty downright sort of question, and my doctor looked rather taken aback.

"'Well,' he said, 'as I fancy your motive in inquiring into the question must be mere curiosity, I think I may tell you my opinion with tolerable freedom. So, Mr., Mr. Dyson? if you want to know my theory, it is this: I believe that Dr. Black killed his wife.'

"'But the verdict,' I answered, 'the verdict was given from your own evidence.'

"'Quite so; the verdict was given in accordance with the evidence of my colleague and myself, and, under the circumstances, I think the jury acted very sensibly. In fact, I don't see what else they could have done. But I stick to my opinion, mind you, and I say this also. I don't wonder at Black's doing what I firmly believe he did. I think he was justified.'

"'Justified! How could that be?' I asked. I was astonished, as you may imagine, at the answer I had got. The doctor wheeled round his chair and looked steadily at me for a moment before he answered.

"'I suppose you are not a man of science yourself? No; then it would be of no use my going into detail. I have always been firmly opposed myself to any partnership between physiology and psychology. I believe that both are bound to suffer. No one recognizes more decidedly than I do the impassable gulf, the fathomless abyss that separates the world of consciousness from the sphere of matter. We know that every change of consciousness is accompanied by a rearrangement of the molecules in the grey matter; and that is all. What the link between them is, or why they occur together, we do not know, and most authorities believe that we never can know. Yet, I will tell you that as I did my work, the knife in my hand, I felt convinced, in spite of all theories, that what lay before me was not the brain of a dead woman—not the brain of a human being at all. Of course I saw the face; but it was quite placid, devoid of all expression. It must have been a beautiful face, no doubt, but I can honestly say that I would not have looked in that face when there was life behind it for a thousand guineas, no, nor for twice that sum.'

"'My dear sir,' I said, 'you surprise me extremely. You say that it was not the brain of a human being. What was it, then?'

"'The brain of a devil.' He spoke quite coolly, and never moved a muscle. 'The brain of a devil,' he repeated, 'and I have no doubt that Black found some way of putting an end to it. I don't blame him if he did. Whatever Mrs. Black was, she was not fit to stay in this world. Will you have anything more? No? Good-night, good-night.'

"It was a queer sort of opinion to get from a man of science, wasn't it? When he was saying that he would not have looked on that face when alive for a thousand guineas, or two thousand guineas, I was thinking of the face I had seen, but I said nothing. I went again to Harlesden, and passed from one shop to another, making small purchases, and trying to find out whether there was anything about the Blacks which was not already common property, but there was very little to hear. One of the tradesmen to whom I spoke said he had known the dead woman well; she used to buy of him such quantities of grocery as were required for their small household, for they never kept a servant, but had a charwoman in occasionally, and she had not seen Mrs. Black for months before she died. According to this man Mrs. Black was 'a nice lady,' always kind and considerate, and so fond of her husband and he of her, as every one thought. And yet, to put the doctor's opinion on one side, I knew what I had seen. And then after thinking it all over, and putting one thing with another, it seemed to me that the only person likely to give me much assistance would be Black himself, and I made up my mind to find him. Of course he wasn't to be found in Harlesden; he had left, I was told, directly after the funeral. Everything in the house had been sold, and one fine day Black got into the train with a small portmanteau, and went, nobody knew where. It was a chance if he were ever heard of again, and it was by a mere chance that I came across him at last. I was walking one day along Gray's Inn Road, not bound for anywhere in particular, but looking about me, as usual, and holding on to my hat, for it was a gusty day in early March, and the wind was making the treetops in the Inn rock and quiver. I had come up from the Holborn end, and I had almost got to Theobald's Road when I noticed a man walking in front of me, leaning on a stick, and to all appearance very feeble. There was something about his look that made me curious, I don't know why, and I began to walk briskly with the idea of overtaking him, when of a sudden his hat blew off and came bounding along the pave-ment to my feet. Of course I rescued the hat, and gave it a glance as I went towards its owner. It was a biography in itself; a Piccadilly maker's name in the inside, but I don't think a beggar would have picked it out of the gutter. Then I looked up and saw Dr. Black of Harlesden waiting for me. A queer thing, wasn't it? But, Salisbury, what a change! When I saw Dr. Black come down the steps of his house at Harlesden he was an upright man, walking firmly with well-built limbs; a man, I should say, in the prime of his life. And now before me there crouched this wretched creature, bent and feeble, with shrunken cheeks, and hair that was whitening fast, and limbs that trembled and shook together, and misery in his eyes. He thanked me for bringing him his hat, saying, 'I don't think I should ever have got it; I can't run much now. A gusty day, sir, isn't it?' and with this he was turning away, but by little and little I contrived to draw him into the current of conversation, and we walked together eastward. I think the man would have been glad to get rid of me; but I didn't intend to let him go, and he stopped at last in front of a miserable house in a miserable street. It was, I verily believe, one of the most wretched quarters I have ever seen: houses that must have been sordid and hideous enough when new, that had gathered foulness with every year, and now seemed to lean and totter to their fall. 'I live up there,' said Black, pointing to the tiles, 'not in the front—in the back. I am very quiet there. I won't ask you to come in now, but perhaps some other day——' I caught him up at that, and told him I should be only too glad to come and see him. He gave me an odd sort of glance, as if he were wondering what on earth I or anybody else could care about him, and I left him fumbling with his latch-key. I think you will say I did pretty well when I tell you that within a few weeks I had made myself an intimate friend of Black's. I shall never forget the first time I went to his room; I hope I shall never see such abject, squalid misery again. The foul paper, from which all pattern or trace of a pattern had long vanished, subdued and penetrated with the grime of the evil street, was hanging in mouldering pennons from the wall. Only at the end of the room was it possible to stand upright, and the sight of the wretched bed and the odour of corruption that pervaded the place made me turn faint and sick. Here I found him munching a piece of bread; he seemed surprised to find that I had kept my promise, but he gave me his chair and sat on the bed while we talked. I used to go to see him often, and we had long conversations together, but he never mentioned Harlesden or his wife. I fancy that he supposed me ignorant of the matter, or thought that if I had heard of it, I should never connect the respectable Dr. Black of Harlesden with a poor garreteer in the backwoods of London. He was a strange man, and as we sat together smoking, I often wondered whether he were mad or sane, for I think the wildest dreams of Paracelsus and the Rosicrucians would appear plain and sober fact compared with the theories I have heard him earnestly

advance in that grimy den of his. I once ventured to hint something
of the sort to him. I suggested that something he had said was in
flat contradiction to all science and all experience. 'No,' he
answered, 'not all experience, for mine counts for something. I am
no dealer in unproved theories; what I say I have proved for myself,
and at a terrible cost. There is a region of knowledge which you will
never know, which wise men seeing from afar off shun like the
plague, as well they may, but into that region I have gone. If you
knew, if you could even dream of what may be done, of what one
or two men have done in this quiet world of ours, your very soul
would shudder and faint within you. What you have heard from me
has been but the merest husk and outer covering of true science—
that science which means death, and that which is more awful than
death, to those who gain it. No, when men say that there are strange
things in the world, they little know the awe and the terror that
dwell always with them and about them.' There was a sort of fascination about the man that drew me to him, and I was quite sorry to
have to leave London for a month or two; I missed his odd talk. A
few days after I came back to town I thought I would look him up,
but when I gave the two rings at the bell that used to summon him,
there was no answer. I rang and rang again, and was just turning to
go away, when the door opened and a dirty woman asked me what
I wanted. From her look I fancy she took me for a plain-clothes
officer after one of her lodgers, but when I inquired if Mr. Black
were in, she gave me a stare of another kind. 'There's no Mr. Black
lives here,' she said. 'He's gone. He's dead this six weeks. I always
thought he was a bit queer in his head, or else had been and got
into some trouble or other. He used to go out every morning from
ten till one, and one Monday morning we heard him come in, and
go into his room and shut the door, and a few minutes after, just as
we was a-sitting down to our dinner, there was such a scream that
I thought I should have gone right off. And then we heard a stamping, and down he came, raging and cursing most dreadful, swearing he had been robbed of something that was worth millions. And
then he just dropped down in the passage, and we thought he was
dead. We got him up to his room, and put him on his bed, and I just
sat there and waited, while my 'usband he went for the doctor. And
there was the winder wide open, and a little tin box he had lying on
the floor open and empty, but of course nobody could possible have
got in at the winder, and as for him having anything that was worth

anything, it's nonsense, for he was often weeks and weeks behind with his rent, and my 'usband he threatened often and often to turn him into the street, for, as he said, we've got a living to myke like other people—and, of course, that's true; but, somehow, I didn't like to do it, though he was an odd kind of a man, and I fancy had been better off. And then the doctor came and looked at him, and said as he couldn't do nothing, and that night he died as I was a-sitting by his bed; and I can tell you that, with one thing and another, we lost money by him, for the few bits of clothes as he had were worth next to nothing when they came to be sold.' I gave the woman half a sovereign for her trouble, and went home thinking of Dr. Black and the epitaph she had made him, and wondering at his strange fancy that he had been robbed. I take it that he had very little to fear on that score, poor fellow; but I suppose that he was really mad, and died in a sudden access of his mania. His landlady said that once or twice when she had had occasion to go into his room (to dun the poor wretch for his rent, most likely), he would keep her at the door for about a minute, and that when she came in she would find him putting away his tin box in the corner by the window; I suppose he had become possessed with the idea of some great treasure, and fancied himself a wealthy man in the midst of all his misery. *Explicit,* my tale is ended, and you see that though I knew Black, I know nothing of his wife or of the history of her death.—That's the Harlesden case, Salisbury, and I think it interests me all the more deeply because there does not seem the shadow of a possibility that I or any one else will ever know more about it. What do you think of it?"

"Well, Dyson, I must say that I think you have contrived to surround the whole thing with a mystery of your own making. I go for the doctor's solution: Black murdered his wife, being himself in all probability an undeveloped lunatic."

"What? Do you believe, then, that this woman was something too awful, too terrible to be allowed to remain on the earth? You will remember that the doctor said it was the brain of a devil?"

"Yes, yes, but he was speaking, of course, metaphorically. It's really quite a simple matter if you only look at it like that."

"Ah, well, you may be right; but yet I am sure you are not. Well, well, it's no good discussing it any more. A little more Benedictine? That's right; try some of this tobacco. Didn't you say that you had been bothered by something—something which happened that night we dined together?"

"Yes, I have been worried, Dyson, worried a great deal. I——
But it's such a trivial matter—indeed, such an absurdity—that I
feel ashamed to trouble you with it."

"Never mind, let's have it, absurd or not."

With many hesitations, and with much inward resentment of the
folly of the thing, Salisbury told his tale, and repeated reluctantly
the absurd intelligence and the absurder doggerel of the scrap of
paper, expecting to hear Dyson burst out into a roar of laughter.

"Isn't it too bad that I should let myself be bothered by such stuff
as that?" he asked, when he had stuttered out the jingle of once,
and twice, and thrice.

Dyson had listened to it all gravely, even to the end, and medi-
tated for a few minutes in silence.

"Yes," he said at length, "it was a curious chance, your taking
shelter in that archway just as those two went by. But I don't know
that I should call what was written on the paper nonsense; it is
bizarre certainly, but I expect it has a meaning for somebody. Just
repeat it again, will you, and I will write it down. Perhaps we might
find a cipher of some sort, though I hardly think we shall."

Again had the reluctant lips of Salisbury slowly to stammer out
the rubbish that he abhorred, while Dyson jotted it down on a slip
of paper.

"Look over it, will you?" he said, when it was done; "it may be
important that I should have every word in its place. Is that all right?"

"Yes; that is an accurate copy. But I don't think you will get much
out of it. Depend upon it, it is mere nonsense, a wanton scribble.
I must be going now, Dyson. No, no more; that stuff of yours is
pretty strong. Good-night."

"I suppose you would like to hear from me, if I did find out
anything?"

"No, not I; I don't want to hear about the thing again. You may
regard the discovery, if it is one, as your own."

"Very well. Good-night."

IV

A good many hours after Salisbury had returned to the company
of the green rep chairs, Dyson still sat at his desk, itself a Japanese
romance, smoking many pipes, and meditating over his friend's
story. The bizarre quality of the inscription which had annoyed

Salisbury was to him an attraction, and now and again he took it up and scanned thoughtfully what he had written, especially the quaint jingle at the end. It was a token, a symbol, he decided, and not a cipher, and the woman who had flung it away was in all probability entirely ignorant of its meaning; she was but the agent of the "Sam" she had abused and discarded, and he too was again the agent of some one unknown; possibly of the individual styled Q, who had been forced to visit his French friends. But what to make of "Traverse Handel S." Here was the root and source of the enigma, and not all the tobacco of Virginia seemed likely to suggest any clue here. It seemed almost hopeless, but Dyson regarded himself as the Wellington of mysteries, and went to bed feeling assured that sooner or later he would hit upon the right track. For the next few days he was deeply engaged in his literary labours, labours which were a profound mystery even to the most intimate of his friends, who searched the railway bookstalls in vain for the result of so many hours spent at the Japanese bureau in company with strong tobacco and black tea. On this occasion Dyson confined himself to his room for four days, and it was with genuine relief that he laid down his pen and went out into the streets in quest of relaxation and fresh air. The gas-lamps were being lighted, and the fifth edition of the evening papers was being howled through the streets, and Dyson, feeling that he wanted quiet, turned away from the clamorous Strand, and began to trend away to the north-west. Soon he found himself in streets that echoed to his footsteps, and crossing a broad new thoroughfare, and verging still to the west, Dyson discovered that he had penetrated to the depths of Soho. Here again was life; rare vintages of France and Italy, at prices which seemed contemptibly small, allured the passer-by; here were cheeses, vast and rich, here olive oil, and here a grove of Rabelaisian sausages; while in a neighbouring shop the whole press of Paris appeared to be on sale. In the middle of the roadway a strange miscellany of nations sauntered to and fro, for there cab and hansom rarely ventured; and from window over window the inhabitants looked forth in pleased contemplation of the scene. Dyson made his way slowly along, mingling with the crowd on the cobble-stones, listening to the queer babel of French and German, and Italian and English, glancing now and again at the shop windows with their levelled batteries of bottles, and had almost gained the end of the street, when his attention was arrested by a small

shop at the corner, a vivid contrast to its neighbours. It was the typical shop of the poor quarter; a shop entirely English. Here were
vended tobacco and sweets, cheap pipes of clay and cherry-wood;
penny exercise books and penholders jostled for precedence with
comic songs, and story papers with appalling cuts showed that
romance claimed its place beside the actualities of the evening
paper, the bills of which fluttered at the doorway. Dyson glanced
up at the name above the door, and stood by the kennel trembling,
for a sharp pang, the pang of one who has made a discovery, had for
a moment left him incapable of motion. The name over the shop
was Travers. Dyson looked up again, this time at the corner of the
wall above the lamp-post, and read in white letters on a blue
ground the words "Handel Street, W. C." and the legend was
repeated in fainter letters just below. He gave a little sigh of satisfaction, and without more ado walked boldly into the shop, and
stared full in the face of the fat man who was sitting behind the
counter. The fellow rose to his feet, and returned the stare a little
curiously, and then began in stereotyped phrase—

"What can I do for you, sir?"

Dyson enjoyed the situation and a dawning perplexity on the
man's face. He propped his stick carefully against the counter and
leaning over it, said slowly and impressively—

"Once around the grass, and twice around the lass, and thrice
around the maple-tree."

Dyson had calculated on his words producing an effect, and he
was not disappointed. The vendor of the miscellanies gasped,
open-mouthed like a fish, and steadied himself against the counter.
When he spoke, after a short interval, it was in a hoarse mutter,
tremulous and unsteady.

"Would you mind saying that again, sir? I didn't quite catch it."

"My good man, I shall most certainly do nothing of the kind. You
heard what I said perfectly well. You have got a clock in your shop,
I see; an admirable timekeeper, I have no doubt. Well, I give you a
minute by your own clock."

The man looked about him in a perplexed indecision, and Dyson
felt that it was time to be bold.

"Look here, Travers, the time is nearly up. You have heard of Q,
I think. Remember, I hold your life in my hands. Now!"

Dyson was shocked at the result of his own audacity. The man shrank and shrivelled in terror, the sweat poured down a face of ashy white, and he held up his hands before him.

"Mr. Davies, Mr. Davies, don't say that—don't for Heaven's sake. I didn't know you at first, I didn't indeed. Good God! Mr. Davies, you wouldn't ruin me? I'll get it in a moment."

"You had better not lose any more time."

The man slunk piteously out of his own shop, and went into a back parlour. Dyson heard his trembling fingers fumbling with a bunch of keys, and the creak of an opening box. He came back presently with a small package neatly tied up in brown paper in his hands, and still, full of terror, handed it to Dyson.

"I'm glad to be rid of it," he said, "I'll take no more jobs of this sort."

Dyson took the parcel and his stick, and walked out of the shop with a nod, turning round as he passed the door. Travers had sunk into his seat, his face still white with terror, with one hand over his eyes, and Dyson speculated a good deal as he walked rapidly away as to what queer chords those could be on which he had played so roughly. He hailed the first hansom he could see and drove home, and when he had lit his hanging lamp, and laid his parcel on the table, he paused for a moment, wondering on what strange thing the lamp-light would soon shine. He locked his door, and cut the strings, and unfolded the paper layer after layer, and came at last to a small wooden box, simply but solidly made. There was no lock, and Dyson had simply to raise the lid, and as he did so he drew a long breath and started back. The lamp seemed to glimmer feebly like a single candle, but the whole room blazed with light—and not with light alone, but with a thousand colours, with all the glories of some painted window; and upon the walls of his room and on the familiar furniture, the glow flamed back and seemed to flow again to its source, the little wooden box. For there upon a bed of soft wool lay the most splendid jewel, a jewel such as Dyson had never dreamed of, and within it shone the blue of far skies, and the green of the sea by the shore, and the red of the ruby, and deep violet rays, and in the middle of all it seemed aflame as if a fountain of fire rose up, and fell, and rose again with sparks like stars for drops. Dyson gave a long deep sigh, and dropped into his chair, and put his hands over his eyes to think. The jewel was like an opal, but from a long experience of the shop windows he knew there was no such thing as an opal one quarter or one eighth of its size. He looked at the stone again, with a feeling that was almost awe, and placed it gently on the table under the lamp, and watched the wonderful flame that shone and sparkled in its centre, and then turned to the box, curious to know whether it might contain other marvels. He lifted the bed of wool on which the opal had reclined, and saw beneath, no more jewels, but a little old pocket-book, worn and shabby with use. Dyson opened it at the first leaf, and dropped the book again, appalled. He had read the name of the owner, neatly written in blue ink:

STEVEN BLACK, M.D.,
Oranmore,
Devon Road,
Harlesden.

It was several minutes before Dyson could bring himself to open the book a second time; he remembered the wretched exile in his garret; and his strange talk, and the memory too of the face he had seen at the window, and of what the specialist had said, surged up in his mind, and as he held his finger on the cover, he shivered, dreading what might be written within. When at last he held it in his hand, and turned the pages, he found that the first two leaves were blank, but the third was covered with clear, minute writing, and Dyson began to read with the light of the opal flaming in his eyes.

V

"Ever since I was a young man"—the record began—"I devoted all my leisure and a good deal of time that ought to have been given to other studies to the investigation of curious and obscure branches of knowledge. What are commonly called the pleasures of life had never any attractions for me, and I lived alone in London, avoiding my fellow students, and in my turn avoided by them as a man self-absorbed and unsympathetic. So long as I could gratify my desire of knowledge of a peculiar kind, knowledge of which the very existence is a profound secret to most men, I was intensely happy, and I have often spent whole nights sitting in the darkness of my room, and thinking of the strange world on the brink of which I trod. My professional studies, however, and the necessity of obtaining a degree, for some time forced my more obscure employment into the background, and soon after I had qualified I met Agnes, who became my wife. We took a new house in this remote suburb, and I began the regular routine of a sober practice, and for some months lived happily enough, sharing in the life about me, and only thinking at odd intervals of that occult science which had once fascinated my whole being. I had learnt enough of the paths I had begun to tread to know that they were beyond all expression difficult and dangerous, that to persevere meant in all probability the wreck of a life, and that they led to regions so terrible, that the mind of man shrinks appalled at the very thought. Moreover, the quiet and the peace I had enjoyed since my marriage had wiled me away to a great extent from places where I knew no peace could dwell. But suddenly—I think indeed it was the work of a single night, as I lay awake on my bed gazing into the darkness—suddenly, I say, the old desire, the former longing, returned, and returned with a force that had been intensified ten times by its absence; and when the day dawned and I looked out of the window, and saw with haggard eyes the sunrise in the east, I knew that my doom had been pronounced; that as I had gone far, so now I must go farther with unfaltering steps. I turned to the bed where my wife was sleeping peacefully, and lay down again, weeping bitter tears, for the sun had set on our happy life and had risen with a dawn of terror to us both. I will not set down here in minute detail what followed; outwardly I went about the day's labour as before, saying nothing to my wife. But she soon saw that I had changed; I spent my spare time in a room which I had fitted up as a laboratory, and often I crept upstairs in the grey dawn of the morning, when the light of many lamps still glowed over London; and each night I had stolen a step nearer to that great abyss which I was to bridge over, the gulf between the world of consciousness and the world of matter. My experiments were many and complicated in their nature, and it was some months before I realized whither they all pointed, and when this was borne in upon me in a moment's time, I felt my face whiten and my heart still within me. But the power to draw back, the power to stand before the doors that now opened wide before me and not to enter in, had long ago been absent; the way was closed, and I could only pass onward. My position was as utterly hopeless as that of the prisoner in an utter dungeon, whose only light is that of the dungeon above him; the doors were shut and escape was impossible. Experiment after experiment gave the same result, and I knew, and shrank even as the thought passed through my mind, that in the work I had to do there must be elements which no laboratory could furnish, which no scales could ever measure. In that work, from which even I doubted to escape with life, life itself must enter; from some human being there must be drawn that essence which men call the soul, and in its place (for in the scheme of the world there is no vacant chamber)—in its place would enter in what the lips can hardly utter, what the mind cannot conceive without a horror more awful than the horror of death itself. And when I knew this, I knew also on whom this fate would fall; I looked into my wife's eyes. Even at that hour, if I had gone out and taken a rope and hanged myself, I might have escaped, and she also, but in no other way. At last I told her all. She shuddered, and wept, and called on her dead mother for help, and asked me if I had no mercy, and I could only sigh. I concealed nothing from her; I told her what she would become, and what would enter in where her life had been; I told her of all the shame and of all the horror. You who will read this when I am dead—if indeed I allow this record to survive—you who have opened the box and have seen what lies there, if you could understand what lies hidden in that opal! For one night my wife consented to what I asked of her, consented with the tears running down her beautiful face, and hot shame flushing red over her neck and breast, consented to undergo this for me. I threw open the window, and we looked together at the sky and the dark earth for the last time; it was a fine star-light night, and there was a pleasant breeze blowing, and I kissed her on her lips, and her tears ran down upon my face. That night she came down to my laboratory, and there, with shutters bolted and barred down, with curtains drawn thick and close, so that the very stars might be shut out from the sight of that room, while the crucible hissed and boiled over the lamp, I did what had to be done, and led out what was no longer a woman. But on the table the opal flamed and sparkled with such light as no eyes of man have ever gazed on, and the rays of the flame that was within it flashed and glittered, and shone even to my heart. My wife had only asked one thing of me; that when there came at last what I had told her, I would kill her. I have kept that promise."

There was nothing more. Dyson let the little pocket-book fall, and turned and looked again at the opal with its flaming inmost light, and then with unutterable irresistible horror surging up in his heart, grasped the jewel, and flung it on the ground, and trampled it beneath his heel. His face was white with terror as he turned away, and for a moment stood sick and trembling, and then with a start he leapt across the room and steadied himself against the door. There was an angry hiss, as of steam escaping under great pressure, and as he gazed, motionless, a volume of heavy yellow smoke was slowly issuing from the very centre of the jewel, and wreathing itself in snakelike coils above it. And then a thin white flame burst forth from the smoke, and shot up into the air and vanished; and on the ground there lay a thing like a cinder, black and crumbling to the touch.

The Man Whom the Trees Loved

Algernon Blackwood

I

HE painted trees as by some special divining instinct of their essential qualities. He understood them. He knew why in an oak forest, for instance, each individual was utterly distinct from its fellows, and why no two beeches in the whole world were alike. People asked him down to paint a favourite lime or silver birch, for he caught the individuality of a tree as some catch the individuality of a horse. How he managed it was something of a puzzle, for he never had painting lessons, his drawing was often wildly inaccurate, and, while his perception of a Tree Personality was true and vivid, his rendering of it might almost approach the ludicrous. Yet the character and personality of that particular tree stood there alive beneath his brush—shining, frowning, dreaming, as the case might be, friendly or hostile, good or evil. It emerged.

There was nothing else in the wide world that he could paint; flowers and landscapes he only muddled away into a smudge; with people he was helpless and hopeless; also with animals. Skies he could sometimes manage, or effects of wind in foliage, but as a rule he left these all severely alone. He kept to trees, wisely following an instinct that was guided by love. It was quite arresting, this way he had of making a tree look almost like a being—alive. It approached the uncanny.

"Yes, Sanderson knows what he's doing when he paints a tree!" thought old David Bittacy, C. B., late of the Woods and Forests. "Why, you can almost hear it rustle. You can smell the thing. You can hear the rain drip through its leaves. You can almost see the branches move. It grows." For in this way somewhat he expressed his satisfaction, half to persuade himself that the twenty guineas were well spent (since his wife thought otherwise), and half to explain this uncanny reality of life that lay in the fine old cedar framed above his study table.

Yet in the general view the mind of Mr. Bittacy was held to be austere, not to say morose. Few divined in him the secretly tenacious love of nature that had been fostered by years spent in the forests and jungles of the eastern world. It was odd for an Englishman, due possibly to that Eurasian ancestor. Surreptitiously, as though half ashamed of it, he had kept alive a sense of beauty that hardly belonged to his type, and was unusual for its vitality. Trees, in particular, nourished it. He, also, understood trees, felt a subtle sense of communion with them, born perhaps of those years he had lived in caring for them, guarding, protecting, nursing, years of solitude among their great shadowy presences. He kept it largely to himself, of course, because he knew the world he lived in. He also kept it from his wife—to some extent. He knew it came between them, knew that she feared it, was opposed. But what he did not know, or realise at any rate, was the extent to which she grasped the power which they wielded over his life. Her fear, he judged, was simply due to those years in India, when for weeks at a time his calling took him away from her into the jungle forests, while she remained at home dreading all manner of evils that might befall him. This, of course, explained her instinctive opposition to the passion for woods that still influenced and clung to him. It was a natural survival of those anxious days of waiting in solitude for his safe return.

For Mrs. Bittacy, daughter of an evangelical clergyman, was a self-sacrificing woman, who in most things found a happy duty in sharing her husband's joys and sorrows to the point of self-obliteration. Only in this matter of the trees she was less successful than in others. It remained a problem difficult of compromise.

He knew, for instance, that what she objected to in this portrait of the cedar on their lawn was really not the price he had given for it, but the unpleasant way in which the transaction emphasised this breach between their common interests—the only one they had, but deep.

Sanderson, the artist, earned little enough money by his strange talent; such cheques were few and far between. The owners of fine or interesting trees who cared to have them painted singly were rare indeed; and the "studies" that he made for his own delight he also kept for his own delight. Even were there buyers, he would not sell them. Only a few, and these peculiarly intimate friends, might even see them, for he disliked to hear the undiscerning criticisms of those who did not understand. Not that he minded laughter at his craftmanship—he admitted it with scorn—but that remarks about the personality of the tree itself could easily wound or anger him. He resented slighting observations concerning them, as though insults offered to personal friends who could not answer for themselves. He was instantly up in arms.

"It really *is* extraordinary," said a Woman who Understood, "that you can make that cypress seem an individual, when in reality all cypresses are so *exactly* alike."

And though the bit of calculated flattery had come so near to saying the right, true thing, Sanderson flushed as though she had slighted a friend beneath his very nose. Abruptly he passed in front of her and turned the picture to the wall.

"Almost as queer," he answered rudely, copying her silly emphasis, "as that *you* should have imagined individuality in your husband, Madame, when in reality all men are so *exactly* alike!"

Since the only thing that differentiated her husband from the mob was the money for which she had married him, Sanderson's relations with that particular family terminated on the spot, chance of prospective 'orders' with it. His sensitiveness, perhaps, was morbid. At any rate the way to reach his heart lay through his trees. He might be said to love trees. He certainly drew a splendid inspiration from them, and the source of a man's inspiration, be it music, religion, or a woman, is never a safe thing to criticise.

"I do think, perhaps, it was just a little extravagant, dear," said Mrs. Bittacy, referring to the cedar cheque, "when we want a lawn-mower so badly too. But, as it gives you such pleasure——"

"It reminds me of a certain day, Sophia," replied the old gentleman, looking first proudly at herself, then fondly at the picture, "now long gone by. It reminds me of another tree—that Kentish lawn in the spring, birds singing in the lilacs, and some one in a muslin frock waiting patiently beneath a certain cedar—not the one in the picture, I know, but——"

"I was not waiting," she said indignantly, "I was picking fir-cones for the schoolroom fire——"

"Fir-cones, my dear, do not grow on cedars, and schoolroom fires were not made in June in my young days."

"And anyhow it isn't the same cedar."

"It has made me fond of all cedars for its sake," he answered, "and it reminds me that you are the same young girl still———"

She crossed the room to his side, and together they looked out of the window where, upon the lawn of their Hampshire cottage, a ragged Lebanon stood in solitary state.

"You're as full of dreams as ever," she said gently, "and I don't regret the cheque a bit—really. Only it would have been more real if it had been the original tree, wouldn't it?"

"That was blown down years ago. I passed the place last year, and there's not a sign of it left," he replied tenderly. And presently, when he released her from his side, she went up to the wall and carefully dusted the picture Sanderson had made of the cedar on their present lawn. She went all round the frame with her tiny handkerchief, standing on tiptoe to reach the top rim.

"What I like about it," said the old fellow to himself when his wife had left the room, "is the way he has made it live. All trees have it, of course, but a cedar taught it to me first—the 'something' trees possess that make them know I'm there when I stand close and watch. I suppose I felt it then because I was in love, and love reveals life everywhere." He glanced a moment at the Lebanon looming gaunt and sombre through the gathering dusk. A curious wistful expression danced a moment through his eyes. "Yes, Sanderson has seen it as it is," he murmured, "solemnly dreaming there its dim hidden life against the Forest edge, and as different from that other tree in Kent as I am from—from the vicar, say. It's quite a stranger, too. I don't know anything about it really. That other cedar I loved; this old fellow I respect. Friendly though—yes, on the whole quite friendly. He's painted the friendliness right enough. He saw that. I'd like to know that man better," he added. "I'd like to ask him how he saw so clearly that it stands there between this cottage and the Forest—yet somehow more in sympathy with us than with the mass of woods behind—a sort of go-between. *That* I never noticed before. I see it now—through his eyes. It stands there like a sentinel—protective rather."

He turned away abruptly to look through the window. He saw the great encircling mass of gloom that was the Forest, fringing their little lawn. It pressed up closer in the darkness. The prim garden with its formal beds of flowers seemed an impertinence almost—some little coloured insect that sought to settle on a sleeping monster—some gaudy fly that danced impudently down the edge of a great river that could engulf it with a toss of its smallest wave. That Forest with its thousand years of growth and its deep spreading being was some such slumbering monster, yes. Their cottage and garden stood too near its running lip. When the winds were strong and lifted its shadowy skirts of black and purple. . . . He loved this feeling of the Forest Personality; he had always loved it.

"Queer," he reflected, "awfully queer, that trees should bring me such a sense of dim, vast living! I used to feel it particularly, I remember, in India; in Canadian woods as well; but never in little English woods till here. And Sanderson's the only man I ever knew who felt it too. He's never said so, but there's the proof," and he turned again to the picture that he loved. A thrill of unaccustomed life ran through him as he looked. "I wonder, by Jove, I wonder," his thoughts ran on, "whether a tree—er—in any lawful meaning of the term can be— alive. I remember some writing fellow telling me long ago that trees had once been moving things, animal organisms of some sort, that had stood so long feeding, sleeping, dreaming, or something, in the same place, that they had lost the power to get away . . . !"

Fancies flew pell-mell about his mind, and, lighting a cheroot, he dropped into an armchair beside the open window and let them play. Outside the blackbirds whistled in the shrubberies across the lawn. He smelt the earth and trees and flowers, the perfume of mown grass, and the bits of open heath-land far away in the heart of the woods. The summer wind stirred very faintly through the leaves. But the great New Forest hardly raised her sweeping skirts of black and purple shadow.

Mr. Bittacy, however, knew intimately every detail of that wilderness of trees within. He knew all the purple coombs splashed with yellow waves of gorse; sweet with juniper and myrtle, and gleaming with clear and dark-eyed pools that watched the sky. There hawks hovered, circling hour by hour, and the flicker of the peewit's flight with its melancholy, petulant cry, deepened the sense of stillness. He knew the solitary pines, dwarfed, tufted, vigorous, that sang to every lost wind, travellers like the gipsies who pitched their bush-like tents beneath them; he knew the shaggy ponies, with foals like baby centaurs; the chattering jays, the milky call of cuckoos in the spring, and the boom of the bittern from the lonely marshes. The undergrowth of watching hollies, he knew too, strange and mysterious, with their dark, suggestive beauty, and the yellow shimmer of their pale dropped leaves.

Here all the Forest lived and breathed in safety, secure from mutilation. No terror of the axe could haunt the peace of its vast subconscious life, no terror of devastating Man afflict it with the dread of premature death. It knew itself supreme; it spread and preened itself without concealment. It set no spires to carry warnings, for no wind brought messages of alarm as it bulged outwards to the sun and stars.

But, once its leafy portals left behind, the trees of the countryside were otherwise. The houses threatened them; they knew themselves in danger. The roads were no longer glades of silent turf, but noisy, cruel ways by which men came to attack them. They were civilised, cared for—but cared for in order that some day they might be put to death. Even in the villages, where the solemn and immemorial repose of giant chestnuts aped security, the tossing of a silver birch against their mass, impatient in the littlest wind, brought warning. Dust clogged their leaves. The inner humming of their quiet life became inaudible beneath the scream and shriek of clattering traffic. They longed and prayed to enter the great Peace of the Forest yonder, but they could not move. They knew, moreover, that the Forest with its august, deep splendour despised and pitied them. They were a thing of artificial gardens, and belonged to beds of flowers all forced to grow one way. . . .

"I'd like to know that artist fellow better," was the thought upon which he returned at length to the things of practical life. "I wonder if Sophia would mind him here for a bit—?" He rose with the sound of the gong, brushing the ashes from his speckled waistcoat. He pulled the waistcoat down. He was slim and spare in figure, active in his movements. In the dim light, but for that silvery moustache, he might easily have passed for a man of forty. "I'll suggest it to her anyhow," he decided on his way upstairs to dress. His thought really was that Sanderson could probably explain this world of things he had always felt about—trees. A man who could paint the soul of a cedar in that way must know it all.

"Why not?" she gave her verdict later over the bread-and-butter pudding; "unless you think he'd find it dull without companions."

"He would paint all day in the Forest, dear. I'd like to pick his brains a bit, too, if I could manage it."

"You can manage anything, David," was what she answered, for this elderly childless couple used an affectionate politeness long since deemed old-fashioned. The remark, however, displeased her, making her feel uneasy, and she did not notice his rejoinder, smiling his pleasure and content—"Except yourself and our bank account, my dear." This passion of his for trees was of old a bone of contention, though very mild contention. It frightened her. That was the truth. The Bible, her Baedeker for earth and heaven, did not mention it. Her husband, while humouring her, could never alter that instinctive dread she had. He soothed, but never changed her. She liked the woods, perhaps as spots for shade and picnics, but she could not, as he did, love them.

And after dinner, with a lamp beside the open window, he read aloud from *The Times* the evening post had brought, such fragments as he thought might interest her. The custom was invariable, except on Sundays, when, to please his wife, he dozed over Tennyson or Farrar as their mood might be. She knitted while he read, asked gentle questions, told him his voice was a "lovely reading voice," and enjoyed the little discussions that occasions prompted because he always let her win them with "Ah, Sophia, I had never thought of it quite in *that* way before; but now you mention it I must say I think there's something in it. . . ."

For David Bittacy was wise. It was long after marriage, during his months of loneliness spent with trees and forests in India, his wife waiting at home in the Bungalow, that his other, deeper side had developed the strange passion that she could not understand. And after one or two serious attempts to let her share it with him, he had given up and learned to hide it from her. He learned, that is, to speak of it only casually; for since she knew it was there, to keep silence altogether would only increase her pain. So from time to time he skimmed the surface just to let her show him where he was wrong and think she won the day. It remained a debatable land of compromise. He listened with patience to her criticisms, her excursions and alarms, knowing that while it gave her satisfaction, it could not change himself. The thing lay in him too deep and true for change. But, for peace' sake, some meeting-place was desirable, and he found it thus.

It was her one fault in his eyes, this religious mania carried over from her upbringing, and it did no serious harm. Great emotion could shake it sometimes out of her. She clung to it because her father taught it her and not because she had thought it out for herself. Indeed, like many women, she never really *thought* at all, but merely reflected the images of others' thinking which she had learned to see. So, wise in his knowledge of human nature, old David Bittacy accepted the pain of being obliged to keep a portion of his inner life shut off from the woman he deeply loved. He regarded her little biblical phrases as oddities that still clung to a rather fine, big soul—like horns and little useless things some animals have not yet lost in the course of evolution while they have outgrown their use.

"My dear, what is it? You frightened me!" She asked it suddenly, sitting up so abruptly that her cap dropped sideways almost to her ear. For David Bittacy behind his crackling paper had uttered a sharp exclamation of surprise. He had lowered the sheet and was staring at her over the tops of his gold glasses.

"Listen to this, if you please," he said, a note of eagerness in his voice, "listen to this, my dear Sophia. It's from an address by Francis Darwin before the Royal Society. He is president, you know, and son of the great Darwin. Listen carefully, I beg you. It is *most* significant."

"I *am* listening, David," she said with some astonishment, looking up. She stopped her knitting. For a second she glanced behind her. Something had suddenly changed in the room, and it made her feel wide awake, though before she had been almost dozing. Her husband's voice and manner had introduced this new thing. Her instincts rose in warning. "*Do* read it, dear." He took a deep breath, looking first again over the rims of his glasses to make quite sure of her attention. He had evidently come across something of genuine interest, although herself she often found the passages from these "Addresses" somewhat heavy.

In a deep, emphatic voice he read aloud:

"'It is impossible to know whether or not plants are conscious; but it is consistent with the doctrine of continuity that in all living things there is something psychic, and if we accept this point of view——'"

"*If*," she interrupted, scenting danger.

He ignored the interruption as a thing of slight value he was accustomed to.

"'If we accept this point of view,'" he continued, "'we must believe that in plants there exists a faint copy of *what we know as consciousness in ourselves.*'"

He laid the paper down and steadily stared at her. Their eyes met. He had italicised the last phrase.

For a minute or two his wife made no reply or comment. They stared at one another in silence. He waited for the meaning of the words to reach her understanding with full import. Then he turned and read them again in part, while she, released from that curious driving look in his eyes, instinctively again glanced over her shoulder round the room. It was almost as if she felt some one had come in to them unnoticed.

"We must believe that in plants there exists a faint copy of what we know as consciousness in ourselves."

"*If,*" she repeated lamely, feeling before the stare of those questioning eyes she must say something, but not yet having gathered her wits together quite.

"*Consciousness,*" he rejoined. And then he added gravely: "That, my dear, is the statement of a scientific man of the Twentieth Century."

Mrs. Bittacy sat forward in her chair so that her silk flounces crackled louder than the newspaper. She made a characteristic little sound between sniffing and snorting. She put her shoes closely together, with her hands upon her knees.

"David," she said quietly, "I think these scientific men are simply losing their heads. There is nothing in the Bible that I can remember about any such thing whatsoever."

"Nothing, Sophia, that I can remember either," he answered patiently. Then, after a pause, he added, half to himself perhaps more than to her: "And, now that I come to think about it, it seems that Sanderson once said something to me that was similar."

"Then Mr. Sanderson is a wise and thoughtful man, and a safe man," she quickly took him up, "if he said that."

For she thought her husband referred to her remark about the Bible, and not to her judgment of the scientific men. And he did not correct her mistake.

"And plants, you see, dear, are not the same thing as trees," she drove her advantage home, "not quite, that is."

"I agree," said David quietly; "but both belong to the great vegetable kingdom."

There was a moment's pause before she answered.

"Pah! the vegetable kingdom, indeed!" She tossed her pretty old head. And into the words she put a degree of contempt that, could the vegetable kingdom have heard it, might have made it feel ashamed for covering a third of the world with its wonderful tangled network of roots and branches, delicate shaking leaves, and its millions of spires that caught the sun and wind and rain. Its very right to existence seemed in question.

II

Sanderson accordingly came down, and on the whole his short visit was a success. Why he came at all was a mystery to those who heard of it, for he never paid visits and was certainly not the kind of man to court a customer. There must have been something in Bittacy he liked.

Mrs. Bittacy was glad when he left. He brought no dress-suit for one thing, not even a dinner-jacket, and he wore very low collars with big balloon ties like a Frenchman, and let his hair grow longer than was nice, she felt. Not that these things were important, but that she considered them symptoms of something a little disordered. The ties were unnecessarily flowing.

For all that he was an interesting man, and, in spite of his eccentricities of dress and so forth, a gentleman. "Perhaps," she reflected in her genuinely charitable heart, "he had other uses for the twenty guineas, an invalid sister or an old mother to support!" She had no notion of the cost of brushes, frames, paints, and canvases. Also she forgave him much for the sake of his beautiful eyes and his eager enthusiasm of manner. So many men of thirty were already blasé.

Still, when the visit was over, she felt relieved. She said nothing about his coming a second time, and her husband, she was glad to notice, had likewise made no suggestion. For, truth to tell, the way the younger man engrossed the older, keeping him out for hours in the Forest, talking on the lawn in the blazing sun, and in the evenings when the damp of dusk came creeping out from the surrounding woods, all regardless of his age and usual habits, was not quite to her taste. Of course, Mr. Sanderson did not know how easily those attacks of Indian fever came back, but David surely might have told him.

They talked trees from morning to night. It stirred in her the old subconscious trail of dread, a trail that led ever into the darkness of big woods; and such feelings, as her early evangelical training taught her, were temptings. To regard them in any other way was to play with danger.

Her mind, as she watched these two, was charged with curious thoughts of dread she could not understand, yet feared the more on that account. The way they studied that old mangy cedar was a trifle unnecessary, unwise, she felt. It was disregarding the sense of proportion which deity had set upon the world for men's safe guidance.

Even after dinner they smoked their cigars upon the low branches that swept down and touched the lawn, until at length she insisted on their coming in. Cedars, she had somewhere heard, were not safe after sundown; it was not wholesome to be too near them; to sleep beneath them was even dangerous, though what the precise danger was she had forgotten. The upas was the tree she really meant.

At any rate she summoned David in, and Sanderson came presently after him.

For a long time, before deciding on this peremptory step, she had watched them surreptitiously from the drawing-room window— her husband and her guest. The dusk enveloped them with its damp veil of gauze. She saw the glowing tips of their cigars, and heard the drone of voices. Bats flitted overhead, and big, silent moths whirred softly over the rhododendron blossoms. And it came suddenly to her, while she watched, that her husband had somehow altered these last few days—since Mr. Sanderson's arrival in fact. A change had come over him, though what it was she could not say. She hesitated, indeed, to search. That was the instinctive dread operating in her. Provided it passed she would rather not know. Small things, of course, she noticed; small outward signs. He had neglected *The Times* for one thing, left off his speckled waistcoats for another. He was absent-minded sometimes; showed vagueness in practical details where hitherto he showed decision. And—he had begun to talk in his sleep again.

These and a dozen other small peculiarities came suddenly upon her with the rush of a combined attack. They brought with them a faint distress that made her shiver. Momentarily her mind was startled, then confused, as her eyes picked out the shadowy figures in the dusk, the cedar covering them, the Forest close at their backs. And then, before she could think, or seek internal guidance as her habit was, this whisper, muffled and very hurried, ran across her brain: "It's Mr. Sanderson. Call David in at once!"

And she had done so. Her shrill voice crossed the lawn and died away into the Forest, quickly smothered. No echo followed it. The sound fell dead against the rampart of a thousand listening trees.

"The damp is so very penetrating, even in summer," she murmured when they came obediently. She was half surprised at her own audacity, half repentant. They came so meekly at her call. "And my husband is sensitive to fever from the East. No, *please* do not throw away your cigars. We can sit by the open window and enjoy the evening while you smoke."

She was very talkative for a moment; subconscious excitement was the cause.

"It is so still—so wonderfully still," she went on, as no one spoke, "so peaceful, and the air so very sweet . . . and God is always near to those who need His aid." The words slipped out before she realised quite what she was saying, yet fortunately, in time to lower her voice, for no one heard them. They were, perhaps, an instinctive expression of relief. It flustered her that she could have said the thing at all.

Sanderson brought her shawl and helped to arrange the chairs; she thanked him in her old-fashioned, gentle way, declining the lamps which he had offered to light. "They attract the moths and insects so, I think!"

The three of them sat there in the gloaming, Mr. Bittacy's white moustache and his wife's yellow shawl gleaming at either end of the little horseshoe, Sanderson with his wild black hair and shining eyes midway between them. The painter went on talking softly, continuing evidently the conversation begun with his host beneath the cedar. Mrs. Bittacy, on her guard, listened—uneasily.

"For trees, you see, rather conceal themselves in daylight. They reveal themselves fully only after sunset. I never *know* a tree," he bowed here slightly towards the lady as though to apologise for something he felt she would not quite understand or like, "until I've seen it in the night. Your cedar, for instance," looking towards her husband again so that Mrs. Bittacy caught the gleaming of his turned eyes, "I failed with badly at first, because I did it in the morning. You shall see to-morrow what I mean—that first sketch is upstairs in my portfolio; it's quite another tree to the one you bought. That view"—he leaned forward, lowering his voice—"I caught one morning about two o'clock in very faint moonlight and the stars. I saw the naked being of the thing——"

"You mean that you went out, Mr. Sanderson, at that hour?" the old lady asked with astonishment and mild rebuke. She did not care particularly for his choice of adjectives either.

"I fear it was rather a liberty to take in another's house, perhaps," he answered courteously. "But, having chanced to wake, I saw the tree from my window, and made my way downstairs."

"It's a wonder Boxer didn't bite you; he sleeps loose in the hall," she said.

"On the contrary. The dog came out with me. I hope," he added, "the noise didn't disturb you, though it's rather late to say so. I feel quite guilty." His white teeth showed in the dusk as he smiled. A smell of earth and flowers stole in through the window on a breath of wandering air.

Mrs. Bittacy said nothing at the moment. "We both sleep like tops," put in her husband, laughing. "You're a courageous man, though, Sanderson; and, by Jove, the picture justifies you. Few artists would have taken so much trouble, though I read once that Holman Hunt, Rossetti, or some one of that lot, painted all night in his orchard to get an effect of moonlight that he wanted."

He chattered on. His wife was glad to hear his voice; it made her feel more easy in her mind. But presently the other held the floor again, and her thoughts grew darkened and afraid. Instinctively she feared the influence on her husband. The mystery and wonder that lie in woods, in forests, in great gatherings of trees everywhere, seemed so real and present while he talked.

"The Night transfigures all things in a way," he was saying; "but nothing so searchingly as trees. From behind a veil that sunlight hangs before them in the day they emerge and show themselves. Even buildings do that—in a measure—but trees particularly. In the daytime they sleep; at night they wake, they manifest, turn active—live. You remember," turning politely again in the direction of his hostess, "how clearly Henley understood that?"

"That socialist person, you mean?" asked the lady. Her tone and accent made the substantive sound criminal. It almost hissed, the way she uttered it.

"The poet, yes," replied the artist tactfully, "the friend of Stevenson, you remember, Stevenson who wrote those charming children's verses."

He quoted in a low voice the lines he meant. It was, for once, the time, the place, and the setting all together. The words floated out across the lawn towards the wall of blue darkness where the big

Forest swept the little garden with its league-long curve that was like the shore-line of a sea. A wave of distant sound that was like surf accompanied his voice, as though the wind was fain to listen too:

> Not to the staring Day,
> For all the importunate questionings he pursues
> In his big, violent voice,
> Shall those mild things of bulk and multitude,
> The trees—God's sentinels . . .
> Yield of their huge, unutterable selves.

> •   •   •   •   •   •

> But at the word
> Of the ancient, sacerdotal Night,
> Night of the many secrets, whose effect—
> Transfiguring, hierophantic, dread—
> Themselves alone may fully apprehend,
> They tremble and are changed:
> In each the uncouth, individual soul
> Looms forth and glooms
> Essential, and, their bodily presences
> Touched with inordinate significance,
> Wearing the darkness like a livery
> Of some mysterious and tremendous guild,
> They brood—they menace—they appal.

The voice of Mrs. Bittacy presently broke the silence that followed.

"I like that part about God's sentinels," she murmured. There was no sharpness in her tone; it was hushed and quiet. The truth, so musically uttered, muted her shrill objections though it had not lessened her alarm. Her husband made no comment; his cigar, she noticed, had gone out.

"And old trees in particular," continued the artist, as though to himself, "have very definite personalities. You can offend, wound, please them; the moment you stand within their shade you feel whether they come out to you, or whether they withdraw." He turned abruptly towards his host. "You know that singular essay of Prentice Mulford's, no doubt, "God in the Trees"—extravagant perhaps, but yet with a fine true beauty in it? You've never read it, no?" he asked.

But it was Mrs. Bittacy who answered; her husband keeping his curious deep silence.

"I never did!" It fell like a drip of cold water from the face muffled in the yellow shawl; even a child could have supplied the remainder of the unspoken thought.

"Ah," said Sanderson gently, "but there *is* 'God' in the trees, God in a very subtle aspect and sometimes—I have known the trees express it too—that which is *not* God—dark and terrible. Have you ever noticed, too, how clearly trees show what they want—choose their companions, at least? How beeches, for instance, allow no life too near them—birds or squirrels in their boughs, nor any growth beneath? The silence in the beech wood is quite terrifying often! And how pines like bilberry bushes at their feet and sometimes little oaks—all trees making a clear, deliberate choice, and holding firmly to it? Some trees obviously—it's very strange and marked—seem to prefer the human."

The old lady sat up crackling, for this was more than she could permit. Her stiff silk dress emitted little sharp reports.

"We know," she answered, "that He was said to have walked in the garden in the cool of the evening"—the gulp betrayed the effort that it cost her—"but we are nowhere told that He hid in the trees, or anything like that. Trees, after all, we must remember, are only large vegetables."

"True," was the soft answer, "but in everything that grows, has life, that is, there's mystery past all finding out. The wonder that lies hidden in our own souls lies also hidden, I venture to assert, in the stupidity and silence of a mere potato."

The observation was not meant to be amusing. It was *not* amusing. No one laughed. On the contrary, the words conveyed in too literal a sense the feeling that haunted all that conversation. Each one in his own way realised—with beauty, with wonder, with alarm—that the talk had somehow brought the whole vegetable kingdom nearer to that of man. Some link had been established between the two. It was not wise, with that great Forest listening at their very doors, to speak so plainly. The Forest edged up closer while they did so.

And Mrs. Bittacy, anxious to interrupt the horrid spell, broke suddenly in upon it with a matter-of-fact suggestion. She did not like her husband's prolonged silence, stillness. He seemed so negative—so changed.

"David," she said, raising her voice, "I think you're feeling the dampness. It's grown chilly. The fever comes so suddenly, you know, and it might be wise to take the tincture. I'll go and get it, dear, at once. It's better." And before he could object she had left the room to bring the homeopathic dose that she believed in, and that, to please her, he swallowed by the tumbler-full from week to week.

And the moment the door closed behind her, Sanderson began again, though now in quite a different tone. Mr. Bittacy sat up in his chair. The two men obviously resumed the conversation—the real conversation interrupted beneath the cedar—and left aside the sham one which was so much dust merely thrown in the old lady's eyes.

"Trees love you, that's the fact," he said earnestly. "Your service to them all these years abroad has made them know you."

"Know me?"

"Made them, yes,"—he paused a moment, then added,—"made them *aware of your presence; aware* of a force outside themselves that deliberately seeks their welfare, don't you see?"

"By Jove, Sanderson—!" This put into plain language actual sensations he had felt, yet had never dared to phrase in words before. "They get into touch with me, as it were?" he ventured, laughing at his own sentence, yet laughing only with his lips.

"Exactly," was the quick, emphatic reply. "They seek to blend with something they feel instinctively to be good for them, helpful to their essential beings, encouraging to their best expression—their life."

"Good Lord, Sir!" Bittacy heard himself saying, "but you're putting my own thoughts into words. D'you know, I've felt something like that for years. As though—" he looked round to make sure his wife was not there, then finished the sentence—"as though the trees were after me!"

"'Amalgamate' seems the best word, perhaps," said Sanderson slowly. "They would draw you to themselves. Good forces, you see, always seek to merge; evil to separate; that's why Good in the end must always win the day—everywhere. The accumulation in the long run becomes overwhelming. Evil tends to separation, dissolution, death. The comradeship of trees, their instinct to run together, is a vital symbol. Trees in a mass are good; alone, you may take it generally, are—well, dangerous. Look at a monkey-puzzler, or better still, a holly. Look at it, watch it, understand it. Did you ever see more plainly an evil thought made visible? They're wicked. Beautiful too, oh yes! There's a strange, miscalculated beauty often in evil——"

"That cedar, then——?"

"Not evil, no; but alien, rather. Cedars grow in forests all together. The poor thing has drifted, that is all."

They were getting rather deep. Sanderson, talking against time, spoke so fast. It was too condensed. Bittacy hardly followed that last bit. His mind floundered among his own less definite, less sorted thoughts, till presently another sentence from the artist startled him into attention again.

"That cedar will protect you here, though, because you both have humanised it by your thinking so lovingly of its presence. The others can't get past it, as it were."

"Protect me!" he exclaimed. "Protect me from their love?"

Sanderson laughed. "We're getting rather mixed," he said; "we're talking of one thing in the terms of another really. But what I mean is—you see—that their love for you, their 'awareness' of your personality and presence involves the idea of winning you—across the border—into themselves—into their world of living. It means, in a way, taking you over."

The ideas the artist started in his mind ran furious wild races to and fro. It was like a maze sprung suddenly into movement. The whirling of the intricate lines bewildered him. They went so fast, leaving but half an explanation of their goal. He followed first one, then another, but a new one always dashed across to intercept before he could get anywhere.

"But India," he said, presently in a lower voice, "India is so far away—from this little English forest. The trees, too, are utterly different for one thing?"

The rustle of skirts warned of Mrs. Bittacy's approach. This was a sentence he could turn round another way in case she came up and pressed for explanation.

"There is communion among trees all the world over," was the strange quick reply. "They always know."

"They always know! You think then——?"

"The winds, you see—the great, swift carriers! They have their ancient rights of way about the world. An easterly wind, for instance, carrying on stage by stage as it were—linking dropped messages and meanings from land to land like the birds—an easterly wind——"

Mrs. Bittacy swept in upon them with the tumbler—

"There, David," she said, "that will ward off any beginnings of attack. Just a spoonful, dear. Oh, oh! not *all!*" for he had swallowed half the contents at a single gulp as usual; "another dose before you go to bed, and the balance in the morning, first thing when you wake."

She turned to her guest, who put the tumbler down for her upon a table at his elbow. She had heard them speak of the east wind. She emphasised the warning she had misinterpreted. The private part of the conversation came to an abrupt end.

"It is the one thing that upsets him more than any other—an east wind," she said, "and I am glad, Mr. Sanderson, to hear you think so too."

<h1 style="text-align:center">III</h1>

A deep hush followed, in the middle of which an owl was heard calling its muffled note in the forest. A big moth whirred with a soft collision against one of the windows. Mrs. Bittacy started slightly, but no one spoke. Above the trees the stars were faintly visible. From the distance came the barking of a dog.

Bittacy, relighting his cigar, broke the little spell of silence that had caught all three.

"It's rather a comforting thought," he said, throwing the match out of the window, "that life is about us everywhere, and that there is really no dividing line between what we call organic and inorganic."

"The universe, yes," said Sanderson, "is all one, really. We're puzzled by the gaps we cannot see across, but as a fact, I suppose, there are no gaps at all."

Mrs. Bittacy rustled ominously, holding her peace meanwhile. She feared long words she did not understand. Beelzebub lay hid among too many syllables.

"In trees and plants especially, there dreams an exquisite life that no one yet has proved unconscious."

"Or conscious either, Mr. Sanderson," she neatly interjected. "It's only man that was made after His image, not shrubberies and things. . . . "

Her husband interposed without delay.

"It is not necessary," he explained suavely, "to say that they're alive in the sense that we are alive. At the same time," with an eye to his wife, "I see no harm in holding, dear, that all created things contain some measure of His life Who made them. It's only beautiful to hold

that He created nothing dead. We are not pantheists for all that!" he
added soothingly.

"Oh, no! Not that, I hope!" The word alarmed her. It was worse
than pope. Through her puzzled mind stole a stealthy, dangerous
thing . . . like a panther.

"I like to think that even in decay there's life," the painter murmured. "The falling apart of rotten wood breeds sentiency; there's
force and motion in the falling of a dying leaf, in the breaking up
and crumbling of everything indeed. And take an inert stone: it's
crammed with heat and weight and potencies of all sorts. What
holds its particles together indeed? We understand it as little as
gravity or why a needle always turns to the 'North.' Both things may
be a mode of life. . . . "

"You think a compass has a soul, Mr. Sanderson?" exclaimed the
lady with a crackling of her silk flounces that conveyed a sense of
outrage even more plainly than her tone. The artist smiled to himself in the darkness, but it was Bittacy who hastened to reply.

"Our friend merely suggests that these mysterious agencies," he
said quietly, "may be due to some kind of life we cannot understand. Why should water only run downhill? Why should trees
grow at right angles to the surface of the ground and towards the
sun? Why should the worlds spin for ever on their axes? Why
should fire change the form of everything it touches without really
destroying them? To say these things follow the law of their being
explains nothing. Mr. Sanderson merely suggests—poetically, my
dear, of course—that these may be manifestations of life, though
life at a different stage to ours."

"The '*breath* of life,' we read, 'He breathed into them.' These
things do not breathe." She said it with triumph.

Then Sanderson put in a word. But he spoke rather to himself or
to his host than by way of serious rejoinder to the ruffled lady.

"But plants do breathe too, you know," he said. "They breathe,
they eat, they digest, they move about, and they adapt themselves
to their environment as men and animals do. They have a nervous
system too . . . at least a complex system of nuclei which have some
of the qualities of nerve cells. They may have memory too.
Certainly, they know definite action in response to stimulus. And
though this may be physiological, no one has proved that it is only
that, and not—psychological."

He did not notice, apparently, the little gasp that was audible behind the yellow shawl. Bittacy cleared his throat, threw his extinguished cigar upon the lawn, crossed and recrossed his legs.

"And in trees," continued the other, "behind a great forest, for instance," pointing towards the woods, "may stand a rather splendid Entity that manifests through all the thousand individual trees—some huge collective life, quite as minutely and delicately organised as our own. It might merge and blend with ours under certain conditions, so that we could understand it by *being* it, for a time at least. It might even engulf human vitality into the immense whirlpool of its own vast dreaming life. The pull of a big forest on a man can be tremendous and utterly overwhelming."

The mouth of Mrs. Bittacy was heard to close with a snap. Her shawl, and particularly her crackling dress, exhaled the protest that burned within her like a pain. She was too distressed to be overawed, but at the same time too confused 'mid the litter of words and meanings half understood, to find immediate phrases she could use. Whatever the actual meaning of his language might be, however, and whatever subtle dangers lay concealed behind them meanwhile, they certainly wove a kind of gentle spell with the glimmering darkness that held all three delicately enmeshed there by that open window. The odours of dewy lawn, flowers, trees, and earth formed part of it.

"The moods," he continued, "that people waken in us are due to their hidden life affecting our own. Deep calls to deep. A person, for instance, joins you in an empty room: you both instantly change. The new arrival, though in silence, has caused a change of mood. May not the moods of Nature touch and stir us in virtue of a similar prerogative? The sea, the hills, the desert, wake passion, joy, terror, as the case may be; for a few, perhaps," he glanced significantly at his host so that Mrs. Bittacy again caught the turning of his eyes, "emotions of a curious, flaming splendour that are quite nameless. Well . . . whence come these powers? Surely from nothing that is . . . dead! Does not the influence of a forest, its sway and strange ascendancy over certain minds, betray a direct manifestation of life? It lies otherwise beyond all explanation, this mysterious emanation of big woods. Some natures, of course, deliberately invite it. The authority of a host of trees,"—his voice grew almost solemn as he said the words—"is something not to be denied. One feels it here, I think, particularly."

There was considerable tension in the air as he ceased speaking. Mr. Bittacy had not intended that the talk should go so far. They had drifted. He did not wish to see his wife unhappy or afraid, and he was aware—acutely so—that her feelings were stirred to a point he did not care about. Something in her, as he put it, was "working up" towards explosion.

He sought to generalise the conversation, diluting this accumulated emotion by spreading it.

"The sea is His and He made it," he suggested vaguely, hoping Sanderson would take the hint, "and with the trees it is the same. . . ."

"The whole gigantic vegetable kingdom, yes," the artist took him up, "all at the service of man, for food, for shelter and for a thousand purposes of his daily life. Is it not striking what a lot of the globe they cover . . . exquisitely organised life, yet stationary, always ready to our hand when we want them, never running away? But the taking them, for all that, not so easy. One man shrinks from picking flowers, another from cutting down trees. And, it's curious that most of the forest tales and legends are dark, mysterious, and somewhat ill-omened. The forest-beings are rarely gay and harmless. The forest life was felt as terrible. Tree-worship still survives to-day. Woodcutters . . . those who take the life of trees . . . you see, a race of haunted men. . . ."

He stopped abruptly, a singular catch in his voice. Bittacy felt something even before the sentences were over. His wife, he knew, felt it still more strongly. For it was in the middle of the heavy silence following upon these last remarks, that Mrs. Bittacy, rising with a violent abruptness from her chair, drew the attention of the others to something moving towards them across the lawn. It came silently. In outline it was large and curiously spread. It rose high, too, for the sky above the shrubberies, still pale gold from the sunset, was dimmed by its passage. She declared afterwards that it moved in "looping circles," but what she perhaps meant to convey was "spirals."

She screamed faintly. "It's come at last! And it's you that brought it!"

She turned excitedly, half afraid, half angry, to Sanderson. With a breathless sort of gasp she said it, politeness all forgotten. "I knew it . . . if you went on. I knew it. Oh! Oh!" And she cried again, "Your talking has brought it out!" The terror that shook her voice was rather dreadful.

But the confusion of her vehement words passed unnoticed in the first surprise they caused. For a moment nothing happened.

"What is it you think you see, my dear?" asked her husband,

startled. Sanderson said nothing. All three leaned forward, the men still sitting, but Mrs. Bittacy had rushed hurriedly to the window, placing herself of a purpose, as it seemed, between her husband and the lawn. She pointed. Her little hand made a silhouette against the sky, the yellow shawl hanging from the arm like a cloud.

"Beyond the cedar—between it and the lilacs." The voice had lost its shrillness; it was thin and hushed. "There . . . now you see it going round upon itself again—going back, thank God! . . . going back to the Forest." It sank to a whisper, shaking. She repeated, with a great dropping sigh of relief—"Thank God! I thought . . . at first . . . it was coming here . . . to us! . . . David . . . to *you!*"

She stepped back from the window, her movements confused, feeling in the darkness for the support of a chair, and finding her husband's outstretched hand instead. "Hold me, dear, hold me, please . . . tight. Do not let me go." She was in what he called afterwards "a regular state." He drew her firmly down upon her chair again.

"Smoke, Sophie, my dear," he said quickly, trying to make his voice calm and natural. "I see it, yes. It's smoke blowing over from the gardener's cottage. . . . "

"But, David,"—and there was a new horror in her whisper now—"it made a noise. It makes it still. I hear it swishing." Some such word she used—swishing, sishing, rushing, or something of the kind. "David, I'm very frightened. It's something awful! That man has called it out . . . !"

"Hush, hush," whispered her husband. He stroked her trembling hand beside him.

"It is in the wind," said Sanderson, speaking for the first time, very quietly. The expression on his face was not visible in the gloom, but his voice was soft and unafraid. At the sound of it, Mrs. Bittacy started violently again. Bittacy drew his chair a little forward to obstruct her view of him. He felt bewildered himself, a little, hardly knowing quite what to say or do. It was all so very curious and sudden.

But Mrs. Bittacy was badly frightened. It seemed to her that what she saw came from the enveloping forest just beyond their little garden. It emerged in a sort of secret way, moving towards them as with a purpose, stealthily, difficultly. Then something stopped it. It could not advance beyond the cedar. The cedar—this impression remained with her afterwards too—prevented, kept it back. Like a rising sea the Forest had surged a moment in their direction through the covering darkness, and this visible movement was its first wave. Thus to her mind it seemed . . . like that mysterious turn of the tide that used to frighten and mystify her in childhood on the sands. The outward surge of some enormous Power was what she felt . . . something to which every instinct in her being rose in opposition because it threatened her and hers. In that moment she realised the Personality of the Forest . . . menacing.

In the stumbling movement that she made away from the window and towards the bell she barely caught the sentence Sanderson—or was it her husband?—murmured to himself: "It came because we talked of it; our thinking made it aware of us and brought it out. But the cedar stops it. It cannot cross the lawn, you see. . . . "

All three were standing now, and her husband's voice broke in with authority while his wife's fingers touched the bell.

"My dear, I should *not* say anything to Thompson." The anxiety he felt was manifest in his voice, but his outward composure had returned. "The gardener can go. . . . "

Then Sanderson cut him short. "Allow me," he said quickly. "I'll see if anything's wrong." And before either of them could answer or object, he was gone, leaping out by the open window. They saw his figure vanish with a run across the lawn into the darkness.

A moment later the maid entered, in answer to the bell, and with her came the loud barking of the terrier from the hall.

"The lamps," said her master shortly, and as she softly closed the door behind her, they heard the wind pass with a mournful sound of singing round the outer walls. A rustle of foliage from the distance passed within it.

"You see, the wind *is* rising. It *was* the wind!" He put a comforting arm about her, distressed to feel that she was trembling. But he knew that he was trembling too, though with a kind of odd elation rather than alarm. "And it *was* smoke that you saw coming from Stride's cottage, or from the rubbish heaps he's been burning in the kitchen garden. The noise we heard was the branches rustling in the wind. Why should you be so nervous?"

A thin whispering voice answered him:

"I was afraid for *you,* dear. Something frightened me for *you.* That man makes me feel so uneasy and uncomfortable for his influence upon you. It's very foolish, I know. I think . . . I'm tired; I feel so overwrought and restless." The words poured out in a hurried jumble and she kept turning to the window while she spoke.

"The strain of having a visitor," he said soothingly, "has taxed you. We're so unused to having people in the house. He goes to-morrow." He warmed her cold hands between his own, stroking them tenderly. More, for the life of him, he could not say or do. The joy of a strange, internal excitement made his heart beat faster. He knew not what it was. He knew only, perhaps, whence it came.

She peered close into his face through the gloom, and said a curious thing. "I thought, David, for a moment . . . you seemed . . . different. My nerves are all on edge to-night." She made no further reference to her husband's visitor.

A sound of footsteps from the lawn warned of Sanderson's return, as he answered quickly in a lowered tone—"There's no need to be afraid on my account, dear girl. There's nothing wrong with me, I assure you; I never felt so well and happy in my life."

Thompson came in with the lamps and brightness, and scarcely had she gone again when Sanderson in turn was seen climbing through the window.

"There's nothing," he said lightly, as he closed it behind him. "Somebody's been burning leaves, and the smoke is drifting a little through the trees. The wind," he added, glancing at his host a moment significantly, but in so discreet a way that Mrs. Bittacy did not observe it, "the wind, too, has begun to roar . . . in the Forest . . . further out."

But Mrs. Bittacy noticed about him two things which increased her uneasiness. She noticed the shining of his eyes, because a similar light had suddenly come into her husband's; and she noticed, too, the apparent depth of meaning he put into those simple words that "the wind had begun to roar in the Forest . . . further out." Her mind retained the disagreeable impression that he meant more than he said. In his tone lay quite another implication. It was not actually "wind" he spoke of, and it would not remain "further out" . . . rather, it was coming in. Another impression she got too—still more unwelcome—was that her husband understood his hidden meaning.

IV

"David, dear," she observed gently as soon as they were alone upstairs, "I have a horrible uneasy feeling about that man. I cannot get rid of it." The tremor in her voice caught all his tenderness.

He turned to look at her. "Of what kind, my dear? You're so imaginative sometimes, aren't you?"

"I think," she hesitated, stammering a little, confused, still frightened, "I mean—isn't he a hypnotist, or full of those theofosical ideas, or something of the sort? You know what I mean—"

He was too accustomed to her little confused alarms to explain them away seriously as a rule, or to correct her verbal inaccuracies, but to-night he felt she needed careful, tender treatment. He soothed her as best he could.

"But there's no harm in that, even if he is," he answered quietly. "Those are only new names for very old ideas, you know, dear." There was no trace of impatience in his voice.

"That's what I mean," she replied, the texts he dreaded rising in an unuttered crowd behind the words. "He's one of those things that we are warned would come—one of those Latter-Day things." For her mind still bristled with the bogeys of Antichrist and Prophecy, and she had only escaped the Number of the Beast, as it were, by the skin of her teeth. The Pope drew most of her fire usually, because she could understand him; the target was plain and she could shoot. But this tree-and-forest business was so vague and horrible. It terrified her. "He makes me think," she went on, "of Principalities and Powers in high places, and of things that walk in darkness. I did *not* like the way he spoke of trees getting alive in the night, and all that; it made me think of wolves in sheep's clothing. And when I saw that awful thing in the sky above the lawn—"

But he interrupted her at once, for that was something he had decided it was best to leave unmentioned. Certainly it was better not discussed.

"He only meant, I think, Sophie," he put in gravely, yet with a little smile, "that trees may have a measure of conscious life—rather a nice idea on the whole, surely,—something like that bit we read in the *Times* the other night, you remember—and that a big forest may possess a sort of Collective Personality. Remember, he's an artist, and poetical."

"It's dangerous," she said emphatically. "I feel it's playing with fire, unwise, unsafe—"

"Yet all to the glory of God," he urged gently. "We must not shut our ears and eyes to knowledge—of any kind, must we?"

"With you, David, the wish is always farther than the thought," she rejoined. For, like the child who thought that "suffered under

Pontius Pilate" was "suffered under a bunch of violets," she heard her proverbs phonetically and reproduced them thus. She hoped to convey her warning in the quotation. "And we must always try the spirits whether they be of God," she added tentatively.

"Certainly, dear, we can always do that," he assented, getting into bed.

But, after a little pause, during which she blew the light out, David Bittacy settling down to sleep with an excitement in his blood that was new and bewilderingly delightful, realised that perhaps he had not said quite enough to comfort her. She was lying awake by his side, still frightened. He put his head up in the darkness.

"Sophie," he said softly, "you must remember, too, that in any case between us and—and all that sort of thing—there is a great gulf fixed, a gulf that cannot be crossed—er—while we are still in the body."

And hearing no reply, he satisfied himself that she was already asleep and happy. But Mrs. Bittacy was not asleep. She heard the sentence, only she said nothing because she felt her thought was better unexpressed. She was afraid to hear the words in the darkness. The Forest outside was listening and might hear them too— the Forest that was "roaring further out."

And the thought was this: That gulf, of course, existed, but Sanderson had somehow bridged it.

It was much later that night when she awoke out of troubled, uneasy dreams and heard a sound that twisted her very nerves with fear. It passed immediately with full waking, for, listen as she might, there was nothing audible but the inarticulate murmur of the night. It was in her dreams she heard it, and the dreams had vanished with it. But the sound was recognisable, for it was that rushing noise that had come across the lawn; only this time closer. Just above her face while she slept had passed this murmur as of rustling branches in the very room, a sound of foliage whispering. "A going in the tops of the mulberry trees," ran through her mind. She had dreamed that she lay beneath a spreading tree somewhere, a tree that whispered with ten thousand soft lips of green; and the dream continued for a moment even after waking.

She sat up in bed and stared about her. The window was open at the top; she saw the stars; the door, she remembered, was locked as usual; the room, of course, was empty. The deep hush of the summer night lay over all, broken only by another sound that now issued from the shadows close beside the bed, a human sound, yet unnatural, a sound that seized the fear with which she had waked and instantly increased it. And, although it was one she recognised as familiar, at first she could not name it. Some seconds certainly passed—and, they were very long ones—before she understood that it was her husband talking in his sleep.

The direction of the voice confused and puzzled her, moreover, for it was not, as she first supposed, beside her. There was distance in it. The next minute, by the light of the sinking candle flame, she saw his white figure standing out in the middle of the room, half-way towards the window. The candle-light slowly grew. She saw him move then nearer to the window, with arms outstretched. His speech was low and mumbled, the words running together too much to be distinguishable.

And she shivered. To her, sleep-talking was uncanny to the point of horror; it was like the talking of the dead, mere parody of a living voice, unnatural.

"David!" she whispered, dreading the sound of her own voice, and half afraid to interrupt him and see his face. She could not bear the sight of the wide-opened eyes. "David, you're walking in your sleep. Do—come back to bed, dear, *please!*"

Her whisper seemed so dreadfully loud in the still darkness. At the sound of her voice he paused, then turned slowly round to face her. His widely-opened eyes stared into her own without recognition; they looked through her into something beyond; it was as though he knew the direction of the sound, yet could not see her. They were shining, she noticed, as the eyes of Sanderson had shone several hours ago; and his face was flushed, distraught. Anxiety was written upon every feature. And, instantly, recognising that the fever was upon him, she forgot her terror temporarily in practical considerations. He came back to bed without waking. She closed his eyelids. Presently he composed himself quietly to sleep, or rather to deeper sleep. She contrived to make him swallow something from the tumbler beside the bed.

Then she rose very quietly to close the window, feeling the night air blow in too fresh and keen. She put the candle where it could not reach him. The sight of the big Baxter Bible beside it comforted her a little, but all through her under-being ran the warnings of a curious alarm. And it was while in the act of fastening the catch with one hand and pulling the string of the blind with the other, that her husband sat up again in bed and spoke in words this time that were distinctly audible. The eyes had opened wide again. He pointed. She stood stock still and listened, her shadow distorted on the blind. He did not come out towards her as at first she feared.

The whispering voice was very clear, horrible, too, beyond all she had ever known.

"They are roaring in the Forest further out . . . and I . . . must go and see." He stared beyond her as he said it, to the woods. "They are needing me. They sent for me. . . . " Then his eyes wandering back again to things within the room, he lay down, his purpose suddenly changed. And that change was horrible as well, more horrible, perhaps, because of its revelation of another detailed world he moved in far away from her.

The singular phrase chilled her blood; for a moment she was utterly terrified. That tone of the somnambulist, differing so slightly yet so distressingly from normal, waking speech, seemed to her somehow wicked. Evil and danger lay waiting thick behind it. She leaned against the window-sill, shaking in every limb. She had an awful feeling for a moment that something was coming in to fetch him.

"Not yet, then," she heard in a much lower voice from the bed, "but later. It will be better so. . . . I shall go later. . . . "

The words expressed some fringe of these alarms that had haunted her so long, and that the arrival and presence of Sanderson seemed to have brought to the very edge of a climax she could not even dare to think about. They gave it form; they brought it closer; they sent her thoughts to her Deity in a wild, deep prayer for help and guidance. For here was a direct, unconscious betrayal of a world of inner purposes and claims her husband recognised while he kept them almost wholly to himself.

By the time she reached his side and knew the comfort of his touch, the eyes had closed again, this time of their own accord, and the head lay calmly back upon the pillows. She gently straightened the bed clothes. She watched him for some minutes, shading the candle carefully with one hand. There was a smile of strangest peace upon the face.

Then, blowing out the candle, she knelt down and prayed before getting back into bed. But no sleep came to her. She lay awake all night thinking, wondering, praying, until at length with the chorus of the birds and the glimmer of the dawn upon the green blind, she fell into a slumber of complete exhaustion.

But while she slept the wind continued roaring in the Forest further out. The sound came closer—sometimes very close indeed.

V

With the departure of Sanderson the significance of the curious incidents waned, because the moods that had produced them passed away. Mrs. Bittacy soon afterwards came to regard them as some growth of disproportion that had been very largely, perhaps, in her own mind. It did not strike her that this change was sudden, for it came about quite naturally. For one thing her husband never spoke of the matter, and for another she remembered how many things in life that had seemed inexplicable and singular at the time turned out later to have been quite commonplace.

Most of it, certainly, she put down to the presence of the artist and to his wild, suggestive talk. With his welcome removal, the world turned ordinary again and safe. The fever, though it lasted as usual a short time only, had not allowed of her husband's getting up to say good-bye, and she had conveyed his regrets and adieux. In the morning Mr. Sanderson had seemed ordinary enough. In his town hat and gloves, as she saw him go, he seemed tame and unalarming.

"After all," she thought as she watched the pony-cart bear him off, "he's only an artist!" What she had thought he might be otherwise her slim imagination did not venture to disclose. Her change of feeling was wholesome and refreshing. She felt a little ashamed of her behaviour. She gave him a smile—genuine because the relief she felt was genuine—as he bent over her hand and kissed it, but she did not suggest a second visit, and her husband, she noted with satisfaction and relief, had said nothing either.

The little household fell again into the normal and sleepy routine to which it was accustomed. The name of Arthur Sanderson was rarely if ever mentioned. Nor, for her part, did she mention to her husband the incident of his walking in his sleep and the wild words he used. But to forget it was equally impossible. Thus it lay buried deep within her like a centre of some unknown disease of which it was a mysterious symptom, waiting to spread at the first favourable opportunity. She prayed against it every night and morning; prayed that she might forget it—that God would keep her husband safe from harm.

For in spite of much surface foolishness that many might have read as weakness, Mrs. Bittacy had balance, sanity, and a fine deep faith. She was greater than she knew. Her love for her husband and her God were somehow one, an achievement only possible to a single-hearted nobility of soul.

There followed a summer of great violence and beauty; of beauty, because the refreshing rains at night prolonged the glory of the spring and spread it all across July, keeping the foliage young and sweet; of violence, because the winds that tore about the south of England brushed the whole country into dancing movement. They swept the woods magnificently, and kept them roaring with a perpetual grand voice. Their deepest notes seemed never to leave the sky. They sang and shouted, and torn leaves raced and fluttered through the air long before their usually appointed time. Many a tree, after days of this roaring and dancing, fell exhausted to the ground. The cedar on the lawn gave up two limbs that fell upon successive days, at the same hour too—just before dusk. The wind often makes its most boisterous effort at that time, before it drops with the sun, and these two huge branches lay in dark ruin covering half the lawn. They spread across it and towards the house. They left an ugly gaping space upon the tree, so that the Lebanon looked unfinished, half destroyed, a monster shorn of its old-time comeliness and splendour. Far more of the Forest was now visible than before; it peered through the breach of the broken defences. They could see from the windows of the house now—especially from the drawing-room and bedroom windows—straight out into the glades and depths beyond.

Mrs. Bittacy's niece and nephew, who were staying on a visit at the time, enjoyed themselves immensely helping the gardeners carry off the fragments. It took two days to do this, for Mr. Bittacy insisted on the branches being moved entire. He would not allow them to be chopped; also, he would not consent to their use as firewood. Under his superintendence the unwieldy masses were dragged to the edge of the garden and arranged upon the frontier line between the Forest and the lawn. The children were delighted with the scheme. They entered into it with enthusiasm. At all costs this defence against the inroads of the Forest must be made secure.

They caught their uncle's earnestness, felt even something of a hidden motive that he had; and the visit, usually rather dreaded, became the visit of their lives instead. It was Aunt Sophia this time who seemed discouraging and dull.

"She's got so old and funny," opined Stephen.

But Alice, who felt in the silent displeasure of her aunt some secret thing that half alarmed her, said:

"I think she's afraid of the woods. She never comes into them with us, you see."

"All the more reason then for making this wall impreg—all fat and thick and solid," he concluded, unable to manage the longer word. "Then nothing—simply *nothing*—can get through. Can't it, Uncle David?"

And Mr. Bittacy, jacket discarded and working in his speckled waistcoat, went puffing to their aid, arranging the massive limb of the cedar like a hedge.

"Come on," he said, "whatever happens, you know, we must finish before it's dark. Already the wind is roaring in the Forest further out." And Alice caught the phrase and instantly echoed it. "Stevie," she cried below her breath, "look sharp, you lazy lump. Didn't you hear what Uncle David said? It'll come in and catch us before we've done!"

They worked like Trojans, and, sitting beneath the wistaria tree that climbed the southern wall of the cottage, Mrs. Bittacy with her knitting watched them, calling from time to time insignificant messages of counsel and advice. The messages passed, of course, unheeded. Mostly, indeed, they were unheard, for the workers were too absorbed. She warned her husband not to get too hot, Alice not to tear her dress, Stephen not to strain his back with pulling. Her mind hovered between the homeopathic medicine-chest upstairs and her anxiety to see the business finished.

For this breaking up of the cedar had stirred again her slumbering alarms. It revived memories of the visit of Mr. Sanderson that had been sinking into oblivion; she recalled his queer and odious way of talking, and many things she hoped forgotten drew their heads up from that subconscious region to which all forgetting is impossible. They looked at her and nodded. They were full of life; they had no intention of being pushed aside and buried permanently. "Now look!" they whispered, "didn't we tell you so?" They had been merely waiting the right moment to assert their presence.

And all her former vague distress crept over her. Anxiety, uneasiness returned. That dreadful sinking of the heart came too.

This incident of the cedar's breaking up was actually so unimportant, and yet her husband's attitude towards it made it so significant.
There was nothing that he said in particular, or did, or left undone
that frightened her, but his general air of earnestness seemed so
unwarranted. She felt that he deemed the thing important. He was
so exercised about it. This evidence of sudden concern and interest,
buried all the summer from her sight and knowledge, she realised
now had been buried purposely; he had kept it intentionally concealed. Deeply submerged in him there ran this tide of other
thoughts, desires, hopes. What were they? Whither did they lead?
The accident to the tree betrayed it most unpleasantly; and, doubtless, more than he was aware.

She watched his grave and serious face as he worked there with
the children, and as she watched she felt afraid. It vexed her that
the children worked so eagerly. They unconsciously supported him.
The thing she feared she would not even name. But it was waiting.

Moreover, as far as her puzzled mind could deal with a dread so
vague and incoherent, the collapse of the cedar somehow brought
it nearer. The fact that, all so ill-explained and formless, the thing
yet lay in her consciousness, out of reach but moving and alive,
filled her with a kind of puzzled, dreadful wonder. Its presence was
so very real, its power so gripping, its partial concealment so abominable. Then, out of the dim confusion, she grasped one thought
and saw it stand quite clear before her eyes. She found difficulty in
clothing it in words, but its meaning perhaps was this: That cedar
stood in their life for something friendly; its downfall meant disaster; a sense of some protective influence about the cottage, and
about her husband in particular, was thereby weakened.

"Why do you fear the big winds so?" he had asked her several
days before, after a particularly boisterous day; and the answer she
gave surprised her while she gave it. One of those heads poked up
unconsciously, and let slip the truth:

"Because, David, I feel they—bring the Forest with them," she
faltered. "They blow something from the trees—into the mind—
into the house."

He looked at her keenly for a moment.

"That must be why I love them then," he answered. "They blow
the souls of the trees about the sky like clouds."

The conversation dropped. She had never heard him talk in quite that way before.

And another time, when he had coaxed her to go with him down one of the nearer glades, she asked why he took the small hand-axe with him, and what he wanted it for.

"To cut the ivy that clings to the trunks and takes their life away," he said.

"But can't the verdurers do that?" she asked. "That's what they're paid for, isn't it?"

Whereupon he explained that ivy was a parasite the trees knew not how to fight alone, and that the verdurers were careless and did not do it thoroughly. They gave a chop here and there, leaving the tree to do the rest for itself if it could.

"Besides, I like to do it for them. I love to help them and protect," he added, the foliage rustling all about his quiet words as they went.

And these stray remarks, as his attitude towards the broken cedar, betrayed this curious, subtle change that was going forward in his personality. Slowly and surely all the summer it had increased.

It was growing—the thought startled her horribly—just as a tree grows, the outer evidence from day to day so slight as to be unnoticeable, yet the rising tide so deep and irresistible. The alteration spread all through and over him, was in both mind and actions, sometimes almost in his face as well. Occasionally, thus, it stood up straight outside himself and frightened her. His life was somehow becoming linked so intimately with trees, and with all that trees signified. His interests became more and more their interests, his activity combined with theirs, his thoughts and feelings theirs, his purpose, hope, desire, his fate——

His fate! The darkness of some vague, enormous terror dropped its shadow on her when she thought of it. Some instinct in her heart she dreaded infinitely more than death—for death meant sweet translation for his soul—came gradually to associate the thought of him with the thought of trees, in particular with these Forest trees. Sometimes, before she could face the thing, argue it away, or pray it into silence, she found the thought of him running swiftly through her mind like a thought of the Forest itself, the two most intimately linked and joined together, each a part and complement of the other, one being.

The idea was too dim for her to see it face to face. Its mere

possibility dissolved the instant she focussed it to get the truth
behind it. It was too utterly elusive, mad, protæan. Under the
attack of even a minute's concentration the very meaning of it vanished, melted away. The idea lay really behind any words that she
could ever find, beyond the touch of definite thought. Her mind
was unable to grapple with it. But, while it vanished, the trail of its
approach and disappearance flickered a moment before her shaking vision. The horror certainly remained.

Reduced to the simple human statement that her temperament
sought instinctively, it stood perhaps at this: Her husband loved
her, and he loved the trees as well; but the trees came first, claimed
parts of him she did not know. *She* loved her God and him. *He*
loved the trees and her.

Thus, in guise of some faint, distressing compromise, the matter
shaped itself for her perplexed mind in the terms of conflict. A
silent, hidden battle raged, but as yet raged far away. The breaking
of the cedar was a visible outward fragment of a distant and mysterious encounter that was coming daily closer to them both. The
wind, instead of roaring in the Forest further out, now came nearer,
booming in fitful gusts about its edge and frontiers.

Meanwhile the summer dimmed. The autumn winds went sighing through the woods; leaves turned to golden red, and the evenings
were drawing in with cosy shadows before the first sign of anything
seriously untoward made its appearance. It came then with a flat,
decided kind of violence that indicated mature preparation beforehand. It was not impulsive nor ill-considered. In a fashion it seemed
expected, and indeed inevitable. For within a fortnight of their
annual change to the little village of Seillans above St. Raphael—a
change so regular for the past ten years that it was not even discussed between them—David Bittacy abruptly refused to go.

Thompson had laid the tea-table, prepared the spirit lamp
beneath the urn, pulled down the blinds in that swift and silent way
she had, and left the room. The lamps were still unlit. The fire-light
shone on the chintz armchairs, and Boxer lay asleep on the black
horse-hair rug. Upon the walls the gilt picture frames gleamed
faintly, the pictures themselves indistinguishable. Mrs. Bittacy had
warmed the teapot and was in the act of pouring the water in to
heat the cups when her husband, looking up from his chair across
the hearth, made the abrupt announcement:

"My dear," he said, as though following a train of thought of which she only heard this final phrase, "it's really quite impossible for me to go."

And so abrupt, inconsequent, it sounded that she at first misunderstood. She thought he meant go out into the garden or the woods. But her heart leaped all the same. The tone of his voice was ominous.

"Of course not," she answered, "it would be *most* unwise. Why should you——?" She referred to the mist that always spread on autumn nights upon the lawn; but before she finished the sentence she knew that *he* referred to something else. And her heart then gave its second horrible leap.

"David! You mean abroad?" she gasped.

"I mean abroad, dear, yes."

It reminded her of the tone he used when saying good-bye years ago, before one of those jungle expeditions she dreaded. His voice then was so serious, so final. It was serious and final now. For several moments she could think of nothing to say. She busied herself with the teapot. She had filled one cup with hot water till it overflowed, and she emptied it slowly into the slop-basin, trying with all her might not to let him see the trembling of her hand. The firelight and the dimness of the room both helped her. But in any case he would hardly have noticed it. His thoughts were far away. . . .

VI

Mrs. Bittacy had never liked their present home. She preferred a flat, more open country that left approaches clear. She liked to see things coming. This cottage on the very edge of the old hunting grounds of William the Conqueror had never satisfied her ideal of a safe and pleasant place to settle down in. The sea-coast, with treeless downs behind and a clear horizon in front, as at Eastbourne, say, was her ideal of a proper home.

It was curious, this instinctive aversion she felt to being shut in— by trees especially; a kind of claustrophobia almost; probably due, as has been said, to the days in India when the trees took her husband off and surrounded him with dangers. In those weeks of solitude the feeling had matured. She had fought it in her fashion, but never conquered it. Apparently routed, it had a way of creeping back in other forms. In this particular case, yielding to his strong desire, she thought the battle won, but the terror of the trees came back before the first month had passed. They laughed in her face.

She never lost knowledge of the fact that the leagues of forest lay about their cottage like a mighty wall, a crowding, watching, listening presence that shut them in from freedom and escape. Far from morbid naturally, she did her best to deny the thought, and so simple and unartificial was her type of mind that for weeks together she would wholly lose it. Then, suddenly it would return upon her with a rush of bleak reality. It was not only in her mind; it existed apart from any mere mood; a separate fear that walked alone; it came and went, yet when it went—went only to watch her from another point of view. It was in abeyance—hidden round the corner.

The Forest never let her go completely. It was ever ready to encroach. All the branches, she sometimes fancied, stretched one way—towards their tiny cottage and garden, as though it sought to draw them in and merge them in itself. Its great, deep-breathing soul resented the mockery, the insolence, the irritation of the prim garden at its very gates. It would absorb and smother them if it could. And every wind that blew its thundering message over the huge sounding-board of the million, shaking trees conveyed the purpose that it had. They had angered its great soul. At its heart was this deep, incessant roaring.

All this she never framed in words; the subtleties of language lay far beyond her reach. But instinctively she felt it; and more besides. It troubled her profoundly. Chiefly, moreover, for her husband. Merely for herself, the nightmare might have left her cold. It was David's peculiar interest in the trees that gave the special invitation.

Jealousy, then, in its most subtle aspect came to strengthen this aversion and dislike, for it came in a form that no reasonable wife could possibly object to. Her husband's passion, she reflected, was natural and inborn. It had decided his vocation, fed his ambition, nourished his dreams, desires, hopes. All his best years of active life had been spent in the care and guardianship of trees. He knew them, understood their secret life and nature, "managed" them intuitively as other men "managed" dogs and horses. He could not live for long away from them without a strange, acute nostalgia that stole his peace of mind and consequently his strength of body. A forest made him happy and at peace; it nursed and fed and soothed his deepest moods. Trees influenced the sources of his life, lowered or raised the very heart-beat in him. Cut off from them he languished as a lover of the sea can droop inland, or a mountaineer may pine in the flat monotony of the plains.

This she could understand, in a fashion at least, and make allowances for. She had yielded gently, even sweetly, to his choice of their English home; for in the little island there is nothing that suggests the woods of wilder countries so nearly as the New Forest. It has the genuine air and mystery, the depth and splendour, the loneliness, and here and there the strong, untamable quality of old-time forests as Bittacy of the Department knew them.

In a single detail only had he yielded to her wishes. He consented to a cottage on the edge, instead of in the heart of it. And for a dozen years now they had dwelt in peace and happiness at the lips of this great spreading thing that covered so many leagues with its tangle of swamps and moors and splendid ancient trees.

Only with the last two years or so—with his own increasing age, and physical decline perhaps—had come this marked growth of passionate interest in the welfare of the Forest. She had watched it grow, at first had laughed at it, then talked sympathetically so far as sincerity permitted, then had argued mildly, and finally come to realise that its treatment lay altogether beyond her powers, and so had come to fear it with all her heart.

The six weeks they annually spent away from their English home, each regarded very differently, of course. For her husband it meant a painful exile that did his health no good; he yearned for his trees— the sight and sound and smell of them; but for herself it meant release from a haunting dread—escape. To renounce those six weeks by the sea on the sunny, shining coast of France, was almost more than this little woman, even with her unselfishness, could face.

After the first shock of the announcement, she reflected as deeply as her nature permitted, prayed, wept in secret—and made up her mind. Duty, she felt clearly, pointed to renouncement. The discipline would certainly be severe—she did not dream at the moment how severe!—but this fine, consistent little Christian saw it plain; she accepted it, too, without any sighing of the martyr, though the courage she showed was of the martyr order. Her husband should never know the cost. In all but this one passion his unselfishness was ever as great as her own. The love she had borne him all these years, like the love she bore her anthropomorphic deity, was deep and real. She loved to suffer for them both. Besides, the way her husband had put it to her was singular. It did not take the form of a mere selfish predilection. Something higher than two wills in conflict seeking compromise was in it from the beginning.

"I feel, Sophia, it would be really more than I could manage," he said slowly, gazing into the fire over the tops of his stretched-out muddy boots. "My duty and my happiness lie here with the Forest and with you. My life is deeply rooted in this place. Something I can't define connects my inner being with these trees, and separation would make me ill—might even kill me. My hold on life would weaken; here is my source of supply. I cannot explain it better than that." He looked up steadily into her face across the table so that she saw the gravity of his expression and the shining of his steady eyes.

"David, you feel it as strongly as that!" she said, forgetting the tea things altogether.

"Yes," he replied, "I do. And it's not of the body only; I feel it in my soul."

The reality of what he hinted at crept into that shadow-covered room like an actual Presence and stood beside them. It came not by the windows or the door, but it filled the entire space between the walls and ceiling. It took the heat from the fire before her face. She felt suddenly cold, confused a little, frightened. She almost felt the rush of foliage in the wind. It stood between them.

"There are things—some things," she faltered, "we are not intended to know, I think." The words expressed her general attitude to life, not alone to this particular incident.

And after a pause of several minutes, disregarding the criticism as though he had not heard it—"I cannot explain it better than that, you see," his grave voice answered. "There *is* this deep, tremendous link,—some secret power they emanate that keeps me well and happy and—alive. If you cannot understand, I feel at least you may be able to—forgive." His tone grew tender, gentle, soft. "My selfishness, I know, must seem quite unforgivable. I cannot help it somehow; these trees, this ancient Forest, both seem knitted into all that makes me live, and if I go——"

There was a little sound of collapse in his voice. He stopped abruptly, and sank back in his chair. And, at that, a distinct lump came up into her throat which she had great difficulty in managing while she went over and put her arms about him.

"My dear," she murmured, "God will direct. We will accept His guidance. He has always shown the way before."

"My selfishness afflicts me——" he began, but she would not let him finish.

"David, He will direct. Nothing shall harm you. You've never once been selfish, and I cannot bear to hear you say such things. The way will open that is best for you—for both of us." She kissed him; she would not let him speak; her heart was in her throat, and she felt for him far more than for herself.

And then he had suggested that she should go alone perhaps for a shorter time, and stay in her brother's villa with the children, Alice and Stephen. It was always open to her as she well knew.

"You need the change," he said, when the lamps had been lit and the servant had gone out again; "you need it as much as I dread it. I could manage somehow till you returned, and should feel happier that way if you went. I cannot leave this Forest that I love so well. I even feel, Sophie dear"—he sat up straight and faced her as he half whispered it—"that I can *never* leave it again. My life and happiness lie here together."

And even while scorning the idea that she could leave him alone with the Influence of the Forest all about him to have its unimpeded way, she felt the pangs of that subtle jealousy bite keen and close. He loved the Forest better than herself, for he placed it first. Behind the words, moreover, hid the unuttered thought that made her so uneasy. The terror Sanderson had brought revived and shook its wings before her very eyes. For the whole conversation, of which this was a fragment, conveyed the unutterable implication that while he could not spare the trees, they equally could not spare him. The vividness with which he managed to conceal and yet betray the fact brought a profound distress that crossed the border between presentiment and warning into positive alarm.

He clearly felt that the trees would miss him—the trees he tended, guarded, watched over, loved.

"David, I shall stay here with you. I think you need me really,—don't you?" Eagerly, with a touch of heart-felt passion, the words poured out.

"Now more than ever, dear. God bless you for your sweet unselfishness. And your sacrifice," he added, "is all the greater because you cannot understand the thing that makes it necessary for me to stay."

"Perhaps in the spring instead——" she said, with a tremor in the voice.

"In the spring—perhaps," he answered gently, almost beneath his breath. "For they will not need me then. All the world can love them in the spring. It's in the winter that they're lonely and neglected. I wish to stay with them particularly then. I even feel I ought to—and I must."

And in this way, without further speech, the decision was made. Mrs. Bittacy, at least, asked no more questions. Yet she could not bring herself to show more sympathy than was necessary. She felt, for one thing, that if she did, it might lead him to speak freely, and to tell her things she could not possibly bear to know. And she dared not take the risk of that.

VII

This was at the end of summer, but the autumn followed close. The conversation really marked the threshold between the two seasons, and marked at the same time the line between her husband's negative and aggressive state. She almost felt she had done wrong to yield; he grew so bold, concealment all discarded. He went, that is, quite openly to the woods, forgetting all his duties, all his former occupations. He even sought to coax her to go with him. The hidden thing blazed out without disguise. And, while she trembled at his energy, she admired the virile passion he displayed. Her jealousy had long ago retired before her fear, accepting the second place. Her one desire now was to protect. The wife turned wholly mother.

He said so little, but—he hated to come in. From morning to night he wandered in the Forest; often he went out after dinner; his mind was charged with trees—their foliage, growth, development; their wonder, beauty, strength; their loneliness in isolation, their power in a herded mass. He knew the effect of every wind upon them; the danger from the boisterous north, the glory from the west, the eastern dryness, and the soft, moist tenderness that a south wind left upon their thinning boughs. He spoke all day of their sensations: how they drank the fading sunshine, dreamed in the moonlight, thrilled to the kiss of stars. The dew could bring them half the passion of the night, but frost sent them plunging beneath the ground to dwell with hopes of a later coming softness in their roots. They nursed the life they carried—insects, larvae, chrysalis—and when the skies above them melted, he spoke of them standing "motionless in an ecstasy of rain," or in the noon of sun-shine "self-poised upon their prodigy of shade."

And once in the middle of the night she woke at the sound of his voice, and heard him—wide awake, not talking in his sleep—but talking towards the window where the shadow of the cedar fell at noon:

> O art thou sighing for Lebanon
> In the long breeze that streams to thy delicious East?
> Sighing for Lebanon,
> Dark cedar;

and, when, half charmed, half terrified, she turned and called to him by name, he merely said—

"My dear, I felt the loneliness—suddenly realised it—the alien desolation of that tree, set here upon our little lawn in England when all her Eastern brothers call to her in sleep." And the answer seemed so queer, so "un-evangelical," that she waited in silence till he slept again. The poetry passed her by. It seemed unnecessary and out of place. It made her ache with suspicion, fear, jealousy.

The fear, however, seemed somehow all lapped up and banished soon afterwards by her unwilling admiration of the rushing splendour of her husband's state. Her anxiety, at any rate, shifted from the religious to the medical. She thought he might be losing his steadiness of mind a little. How often in her prayers she offered thanks for the guidance that had made her stay with him to help and watch is impossible to say. It certainly was twice a day.

She even went so far once, when Mr. Mortimer, the vicar, called, and brought with him a more or less distinguished doctor—as to tell the professional man privately some symptoms of her husband's queerness. And his answer that there was "nothing he could prescribe for" added not a little to her sense of unholy bewilderment. No doubt Sir James had never been "consulted" under such unorthodox conditions before. His sense of what was becoming naturally overrode his acquired instincts as a skilled instrument that might help the race.

"No fever, you think?" she asked insistently with hurry, deter-mined to get something from him.

"Nothing that *I* can deal with, as I told you, Madam," replied the offended allopathic Knight.

Evidently he did not care about being invited to examine patients in this surreptitious way before a teapot on the lawn, chance of a fee most problematical. He liked to see a tongue and feel a thumping pulse; to know the pedigree and bank account of his questioner as well. It was most unusual, in abominable taste besides. Of course it was. But the drowning woman seized the only straw she could.

For now the aggressive attitude of her husband overcame her to the point where she found it difficult even to question him. Yet in the house he was so kind and gentle, doing all he could to make her sacrifice as easy as possible.

"David, you really *are* unwise to go out now. The night is damp and very chilly. The ground is soaked in dew. You'll catch your death of cold."

His face lightened. "Won't you come with me, dear,—just for once? I'm only going to the corner of the hollies to see the beech that stands so lonely by itself."

She had been out with him in the short dark afternoon, and they had passed that evil group of hollies where the gipsies camped. Nothing else would grow there, but the hollies throve upon the stony soil.

"David, the beech is all right and safe." She had learned his phraseology a little, made clever out of due season by her love. "There's no wind to-night."

"But it's rising," he answered, "rising in the east. I heard it in the bare and hungry larches. They need the sun and dew, and always cry out when the wind's upon them from the east."

She sent a short unspoken prayer most swiftly to her deity as she heard him say it. For every time now, when he spoke in this familiar, intimate way of the life of the trees, she felt a sheet of cold fasten tight against her very skin and flesh. She shivered. How *could* he possibly know such things?

Yet, in all else, and in the relations of his daily life, he was sane and reasonable, loving, kind and tender. It was only on the subject of the trees he seemed unhinged and queer. Most curiously it seemed that, since the collapse of the cedar they both loved, though in different fashion, his departure from the normal had increased. Why else did he watch them as a man might watch a sickly child? Why did he linger especially in the dusk to catch their "mood of night" as he called it? Why think so carefully upon them when the frost was threatening or the wind appeared to rise?

As she put it so frequently now to herself—How could he possibly *know* such things?

He went. As she closed the front door after him she heard the distant roaring in the Forest. . . .

And then it suddenly struck her: How could she know them too?

It dropped upon her like a blow that she felt at once all over, upon body, heart and mind. The discovery rushed out from its ambush to overwhelm. The truth of it, making all arguing futile, numbed her faculties. But though at first it deadened her, she soon revived, and her being rose into aggressive opposition. A wild yet calculated courage like that which animates the leaders of splendid forlorn hopes flamed in her little person—flamed grandly, and invincible. While knowing herself insignificant and weak, she knew at the same time that power at her back which moves the worlds. The faith that filled her was the weapon in her hands, and the right by which she claimed it; but the spirit of utter, selfless sacrifice that characterised her life was the means by which she mastered its immediate use. For a kind of white and faultless intuition guided her to the attack. Behind her stood her Bible and her God.

How so magnificent a divination came to her at all may well be a matter for astonishment, though some clue of explanation lies, perhaps, in the very simpleness of her nature. At any rate, she saw quite clearly certain things; saw them in moments only—after prayer, in the still silence of the night, or when left alone those long hours in the house with her knitting and her thoughts—and the guidance which then flashed into her remained, even after the manner of its coming was forgotten.

They came to her, these things she saw, formless, wordless; she could not put them into any kind of language; but by the very fact of being uncaught in sentences they retained their original clear vigour.

Hours of patient waiting brought the first, and the others followed easily afterwards, by degrees, on subsequent days, a little and a little. Her husband had been gone since early morning, and had taken his luncheon with him. She was sitting by the tea things, the cups and teapot warmed, the muffins in the fender keeping hot, all ready for his return, when she realised quite abruptly that this thing which took him off, which kept him out so many hours day after day, this thing that was against her own little will and instincts—was enormous as the sea. It was no mere prettiness of single Trees, but something massed and mountainous. About her rose the wall of its huge opposition to the sky, its scale gigantic, its power utterly prodigious. What she knew of it hitherto as green and delicate forms waving and rustling in the winds was but, as it were, the spray of foam that broke into sight upon the nearer edge of viewless depths far, far away. The trees, indeed, were sentinels set visibly about the limits of a camp that itself remained invisible. The awful hum and murmur of the main body in the distance passed into that still room about her with the firelight and hissing kettle. Out yonder—in the Forest further out—the thing that was ever roaring at the centre was dreadfully increasing.

The sense of definite battle, too—battle between herself and the Forest for his soul—came with it. Its presentment was as clear as though Thompson had come into the room and quietly told her that the cottage was surrounded. "Please, ma'am, there are trees come up about the house," she might have suddenly announced. And equally might have heard her own answer: "It's all right, Thompson. The main body is still far away."

Immediately upon its heels, then, came another truth, with a close reality that shocked her. She saw that jealousy was not confined to the human and animal world alone, but ran through all creation. The Vegetable Kingdom knew it too. So-called inanimate nature shared it with the rest. Trees felt it. This Forest just beyond the window—standing there in the silence of the autumn evening across the little lawn—this Forest understood it equally. The remorseless, branching power that sought to keep exclusively for itself the thing it loved and needed, spread like a running desire through all its million leaves and stems and roots. In humans, of course, it was consciously directed; in animals it acted with frank instinctiveness; but in trees this jealousy rose in some blind tide of impersonal and unconscious wrath that would sweep opposition from its path as the wind sweeps powdered snow from the surface of the ice. Their number was a host with endless reinforcements, and once it realised its passion was returned the power increased. . . . Her husband loved the trees. . . . They had become aware of it. . . . They would take him from her in the end. . . .

Then, while she heard his footsteps in the hall and the closing of the front door, she saw a third thing clearly;—realised the widening of the gap between herself and him. This other love had made it. All these weeks of the summer when she felt so close to him, now especially when she had made the biggest sacrifice of her life to stay by his side and help him, he had been slowly, surely—drawing away. The estrangement was here and now—a fact accomplished. It had been all this time maturing; there yawned this broad deep space between them. Across the empty distance she saw the change in merciless perspective. It revealed his face and figure, dearly-loved, once fondly worshipped, far on the other side in shadowy distance, small, the back turned from her, and moving while she watched— moving away from her.

They had their tea in silence then. She asked no questions, he volunteered no information of his day. The heart was big within her, and the terrible loneliness of age spread through her like a rising icy mist. She watched him, filling all his wants. His hair was untidy and his boots were caked with blackish mud. He moved with a restless, swaying motion that somehow blanched her cheek and sent a miserable shivering down her back. It reminded her of trees. His eyes were very bright.

He brought in with him an odour of the earth and forest that seemed to choke her and make it difficult to breathe; and—what she noticed with a climax of almost uncontrollable alarm—upon his face beneath the lamplight shone traces of a mild, faint glory that made her think of moonlight falling upon a wood through speckled shadows. It was his new-found happiness that shone there, a happiness uncaused by her and in which she had no part.

In his coat was a spray of faded yellow beech leaves. "I brought this from the Forest to you," he said, with all the air that belonged to his little acts of devotion long ago. And she took the spray of leaves mechanically with a smile and a murmured "thank you, dear," as though he had unknowingly put into her hands the weapon for her own destruction and she had accepted it.

And when the tea was over and he left the room, he did not go to his study, or to change his clothes. She heard the front door softly shut behind him as he again went out towards the Forest.

A moment later she was in her room upstairs, kneeling beside the bed—the side he slept on—and praying wildly through a flood of tears that God would save and keep him to her. Wind brushed the window panes behind her while she knelt.

VIII

One sunny November morning, when the strain had reached a pitch that made repression almost unmanageable, she came to an impulsive decision, and obeyed it. Her husband had again gone out with luncheon for the day. She took adventure in her hands and followed him. The power of seeing-clear was strong upon her, forcing her up to some unnatural level of understanding. To stay indoors and wait inactive for his return seemed suddenly impossible. She meant to know what he knew, feel what he felt, put herself in his place. She would dare the fascination of the Forest—share it with him. It was greatly daring; but it would give her greater understanding how to help and save him and therefore greater Power. She went upstairs a moment first to pray.

In a thick, warm skirt, and wearing heavy boots—those walking boots she used with him upon the mountains about Seillans—she left the cottage by the back way and turned towards the Forest. She could not actually follow him, for he had started off an hour before and she knew not exactly his direction. What was so urgent in her was the wish to be with him in the woods, to walk beneath leafless branches just as he did: to be there when he was there, even though not together. For it had come to her that she might thus share with him for once this horrible mighty life and breathing of the trees he loved. In winter, he had said, they needed him particularly; and winter now was coming. Her love *must* bring her something of what he felt himself—the huge attraction, the suction and the pull of all the trees. Thus, in some vicarious fashion, she might share, though unknown to himself, this very thing that was taking him away from her. She might thus even lessen its attack upon himself.

The impulse came to her clairvoyantly, and she obeyed without a sign of hesitation. Deeper comprehension would come to her of the whole awful puzzle. And come it did, yet not in the way she imagined and expected.

The air was very still, the sky a cold pale blue, but cloudless. The entire Forest stood silent, at attention. It knew perfectly well that she had come. It knew the moment when she entered; watched and followed her; and behind her something dropped without a sound and shut her in. Her feet upon the glades of mossy grass fell

silently, as the oaks and beeches shifted past in rows and took up
their positions at her back. It was not pleasant, this way they grew
so dense behind her the instant she had passed. She realised that
they gathered in an ever-growing army, massed, herded, trooped,
between her and the cottage, shutting off escape. They let her pass
so easily, but to get out again she would know them differently—
thick, crowded, branches all drawn and hostile. Already their
increasing numbers bewildered her. In front, they looked so sparse
and scattered, with open spaces where the sunshine fell; but when
she turned it seemed they stood so close together, a serried army,
darkening the sunlight. They blocked the day, collected all the
shadows, stood with their leafless and forbidding rampart like the
night. They swallowed down into themselves the very glade by
which she came. For when she glanced behind her—rarely—the
way she had come was shadowy and lost.

Yet the morning sparkled overhead, and a glance of excitement ran
quivering through the entire day. It was what she always knew as
"children's weather," so clear and harmless, without a sign of danger,
nothing ominous to threaten or alarm. Steadfast in her purpose, looking back as little as she dared, Sophia Bittacy marched slowly and
deliberately into the heart of the silent woods, deeper, ever deeper. . . .

And then, abruptly, in an open space where the sunshine fell
unhindered, she stopped. It was one of the breathing-places of the
forest. Dead, withered bracken lay in patches of unsightly grey.
There were bits of heather too. All round the trees stood looking
on—oak, beech, holly, ash, pine, larch, with here and there small
groups of juniper. On the lips of this breathing-space of the woods
she stopped to rest, disobeying her instinct for the first time. For
the other instinct in her was to go on. She did not really want
to rest.

This was the little act that brought it to her—the wireless message from a vast Emitter.

"I've been stopped," she thought to herself with a horrid qualm.

She looked about her in this quiet, ancient place. Nothing
stirred. There was no life nor sign of life; no birds sang; no rabbits
scuttled off at her approach. The stillness was bewildering, and
gravity hung down upon it like a heavy curtain. It hushed the heart
in her. Could this be part of what her husband felt—this sense of
thick entanglement with stems, boughs, roots, and foliage?

"This has always been as it is now," she thought, yet not knowing

why she thought it. "Ever since the Forest grew it has been still and
secret here. It has never changed." The curtain of silence drew
closer while she said it, thickening round her. "For a thousand
years—I'm here with a thousand years. And behind this place stand
all the forests of the world!"

So foreign to her temperament were such thoughts, and so alien
to all she had been taught to look for in Nature, that she strove
against them. She made an effort to oppose. But they clung and
haunted just the same; they refused to be dispersed. The curtain
hung dense and heavy as though its texture thickened. The air with
difficulty came through.

And then she thought that curtain stirred. There was movement
somewhere. That obscure dim thing which ever broods behind the
visible appearances of trees came nearer to her. She caught her
breath and stared about her, listening intently. The trees, perhaps
because she saw them more in detail now, it seemed to her had
changed. A vague, faint alteration spread over them, at first so
slight she scarcely would admit it, then growing steadily, though
still obscurely, outwards. "They tremble and are changed," flashed
through her mind the horrid line that Sanderson had quoted. Yet
the change was graceful for all the uncouthness attendant upon the
size of so vast a movement. They had turned in her direction. That
was it. *They saw her.*

In this way the change expressed itself in her groping, terrified
thought. Till now it had been otherwise: she had looked at them
from her own point of view; now they looked at her from theirs.
They stared her in the face and eyes; they stared at her all over. In
some unkind, resentful, hostile way, they watched her. Hitherto in
life she had watched them variously, in superficial ways, reading
into them what her own mind suggested. Now they read into her
the things they actually *were,* and not merely another's interpreta-
tion of them.

They seemed in their motionless silence there instinct with life,
a life, moreover, that breathed about her a species of terrible soft
enchantment that bewitched. It branched all through her, climbing
to the brain. The Forest held her with its huge and giant fascination. In this secluded breathing-spot that the centuries had left
untouched, she had stepped close against the hidden pulse of the
whole collective mass of them. They were aware of her and had
turned to gaze with their myriad, vast sight upon the intruder. They

shouted at her in the silence. For she wanted to look back at them, but it was like staring at a crowd, and her glance merely shifted from one tree to another, hurriedly, finding in none the one she sought. They saw her so easily, each and all. The rows that stood behind her also stared. But she could not return the gaze. Her husband, she realised, could. And their steady stare shocked her as though in some sense she knew that she was naked. They saw so much of her: she saw of them—so little.

Her efforts to return their gaze were pitiful. The constant shifting increased her bewilderment. Conscious of this awful and enormous sight all over her, she let her eyes first rest upon the ground; and then she closed them altogether. She kept the lids as tight together as ever they would go.

But the sight of the trees came even into that inner darkness behind the fastened lids, for there was no escaping it. Outside, in the light, she still knew that the leaves of the hollies glittered smoothly, that the dead foliage of the oaks hung crisp in the air above her, that the needles of the little junipers were pointing all one way. The spread perception of the Forest was focussed on herself, and no mere shutting of the eyes could hide its scattered yet concentrated stare—the all-inclusive vision of great woods.

There was no wind, yet here and there a single leaf hanging by its dried-up stalk shook all alone with great rapidity—rattling. It was the sentry drawing attention to her presence. And then, again, as once long weeks before, she felt their Being as a tide about her. The tide had turned. That memory of her childhood sands came back, when the nurse said, "The tide has turned now; we must go in," and she saw the mass of piled-up waters, green and heaped to the horizon, and realised that it was slowly coming in. The gigantic mass of it, too vast for hurry, loaded with massive purpose, she used to feel, was moving towards herself. The fluid body of the sea was creeping along beneath the sky to the very spot upon the yellow sands where she stood and played. The sight and thought of it had always overwhelmed her with a sense of awe—as though her puny self were the object of the whole sea's advance. "The tide has turned; we had better now go in."

This was happening now about her—the same thing was happening in the woods—slow, sure, and steady, and its motion as little discernible as the sea's. The tide had turned. The small human presence that had ventured among its green and mountainous depths, moreover, was its objective.

That all was clear within her while she sat and waited with tight-shut lids. But the next moment she opened her eyes with a sudden realization of something more. The presence that it sought was after all not hers. It was the presence of some one other than herself. And then she understood. Her eyes had opened with a click, it seemed; but the sound, in reality, was outside herself. Across the clearing where the sunshine lay so calm and still, she saw the figure of her husband moving among the trees—a man, like a tree, walking.

With hands behind his back, and head uplifted, he moved quite slowly, as though absorbed in his own thoughts. Hardly fifty paces separated them, but he had no inkling of her presence there so near. With mind intent and senses all turned inwards, he marched past her like a figure in a dream, and like a figure in a dream she saw him go. Love, yearning, pity rose in a storm within her, but as in nightmare she found no words or movement possible. She sat and watched him go—go from her—go into the deeper reaches of the green enveloping woods. Desire to save, to bid him stop and turn, ran in a passion through her being, but there was nothing she could do. She saw him go away from her, go of his own accord and willingly beyond her; she saw the branches drop about his steps and hide him. His figure faded out among the speckled shade and sunlight. The trees covered him. The tide just took him, all unresisting and content to go. Upon the bosom of the green soft sea he floated away beyond her reach of vision. Her eyes could follow him no longer. He was gone.

And then for the first time she realised, even at that distance, that the look upon his face was one of peace and happiness—rapt, and caught away in joy, a look of youth. That expression now he never showed to her. But she *had* known it. Years ago, in the early days of their married life, she had seen it on his face. Now it no longer obeyed the summons of her presence and her love. The woods alone could call it forth; it answered to the trees; the Forest had taken every part of him—from her—his very heart and soul. . . .

Her sight that had plunged inwards to the fields of faded memory now came back to outer things again. She looked about her, and her love, returning empty-handed and unsatisfied, left her open to the invading of the bleakest terror she had ever known. That such things could be real and happen found her helpless utterly. Terror invaded the quietest corners of her heart, that had never yet known quailing. She could not—for moments at any rate—reach either her Bible or her God. Desolate in an empty world of fear she sat with eyes too

dry and hot for tears, yet with a coldness as of ice upon her very
flesh. She stared, unseeing, about her. That horror which stalks in
the stillness of the noonday, when the glare of an artificial sunshine
lights up the motionless trees, moved all about her. In front and
behind she was aware of it. Beyond this stealthy silence, just within
the edge of it, the things of another world were passing. But she
could not know them. Her husband knew them, knew their beauty
and their awe, yes, but for her they were out of reach. She might not
share with him the very least of them. It seemed that behind and
through the glare of this wintry noonday in the heart of the woods
there brooded another universe of life and passion, for her all unexpressed. The silence veiled it, the stillness hid it; but he moved with
it all and understood. His love interpreted it.

She rose to her feet, tottered feebly, and collapsed again upon
the moss. Yet for herself she felt no terror; no little personal fear
could touch her whose anguish and deep longing streamed all out
to him whom she so bravely loved. In this time of utter self-
forgetfulness, when she realised that the battle was hopeless, thinking she had lost even her God, she found Him again quite close
beside her like a little Presence in this terrible heart of the hostile
Forest. But at first she did not recognise that He was there; she did
not know Him in that strangely unacceptable guise. For He stood
so very close, so very intimate, so very sweet and comforting, and
yet so hard to understand—as Resignation.

Once more she struggled to her feet, and this time turned suc-
cessfully and slowly made her way along the mossy glade by which
she came. And at first she marvelled, though only for a moment, at
the ease with which she found the path. For a moment only,
because almost at once she saw the truth. The trees were glad that
she should go. They helped her on her way. The Forest did not
want her.

The tide was coming in, indeed, yet not for her.

And so, in another of those flashes of clear-vision that of late had
lifted life above the normal level, she saw and understood the
whole terrible thing complete.

Till now, though unexpressed in thought or language, her fear
had been that the woods her husband loved would somehow take
him from her—to merge his life in theirs—even to kill him in some
mysterious way. This time she saw her deep mistake, and so seeing,

let in upon herself the fuller agony of horror. For their jealousy was not the petty jealousy of animals or humans. They wanted him because they loved him, but they did not want him dead. Full charged with his splendid life and enthusiasm they wanted him. They wanted him—alive.

It was she who stood in their way, and it was she whom they intended to remove.

This was what brought the sense of abject helplessness. She stood upon the sands against an entire ocean slowly rolling in against her. For, as all the forces of a human being combine unconsciously to eject a grain of sand that has crept beneath the skin to cause discomfort, so the entire mass of what Sanderson had called the Collective Consciousness of the Forest strove to eject this human atom that stood across the path of its desire. Loving her husband, she had crept beneath its skin. It was her they would eject and take away; it was her they would destroy, not him. Him, whom they loved and needed, they would keep alive. They meant to take him living.

She reached the house in safety, though she never remembered how she found her way. It was made all simple for her. The branches almost urged her out.

But behind her, as she left the shadowed precincts, she felt as though some towering Angel of the Woods let fall across the threshold the flaming sword of a countless multitude of leaves that formed behind her a barrier, green, shimmering, and impassable. Into the Forest she never walked again.

•   •   •   •   •   •

And she went about her daily duties with a calm and quietness that was a perpetual astonishment even to herself, for it hardly seemed of this world at all. She talked to her husband when he came in for tea—after dark. Resignation brings a curious large courage—when there is nothing more to lose. The soul takes risks, and dares. Is it a curious short-cut sometimes to the heights?

"David, I went into the Forest, too, this morning; soon after you I went. I saw you there."

"Wasn't it wonderful?" he answered simply, inclining his head a little. There was no surprise or annoyance in his look; a mild and gentle *ennui* rather. He asked no real question. She thought of some garden tree the wind attacks too suddenly, bending it over when it does not want to bend—the mild unwillingness with which it yields. She often saw him this way now, in the terms of trees.

"It was very wonderful indeed, dear, yes," she replied low, her voice not faltering though indistinct. "But for me it was too—too strange and big."

The passion of tears lay just below the quiet voice all unbetrayed. Somehow she kept them back.

There was a pause, and then he added:

"I find it more and more so every day." His voice passed through the lamp-lit room like a murmur of the wind in branches. The look of youth and happiness she had caught upon his face out there had wholly gone, and an expression of weariness was in its place, as of a man distressed vaguely at finding himself in uncongenial surroundings where he is slightly ill at ease. It was the house he hated—coming back to rooms and walls and furniture. The ceilings and closed windows confined him. Yet, in it, no suggestion that he found *her* irksome. Her presence seemed of no account at all; indeed, he hardly noticed her. For whole long periods he lost her, did not know that she was there. He had no need of her. He lived alone. Each lived alone.

The outward signs by which she recognised that the awful battle was against her and the terms of surrender accepted were pathetic. She put the medicine-chest away upon the shelf; she gave the orders for his pocket-luncheon before he asked; she went to bed alone and early, leaving the front door unlocked, with milk and bread and butter in the hall beside the lamp—all concessions that she felt impelled to make. For more and more, unless the weather was too violent, he went out after dinner even, staying for hours in the woods. But she never slept until she heard the front door close below, and knew soon afterwards his careful step come creeping up the stairs and into the room so softly. Until she heard his regular deep breathing close beside her, she lay awake. All strength or desire to resist had gone for good. The thing against her was too huge and powerful. Capitulation was complete, a fact accomplished. She dated it from the day she followed him to the Forest.

Moreover, the time for evacuation—her own evacuation—seemed approaching. It came stealthily ever nearer, surely and slowly as the rising tide she used to dread. At the high-water mark she stood waiting calmly—waiting to be swept away. Across the lawn all those terrible days of early winter the encircling Forest watched it come, guiding its silent swell and currents towards her feet. Only she never once gave up her Bible or her praying. This complete resignation, moreover, had somehow brought to her a strange great understanding, and if she could not share her husband's horrible abandonment to powers outside himself, she could, and did, in some half-groping way grasp at shadowy meanings that might make such abandonment—possible, yes, but more than merely possible—in some extraordinary sense not evil.

Hitherto she had divided the beyond-world into two sharp halves—spirits good or spirits evil. But thoughts came to her now, on soft and very tentative feet, like the footsteps of the gods which are on wool, that besides these definite classes, there might be other Powers as well, belonging definitely to neither one nor other. Her thought stopped dead at that. But the big idea found lodgment in her little mind, and, owing to the largeness of her heart, remained there unejected. It even brought a certain solace with it.

The failure—or unwillingness, as she preferred to state it—of her God to interfere and help, that also she came in a measure to understand. For here, she found it more and more possible to imagine, was perhaps no positive evil at work, but only something that usually stands away from humankind, something alien and not commonly recognised. There *was* a gulf fixed between the two, and Mr. Sanderson *had* bridged it, by his talk, his explanations, his attitude of mind. Through these her husband had found the way into it. His temperament and natural passion for the woods had prepared the soul in him, and the moment he saw the way to go he took it—the line of least resistance. Life was, of course, open to all, and her husband had the right to choose it where he would. He had chosen it—away from her, away from other men, but not necessarily away from God. This was an enormous concession that she skirted, never really faced; it was too revolutionary to face. But its possibility peeped into her bewildered mind. It might delay his progress, or it might advance it. Who could know? And why should God, who ordered all things with such magnificent detail, from the pathway of a sun to the falling of a sparrow, object to his free choice, or interfere to hinder him and stop?

She came to realise resignation, that is, in another aspect. It gave her comfort, if not peace. She fought against all belittling of her God. It was, perhaps, enough that He—knew.

"You are not alone, dear, in the trees out there?" she ventured one night, as he crept on tiptoe into the room not far from midnight. "God is with you?"

"Magnificently," was the immediate answer, given with enthusiasm, "for He is everywhere. And I only wish that you——"

But she stuffed the clothes against her ears. That invitation on his lips was more than she could bear to hear. It seemed like asking her to hurry to her own execution. She buried her face among the sheets and blankets, shaking all over like a leaf.

IX

And so the thought that she was the one to go remained and grew. It was, perhaps, first sign of that weakening of the mind which indicated the singular manner of her going. For it was her mental opposition, the trees felt, that stood in their way. Once that was overcome, obliterated, her physical presence did not matter. She would be harmless.

Having accepted defeat, because she had come to feel that his obsession was not actually evil, she accepted at the same time the conditions of an atrocious loneliness. She stood now from her husband farther than from the moon. They had no visitors. Callers were few and far between, and less encouraged than before. The empty dark of winter was before them. Among the neighbours was none in whom, without disloyalty to her husband, she could confide. Mr. Mortimer, had he been single, might have helped her in this desert of solitude that preyed upon her mind, but his wife was there the obstacle; for Mrs. Mortimer wore sandals, believed that nuts were the complete food of man, and indulged in other idiosyncrasies that classed her inevitably among the "latter signs" which Mrs. Bittacy had been taught to dread as dangerous. She stood most desolately alone.

Solitude, therefore, in which the mind unhindered feeds upon its own delusions, was the assignable cause of her gradual mental disruption and collapse.

With the definite arrival of the colder weather her husband gave up his rambles after dark; evenings were spent together over the fire; he read *The Times;* they even talked about their postponed visit abroad in the coming spring. No restlessness was on him at the change; he seemed content and easy in his mind; spoke little of the trees and woods; enjoyed far better health than if there had been change of scene, and to herself was tender, kind, solicitous over trifles, as in the distant days of their first honeymoon.

But this deep calm could not deceive her; it meant, she fully understood, that he felt sure of himself, sure of her, and sure of the trees as well. It all lay buried in the depths of him, too secure and deep, too intimately established in his central being to permit of those surface fluctuations which betray disharmony within. His life was hid with trees. Even the fever, so dreaded in the damp of winter, left him free. She now knew why. The fever was due to their efforts to obtain him, his efforts to respond and go—physical results of a fierce unrest he had never understood till Sanderson came with his wicked explanations. Now it was otherwise. The bridge was made. And—he had gone.

And she, brave, loyal, and consistent soul, found herself utterly alone, even trying to make his passage easy. It seemed that she stood at the bottom of some huge ravine that opened in her mind, the walls whereof instead of rock were trees that reached enormous to the sky, engulfing her. God alone knew that she was there. He watched, permitted, even perhaps approved. At any rate—He knew.

During those quiet evenings in the house, moreover, while they sat over the fire listening to the roaming winds about the house, her husband knew continual access to the world his alien love had furnished for him. Never for a single instant was he cut off from it. She gazed at the newspaper spread before his face and knees, saw the smoke of his cheroot curl up above the edge, noticed the little hole in his evening socks, and listened to the paragraphs he read aloud as of old. But this was all a veil he spread about himself of purpose. Behind it—he escaped. It was the conjurer's trick to divert the sight to unimportant details while the essential thing went forward unobserved. He managed wonderfully; she loved him for the pains he took to spare her distress; but all the while she knew that the body lolling in that armchair before her eyes contained the merest fragment of his actual self. It was little better than a corpse. It was an empty shell. The essential soul of him was out yonder with the Forest—farther out near that ever-roaring heart of it.

And, with the dark, the Forest came up boldly and pressed against the very walls and windows, peering in upon them, joining hands above the slates and chimneys. The winds were always walking on

the lawn and gravel paths; steps came and went and came again;
some one seemed always talking in the woods, some one was in the
building too. She passed them on the stairs, or running soft and
muffled, very large and gentle, down the passages and landings
after dusk, as though loose fragments of the Day had broken off
and stayed there caught among the shadows, trying to get out. They
blundered silently all about the house. They waited till she passed,
then made a run for it. And her husband always knew. She saw him
more than once deliberately avoid them—because *she* was there.
More than once, too, she saw him stand and listen when he thought
she was not near, then heard herself the long bounding stride of
their approach across the silent garden. Already *he* had heard them
in the windy distance of the night, far, far away. They sped, she well
knew, along that glade of mossy turf by which she last came out; it
cushioned their tread exactly as it had cushioned her own.

It seemed to her the trees were always in the house with him,
and in their very bedroom. He welcomed them, unaware that she
also knew, and trembled.

One night in their bedroom it caught her unawares. She woke
out of deep sleep and it came upon her before she could gather her
forces for control.

The day had been wildly boisterous, but now the wind had
dropped; only its rags went fluttering through the night. The rays
of the full moon fell in a shower between the branches. Overhead
still raced the scud and wrack, shaped like hurrying monsters; but
below the earth was quiet. Still and dripping stood the hosts of
trees. Their trunks gleamed wet and sparkling where the moon
caught them. There was a strong smell of mould and fallen leaves.
The air was sharp—heavy with odour.

And she knew all this the instant that she woke; for it seemed to
her that she had been elsewhere—following her husband—as
though she had been *out!* There was no dream at all, merely this
definite, haunting certainty. It dived away, lost, buried in the night.
She sat upright in bed. She had come back.

The room shone pale in the moonlight reflected through the
windows, for the blinds were up, and she saw her husband's form
beside her, motionless in deep sleep. But what caught her unawares
was the horrid thing that by this fact of sudden, unexpected waking
she had surprised these other things in the room, beside the very
bed, gathered close about him while he slept. It was their dreadful

boldness—herself of no account as it were—that terrified her into screaming before she could collect her powers to prevent. She screamed before she realised what she did—a long, high shriek of terror that filled the room, yet made so little actual sound. For wet and shimmering presences stood grouped all round that bed. She saw their outline underneath the ceiling, the green, spread bulk of them, their vague extension over walls and furniture. They shifted to and fro, massed yet translucent, mild yet thick, moving and turning within themselves to a hushed noise of multitudinous soft rustling. In their sound was something very sweet and winning that fell into her with a spell of horrible enchantment. They were so mild, each one alone, yet so terrific in their combination. Cold seized her. The sheets against her body turned to ice.

She screamed a second time, though the sound hardly issued from her throat. The spell sank deeper, reaching to the heart; for it softened all the currents of her blood and took life from her in a stream—towards themselves. Resistance in that moment seemed impossible.

Her husband then stirred in his sleep, and woke. And, instantly, the forms drew up, erect, and gathered themselves in some amazing way together. They lessened in extent—then scattered through the air like an effect of light when shadows seek to smother it. It was tremendous, yet most exquisite. A sheet of pale-green shadow that yet had form and substance filled the room. There was a rush of silent movement, as the Presences drew past her through the air,—and they were gone.

But, clearest of all, she saw the manner of their going; for she recognised in their tumult of escape by the window open at the top, the same wide "looping circles"—spirals as it seemed—that she had seen upon the lawn those weeks ago when Sanderson had talked. The room once more was empty.

In the collapse that followed, she heard her husband's voice, as though coming from some great distance. Her own replies she heard as well. Both were so strange and unlike their normal speech, the very words unnatural:

"What is it, dear? Why do you wake me *now?*" And his voice whispered it with a sighing sound, like wind in pine boughs.

"A moment since something went past me through the air of the room. Back to the night outside it went." Her voice, too, held the same note as of wind entangled among too many leaves.

"My dear, it *was* the wind."

"But it called, David. It was calling *you*—by name!"

"The stir of the branches, dear, was what you heard. Now, sleep again, I beg you, sleep."

"It had a crowd of eyes all through and over it—before and behind—" Her voice grew louder. But his own in reply sank lower, far away, and oddly hushed.

"The moonlight, dear, upon the sea of twigs and boughs in the rain, was what you saw."

"But it frightened me. I've lost my God—and you—I'm cold as death!"

"My dear, it is the cold of the early morning hours. The whole world sleeps. Now sleep again yourself."

He whispered close to her ear. She felt his hand stroking her. His voice was soft and very soothing. But only a part of him was there; only a part of him was speaking; it was a half-emptied body that lay beside her and uttered these strange sentences, even forcing her own singular choice of words. The horrible, dim enchantment of the trees was close about them in the room—gnarled, ancient, lonely trees of winter, whispering round the human life they loved.

"And let me sleep again," she heard him murmur as he settled down among the clothes, "sleep back into that deep, delicious peace from which you called me. . . ."

His dreamy, happy tone, and that look of youth and joy she discerned upon his features even in the filtered moonlight, touched her again as with the spell of those shining, mild green presences. It sank down into her. She felt sleep grope for her. On the threshold of slumber one of those strange vagrant voices that loss of consciousness lets loose cried faintly in her heart—

"There is joy in the Forest over one sinner that———"

Then sleep took her before she had time to realise even that she was vilely parodying one of her most precious texts, and that the irreverence was ghastly. . . .

And though she quickly slept again, her sleep was not as usual, dreamless. It was not woods and trees she dreamed of, but a small and curious dream that kept coming again and again upon her: that she stood upon a wee, bare rock in the sea, and that the tide was rising. The water first came to her feet, then to her knees, then to her waist. Each time the dream returned, the tide seemed higher. Once it rose to her neck, once even to her mouth, covering her lips for a moment so that she could not breathe. She did not wake between the dreams; a period of drab and dreamless slumber intervened. But, finally, the water rose above her eyes and face, completely covering her head.

And then came explanation—the sort of explanation dreams bring. She understood. For, beneath the water, she had seen the world of seaweed rising from the bottom of the sea like a forest of dense green—long, sinuous stems, immense thick branches, millions of feelers spreading through the darkened watery depths the power of their ocean foliage. The Vegetable Kingdom was even in the sea. It was everywhere. Earth, air, and water helped it, way of escape there was none.

And even underneath the sea she heard that terrible sound of roaring—was it surf or wind or voices?—further out, yet coming steadily towards her.

And so, in the loneliness of that drab English winter, the mind of Mrs. Bittacy, preying upon itself, and fed by constant dread, went lost in disproportion. Dreariness filled the weeks with dismal, sunless skies and a clinging moisture that knew no wholesome tonic of keen frosts. Alone with her thoughts, both her husband and her God withdrawn into distance, she counted the days to Spring. She groped her way, stumbling down the long dark tunnel. Through the arch at the far end lay a brilliant picture of the violet sea sparkling on the coast of France. There lay safety and escape for both of them, could she but hold on. Behind her the trees blocked up the other entrance. She never once looked back.

She drooped. Vitality passed from her, drawn out and away as by some steady suction. Immense and incessant was this sensation of her powers draining off. The taps were all turned on. Her personality, as it were, streamed steadily away, coaxed outwards by this Power that never wearied and seemed inexhaustible. It won her as the full moon wins the tide. She waned; she faded; she obeyed.

At first she watched the process, and recognised exactly what was going on. Her physical life, and that balance of the mind which depends on physical well-being, were being slowly undermined. She saw that clearly. Only the soul, dwelling like a star apart from these and independent of them, lay safe somewhere—with her distant God. That she knew—tranquilly. The spiritual love that linked her to her husband was safe from all attack. Later, in His good time, they would merge together again because of it. But, meanwhile, all of her that had kinship with the earth was slowly going. This separation was being remorselessly accomplished. Every part of her the trees could touch was being steadily drained from her. She was being—removed.

After a time, however, even this power of realisation went, so that she no longer "watched the process" or knew exactly what was going on. The one satisfaction she had known—the feeling that it was sweet to suffer for his sake—went with it. She stood utterly alone with this terror of the trees . . . mid the ruins of her broken and disordered mind.

She slept badly; woke in the morning with hot and tired eyes; her head ached dully; she grew confused in thought and lost the clues of daily life in the most feeble fashion. At the same time she lost sight, too, of that brilliant picture at the exit of the tunnel; it faded away into a tiny semicircle of pale light, the violet sea and the sun-shine the merest point of white, remote as a star and equally inaccessible. She knew now that she could never reach it. And through the darkness that stretched behind, the power of the trees came close and caught her, twining about her feet and arms, climbing to her very lips. She woke at night, finding it difficult to breathe. There seemed wet leaves pressed against her mouth, and soft green tendrils clinging to her neck. Her feet were heavy, half rooted, as it were, in deep, thick earth. Huge creepers stretched along the whole of that black tunnel, feeling about her person for points where they might fasten well, as ivy or the giant parasites of the Vegetable Kingdom settle down on the trees themselves to sap their life and kill them.

Slowly and surely the morbid growth possessed her life and held her. She feared those very winds that ran about the wintry forest. They were in league with it. They helped it everywhere.

"Why don't you sleep, dear?" It was her husband now who played the rôle of nurse, tending her little wants with an honest care that at least aped the services of love. He was so utterly unconscious of the raging battle he had caused. "What is it keeps you so wide awake and restless?"

"The winds," she whispered in the dark. For hours she had lain watching the tossing of the trees through the blindless windows. "They go walking and talking everywhere to-night, keeping me awake. And all the time they call so loudly to you."

And his strange whispered answer appalled her for a moment until the meaning of it faded and left her in a dark confusion of the mind that was now becoming almost permanent.

"The trees excite them in the night. The winds are the great swift carriers. Go with them, dear—and not against. You'll find sleep that way if you do."

"The storm is rising," she began, hardly knowing what she said.

"All the more then—go with them. Don't resist. They'll take you to the trees, that's all."

Resist! The word touched on the button of some text that once had helped her.

"Resist the devil and he will flee from you," she heard her whispered answer, and the same second had buried her face beneath the clothes in a flood of hysterical weeping.

But her husband did not seem disturbed. Perhaps he did not hear it, for the wind ran just then against the windows with a booming shout, and the roaring of the Forest farther out came behind the blow, surging into the room. Perhaps, too, he was already asleep again. She slowly regained a sort of dull composure. Her face emerged from the tangle of sheets and blankets. With a growing terror over her—she listened. The storm was rising. It came with a sudden and impetuous rush that made all further sleep for her impossible.

Alone in a shaking world, it seemed, she lay and listened. That storm interpreted for her mind the climax. The Forest bellowed out its victory to the winds; the winds in turn proclaimed it to the Night. The whole world knew of her complete defeat, her loss, her little human pain. This was the roar and shout of victory that she listened to.

For, unmistakably, the trees were shouting in the dark. There were sounds, too, like the flapping of great sails, a thousand at a time, and sometimes reports that resembled more than anything else the distant booming of enormous drums. The trees stood up— the whole beleaguering host of them stood up—and with the uproar of their million branches drummed the thundering message out across the night. It seemed as if they all had broken loose. Their roots swept trailing over field and hedge and roof. They tossed their bushy heads beneath the clouds with a wild, delighted shuffling of great boughs. With trunks upright they raced leaping through the sky. There was upheaval and adventure in the awful sound they made, and their cry was like the cry of a sea that has broken through its gates and poured loose upon the world. . . .

Through it all her husband slept peacefully as though he heard it not. It was, as she well knew, the sleep of the semi-dead. For he was out with all that clamouring turmoil. The part of him that she had lost was there. The form that slept so calmly at her side was but the shell, half emptied. . . .

And when the winter's morning stole upon the scene at length, with a pale, washed sunshine that followed the departing tempest, the first thing she saw, as she crept to the window and looked out, was the ruined cedar lying on the lawn. Only the gaunt and crippled trunk of it remained. The single giant bough that had been left to it lay dark upon the grass, sucked endways towards the Forest by a great wind eddy. It lay there like a mass of drift-wood from a wreck, left by the ebbing of a high spring-tide upon the sands—remnant of some friendly, splendid vessel that once sheltered men.

And in the distance she heard the roaring of the Forest further out. Her husband's voice was in it.

IV. Tales of Fantasy

The King's Messenger

F. Marion Crawford

It was a rather dim daylight dinner. I remember that quite distinctly, for I could see the glow of the sunset over the trees in the
park, through the high window at the west end of the dining-room.
I had expected to find a larger party, I believe, for I recollect being
a little surprised at seeing only a dozen people assembled at table.
It seemed to me that in old times, ever so long ago, when I had last
stayed in that house, there had been as many as thirty or forty
guests. I recognized some of them among a number of beautiful
portraits that hung on the walls. There was room for a great many
because there was only one huge window, at one end, and one large
door at the other. I was very much surprised, too, to see a portrait
of myself, evidently painted about twenty years ago by Lenbach. It
seemed very strange that I should have so completely forgotten the
picture, and that I should not be able to remember having sat for
it. We were good friends, it is true, and he might have painted it
from memory, without my knowledge, but it was certainly strange
that he should never have told me about it. The portraits that hung
in the dining-room were all very good indeed and all, I should say,
by the best painters of that time.

My left-hand neighbor was a lovely young girl whose name I had
forgotten, though I had known her long, and I fancied that she
looked a little disappointed when she saw that I was beside her. On
my right there was a vacant seat, and beyond it sat an elderly woman
with features as hard as the overwhelmingly splendid diamonds she

wore. Her eyes made me think of gray glass marbles cemented into a stone mask. It was odd that her name should have escaped me, too, for I had often met her.

The table looked irregular, and I counted the guests mechanically while I ate my soup. We were only twelve, but the empty chair beside me was the thirteenth place.

I suppose it was not very tactful of me to mention this, but I wanted to say something to the beautiful girl on my left, and no other subject for a general remark suggested itself. Just as I was going to speak I remembered who she was.

"Miss Lorna," I said, to attract her attention, for she was looking away from me toward the door. "I hope you are not superstitious about there being thirteen at table, are you?"

"We are only twelve," she said, in the sweetest voice in the world.

"Yes; but some one else is coming. There's an empty chair here beside me."

"Oh, he doesn't count," said Miss Lorna quietly. "At least, not for everybody. When did you get here? Just in time for dinner, I suppose."

"Yes," I answered. "I'm in luck to be beside you. It seems an age since we were last here together."

"It does indeed!" Miss Lorna sighed and looked at the pictures on the opposite wall. "I've lived a lifetime since I saw you last."

I smiled at the exaggeration. "When you are thirty, you won't talk of having your life behind you," I said.

"I shall never be thirty," Miss Lorna answered, with such an odd little air of conviction that I did not think of anything to say. "Besides, life isn't made up of years or months or hours, or of anything that has to do with time," she continued. "You ought to know that. Our bodies are something better than mere clocks, wound up to show just how old we are at every moment, by our hair turning gray and our teeth falling out and our faces getting wrinkled and yellow, or puffy and red! Look at your own portrait over there. I don't mind saying that you must have been twenty years younger when that was painted, but I'm sure you are just the same man to-day—improved by age, perhaps."

I heard a sweet little echoing laugh that seemed very far away; and indeed I could not have sworn that it rippled from Miss Lorna's beautiful lips, for though they were parted and smiling my impression is that they did not move, even as little as most women's lips are moved by laughter.

"Thank you for thinking me improved," I said. "I find you a little changed, too. I was just going to say that you seem sadder, but you laughed just then."

"Did I? I suppose that's the right thing to do when the play is over, isn't it?"

"If it has been an amusing play," I answered, humoring her.

The wonderful violet eyes turned to me, full of light. "It's not been a bad play. I don't complain."

"Why do you speak of it as over?"

"I'll tell you, because I'm sure you will keep my secret. You will, won't you? We were always such good friends, you and I, even two years ago when I was young and silly. Will you promise not to tell anyone till I'm gone?"

"Gone?"

"Yes. Will you promise?"

"Of course I will. But——" I did not finish the sentence, because Miss Lorna bent nearer to me, so as to speak in a much lower tone. While I listened, I felt her sweet young breath on my cheek.

"I'm going away to-night with the man who is to sit at your other side," she said. "He's a little late—he often is, for he is tremendously busy; but he'll come presently, and after dinner we shall just stroll out into the garden and never come back. That's my secret. You won't betray me, will you?"

Again, as she looked at me, I heard that far-off silver laugh, sweet and low. I was almost too much surprised by what she had told me to notice how still her parted lips were, but that comes back to me now, with many other details.

"My dear Miss Lorna," I said, "do think of your parents before taking such a step!"

"I have thought of them," she answered. "Of course they would never consent, and I am very sorry to leave them, but it can't be helped."

At this moment, as often happens when two people are talking in low tones at a large dinner-table, there was a momentary lull in the general conversation, and I was spared the trouble of making any further answer to what Miss Lorna had told me so unexpectedly, and with such profound confidence in my discretion.

To tell the truth, she would very probably not have listened, whether my words expressed sympathy or protest, for she had turned suddenly pale, and her eyes were wide and dark. The lull in the talk at table was due to the appearance of the man who was to occupy the vacant place beside me.

He had entered the room very quietly, and he made no elaborate apology for being late, as he sat down, bending his head courteously to our hostess and her husband, and smiling in a gentle sort of way as he nodded to the others.

"Please forgive me," he said quietly. "I was detained by a funeral and missed the train."

It was not until he had taken his place that he looked across me at Miss Lorna and exchanged a glance of recognition with her. I noticed that the lady with the hard face and the splendid diamonds, who was at his other side, drew away from him a little, as if not wishing even to let his sleeve brush against her bare arm. It occurred to me at the same time that Miss Lorna must be wishing me anywhere else than between her and the man with whom she was just about to run away, and I wished for their sake and mine that I could change places with him.

He was certainly not like other men, and though few people would have called him handsome there was something about him that instantly fixed the attention; rarely beautiful though Miss Lorna was, almost everyone would have noticed him first on entering the room, and most people, I think, would have been more interested by his face than by hers. I could well imagine that some women might love him, even to distraction, though it was just as easy to understand that others might be strongly repelled by him, and might even fear him.

For my part, I shall not try to describe him as one describes an ordinary man, with a dozen or so adjectives that leave nothing to the imagination but yet offer it no picture that it can grasp. My instinct was to fear him rather than think of him as a possible friend, but I could not help feeling instant admiration for him, as one does at first sight for anything that is very complete, harmonious, and strong. He was dark, and pale with a shadowy pallor I never saw in any other face; the features of thrice-great Hermes were not modeled in more perfect symmetry; his luminous eyes were not unkind, but there was something fateful in them, and they were set very deep under the grand white brow. His age I could not guess, but I should have called him young; standing, I had seen that he was tall and sinewy, and now that he was seated, he had the unmistakable look of a man accustomed to be in authority, to be heard and to be obeyed. His hands were white, his fingers straight, lean, and very strong.

Everyone at the table seemed to know him, but as often happens among civilized people no one called him by name in speaking to him.

"We were beginning to be afraid that you might not get here," said our host.

"Really?" The Thirteenth Guest smiled quietly, but shook his head. "Did you ever know me to break an engagement, under any circumstances?"

The master of the house laughed, though not very cordially, I thought. "No," he answered. "Your reputation for keeping your appointments is proverbial. Even your enemies must admit that."

The Guest nodded and smiled again. Miss Lorna bent toward me.

"What do you think of him?" she asked, almost in a whisper.

"Very striking sort of man," I answered, in a low tone. "But I'm inclined to be a little afraid of him."

"So was I, at first," she said, and I heard the silver laugh again. "But that soon wears off," she went on. "You'll know him better some day!"

"Shall I?"

"Yes; I'm quite sure you will. Oh, I don't pretend that I fell in love with him at first sight! I went through a phase of feeling afraid of him, as almost everyone does. You see, when people first meet him they cannot possibly know how kind and gentle he can be, though he is so tremendously strong. I've heard him called cruel and ruthless and cold, but it's not true. Indeed it's not! He can be as gentle as a woman, and he's the truest friend in all the world."

I was going to ask her to tell me his name, but just then I saw that she was looking at him, across me, and I sat as far back in my chair as I could, so that they might speak to each other if they wished to. Their eyes met, and there was a longing light in both—I could not help glancing from one to the other—and Miss Lorna's sweet lips moved almost imperceptibly, though no sound came from them. I have seen young lovers make that small sign to each other even across a room, the signal of a kiss given and returned in the heart's thoughts.

If she had been less beautiful and young, if the man she loved had not been so magnificently manly, it would have irritated me; but it seemed natural that they should love and not be ashamed of it, and I only hoped that no one else at the table had noticed the tenderly quivering little contraction of the young girl's exquisite mouth.

"You remembered," said the man quietly. "I got your message this morning. Thank you."

"I hope it's not going to be very hard," murmured Miss Lorna, smiling. "Not that it would make any great difference if it were," she added more thoughtfully.

"It's the easiest thing in life," he said, "and I promise that you shall never regret it."

"I trust you," the young girl answered simply.

Then she turned away, for she no doubt felt the awkwardness of talking to him across me of a secret which she had confided to me without letting him know that she had done so. Instinctively I turned to him, feeling that the moment had come for disregarding formality and making his acquaintance, since we were neighbors at table in a friend's house and I had known Miss Lorna so long. Besides, it is always interesting to talk with a man who is just going to do something very dangerous or dramatic and who does not guess that you know what he is about.

"I suppose you motored here from town, as you said you missed the train," I said. "It's a good road, isn't it?"

"Yes, I literally flew," replied the dark man, with his gentle smile. "I hope you're not superstitious about thirteen at table?"

"Not in the least," I answered. "In the first place, I'm a fatalist about everything that doesn't depend on my own free will. As I have not the slightest intention of doing anything to shorten my life, it will certainly not come to an abrupt end by any autosuggestion arising from a silly superstition like that about thirteen."

"Autosuggestion? That's rather a new light on the old belief."

"And secondly," I continued, "I don't believe in death. There is no such thing."

"Really?" My neighbor seemed greatly surprised. "How do you mean?" he asked. "I don't think I understand you."

"I'm sure *I* don't," put in Miss Lorna, and the silver laugh followed. She had overheard the conversation, and some of the others were listening, too.

"You don't kill a book by translating it," I said, rather glad to expound my views. "Death is only a translation of life into another language. That's what I mean."

"That's a most interesting point of view," observed the Thirteenth

Guest thoughtfully. "I never thought of the matter in that way before, though I've often seen the expression 'translated' in epitaphs. Are you sure that you are not indulging in a little paronomasia?"

"What's that?" inquired the hard-faced lady, with all the contempt which a scholarly word deserves in polite society.

"It means punning," I answered. "No, I am not making a pun. Grave subjects do not lend themselves to low forms of humor. I assure you, I am quite in earnest. Death, in the ordinary sense, is not a real phenomenon at all, so long as there is any life in the universe. It's a name we apply to a change we only partly understand."

"Learned discussions are an awful bore," said the hard-faced lady very audibly.

"I don't advise you to argue the question too sharply with your neighbor there," laughed the master of the house, leaning forward and speaking to me. "He'll get the better of you! He's an expert at what you call 'translating people into another language.'"

If the man beside me was a famous surgeon, as our host perhaps meant, it seemed to me that the remark was not in very good taste. He looked more like a soldier.

"Does our friend mean that you are in the army, and that you are a dangerous person?" I asked of him.

"No," he answered quietly. "I'm only a King's Messenger, and in my own opinion I'm not at all dangerous."

"It must be rather an active life," I said, in order to say something; "constantly coming and going, I suppose?"

"Yes, constantly."

I felt that Miss Lorna was watching and listening, and I turned to her, only to find that she was again looking beyond me, at my neighbor, though he did not see her. I remember her face very distinctly as it was just then; the recollection is, in fact, the last impression I retain of her matchless beauty, for I never saw her after that evening.

It is something to have seen one of the most beautiful women in the world gazing at the man who was more to her than life and all it held; it is something I cannot forget. But he did not return her look just then, for he had joined in the general conversation, and very soon afterward he practically absorbed it.

He talked well; more than well, marvelously; for before long even the lady with the hard face was listening spellbound, with the rest of us, to his stories of nations and tales of men, brilliant descriptions, anecdotes of heroism and tenderness that were each a perfect coin from the mint of humanity, with dashes of daring wit, glimpses of a profound insight into the great mystery of the beyond, and now and then a manly comment on life that came straight from the heart: never, in all my long experience, have I heard poet, or scholar, or soldier, or ruler of men talk as he did that evening. And as I listened I was more and more amazed that such a man should be but a simple King's Messenger, as he said he was, earning a poor gentleman's living by carrying his majesty's despatches from London to the ends of the earth, and I made some sad and sober inward reflections on the vast difference between the gift of talking supremely well and the genius a man must have to accomplish even one little thing that may endure in history, in literature, or in art.

"Do you wonder that I love him?" whispered Miss Lorna.

Even in the whisper I heard the glorious pride of the woman who loves altogether and wholly believes that there is no one like her chosen man.

"No," I answered, "for it is no wonder. I only hope——" I stopped, feeling that it would be foolish and unkind to express the doubt I felt.

"You hope that I may not be disappointed," said Miss Lorna, still almost in a whisper. "That was what you were going to say, I'm sure."

I nodded, in spite of myself, and met her eyes; they were full of a wonderful light.

"No one was ever disappointed in him," she murmured—"no living being, neither man, nor woman, nor child. With him I shall have peace and love without end."

"Without end?"

"Yes. Forever and ever!"

After dinner we scattered through the great rooms in the soft evening light of mid-June, and by and by I was standing at an open window, with the mistress of the house, looking out across the garden.

In the distance, Lorna was walking slowly away down the broad avenue with a tall man; and while they were still in sight, though far away, I am sure that I saw his arm steal round her as if he were drawing her on, and her head bent lovingly to his shoulder; and so they glided away into the twilight and disappeared.

Then at last I turned to my hostess. "Do you mind telling me the name of that man who came in late and talked so well?" I asked. "You all seemed to know him like an old friend."

She looked at me in profound surprise. "Do you mean to say that you do not know who he is?" she asked.

"No. I never met him before. He is a most extraordinary man to be only a King's Messenger."

"He is indeed the King's Messenger, my dear friend. His name is Death."

I dreamed this dream one afternoon last summer, dozing in my chair on deck, under the double awning, when the *Alda* was anchored off Goletta, in sight of Carthage, and the cool north breeze was blowing down the deep gulf of Tunis. I must have been wakened by some slight sound from a boat alongside, for when I opened my eyes my man was standing a little way off, evidently waiting till I should finish my nap. He brought me a telegram which had just come on board, and I opened it rather drowsily, not expecting any particular news.

It was from England, from a very dear friend.

Lorna died suddenly last night at Church Hadley.

That was all; the dream had been a message.

"With him I shall have peace and love without end."

Thank God, I hear those words in her own voice, whenever I think of her.

The Unhappy Body

Lord Dunsany

"Why do you not dance with us and rejoice with us?" they said to a certain body. And then that body made the confession of its trouble. It said: "I am united with a fierce and violent soul, that is altogether tyrannous and will not let me rest, and he drags me away from the dances of my kin to make me toil at his detestable work; and he will not let me do the little things, that would give pleasure to the folk I love, but only cares to please posterity when he has done with me and left me to the worms; and all the while he makes absurd demands of affection from those that are near to me, and is too proud even to notice any less than he demands, so that those that should be kind to me all hate me." And the unhappy body burst into tears.

And they said: "No sensible body cares for its soul. A soul is a little thing, and should not rule a body. You should drink and smoke more till he ceases to trouble you." But the body only wept, and said, "Mine is a fearful soul. I have driven him away for a little while with drink. But he will soon come back. Oh, he will soon come back!"

And the body went to bed hoping to rest, for it was drowsy with drink. But just as sleep was near it, it looked up, and there was its soul sitting on the windowsill, a misty blaze of light, and looking into the street.

"Come," said that tyrannous soul, "and look into the street."

"I have need of sleep," said the body.

"But the street is a beautiful thing," the soul said vehemently; "a hundred of the people are dreaming there."

"I am ill through want of rest," the body said.

"That does not matter," the soul said to it. "There are millions

162

like you in the earth, and millions more to go there. The people's dreams are wandering afield; they pass the seas and the mountains of faëry, threading the intricate passes led by their souls; they come to golden temples a-ring with a thousand bells; they pass up steep streets lit by paper lanterns, where the doors are green and small; they know their way to witches' chambers and castles of enchantment; they know the spell that brings them to the causeway along the ivory mountains—on one side looking downward they behold the fields of their youth and on the other lie the radiant plains of the future. Arise and write down what the people dream."

"What reward is there for me," said the body, "if I write down what you bid me?"

"There is no reward," said the soul.

"Then I shall sleep," said the body.

And the soul began to hum an idle song sung by a young man in a fabulous land as he passed a golden city (where fiery sentinels stood), and knew that his wife was within it, though as yet but a little child, and knew by prophecy that furious wars, not yet arisen in far and unknown mountains should roll above him with their dust and thirst before he ever came to that city again—the young man sang it as he passed the gate, and was now dead with his wife a thousand years.

"I cannot sleep for that abominable song," the body cried to the soul.

"Then do as you are commanded," the soul replied. And wearily the body took a pen again. Then the soul spoke merrily as he looked through the window. "There is a mountain lifting sheer above London, part crystal and part mist. Thither the dreamers go when the sound of the traffic has fallen. At first they scarcely dream because of the roar of it, but before midnight it stops, and turns, and ebbs with all its wrecks. Then the dreamers arise and scale the shimmering mountain, and at its summit find the galleons of dream. Thence some sail East, some West, some into the Past and some into the Future, for the galleons sail over the years as well as over the spaces, but mostly they head for the Past and the olden harbours, for thither the sighs of men are mostly turned, and the dream-ships go before them, as the merchantmen before the continual trade-winds go down the African coast. I see the galleons even now raise anchor after anchor; the stars flash by them; they slip out of the night; their prows go gleaming into the twilight of memory, and night soon lies far off, a black cloud hanging low, and faintly spangled with stars, like the harbour and shore of some low-lying land seen afar with its harbour lights."

Dream after dream that soul related as he sat there by the window. He told of tropical forests seen by unhappy men who could not escape from London, and never would—forests made suddenly wondrous by the song of some passing bird flying to unknown aeries and singing an unknown song. He saw the old men lightly dancing to the tune of elfin pipes—beautiful dances with fantastic maidens—all night on moonlit imaginary mountains; he heard far off the music of glittering Springs; he saw the fairness of blossoms of apple and may thirty years fallen; he heard old voices—old tears came glistening back; Romance sat cloaked and crowned upon southern hills, and the soul knew him.

One by one he told the dreams of all that slept in that street. Sometimes he stopped to revile the body because it worked badly and slowly. Its chill fingers wrote as fast as they could, but the soul cared not for that. And so the night wore on till the soul heard tinkling in Oriental skies far footfalls of the morning.

"See now," said the soul, "the dawn that the dreamers dread. The sails of light are paling on those unwreckable galleons; the mariners that steer them slip back into fable and myth; that other sea the traffic is turning now at its ebb, and is about to hide its pallid wrecks, and to come swinging back, with its tumult, at the flow. Already the sunlight flashes in the gulfs behind the east of the world; the gods have seen it from their palace of twilight that they built above the sunrise; they warm their hands at its glow as it streams through their gleaming arches, before it reaches the world; all the gods are there that have ever been, and all the gods that shall be; they sit there in the morning, chanting and praising Man."

"I am numb and very cold for want of sleep," said the body.

"You shall have centuries of sleep," said the soul, "but you must not sleep now, for I have seen deep meadows with purple flowers flaming tall and strange above the brilliant grass, and herds of pure white unicorns that gambol there for joy, and a river running by with a glittering galleon on it, all of gold, that goes from an unknown island to an unknown isle of the sea to take a song from the King of Over-the-Hills to the Queen of Far-Away.

"I will sing that song to you, and you shall write it down."

"I have toiled for you for years," the body said. "Give me now but one night's rest, for I am exceeding weary."

"Oh, go and rest. I am tired of you. I am off," said the soul.

And he arose and went, we know not whither. But the body they laid in the earth. And the next night at midnight the wraiths of the dead came drifting from their tombs to felicitate that body.

"You are free here, you know," they said to their new companion.

"Now I can rest," said the body.

Xélucha

M. P. Shiel

"He goeth after her . . . and knoweth not . . . "
(from a diary)

Three days ago! by heaven, it seems an age. But I am shaken—
my reason is debauched. A while since I fell into a coma precisely resembling an attack of *petit mal.* "Tombs, and worms, and
epitaphs"—that is the fantasy of my dream. At my age, with my
physique, to walk staggery, like a man stricken! But all that will pass:
I must collect myself—my reason is debauched. Three days ago! it
seems an age! Sitting on the floor before an old cista full of letters,
I lighted upon a packet of Cosmo's. Why, I had forgotten them!
they are turning sere! Truly, I can no more call myself a young man.
I sat reading, listlessly, rapt back by memory. But to muse is to be
lost! of *that* evil habit I must wring the neck, or look to perish. Once
more I threaded the mazy sphere-harmony of the minuet, reeled in
the waltz, long pomps of candelabra, the noon-day of the bacchanal,
about me. Cosmo was the very tsar and maharajah of the Sybarites!
the Priap of the *détraqués!* In every unexpected alcove of his
Roman Villa was a couch, raised high, with necessary foot-stool,
flanked and canopied with mirrors of clarified gold. Consumption
fastened upon him; reclining at last at table, he could, till warmed,
scarce lift the wine! his eyes were like glow-worms coiled together!
haloed with vaporous emanations of phosphorus! Desperate, one
could see, was his struggle with the Devourer. But to the end the
princely smile persisted; to the end—to the last day—he continued
among that comic crew unchallenged choragus of all the rites, I will
not say of Paphos, but of Chemos! and Baal-Peor! Warmed, he did

166

not refuse the revel, the dance, the darkened chamber. It was black, that chamber, rayless; approached by a secret passage; in shape circular; the air hot, haunted by odours of balms, bdellium, hints of dulcimer, flute, and all around it ottomans of Morocco. Here Lucy Hill stabbed to the heart Caccofogo, mistaking the scar on his back for the scar of Soriac. In a bath of malachite the Princess Egla, waking late one morning, found Cosmo lying stiffly dead, the bath-water covering him wholly.

"But in God's name, Mérimée!" (so he wrote), "to think of Xélucha dead! Xélucha! Can a moon-beam, then, perish of suppurations? Can the rainbow be eaten by worms? Ha! ha! ha! laugh with me, my friend: *'elle dérangera l'Enfer'!* She will introduce the *pas de tarantule* into Tophet! Xélucha, the feminine! Xelucha recalling the splendid harlots of history! Weep with me—manat rara meas lacrima per genas! expert as Thargelia; cultured as Aspatia; purple as Semiramis. She comprehended the human tabernacle, my friend, its secret springs and tempers, more intimately than any *savant* of Salamanca who breathes. *Tarare*—but Xélucha is not dead! Vitality is not mortal; you cannot wrap flame in a shroud. Xélucha! where, then, is she? Translated, perhaps—rapt to a constellation like the daughter of Leda. She journeyed to Hindostan, accompanied by the train and appurtenance of a Begum, threatening descent upon the Emperor of Tartary. I spoke of the desolation of the West; she kissed me, and promised return. Mentioned you, too, Mérimée—'her Conqueror'—'Mérimée, Destroyer of Woman.' Breaths from the conservatory rioted among her blowing hair, threads of it astray over that thulite tint you know. Costumed cap-à-pie, she had, my friend, the dainty completeness of a daisy mirrored bright in the eye of the browsing brute. A simile of Milton had for years, she said, inflamed the lust of her eye: 'The barren plains of Sericana, where Chinese drive with sails and wind their cany wagons light.' I, and the Sabaeans, she assured me, wrongly considered Flame the whole of being; the other half of things being Aristotle's quintessential Light. In the Ourania Hierarchia and the Faustbook you meet a completeness: burning Seraph, Cherûb full of eyes. Xélucha combined them. She would reconquer the Orient for Dionysius, and return. I heard of her blazing at Delhi; drawn in a chariot by lions. Then this rumour—probably false. Like Odin, Arthur, and the rest, Xélucha—will reappear."

Soon subsequently Cosmo lay down in his balneum of malachite, and slept, having drawn over him the water as a coverlet. I, in England, heard little of Xélucha: first that she was alive, then dead, then had alighted at old Tadmor in the Wilderness, Palmyra now. Nor did I greatly care, Xelucha having long since turned to apples of Sodom in my mouth. Till I sat by the cista of letters and re-read Cosmo, she had for some years passed from my active memories.

The habit is now confirmed in me of spending the greater part of the day in sleep, while by night I wander far and wide through the city under the sedative influence of a tincture which has become necessary to my life. Such an existence of shadow is not without charm; nor, I think, could many minds be subjected to its conditions without elevation, deepened awe. To travel alone with the Primordial cannot but be solemn. The moon is of the hue of the glow-worm; and Night of the sepulchre. Nux bore not less Thanatos than Hypnos, and the bitter tears of Isis redundulate to a flood. At three, if a cab rolls by, the sound has the augustness of thunder. Once, at two, near a corner, I came upon a priest, seated, dead, leering, his legs bent. One arm, supported on a knee, pointed with accusing forefinger upward. By exact observation, I found that he indicated Betelgeuse, the star 'α' of rainy Orion. He was hideously swollen, having perished of dropsy. Thus in all Supremes is a *grotesquerie;* and one of the sons of Night is—Buffo.

In a London square deserted, I imagine, even in the day, I was aware of the metallic, silvery-clinking approach of little shoes. It was three in a morning of winter, a day after my rediscovery of Cosmo. I had stood by a railing, looking at clouds sailing as under the steering of a moon wrapped in cloaks of inclemency. Turning, I saw a little lady, very gloriously dressed. She had walked straight to me. Her head was bare, and crisped with ripples which rolled to a globe, rich with jewels, at her nape. In the redundance of her décolleté development, she resembled Parvati, love-goddess of the luscious fancy of the Brahmin.

She addressed to me the question:

"What are you doing there, darling?"

Her loveliness stirred me, and Night is *bon camarade.* I replied:

"Sunning myself by means of the moon."

"All that is borrowed lustre," she returned, "you have got it from old Drummond's *Flowers of Sion.*"

Looking back, I cannot remember that this reply astonished me, though it should—of course—have done so. I said:

"On my soul, no; but you?"

"You might guess whence *I* come!"

"You are dazzling: you come from Paz."

"Oh, farther than that, my son! Say a subscription ball in Soho."

"Yes? . . . and alone? in the cold? on foot . . . ?"

"Why, I am old, and a philosopher. I can pick you out riding Andromeda yonder from the ridden Ram. They are in error, M'sieur, who suppose an atmosphere on the broad side of the moon. I have reason to believe that on Mars dwells a race whose lids are transparent like glass; so that the eyes are visible during sleep; and every dream moves imaged forth to the beholder in tiny panorama on the iris. You cannot imagine me a mere *fille!* To be escorted is to admit yourself a woman, and that is improper in Nowhere. Young Enos drives an *equipage à quatre,* but Artemis 'walks' alone. Get out of my borrowed light in the name of Diogenes! I am going home."

"Far?"

"Near Piccadilly."

"But a cab?"

"No cabs for *me,* thank you. The distance is a mere nothing. Come."

We set off. My companion at once put an interval between us, quoting from the *Spanish Curate* that the open is an enemy to love. The Talmudists, she twice insisted, rightly held the hand the sacredest part of the person, and at that point also contact was for the moment interdict. Her walk was extremely rapid. I followed. Not a cat was anywhere visible. We reached at length the door of a mansion in St. James's: no light, it seemed tenantless, windows uncurtained, pasted across, some of them, with the words, To Let. My companion, however, flitted up the steps, and, beckoning, passed inward. I, following, slammed the door, and was in darkness. I heard her ascend, and presently a region of glimmer above revealed a stairway, curving broadly up. On that lowest floor where I stood was no carpet, nor furniture; the dust thick. I had begun to mount when, to my surprise, she stood by my side, returned; and whispered:

"To the very top, darling."

She soared nimbly up, anticipating me. Higher, I could no longer doubt that the house was empty but for us. All was a vacuum full of dust and echoes. But at the top light streamed from a door, and I entered a good-sized saloon. I was dazzled by the sudden resplendence of the apartment, at the middle of which was a spread table, square, opulent with gold plate, fruit, dishes; three ponderous chandeliers of electric light above; and I noticed also (what was very *bizarre*) one little candlestick of tin containing an old curve of tallow, on the table. But the impression of the whole was one of gorgeousness not less than Assyrian: an ivory couch at one end of the table had a head-piece of chalcedony forming a sea for the sport of emerald ichthyosauri; copper-coloured hangings, panelled with mirrors, corresponded with a dome of copper; yet this latter, I now remember, produced upon my glance an impression of actual grime. My companion reclined on a sigma couch, raised to the table-level in the Semitic manner, visible to her saffron slippers of satin. She pointed me a seat opposite, the incongruity of whose presence in the midst of this pomp so tickled me, that no power could have kept me from a smile: it was a mean chair, all wood, nor was I long in discovering one leg shorter than its fellows.

She indicated wine in a black bottle, and a tumbler, but herself made no pretence of drinking or eating, lay on hip and elbow, *petite,* resplendent, and gazed gravely upward. I, however, drank.

"You are tired," I said, "one sees that."

"It is precious little that *you see!*" she returned, dreamy, hardly glancing.

"How! your mood is changed, then? You are morose."

"You never, I think, saw a Norse passage-grave?"

"And abrupt."

"Never?"

"A passage-grave? No."

"It is worth a journey! They are circular chambers of stone, covered by earth-mounds, with a 'passage' of slabs connecting them with the outer air. All round the chamber the dead sit, head resting on bent knees, and consult together in silence."

"Drink wine with me, and be less Tartarean."

"You certainly seem to be a fool," she replied with a sardonic iciness. "Is it not, then, highly romantic? They belong, you know, to the Neolithic Age. As the teeth fall, one by one, from the lipless mouths—they are caught by the lap. When the lap thins—they roll to the floor. Thereafter, every tooth that drops all round the chamber sharply breaks the silence."

"Ha! ha! ha!"

"Yes. It is like a century-slow dripping in some cavern of the far subterrene."

"Ha! ha! This wine seems heady! They express themselves in a dialect largely dental."

"The Ape, on the other hand, in a language wholly guttural."

A town-clock tolled four. Our talk was holed with silences, and heavy-paced. The wine's exhalation reached my brain: I saw her through mist, dilating large, uncertain, shrinking again to dainty compactness. But amorousness had died within me.

"Do you know," she asked, "what has been discovered in one of the Danish *Kjökkenmöddings* by a little boy? It was ghastly. The skeleton of a huge fish with human—"

"You are most unhappy."

"Be silent."

"You are full of care."

"I think you a great fool."

"You are racked with misery."

"You are a child. You have not an instinct of the meaning of the words."

"How! Am I not a man? I, too, miserable, careful?"

"You are not, really, *anything*—until you can create."

"Create what?"

"Matter."

"That is foppish. Matter cannot be created, nor destroyed."

"Truly, then, you must be a creature of unusually weak intellect. I see that now. Matter does not exist, then, there is no such thing, really—it is an appearance, a spectrum—every writer not imbecile from Plato to Fichte has, voluntary or involuntary, proved that for your good. To create it is to produce an impression of its reality upon the senses; to destroy it is to wipe a wet rag across a scribbled slate."

"Perhaps. I do not care. Since no one can do it."

"No one? You are mere embryo—"

"Who, then?"

"*Anyone* whose power of Will is equivalent to the gravitating force of a star of the First Magnitude."

"Ha! ha! ha! By heaven, you choose to be facetious. Are there, then, wills of such equivalence?"

"There have been three, the founders of religions. There was a fourth: a cobbler of Herculaneum, whose volition induced the cataclysm of Vesuvius in '79, in direct opposition to the gravity of Sirius. There are more fames than *you* have ever sung, you know. The greater number of disembodied spirits, too, I feel certain—"

"By heaven, I cannot but think you full of sorrow! Poor wight! come, drink with me. The wine is thick and boon. Is it not Setian? It makes you sway and swell before me, I swear, like a purple cloud of evening—"

"But you are mere ponderance!—I did not know that!—you are no companion! your little interest revolves round the lowest centres."

"Come—forget your agonies—"

"What, think you, is the portion of the buried body first sought by the worm?"

"The eyes! the eyes!"

"You are *hideously* wrong—you are so *utterly* at sea—"

"My God!"

She had bent forward with such rage of contradiction as to approach me closely. A loose gown of amber silk, wide-sleeved, had replaced her ball attire, though at what opportunity I could not guess; wondering, I noticed it as she now placed her palms far forth upon the table. A sudden wafture as of orange-flowers, mingled with the faint odour of mortality over-ready for the tomb, greeted my sense. A chill crept upon my flesh.

"You are so *hopelessly* at fault—"

"For God's sake—"

"You are so *miserably* deluded! Not the eyes *at all!*"

"Then, in Heaven's name, what?"

Five tolled from a clock.

"The *Uvula!* that drop of mucous flesh, you know, suspended from the palate above the glottis: they eat through the face-cloth and cheek, or crawl by the lips between defective teeth, filling the mouth. They make straight for it: it is the *deliciae* of the vault."

At her horror of interest I grew sick, at her odour, and her words. Some unspeakable sense of insignificance, of debility, held me dumb.

"You say I am full of sorrows. You say I am racked with woe; that I gnash with anguish. Well, you are a child in intellect. You use words without realisation of meaning like those minds in what Leibnitz calls 'symbolical consciousness.' But suppose it were so—"

"It *is* so."

"You know nothing."

"I see you twist and grind. Your eyes are very pale. I thought they were hazel: they are of the bluishness of phosphorous shimmerings seen in darkness."

"That proves nothing."

"But the 'white' of the sclerotic is dyed to yellow. And you look inward. Why do you look so palely inward, so woe-worn, upon your soul? Why can you speak of nothing but of the sepulchre, and its rottenness? Your eyes seem to me wan with centuries of vigil, with mysteries and millenniums of pain."

"Pain! but you know so *little* of it! you are wind and words! of its philosophy and *rationale* nothing!"

"Who knows?"

"I will give you a hint. Pain is the sub-consciousness in conscious creatures of Eternity, and of eternal loss. The least prick of a pin not Pæan and Æsculapius and the powers of heaven and hell can utterly heal. Of an everlasting loss of wholeness the conscious body is sub-conscious, and 'pain' is its sigh at the tragedy. So with all pain— greater, the greater the loss. The hugest of losses is, of course, the loss of Time. If you lose that, any of it, you plunge at once into the transcendentalisms, the infinitudes, of Loss; if you lose *all of it*—"

"But you so wildly exaggerate! Ha! ha! You rant, I tell you, of common-places with the woe—"

"Hell is where a clear, untrammelled Spirit is sub-conscious of lost Time; where it writhes with envy of the living world; *hating* it for ever, and all the sons of Life!"

"But curb yourself! Drink—I implore—I *implore*—for God's sake—but *once*—"

"To *hasten* to the snare—*that* is woe! to drive your ship upon the *lighthouse* rock—that is Marah! To wake, and feel it irrevocably true that you went after her—*and the dead were there*—and her guests were in the depths of hell—*and you did not know it!*— though you *might* have. Look out upon the houses of the city this dawning day: not one, I tell you, but in it haunts some soul—walking up and down the old theatre of its little Day—goading imagination by a thousand childish tricks, vraisemblances—elaborately duping itself into the fantasy *that it still lives,* that the chance of life is not for ever and for ever lost—yet riving all the time with under-memories of the wasted Summer, the lapsed brief light between the two eternal glooms—riving I say and shriek to you!—riving, *Mérimée, you destroying fiend*—"

She had sprung—*tall* now, she seemed to me—between couch and table.

"Mérimée!" I screamed,—"*my* name, harlot, in your maniac mouth? By God, woman, you terrify me to death!"

I too sprang, the hairs of my head catching stiff horror from my fancies.

"Your name? Can you imagine me ignorant of your name, or anything concerning you? Mérimée! Why, did you not sit yesterday and read of me in a letter of Cosmo's?"

"Ah-h . . . , " hysteria bursting in sob and laughter from my arid lips—"Ah! ha! ha! Xélucha! My memory grows palsied and grey, Xélucha! pity me—my walk is in the very valley of shadow!—senile and sere!—observe my hair, Xélucha, its grizzled growth—trepidant, Xélucha, clouded—I am not the man you knew, Xélucha, in the palaces—of Cosmo! You are Xélucha!"

"You rave, poor worm!" she cried, her face contorted by a species of malicious contempt. "Xélucha died of cholera ten years ago at Antioch. I wiped the froth from her lips. Her nose underwent a green decay before burial. So far sunken into the brain was the left eye—"

"You are—*you are Xélucha!*" I shrieked; "voices now of thunder howl it within my consciousness—and by the holy God, Xélucha, though you blight me with the breath of the hell you are, I shall clasp you,—living or damned—"

I rushed toward her. The word "Madman!" hissed as by the tongues of ten thousand serpents through the chamber, I heard; for a moment to my wild eyes there seemed to rear itself, swelling to the roof, a tower of ragged cloud, and, as my arms closed upon emptiness, I was tossed by the operation of some Behemoth potency backward to a wall of the chamber, where I fell, shocked into insensibility.

When the sun was low toward night, I lay awake, and listlessly observed the grimy roof, and the sordid chair, and the candlestick of tin, and the bottle of which I had drunk. The table was filthy, of deal, uncovered. All bore the appearance of having stood there for years. But for them, the room was void, the vision of luxury thinned to air. Sudden memory flashed upon me. I scrambled to my feet, and ran tottering, bawling, through the evening into the streets.

The Eye Above the Mantel

Frank Belknap Long

I cannot recall to mind the precise place where we met, or even why we met. Perhaps we were assembled merely by chance, or perhaps we dared not consciously acknowledge the purpose which had brought us together. We had drunk a great deal of exceedingly rare and costly wine, and all sense of *proportion* had left us. We blasphemed openly, and uttered prophecies and warnings which none but the gods have a right to utter. We also defied the little gods, and made fun of their tininess, which was unkind.

It seems to me that we were all very young, and students of a lore which has long since perished from the earth, even as the inspired and mystic writings of the Chaldees have sunk into oblivion with the forgotten centuries. I know that we interested ourselves in evolution, and speculated upon the creature which would some day take man's place upon this tiny planet of ours. That such a creature would come, we had not the slightest doubt, and we merely discussed the *way* of his coming.

But there was one among us who took no part in our conversation, but who sat with folded arms and smiling face, listening in silence to all which fell from our lips. He was tall and pale, and yet I cannot, I cannot for my life, describe him, or even hint at the unheard-of characters which marked him as one apart, and which made us fear him with a fear which was more than human, a fear which the Sphinx must have felt when the gods of Egypt went shrieking across the Nile, to mingle with the gods of Greece and the gods of Rome. Of his dress, I remember nothing save that the tails of his coat were immoderately long, and seemed to sweep the floor.

We feared him, and yet we dared not openly show our fear. Our

gestures were violent and affected, and our voices low and constrained. And we looked at him constantly, and yet continued to
talk of the superman. We continued to talk of the superman who
would some day come and destroy the pallid and feeble thing
called vir. And we thought of this superman as some great insect,
with long hairy arms and loathsome, spider-like body, and we shuddered to think of that terrible day not far distant when the old lord
of the earth should stand naked and defenceless before the new,
and send up impotent shrieks to the quiet stars.

It was at this point that the stranger arose, and laughed. I cannot
think that such a laugh was known to the Egyptians, or to the
Medes, or to the Persians, or to any of the lesser peoples who now
dwell within the region of darkness. It was a laugh such as is only
heard in the small hours of the night, when the gods are careless,
and no longer watch over the meditations and manifestations of
man. And the stranger spoke, and his voice was the voice of a daemon, but it was also the voice of an angel. And the stranger spoke,
and his voice was unchaste, but it was holy. And I shuddered, and
drew my coat up over my ears that I might not hear the voice that
seemed to tempt me away from myself. And the others did likewise, but the voice reached us through our clothes.

"As the eye is the window of the soul, so is the eye of this room
the window to that which is to come!"

Upon hearing this we looked at one another, and our faces
assumed expressions at once sinister and indescribable. There was
but one window in that small room, and it was high up over a mantel of gold and onyx under a ceiling of white marble, and through it
the pale light of the wan moon came in thin pencil-like rays.

In a moment we had placed a chair against the wall, a red-plush
chair with arms of black ebony, and were mounting the mantel. But
the mantel was narrow, and could not hold all of us, and seeing this,
we became angry, and fought among ourselves, and quarrelled for
a place on the mantel. And finally we decided to draw lots, and let
fate decide who should be the first to mount, and to gaze through
that little window which admitted the pale light of the wan moon
in thin pencil-like rays.

And so one Amomenon produced a set of jet black dice, and for
five minutes we gambled there under the little window to see who
should be the first to mount. And, may the gods who watch over my
destiny be praised, I *won*, and to me was reserved the privilege and

the right of being the first, the first of all of the children of men, to look through that tiny window, and to view all that lay beyond.

And I mounted with glee, my heart beating within me, and my soul screaming with ecstasy. I mounted slowly, because the writings of Plith, the Babylonian, the ancient and yellow scrolls of Plith, had taught me that haste injures the bodily organs and destroys the faculties of the mind.

At length I reached the little window, and gazed out. I had expected to see a quiet Manhattan street, with yellow and black automobiles sweeping noiselessly by, and gentle lamp-posts shedding melancholy beams upon the well-turned mustaches of pale passers-by, and over all the wan moon which had shed its pale rays into the little room below through the tiny window at which I was now gazing.

But instead I beheld an endless waste stretching out for miles and miles, a quiet, empty waste of gray sandstone, utterly bereft of every living thing. The singing of birds, the drone of insects, and the sighing of the wind against the trees, and against the houses of brick and the palaces of marble—all had ceased, because there were no birds or insects or wind or palaces of marble and houses of brick.

For miles and miles the waste stretched out, and met the sky. And the sky was not blue, but yellow, and shed a yellow light over the gray sandstone. The sky itself shed this light, because there was no sun, or indication that there ever had been a sun. The light came from the sky, from every part of the sky, from out of infinite space came that light. And there were no birds or insects or wind or houses of brick and palaces of marble, but only the waste, endless, stretching away into infinity, crying out unto God.

And a hideous sense of foreboding hung over me, and I groaned inwardly, and was about to turn away from the window. But something arose in the distance—something white and terrible arose in the distance.

From all sides it arose, they arose, myriad white things, and they came forward in even formation. They came forward from the place where the earth met the sky, and they marched with the sure and even step of an invading army.

And when they came near, and I beheld them, I screamed in dismay. For they were all white and tall, and were not like the men I knew. And then it dawned upon me with a fearful suddenness that these were not men at all, but were those of whom the Arabians wrote in letters of blood on secret tablets which have gone the way of all secret tablets.

And I stood with my eyes glued to the window, and watched them advance. I soon noticed that they were not all of the same size, and that the tallest commanded the less tall. I also noticed that they wore no clothes, but were covered with a kind of white fur, and that they were not ashamed of their nakedness. I also noticed that their teeth were black, and their eyes red and inflamed. And then they came very near, almost under the window, and I could hear them talk, and they spoke neither the tongue of Greece nor the tongue of Rome, neither the tongue of England nor the tongue of France, but held discourse in a strange tongue which I could not understand, and which I did not wish to understand.

And they kept coming and coming, and filled up the whole great expanse of gray sandstone, and became a titanic sea of ever-moving white.

And now they filled every square inch of all that land, and there was room for no more, and still some continued to come, crawling over the heads and shoulders of the others. And when at length they came no more, the yellow heavens went colourless, and the stars and the pale moon, which had shed its feeble mercuric light through the low window at which I now stood, became visible.

And then someone below spoke a command. It was uttered in a low voice, and it lacked authority, and yet I knew that it would be obeyed. I knew that the command would be obeyed, because it came from below. And I was not mistaken, for lo, as I stood there, a path was cleared among the multitude of white beings who swayed to and fro under the colourless sky, and the pale moon, and the quiet stars.

And the path was a shocking path, very narrow and uneven, and ever in danger of being closed up by the angry white things that had made it. And the path extended from the window to the place where the earth met the sky. And I kept my face pressed to the window, watching the path.

Of a sudden there arose on the horizon four white figures, but taller than any that had gone before, as tall as the Arabian goddess Aso who rules over the hearts of all brave men. And these four figures came forward, and they carried with them a great thing of bronze and of iron, a great heavy thing of bronze and iron that resembled nothing so much as a cage.

And when they came very near I saw that it *was* a cage, and I cried out to the gods of Seth and Sarmenia to take forever from me my sight, that I might not behold the thing within that cage. For the thing within that cage was hideous to look upon, and was covered with foul yellow mud and dank Charonian vegetation, and it uttered little feeble cries which reminded me of the cries which Heth had uttered when he had been attacked by the lampreys in his master's garden, and had suffered his blood to be drawn off in eighteen different directions at the same time.

But the gods of Seth and Sarmenia heard me not, and my sight never left me, and I was forced to keep my eyes riveted upon the cage of iron and bronze and the loathsome thing within. And while I watched, the white creatures began to torture their captive with little sticks of wood, little sharp sticks which they held in their hands. They poked him in the face, and hit him over the head and shoulders, and called him names which I knew were shocking because of the voice in which they were uttered. But, strange to say, I felt sympathy only for myself, because the creature was too horrid to excite sympathy in either man or beast. And the moon and the stars looked down silently, and said nothing, and the cries of the thing went up to the colourless heavens with no one to protest.

How long I continued to watch them torture the thing, I cannot tell, but it seems to me that for ages and ages, aeons and aeons, the cries rose up to the gods. And at length the light of the moon fell full upon the cage, and the thing within stood out in awful clearness.

And now as I write, my soul becomes delirious, and my heart volcanic, and my mind alone remains calm. For the thing within that cage—I am consumed with fire—I cannot write it—I cannot—this wretched soul—but enough—I will tell all—the thing within that cage was a man, and that man was *Kunos*, my dear, my darling brother! O God, the loathsome thing within covered with dank Charonian vegetation was flesh of my flesh, and bone of my bone!

I tried to turn from the window—I sent up supplications to both the little gods and the big gods; and I even invoked the aid of the sinister and unchaste daemon Roth who dwells within the vile Dagaan charnel house, and who is part ruler of Eld and Nomore. But my prayers were unanswered, and to me of all men was reserved the horrible fate of being forced to gaze upon the living disintegration of a loved one.

And when at length it was over, and dear Kunos had gone his way into the endless void, the gods of Seth and Sarmenia, and of Rosath and Raynald, gave me permission to leave the window. And, with a shriek which I did not recognise as my own, I jumped down from the mantel, and screamed to my companions to cover me with their cloaks, and to shield me from myself. But my companions heard me not, for my companions, alas, were beyond hearing! My companions were beyond hearing and seeing, and they neither heard my cries, nor noticed the agony of my soul.

Stretched out pale and motionless they lay in a neat row upon the cold floor of white marble—stretched out stiff and silent they lay.

And upon the lips of each there was a smile, and upon the breast of each a little red spot—a little, neat, round red spot upon the breast of each. And then with a fearful suddenness it all came to me, and I knew that the Egyptians, and the Medes, and the Assyrians and the Persians were all more cunning than we—all infinitely more cunning than we—because *they* had *known,* and had permitted their civilisations to sink into decay, and had left to the Celt and the Saxon the terrible menace of the superman.

And now I saw him standing there, the new lord of the universe, standing there quiet and silent and sinister over the bodies of those whom he had slain. And then he suddenly seemed to perceive that I was no longer at the window, and he smiled with a sweet smile, and spoke in a voice which was tender and soft.

"You are the last of your kind, and I pity you. Go, and live to revel in the glories of a civilisation which is to come, a civilisation such as you have never known. Go, I say, and wander among the graves of your race, and if you so desire, write the history of my coming!"

And I obeyed.

A Dim-Remembered Story

R. H. Barlow

Dedicated to H. P. Lovecraft

Prologue

I have seen the castle of Yrn, which shall rise in undreamed years, and I have been at night in the wood which usurps a curious ruin. I have witnessed the master-things at their gigantic play, and I have known that last abyss wherein my faltering body might not live. Now I shall write of what happened, and of how these things befell me.

Time, of all things, is most elusive; for no one can know what it actually is. Perhaps time is a creation of Man—and Man is a brief thing upon a fragile sphere. His world is but a single blossom in the garden of the firmament. It might be that if there were no life, Time would not exist. The crystal stars would then remain in their careless pattern—the night sky would be as great and jewel-set, but if no thing watched, if no heart moved in all eternity, by what should Time be reckoned? A scientist has written: "Suppose that everything in the universe should halt—all life cease, the planets pause in their orbits, the atoms and electrons cease their flow, it would appear to us as the next instant, and we should be unaware of the occurrence." He suggests, too, that possibly Time does not run a smooth course; that it may ebb and surge like any stream. In each such abeyance there might be long eternities.

With this is my story linked. What I would say may forever elude me, because it is difficult to put such things in words, but I am getting down this narrative in the hope that someone may understand, or at least believe, it.

In looking down earth's centuries, our minds can summon all the

vanished things—the filth of Villion's Paris, or the tumult of dead
Carthage, or monster-swamps which have seen no mortal in secret
Asia. Pageants are re-staged for us, the noise and colour of forgotten worlds are fixed eternally. Yet because we cannot reach them,
they seem beyond recovery; their ecstasies wholly lost. To you now
who scan this page, I say they are not gone, nor do I affect a paradox. Augustus yet prevails in uncrumbled Rome, and Christian
warriors storm the bearded foe of Acre, on that bright dust-filled
day nine centuries ago. In Posedonis there are lunar rituals, and
Russia's Ivan holds a bloody scepter. These worlds are only around
some crook in the lane of eternity, hidden by a bend in the path
along which our own frail world passes.

Our age is a given point in the inexorable journey—if we might
look ahead, we should see it blotted out by a succeeding epoch.
Then our towns and continents will be as one with those lost earths.
Yet our wars and loves and passions, the shapes and hues of our
existence are set, fixed, in some unknown way. All things that have
been, all that shall be, are together recorded. It is as if everything
in earth's history, each phase and aspect of life, had been ordained
at the great start of things. As if they had occurred, perhaps, at one
mighty instant, so that the beginning and the end are merged. Or
as if each century were an earth separate in space and time and
matter. A thousand earths—a world repeating itself beyond count-
ing, so that things may exist in many avatars and many ages. Worlds
beside us that we cannot reach.

And so with those latter events of earth's career, in the land
before us, we shall come upon them in a destined sequence, through
the rise and triumph and perishing of cultures, through the great
sweep of history, as autumn succeeds the full summer, and tired
leaves fall where once fell blossoms. But if the way might be
opened, the door unsealed, we could go into other realms, to see
and know forbidden things. They are as real, those future years, as
any which our far journeying has passed. This fact I know with a
poignancy none other can share. Do not say the land ahead does
not exist, simply because you cannot see it.

Look tonight at the stars. Let them overwhelm you in the postures
of their bright dance. Face the vastness which they dot like silver
bees, and sound with your own brain the mystery, hazarding at the
inscrutable plan of things. Then you will comprehend my tale.

I

That Is Not Dead . . .

Each muscle of my body twitched weakly as I recovered consciousness. For a moment, as I lingered in the void between sleep
and life, there was a sense of floating—a feeling of disembodiment
that increased as I neared reality and awakening. It was as if I drifted
idly among clouds of red and purple, of green and orange and yellow, mingled with yet other prismatic hues for which I can find no
name. I moved in pleasant languor through a thousand-coloured
realm, knowing it as half a dream and I a dream within it. About
and above me were shapes like those made in our eyes by gazing
too long at the sun. I was ambiguously conscious that all these
forms had such an origin, that they were but a visual rendering of
things whose true nature eluded my sight and comprehension.
Then all the horizon of seething colour faded swiftly, dropped into
organizing patterns, and ebbed about me. Everything was clear in
an abrupt stab of light.

Hot bands were tight about my throbbing head, and I was unable
to rise from the bank of moss whereon I lay. A verdant greenness
smote my retina and shot through trembling eyelids. The green of
a forest luxuriant in plants and trees. This wealth of ferns and matting
vines and thick, olive-coloured trunks was pierced with gilding sunlight. I blinked painfully, and all the jungle wavered into brightness.
Everywhere this monstrous forest loomed, dripping pale sunlight
into leafy strongholds. My weakness seeped away as I sprawled
prone on the rich sward.

How may I convey to you the mysterious beauty of this afternoon
wood? Keats would have worshipped it like a Druid-priest. It was a
green-carpeted gallery guarded by rows of dark, polished pillars, or a
tapestry of gold on silk. There were somewhere bird-voices in ardent
song, and I heard the pleasantly harsh cry of a carrion fowl. But I did
not see the fluttering wings, nor could I discover anything living.

After a little I attempted to rise, but Gulliver bound in Lilliput
could not have had more difficulty. A sword of pain was thrust into
my aching head, as if some blow had felled me. My thoughts
were blurred, and somehow fearing, as I stood wearily to gaze about
me. How had I come into that ancient wood? Clustered with great

bushes among oak boles, it seemed almost tropical in that glamorous
light. Trees leaned in on me, alight with the failing sun, as if they
would impart some woodland secret. It was like waking into a
dream of Arden, or some strange forgotten wood of Arthur's time.
It was as fabulous and richly foliated as lost Eden might have been.
On every side the great trees rose; above, their tops were so netted
as to hide the cobalt sky. They lingered, waiting and silent—tall
goblins circling me with outstretched arms. This wood was strange
and mystical. In the lingering afternoon dark shadows spread, and
tried to blot out the pools of light strewn everywhere.

In what manner had I come to be there? Alien and inscrutable,
my surroundings gave no clue. It was painful and annoying to stand
bewildered and impotent in a strange place. Deprived of recent
memories, weak and bruised, how was I to leave the place and reach
the city? If the visions of a sleeping mind were made reality—and
reality this was—one might know my baffling sensations. I had
never anywhere before seen the place, yet now I stood upon the
grass within a strange, faintly sinister forest, searching with confused eyes for some familiar sight.

The blind eyes of the forest peered back. Leaves and mosses
seemed to watch me, and tortuous black limbs to await my action.
I had wandered many times over half-lost roads and through dark,
unpenetrated regions in the Kansas hill-country. Perhaps, in a state
of partial amnesia, I had got into a secluded portion of the woodland. I could in no other way account for the odd surroundings in
which I found myself. And if that were so, a few hours' walk should
take me to some house or roadway. At either of these, I would be
all right. On the road I might hail some passing car, or at a house I
could quietly learn my position, saying that I had become lost from
a party of campers. By this I should attract little attention to myself,
which was best, if my memory were indeed gone. Already darkness
was settling upon the great world, and this enchanted sunlight
would ebb into dusk before the hour was past.

So, perplexed and irritated and perhaps a little afraid, I wandered into another glade, surrounded by dark bushes. From that
place, which was as unfamiliar as the first, I made my way through
snaring briars, until I came to a third. Each of them was to me a
street in an unfamiliar town; and I added to my bruises the flick of
sharp vines. Soon the futility of this aimless walk forced itself upon
me, and though I could see no smoke, nor any trace of habitation,

beyond the avenue of sunset trees, I determined that my course should lie in one direction. If I should walk long enough, there must certainly be an end to the unpierced forest.

With this thought, I chose a random direction—to the left of the misty, tree-hidden sun, and walked into the brightness. The vegetation surrounding me was very rich, and I wondered that it should remain untouched by men. In these modern times the places seemed fabulous—a wealth of timber that knew no axe. Hoary and untramped, it had been neither cut nor touched by man, as fallen, decaying trees attested.

I had walked some little time before I realized the dangers those unplumed thickets might conceal. I had seen nothing; not even the flutter of those abounding singers; but some thin voice of inner consciousness whispered, *tread quietly;* and a little breeze soughed past, laden with the mysterious scent of the forest.

The rich profusion of the trees began to thin, and I saw the late sky behind dappling greenery. The silence of this vast clear world was rendered more noticeable by the noise of birds, but for some while they remained beyond sight. Now, as I paused a moment, one plump bluejay lit with unexpected quickness on a dark bough before me, and cocked his speculative head. There was something unusual in the short body—something that troubled me, though what it was, I did not know. Startled by the small creature, I smiled at my fright, but when he was gone, my wariness was increased.

Then, at once there was no sound but that of quivering branches, until I heard above it the heavy rustling of some large animal, very near. The wood became to me a place of terror, and the bright sunset failed to assuage my nocturnal fright. I had seen nothing; yet I felt now an unreasonable apprehension, and fled among the oaks and foetal pines. If there had been a real danger, if some creature had trailed my path, that noisy flight imperilled me. It was only an excessive nervousness that caused my dark terror, for nothing followed. After an inward struggle, I slowed my pace, forcing myself into a normal walk. But when I came upon a stout limb beneath the trees, I took it with me as a club.

The trembling of dusk overshadowed the forest when I came upon the second living thing that my long walk revealed. It was, I am certain, a rabbit; though of what breed I hesitate to say. There was only a glimpse of the round grey body before it plunged into the underbrush, but I was greatly disturbed by that sight. When I speak of it, there exists no comparable experience whereby to judge. The little animal was not visibly deformed: it moved with reassuring naturalness, yet there was something definitely wrong about those short, thick legs, and the flattened tail. It was a rabbit, but such a rabbit as might have lived in the years before man's existence, or as the product of cautious experiment in some gleaming laboratory. It was not the sort of animal that should roam a Kansas field.

Yet it was not until I saw those other objects that I received the full shock of implication. Walking in the dim light of that forest, I came upon profuse numbers of wild yellow roses, frail to the touch. And as the red-gold sun hovered in a last farewell, I found among the blossoms a singular thing.

At first glance it was no more than a rock, albeit a rock of curious evenness and regularity. But as I examined it the fact became apparent that this moss-hidden block, beneath the guarding thorns, had been shaped by deliberate hands. There were traces of an ornate and ineradicable carving. Despite the fleeing daylight, despite the verdant patina of forgotten centuries, I saw a design that was not traced by capricious weathering. This stone was patterned, and had once formed part of a massive wall. I knew this because of the other stones that I found close by. Some were drifted over by decaying leaves and insect-haunted mould, or split by usurping roots. These also were from some lost ruin, the magnitude of which was disturbing. Not because the blocks were so large, but from the number and position of those which were uncovered, and from that greater number betrayed by an exposed corner, or an uncovered edge, I saw that a mighty tower had fallen very long ago in this place. Long ago—and Kansas is a new country. Only a century has gone since white men settled there, and the Indian had no such masonry.

The tower had not collapsed from age and imperfection—that much was clear from the disposition of the ruins. Some force had crushed those blocks into the black soil of the forest; strewn them (like scattered toys) over a great area.

I stood aghast before this evidence of an old, unrecorded catastrophe, and the fears that were to come later began smouldering in my brain. Fragile blossoms piled their fragrant petals over the old ruins, and great trees were sprung everywhere amid them. But even the hoary fingers of time might not conceal what had happened in that place, when the forest was young.

Here a deep gouge, as if made by a clumsy Titan, marred the flowering sod: in another place a whole fragmentary wall, whose stones were broken *across,* lay beneath aspiring bushes. Whatever had happened—an explosion, an earthquake,—the memory of that flaming day had lingered through dark centuries, while vines and flowers crawled and bloomed above the shards of a cryptic doom.

As I have said, the antiquity of this ruin began to trouble me. The fact alone that I was so far from any road seemed disquieting. Perhaps this is the best time to speak of those dim, unshaped fears that crowded my dazed mind. Can you conceive the bitterness of my position? This was not amnesia, for I knew my identity and all the countless details of my commonplace life. There was no stumbling in my reason—I could have described even the pattern of the metalwork in that elevator I so often entered, or the chipped door of my small office. Yet there was some dim barrier . . . a veil enshrouding whatever lay immediately before my wakening.

You know, it was an odd place I found myself in. A place whose existence was unfamiliar to me—and night was close. Then, too, I had discovered things which hinted at a gulf between this place and my previous life. I do not mean that I had any assurance, then—but somehow, everything seemed very unusual in the gloom.

Disturbed and perplexed though I was, there was at first no panic in my bewilderment. Instead, I had an intense and half-suspecting curiosity about a place harbouring such things as I had seen—a place strange, too, in other, less obvious ways. Not even the countless trees seemed normal, though what was unusual about them I could not decide.

Now I shall tell you things as they happened. To this, I will append what I have since guessed or learned. Only in this way can you understand anything of my reactions and emotions. Gradually there was forced upon me the realization that I had undergone something enormously removed from man's experience. In all the years of our race there has been no one else who can narrate such a tale. It was, viewed in the perspective of what we call normality, as alien and catastrophic as the approach of some celestial derelict laden with fiery death. It involved abstrusenesses that might baffle Jeans or Eddington, perplex the greatest of our scientists. For it was a looping, of the real world with another no less real, but more distant than the mind can hold. Distant not in the scale of miles and light-years, but in another, less tangible, less conceivable fashion.

I do not wish to evade, but my fingers are reluctant to form the incredible words; though I underwent the experiences for which those words would stand. Trembling in the grasp of a cosmic nostalgia, my whole frame was wrenched by a shocking, tremendous emotion. I suspected, now, that I was lost indeed; lost forever in some alien eternity. There was a dark whisper of *wrongness* in the darkling glade and that land which surrounded me . . . something hinted incredibly by the aspect of those old fragments and the ruin whose existence had not been mentioned in the town where I grew up, being unknown to anyone of my time. Something hinted again by the nature of the bird that I had seen, and by that curiously— evolved—rabbit.

Though I was spared at first the certainty of my belief, the devastation of that awful knowledge, my whole outlook, my reactions and numb feelings were twisted horribly, like those of a man who has escaped a hideous death, only to realize that he will be maimed during the rest of his life. It was so overwhelming, so incredible, that I was at first unable to realize the blight induced by that change. Recognition of that might only come when I had pondered the matter, and seen in each aspect of life how great and monstrous a transition I had undergone.

Then, while I was torn with grief and horror and dull acquiescence, I heard the clank of metal upon stone. The feeling induced by this sound—ordinarily a common one, and unworthy of notice—is indescribable. For a brief moment I hoped, wildly and incredulously, that all my fears had been the result of a weary body and a mind depressed by unknown surroundings. I wanted dreadfully to believe this, yet in the end I knew that I was unable. What lurked in my outraged brain was a verity, as actual as any memory or knowledge. Such a change in my surroundings, in the very structure and appearance of common plants and animals could mean but a single thing, and that one thing I feared to believe, the while I knew that ultimately I must.

Acceptance of such things does not come fast. There were left to me long periods of suspense and torment—moments which were more terrible, I think, than certainty would have been. It was not until I saw the castle of Yrn that I knelt before the daemonic knowledge and the accompanying pain.

I heard, as I have said, some metallic object ringing through the forest. And hearing it, I knew in a flash of joy and surprise which no fear might stifle, that some one else, some mortal being, had caused that sound in the lonely and morbid wood. This was confirmed by the clear voice of a woman, among unidentifiable sounds.

In a brief moment I hastened through the shadows, coming to a clear space not twenty yards from where I had stood and thought myself alone. The forest resembled a rich wash-drawing by some Dutch master, while a few woolly blossoms trembled about me, shedding their fragrance in the enchanted glade. By the curbing of a stone well there was a figure, blurred in the dark. I knew that it was a woman—the woman whose laughing voice had come to me. She was cupping water in a bowl, and pouring it into a squat red jar that stood beside her.

The hour, if I had been in the city, was that in which street lamps begin to flare out with their mellow, insecure glow, driving the blue and translucent shadows of evening from streets made abruptly mysterious. There, in the forest, I remember that it was very dark, and objects were melting into a blurred unity. I dared not frighten the woman, and so I called out to her from the shelter of an oak. My voice broke the rustle of an evening in a harsh, unexpected way, as if I listened to a stranger, and not as if I spoke myself.

"Don't be alarmed," I repeated, showing myself frankly. But she had dropped the clay vessel in a start of fear, and it splintered on the well-top. She looked up and watched my hesitant advance. My clothing was lamentably torn and soiled, and upon my face were many thin scratches, so that I did not wonder at her distrust. As I walked toward her she drew back with something of defiance in her broad, strong face. Her features were not delicate, nor wholly pleasing, but they held an honest, competent quality, like the face of a young peasant woman.

"Na troiten," she cried anxiously, and her voice quavered. "Na troiten." And her dark eyes searched my face, as she stood motionless.

Then, after a gaze that was also an inspection, she spoke again, and though a sullen resentment darkened her voice, there was less of fear within it.

"Td'lo," she observed suddenly in a syllable I cannot form. "Na troiten!" And she laughed, somehow like a grey bird, reassured.

My brain was sick from that smouldering fear, and perhaps she realized something of my plight, for she spoke not unkindly, and called to some unseen companion.

As she stood before me with an enquiring regard, a younger girl clad also in garments of heavy grey, entered the clearing. The two of them considered me, and spoke together. Then the younger addressed me, but I could only shake my head despairingly.

Fat boughs swayed about us, whispering of the oncoming night. This was far upon us, and the women were veiled by smudging blue. The elder woman touched my arm—her face was broad and somehow bovine without actual ugliness—and turned away. There was nothing to do but follow.

Of my confused mental state, I can hope to convey but little. The sudden, unwarned severance from reality—or what I had known as reality, for if such things might happen, what then was reality?— caused me to experience emotions that few can ever have known. Perhaps it were best to follow only the surface impressions of that frighteningly strange event. I cannot ever tell of the rapture of despair that thronged my dull brain.

So I followed the two grey-clad figures, mysterious in the young moonlight. They might have been the sisters of Clotho as they stole, tall and silent, like dim wraiths through the listening forest. At times the new-spread darkness hid them from me, so that it was difficult to see the path they took.

There is a dim, elusive spirit in the new evening, when the naked realities of day are veiled, and hidden things steal forth to caper with the bat in pearl-grey shadow. The sunlit, familiar aspect of nature is concealed, and mystery breathes in each sentient tree. The ecstasies of dusk are sounded by each exuberant frog and shrill, secretive insect. But quickly the dark triumph of night was banished by a flower-white moon that spun high in the steel-chambered heavens. The cold orb served as our penetrating torch, and by this light I trod the leafy earth. Whatever season ruled this land, it wove the rich death of autumn with blossoming springtide. The chill that caressed me was no harbinger of frost, but a breath of fear from my own heart. My flesh tingled in the seeping moonrays, for it is strange to follow hidden figures in the darkness.

II

—Which Can Eternal Lie,

From their sturdiness I knew that these women led hard lives. Their stride was more assured than mine, as if from customary walking of fields. They knew a simple existence, like the Viking women, or the wives of a pioneering race. Vaguely, almost unconsciously, I identified them with the folk of medieval times—not those of palace gardens, but the sturdy peasant class who made ale and loaves for warring men.

Suddenly, the forest dropped away, and we stood in the flowers of a grass-smooth plain. All about us blooms nodded in the pallid light. White iris beneath the moon. It struck a rich nostalgia in me, for that glow was fascinatingly uncanny. A deluge of death-white pallor shimmered in the air, enveloping the guides like a horde of merging wraiths. How am I to tell of the lunar magic wrought before me? Like clustering moths, the fragile iris melted away to a jewel-dim sky. The moon had frightened all the stars, until they fled in trailing sparks; ahead the firmament was bright with them—each a dead world of jewelled cities hurtling to oblivion.

The women pointed, and I made out a shape that blotted away the sky. The dusky battlements of a crag-hung castle. Rising mountainously from the shimmering field, it pierced the sky with wall and turrets crouching monstrously against the silken universe.

What hands had reared that dark pile I could not guess. Kobaldbuilded, in the darkness the citadel seemed vaster than any building on earth. Only gods might live in such a place of wonder, overlooking mortal worlds. But these cryptic guides were women, and they were leading me through silver fields toward a roadway in the sky. For it seemed that. Sheer as the wind-haunted trails that wind to monasteries in Tibet, the ribbon looped through netted stars.

Up that trail we toiled, the women silent ghosts on the rocky slope. The castle-walls, high above me in the glittering moon, were guarded by a natural fortress of sheer cliffs, save in this one place where the trail was made. It would be a strong foe whose army scaled the grey spires.

Let me tell what I remember of the precipice-upthrust castle when I first beheld it in the warm night. There were many smaller and a single great tower rising with protruding turrets like a faery stronghold on the moon-blotting mountain. The place was built of storm-dark blocks, broidered with aeonian moss. We trod a narrow road between sentinel boulders, and to either hand beyond those boulders, the sustaining cliff fell into darkness. I did not wish to look into the shuddering void, and kept my eyes upturned. The peak on which the castle reared was a flat-topped cone, steeper

than the pyramids of sun-baked Egypt, and guarded on all sides by
the plain.

I was sick with weariness when we stood at last before the gated
wall. The night had been like the colour of lost dreams, and I half-
expected some mailed warrier to confront us in that curiously
mediaeval arch. But instead, the elder woman swung wide a nail-
studded door.

A long grey-hung chamber lit with the orange flame of candles
was revealed as that door swung back. The woman entered before
me, blotting out the rich light.

For a moment their faces were hidden from me, and I wondered
at the ever-present grey. From a night-dim wood to dark castle
hung with smoke-hued tapestries I had been led by figures in the
garb of corpses. This colour was oppressive, and my heart was glad
of the mote-spinning light. About me there were many candles, on
heavy tables of carved wood and upon figured chests that stood
against the wall. The closing door disturbed their patient flame
ever so slightly, and as they settled into calmness, I saw beyond my
guides a man in rich garments.

As he faced me the women drew aside, and I stepped out of the
gloom. He was a man who but recently had passed his youth, and
the plump face had not yet lost a certain handsomeness. This huge
man was clad in a curiously extravagant fashion quite in contrast to
the quiet grey of the women, and his short thick fingers were
ringed with great seals. Something about his dress reminded me of
the gaudy costumes of the fifteenth century, but his clothing, while
very colourful in orange and crimson silk, was less grotesque. Over
tight breeches embroidered with a pattern of ferns he wore a waist-
long coat with puffed sleeves and stiff cuffs of elaborate lace like
that of his collar. A massive chain of flat gold links hung over his
vast shoulders and lay upon his chest. Each segment of this chain
bore a curious cypher.

The man's hair, heavy and flaxen like that of the women, hung
loosely about his collar, clipped in a rough fashion, so that it did not
veil the burning of his eyes. There was a mistrusting civility in that
gaze, and his thick mouth seemed tinged with latent cruelty. He
spoke to me in a voice of great suspicion.

Since I comprehended nothing of his words I shook my head
wearily, and the two women burst into shrill chatter. From their
gestures I judged they told of how I had been found in the shadowed

wood, and of my ignorance regarding their tongue. At any rate, the man did not attempt to speak to me again. Instead, he gave me a strange look and indicated that I was to stay in this room. Then, as I seated myself upon a thick chest of reddish wood, he drew aside a heavy curtain and left me. The women followed, looking back at me in a secret triumph for which I was at a loss to account. It was as if they were pleased at having trapped some malignant but valuable animal.

I remained there for a time, inspecting the room with great curiosity. That such a medieval place might be set in any modern wood was unthinkable—I was as completely severed from the world that I had known as if I had found myself upon another planet. That vertigo, the sense of an ebbing tide that fell away from me as I woke, had tangled all my thoughts, and I only knew that if I had been a victim of amnesia, my wanderings had been far and strange to bring me to this place.

The room was long and narrow, and where no shadowy tapestries were hung, a bleak rock of the same hue was revealed. The roof was vaulted, like cathedrals I had seen in ancient towns, and there was not anywhere a window. This place was old, with the echoes of antiquity in the dark halls and chambers. Great chests of red and brown wood formed all the furniture, save a very solid table in the center of the room; and large hides that had the texture of ape-fur were spread upon the floor.

I had no idea of what these people intended, but despite their curious attitude, I hoped that I had been accepted as a guest for at least this night. While I awaited their return, numberless candles dwindled into little rills of wax, and my weariness increased.

Rising at length, I went to look at those dim hangings, and found that pale designs were worked in threads that tiny spiders might have webbed. The scenes depicted were of great strangeness, and seemed to form a series commencing at the curtained door. But when I tried to catch their theme, I was unable to follow the narrative unfolded. On the first of them a figure knelt before a vibrant glow that radiated swathingly about his averted head and upflung hands. The tapestry was worked with great skill, and I was enchanted by its beauty. Another was a forest-scene with great dim rocks ranged about as if they had once formed the base of a ruined tower; while others dealt with various subjects whose relationship was vague, as if some pictured links were lost. And the last of the weavings was a

mad potpourri of seething colour, like a war-louck's brew. I think
they must have been very old, for some were stained and half-rot-
ten to the touch.

I turned back to the massive table. It was crusted with wax from
a candelabrum, and a platter laden with foodstuffs had been set
upon it by a quiet servant. There was no meat, but many vegetables
were stewed together (some of them unlike any that I had seen)
and I fell to eating hungrily. Before I had finished, the man who
had become my host returned, and I saw his crimson coat beside
me as I looked up.

He plucked my sleeve, and leaving the grey-hung chamber, led
me through a dark passage. The low-burning taper in his thick
hand did not flicker, for here were no more windows, the room I
left. Yet from the plain I had seen a multitude of lights, so there
must be windows elsewhere in this shadowed pile—perhaps in the
place where guardsmen and warriors had their quarters. No thin
arrows might pierce these unbroken walls. I thought of the towers
above, grey in the darkness, save where moonlight drove the shadows into fluttering clots; and I thought again how mighty must a foe
be to overtop these walls. The place was built to withstand prodigious attacks—yet I had seen no garrison, nor any man save this
scarlet-cloaked figure. In what tumultuous halls were the fighting
men, and who served this cryptic lord? Were the women menials,
or did they share his rank and dignity? These questions plagued me
as we neared a heavy door secured by an elaborate system of iron
bolts and chained rings.

My host bent over the catch—I did not see how it was managed—and swung back this time-assaulted door. Then he gave to
me the candle, and vanished in the gloom. I awaited his return, but
after a time, when he did not come back, I stepped across the
threshold, and found myself in a small chamber roofed by pointed
arches. There was a low couch with woven spreads, and beyond this
a window in the facing wall. Tiny stars hung in the unglazed opening, and there were hints of man's fire beyond. I set my candle on
a wooden bench, and looked through the narrow window-slit.

It opened above a walled court, empty and silent in the snowy
moonlight. Beyond these walls I saw the plain, still as if overtaken
by charmed death, save where iris rippled in the breeze, like the
glitter of waves over a dark lake. A woman's voice, singing, disturbed
the stillness. What she sang I shall not ever know, but it was lonely

and thin, and pierced my very soul with rapture. The round moon with its burden of ancient death was not so tragic, as this melody; lamenting the inevitable doom of loveliness, like a mournful Pierrot in autumn's garden. It remembered dimly the scents and colours and the ecstasy of paradise. It was the dirge of water-steeped Atlantis, or the cry of a tortured lover in the night. Long after the voice of passionate despair had ebbed into oblivion, the silence rippled with its memory, and I scrutinized the black horizon to find a key to the singer and her melody.

When I lay at last upon the pillowed couch, sleep came over me, but it was fraught with troubling dreams.

III

And In Strange Aeons . . .

It seems, now, very difficult to make the statement that I have lived for three days in a remote castle, lost in some century for which there is scarcely a name. I have little doubt but that I shall fail in my attempt to convey the peculiar shock of knowing that to be a reality; yet it was a thing as actual, as incontrovertibly real, as the existence of that dusty-sun heated road you rode on today—as certain as the live pounding ocean on a brilliant day.

It was with that curious detachment that comes when one awakens in a strange room that I beheld the morning. My weariness had abated, but a vertigo of strangeness clung oppressively to me. Remembrance of my isolation came. My world was lost as aeon-buried Ur, as the obliterated palaces that perished before Cortez. This morning memories were clearing, and the wrench of my bewildering transition throbbed in a hot brain. I realized wholly; and realizing, accepted the fact, that something—God knows what, for even yet I am uncertain—had precipitated me into realms that only madness can accept. The nostalgia of old centuries overhung me, and momently I feared a confirmation of that besetting dread; feared that I should know absolutely and completely that my old life and surroundings were lost to me—that I was destined to live and perish in this incredible alienation.

Yet, in a while, I was able to force myself from these reflections, and rising, looked from the narrow window. Even the greatest of sorrows cannot last. So brief are man's emotions that when the height of fear or passion has been reached, that emotion ebbs like a tide slipping oceanward.

The sky was gaudy once more, and everywhere leaves of sanguine hue invaded the green ranks. The army of marching trees was flecked with blood. Summer's garment was cast off, and the very grasses were astir in some ineffable expectancy. Over a sky like the rich enamel of an inverted cup there moved a caravan of tumbled clouds—slow and infinitely majestic.

In the courtyard whence that song had come, a young man now walked slowly beneath me, carrying a thin spear. The fresh sun was quieting, and my darkness-nurtured fears perished like fungi brought into the light from an unclean hole. Morning was new, and I was strengthened by the reassurance of day. For a long time I gazed into the dim hills, which were broken by outlined leaves of the closer forest. I must have stayed there a long while, for the sky became a faded powder-blue, and the scattered clouds like chargers whose silk manes overspread the heavens.

My attention was drawn again to the young man below me. He also gazed over the surrounding world, but with a keener scrutiny than mine—a gaze suggesting watchfulness, as if he were a castle guardian. Beneath the foreshortened curls of browning hair, his young body was clad in a green and yellow tunic; and on his metal belt hung a thick blade, hilted with coloured stones. He laid the spear upon a low wall, and toyed with the keen blade of this smaller weapon. I had thought both primitive, until it came to me that all battling must be afoot in this strange place, and from the walls of such a castle a sword might be very potently destructive.

In the vast sky there was no glitter of aeroplane, and only hunting birds glided above the forest. Otherwise, the swollen clouds were white. In this land were there none who had conquered the air? Were all men and all strongholds so near to barbarism?

The man in the courtyard disappeared, and dawn was forgotten by a molten sun. Unanswered, mystified, I left my room in search of the castle lord.

And so for three days I dwelt in the castle, sleeping in that arched room whose shadow is yet on me. In that time I found little explanation of my disturbing change. Roaming through dark halls, I found chambers as old as memory; overhung like all the castle and the land with the wraith of some enormous change. These rooms were furnished unendingly with chests, though they held only dust. Some were used as chairs and some as tables, though most of them were long disused. Apish hides concealed the floors, and there were a few decorative hangings of extreme age. The place had obviously been made to house a great multitude, but now the windowless rooms were given into the keeping of spiders.

I saw no books, but in a high room I found by torchlight the fragments of a damaged manuscript, written in unreadable characters. It bore no pictures and I was unable to discover anything familiar in the text. Of alien tongued warriors I saw many, but the two women did not reappear. So, alone, I peered from dizzy windows at hilly forest-land that rolled away to opalescent mist, and descended forgotten stairways where rubbish hampered my footsteps. There was much that I did not ever understand. The incongruities of this narrative are due only to my faulty comprehension, a situation so different from that which I had known. I was inarticulate and lost, as any savage taken from his tortuous jungle to a dazzling slave town.

When the third day came, I had grown somewhat accustomed to the strange place, and knew the names of the castle-lord and his great fortress, which was Yrn. But there was nothing to show me positively into what years I had come, or the nature of that land. And now I shall not know. The wood, the castle—and that greater thing which came after—these are only fragments in a great mosaic whose design is concealed. This much I know or have surmised. By the natural calendar of stars and forest-growth and other changing guides, I have tried to judge the century and year prevailing in that place of Tomorrow. And it is such that I hesitate to accept it, despite the weight of evidence. It is thrice farther from us than we are from the Thinite Kings of Egypt; it is deeper in the coming years than any past thing of which we have record.

Not centuries, but dozens of centuries barred me from my own world. There are things of great wonder to me, but none so terrible as this. I think that civilization sank to low ebb in that unknown span of years. Brought on by wars unchronicled, by some misty Armageddon of fire and battle and great lumbering machines, the lands and governments were broken into chaotic fragments of which this castle was a part. There must have been others like it, but of them I can only know a little. Countless subjects baffle me— there is so much that I desire to learn of that mysterious place now lost to me forever.

Whether even a guess of a hundred centuries is right, I do not know. Perhaps I underestimate—it may have been a thousand centuries away. Between that time and my own the fires of war spread over a mourning earth, and there were battles so great and terrible that a new Dark Age set in. Mankind slipped far in those years . . . perhaps he may not regain his old supremacy. That also is scribed in the unseen and unguessed volumes of coming things.

All traces of the city that I had known were gone. There were no ruins. No rustly girder or asphalt fragment remained to mark the town now buried underneath a settled wood. Knowledge of the intervening years depends upon the length of time in which a mutation can develop. The bird and hare which I saw (and whose aspect first set loose the roving of my fear) had altered subtly, but considerably. I do not, of course, have any evidence but that it was a local change. Under the new conditions of that vast, crouching forest, evolution may have quickened, so that in a relatively short period those variations might occur. Whatever the answer to this may be, is also a clue to the date of that age into which I was flung.

Some while ago I made a plan of the castle as it was. There were nearly sixty rooms, flanking long hallways, and they were above one another to the extent of three and sometimes five stories, with small tower-rooms. Most of these were empty, though at one time a great host must have quartered there. I found signs carved over certain doors, in the time-blackened wood; which gave me great wonder, for like the words of these people these were unknown. No trace of the English tongue has gone to them, who are our descendents and the inheritors of earth.

On this third day the lord of Yrn was absent when I rose, and I did not see him afterward. To him I came from the outside, and left as strangely. The mystery of my coming and disappearance must have been great to him. For neither time was I warned—abrupt and sudden, the change came, and I was flung through time and space and universes in the great transition.

There were steps leading to a northern tower, and I stood on these when it came to me a second time. At first I seemed to fall, as if the steps had slid beneath me, and a noise like breaking surf was in my ears. The stairs before me writhed; grew dim in a blur of floating colours. Then came a wave of darkness, and a shock that tore my vitals, wrenching each cell of my flesh. It was at once pain and ecstasy and terror. When it returned, all things merged before my sight, and a great radiance supplanted the hall and the many dark steps. A blur of light, as if some god crouched before me, so glorious that my eyes were dimmed. Vibrating, throbbing, this glow set up a curious rhythm which passed to my inmost tissue and was echoed there. I was enslaved by the pure and glowing energy of the hueless light. It was mightier than the power which churns out earth in the frail universe. My heart jerked dizzily, and I felt an expectant lightness. Then I was devoured by the live, hungry radiance, so that in the final vertigo of consciousness my body was distant and my flesh numb.

IV

Even Death May Die

I was caught up in the backwash of that incredible change. Like a swimmer in unknown waters, I was embraced by a moving wave. And upon the peak of that wave I was borne . . . carried into the heart of a black, unsailed ocean. Swiftly, I was swept into that sea, while the image of the castle swayed in my memory like a curtain in the breeze. And then, in a crescendo that was neither visual nor audient, the curtains of the universe rolled back, and before me was the stage upon which universes enact a brief, tragic drama.

Here, all the stars were changed. I was in some altered cosmos— the cosmos of future aeons, when not one star shall remain as we know it. It was hideous and stupefying to find no recognized orb in that realm. The night sky was great, larger than my vision could embrace, and everywhere about me was star-flecked darkness, and at my feet a chasm of night.

I say above and below, for these are terms that come to mind, but there were no true directions. My spirit swung as the hub of a radiating universe.

Freed of matter, I had become a naked consciousness; and this thing is wonderful. My body had passed to its own land, while my spirit, my intellect, my comprehension, dropped to the far abysses before it could return and join with flesh again. Only thus, you understand, could I have experienced the journey into that waiting Ultimate.

Gradually, I seemed to move—blown before a wind out of nowhere . . . and approach the clustered universes, shuddering with stars. To every side, fixed and still in the eternal night, they spread as I moved among them. And drifting ceaselessly, after a great period I found one thing which I had known; one spot dear and marked for me in the indifferent, half-forgotten years of Earth. Like a bubble of heated glass, our sun glowed small and red. And when I saw at last, within the unknown deeps that solar pinpoint, there revolved about it no longer any Earth. The worlds were gone, and our sun dead with the cool of night. Chasms sprawled where anciently green fields and cloud-strewn skies had shut away the ravenous black. Mankind was a dream, and the earth a bright, nostalgic memory. There was no record of how our world perished. Somewhere in the great maze a star winked out. Only that, and all of humanity was gone—the splendid dreams, the bravery of that race which I had known (long since) when it was young. Man, great, assured, and invincible, was now obliterated. For him a last sunset had dappled the orange sky, flared up in false dawning, and sunk at length to embers. Cold embers that no breath might requicken. The horror of that long-evaded Night had cast its shadow over Earth, and she was gone now. Her fragile vision of supremacy had been as naught; her gods and citadels, with all lovely things, gone. Perhaps, for a while after Man was dead such things as Egypt's pyramids endured for cenotaphs to the lost race. Perhaps, here and there about the dead world (now cold eternally, in the End of things) some traces of humanity survived a while.

Yet they all crumbled before the sun's death; and that great ember shot her last rays upon an empty land. Perhaps a few green things were left . . . a few toughened forms of earlier vegetation; plants and vines that struggled like reptiles to remain in the dim sunlight. These things may have been left—but Man was gone. The splendour of his race was forgotten, and the lordly trumpets mute. Then, when unmeasured centuries were done, earth had ceased, and her sun lingered briefly as a cinder, unmarked, in the blackness.

My position was alien and frightful. Lost forever and remote in a hallway of the gods, guided by no thing that man had seen, and facing the horror of the Inevitable, I knew no emotion that mixed ecstasy and terror, and yet other things for which there are no words. How I went from that place, for what centuries my brain was numb, I do not know, but in a time I saw again the unknown and hateful stars above me, glittering like the hoar on some rock-chiselled tomb in a silent land of snow and night.

Everywhere was the black abyss. A monstrousness that grew and burrowed through the cosmos, engulfing faint worlds and brittle suns; sundering and destroying them. A nighted area where Nothingness grew powerful on substance.

Eternities it swelled before me, until I saw that each of the strange new galaxies was vanishing. A last handful of stars melted away in gradual aeons. Reluctant, they went like guests at an ending banquet, until I was alone. Unaccompanied now, I drifted on that unknown ocean through which lay no chartered course; and where the ships of worlds had destroyed themselves on reefs of darkness. Brave, small voyagers, with no captain and no beckoning goal! Tiny wormish lights that crept awhile upon the fields . . . lights that were now forever extinguished.

So I was left in ages of black so great that only blindness might conceive it. It was not an absence of light . . . it was a tangible negation, an unending hue like the shadows of a demon wing. Or it was a crypt—the burial ground of forgotten orbs whose brief lives were glut in the maw of that triumphant abyss.

There would never anywhere again be worlds. I watched for centuries, conscious of this fact. Confronting me was the sum, the purpose and destiny of the galaxies that had spotted that void. My soul shrank from the cataclysm before me, and trembling my conscienceness waited; as if I sat before a darkened stage, seeking the rise of a curtain. But the comedy was played, and all the actors gone. Blank, hideous, supreme, devastating, the eternal naught remained.

I waited, beset with monstrous fancies. Then my searching eyes found a dim light swelling beyond the limit of vision. What it might be, or how far away, I could not tell. There were no worlds to judge by, no scale for measurement. But the light grew; and I saw it to be composed of many separate glowing objects. In that vast chasm their progress was torturingly slow, yet no comet might attain such a speed. It was only that their road was the road of eternity.

I could not, yet, distinguish what form the lights assumed. Was it a band of celestial vagrants? A lost group of wandering stars? There was no answer save only that which patience might bring. Then, for a little, I feared that I was not in the path of the approaching forms, dreaded that they might take a distant course. Gradually, however, they became clear. A band of racing lights, perhaps half a hundred of them. Lights only: hued in green and red and purple. Globular forms of *adhering vibration* . . . elementals. There were before me only the simple balls and that nothingness in which they moved. Pristine matter in a pristine cosmos. They had shape—the simplest; and substance. What that was is beyond ken. And they had colour. But there was no complexity, no kin in their forms to the forms of Earth.

The balls were living. As I watched, they grew tremendously, and shifted like phantasmal sea-things. How much of consciousness they had, I cannot guess. They lived and moved, but their sentience was too different from my own for one to comprehend the other.

Each ball gave off a faint glow, so that as they hung before me they made a coloured pool . . . a dancing, tossing mass of gem-hued radiance. It is hard to fit words to such alien things, and to such a sight. I was a mote in the great desolation. My world was gone, and with it, all worlds. Yet here before me, in the ultimate chill of a naked void, there clustered a group of living lights. Things from infinitely beyond Space; creatures from a place which no faltering word can make real. I feared them, not because they were evil-shaped, or because of their actions, but because they were great—for such greatness is terrible. There was more than fright upon me as I watched the globes at play. They built themselves in pyramids, and rapidly strung out, like a huge necklace athwart eternity. A myriad forms of unearthly geometry diverted them as they rolled and built, separated and shifted in kaleidoscopic array.

About this eerie tableau I felt a dreamful familiarity, as if I had known before the mad gyrations of those living colours. I wrenched a painful memory from darkness; plunged backward into a fearful mind, until I came upon this impression of that vari-coloured bubbling through which my awakening mind had seemed to fall, and first beheld the earthly forest, so long vanished.

Here, at the end of time, when all celestial landmarks were obliterated, when the very firmament had altered, was the same group of tossing colours on a million-fold scale. These playful monstrosities, whose very conception was perverse; gambolling in deformed symmetries, were akin to what I had seen in the land of unconsciousness.

Then, before I could know what ultimate goal the creatures might have, before I might comprehend that quest which led them across the fields of Infinity, an emotional illness came upon me, and I was sick in a dull, indescribable fashion, revolted by the wrongness of that lurking universe. Thus bitter and forlorn is that despair which awaits us.

As my mind turned—for I might not faint, having no body—it

was like seeing black cliffs rise and curve away overhead. I lost all sense of vision, and seemed pressed on every side by a buzzing darkness. Then, slowly, deliberately, everything wheeled about me, so that I hung like a perishing wretch upon the edge of a great chasm. A chasm deeper than the pits of hell, and more evil. Again, with swifter motion, my surroundings revolved; and then life became a series of hideous revolutions backward through time and space. I seemed to experience anew each joy and pain that I had ever known: again and yet again I lived a tortuous life, and the dark years sped in rhythm with a lurching cosmos.

Epilogue

I have begun, lately, to judge something of the force motivating my transition, and to gropingly conceive the nature of those . . . objects . . . inhabiting the lost void to which my dream bore me. Their cosmic errand is unknowable, as is the inconceivable dimension of their reeling, prismatic lair. They are, I believe, the dominating life-form, the ultimate inheritors of our universe. *Perhaps they even created it.* In a part of space lost past the reach of light-years; a place where the farthest comet never swings, these creatures have their world. A nighted world in no sense like our earth-wrought planets . . . a world upon the black Rim—a world that no mind can believe or even dimly picture. It must be a place of very wrong dimensions, existing in some alien eternity. I cannot hazard the nature of such a place, or know whether it be in the aeonian past or vague futurity. It was in only our small portion of infinity that I saw the evanescent forms of the master-things, journeying through galaxies as I might wander along a pebbled beach. But I do know this: that all the laws and barriers of our cosmos are as nothing to them, dwelling as they do in a realm oblique across eternity. For their purposes the master-things somehow turned aside the stream of years, diverted for a space the succession of ages from the rusty channel wherein they flow. And in that celestial maelstrom I was sucked, twisted about, so that when their Gargantuan play was over, I was flung from Time's unknown waters upon the rock-girt coast of alien years. From my own life I was caught up by a violating law, whose course left me for a little upon the future world, and then swept me to the far black reaches of God's infinity. My voyaging was lone and terrible. It took me past the chaos of suns and stars, beyond the nethermost limits of a perishing universe. And in the end I saw those Supreme entities, whose servants are the gods. They linked the end and origin of things, they formed a million-ruled universe as playground, and then set those rules aside.

My first transition was of flesh, but the other passes such material change. When I was swept into the naked and lonely Ultimate, it was as an ego, an intelligence, a consciousness. My flesh could bear the change and stress of thrice five hundred years, but it was for centuries that I swung in the unplumbed void. Years or centuries of aeons—I do not know. Yet it was for a very long while that I watched the symphony, the ecstasy and harmony, of the abyss-things. Visually, perhaps I was not absent at all from my own world. Perhaps I only *flickered* in existence; but in that time I saw a new land and a new universe. I spent a million years in space, or if you like, three days in the old castle.

I am told that I fainted on the street that morning and remained unconscious for some while. I was taken to my brother's home, and remained in a coma for several hours. During this time, my body scarcely held life . . . the pulse was dim and faint, the muscles limp as if I were newly dead. Then, before I woke, groaning as if in torment, I flailed my arms about in mysterious battle.

I know what happened in that time, and I shall tell what I am able. When I fell upon the pavement, I had *already* made the flight into a future world. I had experienced the imperceptible brief physical absence from the year and the world of my people. Yet my first transition, as I have said, was bodily; and the second one of soul, spirit, intelligence—call it what you will. I do not wish to indulge in spurious mysticism, for I merely seek the narration of a verity. So, you will understand that when my outward shape returned to 1936, to the month and day, perhaps to the second from which it came, the *other* component of my entity was swept immensely farther, parting wholly from my body, into the sucking whirlpool of time, whose flotsam is the stars. Into the great distances I went, to Infinity and her sheer end. It was ordained that, like a pendulum, my spirit must complete the far swing, where matter could not go. And thus for a while was my body returned, untenanted, to earth; while I knew the terrors of the abyss, and all the pain thereof.

But somehow more than to any other part of that adventure, my thoughts return to the old castle beyond an unknown wood. It is frightening to think that it will not be built for over fifteen thousand years, for I can remember the sunlight on the open court and the green deeps of that surrounding wood more clearly than this room in which I write. I lived in that castle when it had begun to crumble, and I felt the breeze come over swinging vines and old trees when I stood before the narrow window of my arched chamber. Yet my bones shall be wind-borne dust, and I shall have known rebirth in grass and flowers and dark roots, many centuries before masons lay trowel to the first stone of that edifice. The place where it will rise, in more than a dozen tens of centuries, is now an active city, with steel and glass and concrete walls that seem very permanent. But I know them as ephemera, for my eyes are haunted by the nocturnal wood, by the dark sunset of that land wherein I shall never again be. It saddens me to think of the bright sunshine and the fresh wind that will come long after I am worm-infested. Having seen it I know that in this world about me I can nevermore find zest, desire, or consolation.

But the room is growing chill, and I do not think that I shall write any more.

V. Tales of Pseudo-Science

The Diamond Lens

Fitz-James O'Brien

CHAPTER I

THE BENDING OF THE TWIG

From a very early period of my life the entire bent of my inclinations had been towards microscopic investigations. When I was not more than ten years old, a distant relative of our family, hoping to astonish my inexperience, constructed a simple microscope for me, by drilling in a disk of copper a small hole, in which a drop of pure water was sustained by capillary attraction. This very primitive apparatus, magnifying some fifty diameters, presented, it is true, only indistinct and imperfect forms, but still sufficiently wonderful to work up my imagination to a preternatural state of excitement.

Seeing me so interested in this rude instrument, my cousin explained to me all that he knew about the principles of the microscope, related to me a few of the wonders which had been accomplished through its agency, and ended by promising to send me one regularly constructed, immediately on his return to the city. I counted the days, the hours, the minutes, that intervened between that promise and his departure.

Meantime I was not idle. Every transparent substance that bore the remotest resemblance to a lens I eagerly seized upon, and employed in vain attempts to realize that instrument, the theory of whose construction I as yet only vaguely comprehended. All panes of glass containing those oblate spheroidal knots familiarly known as "bull's eyes" were ruthlessly destroyed, in the hope of obtaining lenses of marvellous power. I even went so far as to extract the crystalline humor from the eyes of fishes and animals, and endeavored to press it into the microscopic service. I plead guilty to having stolen the glasses from my Aunt Agatha's spectacles, with a dim idea of grinding them into lenses of wondrous magnifying properties,—in which attempt it is scarcely necessary to say that I totally failed.

At last the promised instrument came. It was of that order known as Field's simple microscope, and had cost perhaps about fifteen dollars. As far as educational purposes went, a better apparatus could not have been selected. Accompanying it was a small treatise on the microscope,—its history, uses, and discoveries. I comprehended then for the first time the "Arabian Nights Entertainments." The dull veil of ordinary existence that hung across the world seemed suddenly to roll away, and to lay bare a land of enchantments. I felt towards my companions as the seer might feel towards the ordinary masses of men. I held conversations with nature in a tongue which they could not understand. I was in daily communication with living wonders, such as they never imagined in their wildest visions. I penetrated beyond the external portal of things, and roamed through the sanctuaries. Where they beheld only a drop of rain slowly rolling down the window-glass, I saw a universe of beings animated with all the passions common to physical life, and convulsing their minute sphere with struggles as fierce and protracted as those of men. In the common spots of mould, which my mother, good housekeeper that she was, fiercely scooped away from her jam pots, there abode for me, under the name of mildew, enchanted gardens, filled with dells and avenues of the densest foliage and most astonishing verdure, while from the fantastic boughs of these microscopic forests hung strange fruits glittering with green, and silver, and gold.

It was no scientific thirst that at this time filled my mind. It was the pure enjoyment of a poet to whom a world of wonders has been disclosed. I talked of my solitary pleasures to none. Alone with my microscope, I dimmed my sight, day after day and night after night, poring over the marvels which it unfolded to me. I was like one who, having discovered the ancient Eden still existing in all its primitive glory, should resolve to enjoy it in solitude, and never betray to mortal the secret of its locality. The rod of my life was bent at this moment. I destined myself to be a microscopist.

Of course, like every novice, I fancied myself a discoverer. I was ignorant at the time of the thousands of acute intellects engaged in the same pursuit as myself, and with the advantage of instruments a thousand times more powerful than mine. The names of Leeuwenhoek, Williamson, Spencer, Ehrenberg, Schultz, Dujardin, Schact, and Schleiden were then entirely unknown to me, or if known, I was ignorant of their patient and wonderful researches. In every fresh specimen of cryptogamia which I placed beneath my instrument I believed that I discovered wonders of which the world was as yet ignorant. I remember well the thrill of delight and admiration that shot through me the first time that I discovered the common wheel animalcule *(Rotifera vulgaris)* expanding and contracting its flexible spokes, and seemingly rotating through the water. Alas! as I grew older, and obtained some works treating of my favorite study, I found that I was only on the threshold of a science to the investigation of which some of the greatest men of the age were devoting their lives and intellects.

As I grew up, my parents, who saw but little likelihood of anything practical resulting from the examination of bits of moss and drops of water through a brass tube and a piece of glass, were anxious that I should choose a profession. It was their desire that I should enter the counting-house of my uncle, Ethan Blake, a prosperous merchant, who carried on business in New York. This suggestion I decisively combated. I had no taste for trade; I should only make a failure; in short, I refused to become a merchant.

But it was necessary for me to select some pursuit. My parents were staid New England people, who insisted on the necessity of labor; and therefore, although, thanks to the bequest of my poor Aunt Agatha, I should, on coming of age, inherit a small fortune sufficient to place me above want, it was decided that, instead of waiting for this, I should act the nobler part, and employ the intervening years in rendering myself independent.

After much cogitation I complied with the wishes of my family, and selected a profession. I determined to study medicine at the New York Academy. This disposition of my future suited me. A removal from my relatives would enable me to dispose of my time as I pleased without fear of detection. As long as I paid my Academy fees, I might shirk attending the lectures if I chose; and, as I never had the remotest intention of standing an examination, there was no danger of my being "plucked." Besides, a metropolis was the place for me. There I could obtain excellent instruments, the newest publications, intimacy with men of pursuits kindred with my own,—in short, all things necessary to insure a profitable devotion of my life to my beloved science. I had an abundance of money, few desires that were not bounded by my illuminating mirror on one side and my object-glass on the other; what, therefore, was to prevent my becoming an illustrious investigator of the veiled worlds? It was with the most buoyant hope that I left my New England home and established myself in New York.

CHAPTER II

THE LONGING OF A MAN OF SCIENCE

My first step, of course, was to find suitable apartments. These I obtained, after a couple of days' search, in Fourth Avenue; a very pretty second-floor unfurnished, containing sitting-room, bedroom, and a smaller apartment which I intended to fit up as a laboratory. I furnished my lodgings simply, but rather elegantly, and then devoted all my energies to the adornment of the temple of my worship. I visited Pike, the celebrated optician, and passed in review his splendid collection of microscopes,—Field's Compound, Hingham's, Spencer's, Nachet's Binocular (that founded on the principles of the stereoscope), and at length fixed upon that form known as Spencer's Trunnion Microscope, as combining the greatest number of improvements with an almost perfect freedom from tremor. Along with this I purchased every possible accessory,— draw-tubes, micrometers, a *camera-lucida,* lever-stage, achromatic condensers, white cloud illuminators, prisms, parabolic condensers, polarizing apparatus, forceps, aquatic boxes, fishing-tubes, with a host of other articles, all of which would have been useful in the hands of an experienced microscopist, but, as I afterwards discovered, were not of the slightest present value to me. It takes years of practice to know how to use a complicated microscope. The optician looked suspiciously at me as I made these wholesale purchases. He evidently was uncertain whether to set me down as some scientific celebrity or a madman. I think he inclined to the latter belief. I suppose I was mad. Every great genius is mad upon the subject in which he is greatest. The unsuccessful madman is disgraced and called a lunatic.

Mad or not, I set myself to work with a zeal which few scientific students have ever equalled. I had everything to learn relative to the delicate study upon which I had embarked,—a study involving the most earnest patience, the most rigid analytic powers, the steadiest hand, the most untiring eye, the most refined and subtile manipulation.

For a long time half my apparatus lay inactively on the shelves of my laboratory, which was now most amply furnished with every possible contrivance for facilitating my investigations. The fact was that I did not know how to use some of my scientific implements,— never having been taught microscopics,—and those whose use I understood theoretically were of little avail, until by practice I could attain the necessary delicacy of handling. Still, such was the fury of my ambition, such the untiring perseverance of my experiments, that, difficult of credit as it may be, in the course of one year I became theoretically and practically an accomplished microscopist.

During this period of my labors, in which I submitted specimens of every substance that came under my observation to the action of my lenses, I became a discoverer,—in a small way, it is true, for I was very young, but still a discoverer. It was I who destroyed Ehrenberg's theory that the *Volvox globator* was an animal, and proved that his "monads" with stomachs and eyes were merely phases of the formation of a vegetable cell, and were, when they reached their mature state, incapable of the act of conjugation, or any true generative act, without which no organism rising to any stage of life higher than vegetable can be said to be complete. It was I who resolved the singular problem of rotation in cells and hairs of plants into ciliary attraction, in spite of the assertions of Mr. Wenham and others, that my explanation was the result of an optical illusion.

But notwithstanding these discoveries, laboriously and painfully made as they were, I felt horribly dissatisfied. At every step I found myself stopped by the imperfections of my instruments. Like all active microscopists, I gave my imagination full play. Indeed, it is a common complaint against many such, that they supply the defects of their instruments with the creations of their brains. I imagined depths beyond depths in nature which the limited power of my lenses prohibited me from exploring. I lay awake at night constructing imaginary microscopes of immeasurable power, with which I seemed to pierce through all the envelopes of matter down to its original atom. How I cursed those imperfect mediums which necessity through ignorance compelled me to use! How I longed to discover the secret of some perfect lens, whose magnifying power should be limited only by the resolvability of the object, and which at the same time should be free from spherical and chromatic aberrations, in short from all the obstacles over which the poor microscopist finds himself continually stumbling! I felt convinced that the simple microscope, composed of a single lens of such vast yet perfect power was possible of construction. To attempt to bring the compound microscope up to such a pitch would have been commencing at the wrong end; this latter being simply a partially successful endeavor to remedy those very defects of the simple instrument, which, if conquered, would leave nothing to be desired.

It was in this mood of mind that I became a constructive microscopist. After another year passed in this new pursuit, experimenting on every imaginable substance,—glass, gems, flints, crystals, artificial crystals formed of the alloy of various vitreous materials,—in short, having constructed as many varieties of lenses as Argus had eyes, I found myself precisely where I started, with nothing gained save an extensive knowledge of glass-making. I was almost dead with despair. My parents were surprised at my apparent want of progress in my medical studies, (I had not attended one lecture since my arrival in the city,) and the expenses of my mad pursuit had been so great as to embarrass me very seriously.

I was in this frame of mind one day, experimenting in my laboratory on a small diamond,—that stone, from its great refracting power, having always occupied my attention more than any other,—when a young Frenchman, who lived on the floor above me, and who was in the habit of occasionally visiting me, entered the room.

I think that Jules Simon was a Jew. He had many traits of the Hebrew character: a love of jewelry, of dress, and of good living. There was something mysterious about him. He always had something to sell, and yet went into excellent society. When I say sell, I should perhaps have said peddle; for his operations were generally confined to the disposal of single articles,—a picture, for instance, or a rare carving in ivory, or a pair of duelling-pistols, or the dress of a Mexican *caballero.* When I was first furnishing my rooms, he paid me a visit, which ended in my purchasing an antique silver lamp, which he assured me was a Cellini,—it was handsome enough even for that,—and some other knickknacks for my sitting-room. Why Simon should pursue this petty trade I never could imagine. He apparently had plenty of money, and had the *entrée* of the best houses in the city,—taking care, however, I suppose, to drive no bargains within the enchanted circle of the Upper Ten. I came at length to the conclusion that this peddling was but a mask to cover some greater object, and even went so far as to believe my young acquaintance to be implicated in the slave-trade. That, however, was none of my affair.

On the present occasion, Simon entered my room in a state of considerable excitement.

"*Ah! mon ami!*" he cried, before I could even offer him the ordinary salutation, "it has occurred to me to be the witness of the most astonishing things in the world. I promenade myself to the house of Madame—— How does the little animal—*le renard*—name himself in the Latin?"

"Vulpes," I answered.

"Ah! yes,—Vulpes. I promenade myself to the house of Madame Vulpes."

"The spirit medium?"

"Yes, the great medium. Great heavens! what a woman! I write on a slip of paper many of questions concerning affairs the most secret,—affairs that conceal themselves in the abysses of my heart the most profound; and behold! by example! what occurs? This devil of a woman makes me replies the most truthful to all of them. She talks to me of things that I do not love to talk of to myself. What am I to think? I am fixed to the earth!"

"Am I to understand you, M. Simon, that this Mrs. Vulpes replied to questions secretly written by you, which questions related to events known only to yourself?"

"Ah! more than that, more than that," he answered, with an air of some alarm. "She related to me things—But," he added, after a pause, and suddenly changing his manner, "why occupy ourselves with these follies? It was all the biology, without doubt. It goes without saying that it has not my credence.—But why are we here, *mon ami?* It has occurred to me to discover the most beautiful thing as you can imagine,—a vase with green lizards on it, composed by the great Bernard Palissy. It is in my apartment; let us mount. I go to show it to you."

I followed Simon mechanically; but my thoughts were far from Palissy and his enamelled ware, although I, like him, was seeking in the dark a great discovery. This casual mention of the spiritualist, Madame Vulpes, set me on a new track. What if this spiritualism should be really a great fact? What if, through communication with more subtile organisms than my own, I could reach at a single bound the goal, which perhaps a life of agonizing mental toil would never enable me to attain?

While purchasing the Palissy vase from my friend Simon, I was mentally arranging a visit to Madame Vulpes.

CHAPTER III

THE SPIRIT OF LEEUWENHOEK

Two evenings after this, thanks to an arrangement by letter and the promise of an ample fee, I found Madame Vulpes awaiting me at her residence alone. She was a coarse-featured woman, with keen and rather cruel dark eyes, and an exceedingly sensual expression about her mouth and under jaw. She received me in perfect silence, in an apartment on the ground floor, very sparely furnished. In the centre of the room, close to where Mrs. Vulpes sat, there was a common round mahogany table. If I had come for the purpose of sweeping her chimney, the woman could not have looked more indifferent to my appearance. There was no attempt to inspire the visitor with awe. Everything bore a simple and practical aspect. This intercourse with the spiritual world was evidently as familiar an occupation with Mrs. Vulpes as eating her dinner or riding in an omnibus.

"You come for a communication, Mr. Linley?" said the medium, in a dry, business-like tone of voice.

"By appointment,—yes."

"What sort of communication do you want?—a written one?"

"Yes,—I wish for a written one."

"From any particular spirit?"

"Yes."

"Have you ever known this spirit on this earth?"

"Never. He died long before I was born. I wish merely to obtain from him some information which he ought to be able to give better than any other."

"Will you seat yourself at the table, Mr. Linley," said the medium, "and place your hands upon it?"

I obeyed,—Mrs. Vulpes being seated opposite to me, with her hands also on the table. We remained thus for about a minute and a half, when a violent succession of raps came on the table, on the back of my chair, on the floor immediately under my feet, and even on the windowpanes. Mrs. Vulpes smiled composedly.

"They are very strong to-night," she remarked. "You are fortunate." She then continued, "Will the spirits communicate with this gentleman?"

Vigorous affirmative.

"Will the particular spirit he desires to speak with communicate?"

A very confused rapping followed this question.

"I know what they mean," said Mrs. Vulpes, addressing herself to me; "they wish you to write down the name of the particular spirit that you desire to converse with. Is that so?" she added, speaking to her invisible guests.

That it was so was evident from the numerous affirmatory responses. While this was going on, I tore a slip from my pocket-book, and scribbled a name, under the table.

"Will this spirit communicate in writing with this gentleman?" asked the medium once more.

After a moment's pause, her hand seemed to be seized with a violent tremor, shaking so forcibly that the table vibrated. She said that a spirit had seized her hand and would write. I handed her some sheets of paper that were on the table, and a pencil. The latter she held loosely in her hand, which presently began to move over the paper with a singular and seemingly involuntary motion. After a few moments had elapsed, she handed me the paper, on which I found written, in a large, uncultivated hand, the words, "He is not here, but has been sent for." A pause of a minute or so now ensued, during which Mrs. Vulpes remained perfectly silent, but the raps continued at regular intervals. When the short period I mention had elapsed, the hand of the medium was again seized with its convulsive tremor, and she wrote, under this strange influence, a few words on the paper, which she handed to me. They were as follows:—

"I am here. Question me.
"LEEUWENHOEK."

I was astounded. The name was identical with that I had written beneath the table, and carefully kept concealed. Neither was it at all probable that an uncultivated woman like Mrs. Vulpes should know even the name of the great father of microscopics. It may have been biology; but this theory was soon doomed to be destroyed. I wrote on my slip—still concealing it from Mrs. Vulpes—a series of questions, which, to avoid tediousness, I shall place with the responses, in the order in which they occurred:—

I.—Can the microscope be brought to perfection?

SPIRIT.—Yes.

I.—Am I destined to accomplish this great task?

SPIRIT.—You are.

I.—I wish to know how to proceed to attain this end. For the love which you bear to science, help me!

SPIRIT.—A diamond of one hundred and forty carats, submitted to electro-magnetic currents for a long period, will experience a rearrangement of its atoms *inter se,* and from that stone you will form the universal lens.

I.—Will great discoveries result from the use of such a lens?

SPIRIT.—So great that all that has gone before is as nothing.

I.—But the refractive power of the diamond is so immense, that the image will be formed within the lens. How is that difficulty to be surmounted?

SPIRIT.—Pierce the lens through its axis, and the difficulty is obviated. The image will be formed in the pierced space, which will itself serve as a tube to look through. Now I am called. Good night.

I cannot at all describe the effect that these extraordinary communications had upon me. I felt completely bewildered. No biological theory could account for the *discovery* of the lens. The medium might, by means of biological *rapport* with my mind, have gone so far as to read my questions, and reply to them coherently. But biology could not enable her to discover that magnetic currents would so alter the crystals of the diamond as to remedy its previous defects, and admit of its being polished into a perfect lens. Some such theory may have passed through my head, it is true; but if so, I had forgotten it. In my excited condition of mind there was no course left but to become a convert, and it was in a state of the most painful nervous exaltation that I left the medium's house that evening. She accompanied me to the door, hoping that I was satisfied. The raps followed us as we went through the hall, sounding on the balusters, the flooring, and even the lintels of the door. I hastily expressed my satisfaction, and escaped hurriedly into the cool night air. I walked home with but one thought possessing me,—how to obtain a diamond of the immense size required. My entire means multiplied a hundred times over would have been inadequate to its purchase. Besides, such stones are rare, and become historical. I could find such only in the regalia of Eastern or European monarchs.

CHAPTER IV

THE EYE OF MORNING

There was a light in Simon's room as I entered my house. A vague impulse urged me to visit him. As I opened the door of his sitting-room unannounced, he was bending, with his back toward me, over a carcel lamp, apparently engaged in minutely examining some object which he held in his hands. As I entered, he started suddenly, thrust his hand into his breast pocket, and turned to me with a face crimson with confusion.

"What!" I cried, "poring over the miniature of some fair lady? Well, don't blush so much; I won't ask to see it."

Simon laughed awkwardly enough, but made none of the negative protestations usual on such occasions. He asked me to take a seat.

"Simon," said I, "I have just come from Madame Vulpes."

This time Simon turned as white as a sheet, and seemed stupefied, as if a sudden electric shock had smitten him. He babbled some incoherent words, and went hastily to a small closet where he usually kept his liquors. Although astonished at his emotion, I was too preoccupied with my own idea to pay much attention to anything else.

"You say truly when you call Madame Vulpes a devil of a woman," I continued. "Simon, she told me wonderful things to-night, or rather was the means of telling me wonderful things. Ah! if I could only get a diamond that weighed one hundred and forty carats!"

Scarcely had the sigh with which I uttered this desire died upon my lips, when Simon, with the aspect of a wild beast, glared at me savagely, and, rushing to the mantelpiece, where some foreign weapons hung on the wall, caught up a Malay creese, and brandished it furiously before him.

"No!" he cried in French, into which he always broke when excited. "No! you shall not have it! You are perfidious! You have consulted with that demon, and desire my treasure! But I shall die first! Me! I am brave! You cannot make me fear!"

All this, uttered in a loud voice trembling with excitement, astounded me. I saw at a glance that I had accidentally trodden upon the edges of Simon's secret, whatever it was. It was necessary to reassure him.

"My dear Simon," I said, "I am entirely at a loss to know what you mean. I went to Madame Vulpes to consult her on a scientific problem, to the solution of which I discovered that a diamond of the size I just mentioned was necessary. You were never alluded to during the evening, nor, so far as I was concerned, even thought of. What can be the meaning of this outburst? If you happen to have a set of valuable diamonds in your possession, you need fear nothing from me. The diamond which I require you could not possess; or, if you did possess it, you would not be living here."

Something in my tone must have completely reassured him; for his expression immediately changed to a sort of constrained merriment, combined, however, with a certain suspicious attention to my movements. He laughed, and said that I must bear with him; that he was at certain moments subject to a species of vertigo, which betrayed itself in incoherent speeches, and that the attacks passed off as rapidly as they came. He put his weapon aside while making this explanation, and endeavored, with some success, to assume a more cheerful air.

All this did not impose on me in the least. I was too much accustomed to analytical labors to be baffled by so flimsy a veil. I determined to probe the mystery to the bottom.

"Simon," I said, gayly, "let us forget all this over a bottle of Burgundy. I have a case of Lausseure's *Clos Vougeot* down-stairs, fragrant with the odors and ruddy with the sunlight of the Côte d'Or. Let us have up a couple of bottles. What say you?"

"With all my heart," answered Simon, smilingly.

I produced the wine and we seated ourselves to drink. It was of a famous vintage, that of 1848, a year when war and wine throve together,—and its pure but powerful juice seemed to impart renewed vitality to the system. By the time we had half finished the second bottle, Simon's head, which I knew was a weak one, had begun to yield, while I remained calm as ever, only that every draught seemed to send a flush of vigor through my limbs. Simon's utterance became more and more indistinct. He took to singing French *chansons* of a not very moral tendency. I rose suddenly from the table just at the conclusion of one of those incoherent verses, and fixing my eyes on him with a quiet smile, said: "Simon, I have deceived you. I learned your secret this evening. You may as well be frank with me. Mrs. Vulpes, or rather one of her spirits, told me all."

He started with horror. His intoxication seemed for the moment to fade away, and he made a movement towards the weapon that he had a short time before laid down. I stopped him with my hand.

"Monster," he cried, passionately, "I am ruined! What shall I do? You shall never have it! I swear by my mother!"

"I don't want it," I said; "rest secure, but be frank with me. Tell me all about it."

The drunkenness began to return. He protested with maudlin earnestness that I was entirely mistaken,—that I was intoxicated; then asked me to swear eternal secrecy, and promised to disclose the mystery to me. I pledged myself, of course, to all. With an uneasy look in his eyes, and hands unsteady with drink and nervousness, he drew a small case from his breast and opened it. Heavens! How the mild lamp-light was shivered into a thousand prismatic arrows, as it fell upon a vast rose-diamond that glittered in the case! I was no judge of diamonds, but I saw at a glance that this was a gem of rare size and purity. I looked at Simon with wonder, and—must I confess it?—with envy. How could he have obtained this treasure? In reply to my questions, I could just gather from his drunken statements (of which, I fancy, half the incoherence was affected) that he had been superintending a gang of slaves engaged in diamond-washing in Brazil; that he had seen one of them secrete a diamond, but, instead of informing his employers, had quietly watched the negro until he saw him bury his treasure; that he had dug it up and fled with it, but that as yet he was afraid to attempt to dispose of it publicly,—so valuable a gem being almost certain to attract too much attention to its owner's antecedents,—and he had not been able to discover any of those obscure channels by which such matters are conveyed away safely. He added, that, in accordance with the oriental practice, he had named his diamond with the fanciful title of "The Eye of Morning."

While Simon was relating this to me, I regarded the great diamond attentively. Never had I beheld anything so beautiful. All the glories of light, ever imagined or described, seemed to pulsate in its crystalline chambers. Its weight, as I learned from Simon, was exactly one hundred and forty carats. Here was an amazing coincidence. The hand of destiny seemed in it. On the very evening when the spirit of Leeuwenhoek communicates to me the great secret of the microscope, the priceless means which he directs me to employ start up within my easy reach! I determined, with the most perfect deliberation, to possess myself of Simon's diamond.

I sat opposite to him while he nodded over his glass, and calmly revolved the whole affair. I did not for an instant contemplate so foolish an act as a common theft, which would of course be discovered, or at least necessitate flight and concealment, all of which must interfere with my scientific plans. There was but one step to be taken,—to kill Simon. After all, what was the life of a little peddling Jew, in comparison with the interests of science? Human beings are taken every day from the condemned prisons to be experimented on by surgeons. This man, Simon, was by his own confession a criminal, a robber, and I believed on my soul a murderer. He deserved death quite as much as any felon condemned by the laws: why should I not, like government, contrive that his punishment should contribute to the progress of human knowledge?

The means for accomplishing everything I desired lay within my reach. There stood upon the mantelpiece a bottle half full of French laudanum. Simon was so occupied with his diamond, which I had just restored to him, that it was an affair of no difficulty to drug his glass. In a quarter of an hour he was in a profound sleep.

I now opened his waistcoat, took the diamond from the inner pocket in which he had placed it, and removed him to the bed, on which I laid him so that his feet hung down over the edge. I had possessed myself of the Malay creese, which I held in my right hand, while with the other I discovered as accurately as I could by pulsation the exact locality of the heart. It was essential that all the aspects of his death should lead to the surmise of self-murder. I calculated the exact angle at which it was probable that the weapon, if levelled by Simon's own hand, would enter his breast; then with one powerful blow I thrust it up to the hilt in the very spot which I desired to penetrate. A convulsive thrill ran through Simon's limbs. I heard a smothered sound issue from his throat, precisely like the bursting of a large air-bubble, sent up by a diver, when it reaches the surface of the water; he turned half round on his side, and, as if to assist my plans more effectually, his right hand, moved by some mere spasmodic impulse, clasped the handle of the creese, which it remained holding with extraordinary muscular tenacity. Beyond this there was no apparent struggle. The laudanum, I presume, paralyzed the usual nervous action. He must have died instantly.

There was yet something to be done. To make it certain that all suspicion of the act should be diverted from any inhabitant of the house to Simon himself, it was necessary that the door should be found in the morning *locked on the inside.* How to do this, and afterwards escape myself? Not by the window; that was a physical impossibility. Besides, I was determined that the windows *also* should be found bolted. The solution was simple enough. I descended softly to my own room for a peculiar instrument which I had used for holding small slippery substances, such as minute spheres of glass, etc. This instrument was nothing more than a long slender hand-vice, with a very powerful grip, and a considerable leverage, which last was accidentally owing to the shape of the handle. Nothing was simpler than, when the key was in the lock, to seize the end of its stem in this vice, through the keyhole, from the outside, and so lock the door. Previously, however, to doing this, I burned a number of papers on Simon's hearth. Suicides almost always burn papers before they destroy themselves. I also emptied some more laudanum into Simon's glass,—having first removed from it all traces of wine,—cleaned the other wine-glass, and brought the bottles away with me. If traces of two persons drinking had been found in the room, the question naturally would have arisen, Who was the second? Besides, the wine-bottles might have been identified as belonging to me. The laudanum I poured out to account for its presence in his stomach, in case of a *post-mortem* examination. The theory naturally would be, that he first intended to poison himself, but, after swallowing a little of the drug, was either disgusted with its taste, or changed his mind from other motives, and chose the dagger. These arrangements made, I walked out, leaving the gas burning, locked the door with my vice, and went to bed.

Simon's death was not discovered until nearly three in the afternoon. The servant, astonished at seeing the gas burning,—the light

streaming on the dark landing from under the door,—peeped
through the keyhole and saw Simon on the bed. She gave the alarm.
The door was burst open, and the neighborhood was in a fever of
excitement.

Every one in the house was arrested, myself included. There was
an inquest; but no clew to his death beyond that of suicide could be
obtained. Curiously enough, he had made several speeches to his
friends the preceding week, that seemed to point to self-destruction.
One gentleman swore that Simon had said in his presence that "he
was tired of life." His landlord affirmed that Simon, when paying
him his last month's rent, remarked that "he should not pay him rent
much longer." All the other evidence corresponded,—the door
locked inside, the position of the corpse, the burnt papers. As I
anticipated, no one knew of the possession of the diamond by
Simon, so that no motive was suggested for his murder. The jury,
after a prolonged examination, brought in the usual verdict, and the
neighborhood once more settled down into its accustomed quiet.

CHAPTER V

ANIMULA

The three months succeeding Simon's catastrophe I devoted
night and day to my diamond lens. I had constructed a vast galvanic
battery, composed of nearly two thousand pairs of plates,—a higher
power I dared not use, lest the diamond should be calcined. By
means of this enormous engine I was enabled to send a powerful
current of electricity continually through my great diamond, which
it seemed to me gained in lustre every day. At the expiration of a
month I commenced the grinding and polishing of the lens, a work
of intense toil and exquisite delicacy. The great density of the stone,
and the care required to be taken with the curvatures of the sur-
faces of the lens, rendered the labor the severest and most harassing
that I had yet undergone.

At last the eventful moment came; the lens was completed. I stood
trembling on the threshold of new worlds. I had the realization of
Alexander's famous wish before me. The lens lay on the table,
ready to be placed upon its platform. My hand fairly shook as I
enveloped a drop of water with a thin coating of oil of turpentine,

preparatory to its examination,—a process necessary in order to prevent the rapid evaporation of the water. I now placed the drop on a thin slip of glass under the lens, and throwing upon it, by the combined aid of a prism and a mirror, a powerful stream of light, I approached my eye to the minute hold drilled through the axis of the lens. For an instant I saw nothing save what seemed to be an illuminated chaos, a vast luminous abyss. A pure white light, cloudless and serene, and seemingly limitless as space itself, was my first impression. Gently, and with the greatest care, I depressed the lens a few hair's-breadths. The wondrous illumination still continued, but as the lens approached the object a scene of indescribable beauty was unfolded to my view.

I seemed to gaze upon a vast space, the limits of which extended far beyond my vision. An atmosphere of magical luminousness permeated the entire field of view. I was amazed to see no trace of animalculous life. Not a living thing, apparently, inhabited that dazzling expanse. I comprehended instantly that, by the wondrous power of my lens, I had penetrated beyond the grosser particles of aqueous matter, beyond the realms of infusoria and protozoa, down to the original gaseous globule, into whose luminous interior I was gazing, as into an almost boundless dome filled with a supernatural radiance.

It was, however, no brilliant void into which I looked. On every side I beheld beautiful inorganic forms, of unknown texture, and colored with the most enchanting hues. These forms presented the appearance of what might be called, for want of a more specific definition, foliated clouds of the highest rarity; that is, they undulated and broke into vegetable formations, and were tinged with splendors compared with which the gilding of our autumn woodlands is as dross compared with gold. Far away into the illimitable distance stretched long avenues of these gaseous forests, dimly transparent, and painted with prismatic hues of unimaginable brilliancy. The pendent branches waved along the fluid glades until every vista seemed to break through half-lucent ranks of many-colored drooping silken pennons. What seemed to be either fruits or flowers, pied with a thousand hues, lustrous and ever varying, bubbled from the crowns of this fairy foliage. No hills, no lakes, no rivers, no forms animate or inanimate, were to be seen, save those vast auroral copses that floated serenely in the luminous stillness, with leaves and fruits and flowers gleaming with unknown fires, unrealizable by mere imagination.

How strange, I thought, that this sphere should be thus condemned to solitude! I had hoped, at least, to discover some new form of animal life,—perhaps of a lower class than any with which we are at present acquainted, but still, some living organism. I found my newly discovered world, if I may so speak, a beautiful chromatic desert.

While I was speculating on the singular arrangements of the internal economy of Nature, with which she so frequently splinters into atoms our most compact theories, I thought I beheld a form moving slowly through the glades of one of the prismatic forests. I looked more attentively, and found that I was not mistaken. Words cannot depict the anxiety with which I awaited the nearer approach of this mysterious object. Was it merely some inanimate substance, held in suspense in the attenuated atmosphere of the globule? or was it an animal endowed with vitality and motion? It approached, flitting behind the gauzy, colored veils of cloud-foliage, for seconds dimly revealed, then vanishing. At last the violet pennons that trailed nearest to me vibrated; they were gently pushed aside, and the form floated out into the broad light.

It was a female human shape. When I say human, I mean it possessed the outlines of humanity,—but there the analogy ends. Its adorable beauty lifted it illimitable heights beyond the loveliest daughter of Adam.

I cannot, I dare not, attempt to inventory the charms of this divine revelation of perfect beauty. Those eyes of mystic violet, dewy and serene, evade my words. Her long, lustrous hair following her glorious head in a golden wake, like the track sown in heaven by a falling star, seems to quench my most burning phrases with its splendors. If all the bees of Hybla nestled upon my lips, they would still sing but hoarsely the wondrous harmonies of outline that enclosed her form.

She swept out from between the rainbow-curtains of the cloud-trees into the broad sea of light that lay beyond. Her motions were those of some graceful naiad, cleaving, by a mere effort of her will, the clear, unruffled waters that fill the chambers of the sea. She floated forth with the serene grace of a frail bubble ascending through the still atmosphere of a June day. The perfect roundness of her limbs formed suave and enchanting curves. It was like listening to the most spiritual symphony of Beethoven the divine, to watch the harmonious flow of lines. This, indeed, was a pleasure cheaply purchased at any price. What cared I, if I had waded to the portal of this wonder through another's blood? I would have given my own to enjoy one such moment of intoxication and delight.

Breathless with gazing on this lovely wonder, and forgetful for an instant of everything save her presence, I withdrew my eye from the microscope eagerly,—alas! As my gaze fell on the thin slide that lay beneath my instrument, the bright light from mirror and from prism sparkled on a colorless drop of water! There, in that tiny bead of dew, this beautiful being was forever imprisoned. The planet Neptune was not more distant from me than she. I hastened once more to apply my eye to the microscope.

Animula (let me now call her by that dear name which I subsequently bestowed on her) had changed her position. She had again approached the wondrous forest, and was gazing earnestly upwards. Presently one of the trees—as I must call them—unfolded a long ciliary process, with which it seized one of the gleaming fruits that glittered on its summit, and, sweeping slowly down, held it within reach of Animula. The sylph took it in her delicate hand and began to eat. My attention was so entirely absorbed by her, that I could not apply myself to the task of determining whether this singular plant was or was not instinct with volition.

I watched her, as she made her repast, with the most profound attention. The suppleness of her motions sent a thrill of delight through my frame; my heart beat madly as she turned her beautiful eyes in the direction of the spot in which I stood. What would I not have given to have had the power to precipitate myself into that luminous ocean, and float with her through those groves of purple and gold! While I was thus breathlessly following her every movement, she suddenly started, seemed to listen for a moment, and then cleaving the brilliant ether in which she was floating, like a flash of light, pierced through the opaline forest, and disappeared.

Instantly a series of the most singular sensations attacked me. It seemed as if I had suddenly gone blind. The luminous sphere was still before me, but my daylight had vanished. What caused this sudden disappearance? Had she a lover or a husband? Yes, that was the solution! Some signal from a happy fellow-being had vibrated through the avenues of the forest, and she had obeyed the summons.

The agony of my sensations, as I arrived at this conclusion, startled me. I tried to reject the conviction that my reason forced upon me. I battled against the fatal conclusion,—but in vain. It was so. I had no escape from it. I loved an animalcule!

It is true that, thanks to the marvellous power of my microscope, she appeared of human proportions. Instead of presenting the revolting aspect of the coarser creatures, that live and struggle and die, in the more easily resolvable portions of the water-drop, she was fair and delicate and of surpassing beauty. But of what account was all that? Every time that my eye was withdrawn from the instrument, it fell on a miserable drop of water, within which, I must be content to know, dwelt all that could make my life lovely.

Could she but see me once! Could I for one moment pierce the mystical walls that so inexorably rose to separate us, and whisper all that filled my soul, I might consent to be satisfied for the rest of my life with the knowledge of her remote sympathy. It would be something to have established even the faintest personal link to bind us together,—to know that at times, when roaming through those enchanted glades, she might think of the wonderful stranger, who had broken the monotony of her life with his presence, and left a gentle memory in her heart!

But it could not be. No invention of which human intellect was capable could break down the barriers that nature had erected. I might feast my soul upon her wondrous beauty, yet she must always remain ignorant of the adoring eyes that day and night gazed upon her, and, even when closed, beheld her in dreams. With a bitter cry of anguish I fled from the room, and, flinging myself on my bed, sobbed myself to sleep like a child.

CHAPTER VI

THE SPILLING OF THE CUP

I arose the next morning almost at daybreak, and rushed to my microscope. I trembled as I sought the luminous world in miniature that contained my all. Animula was there. I had left the gas-lamp, surrounded by its moderators, burning, when I went to bed the night before. I found the sylph bathing, as it were, with an expression of pleasure animating her features, in the brilliant light which surrounded her. She tossed her lustrous golden hair over her shoulders with innocent coquetry. She lay at full length in the transparent medium, in which she supported herself with ease, and gambolled with the enchanting grace that the nymph Salmacis might have exhibited when she sought to conquer the modest Hermaphroditus. I tried an experiment to satisfy myself if her powers of reflection were developed. I lessened the lamp-light considerably. By the dim light that remained, I could see an expression of pain flit across her face. She looked upward suddenly, and her brows contracted. I flooded the stage of the microscope again with a full stream of light, and her whole expression changed. She sprang forward like some substance deprived of all weight. Her eyes sparkled and her lips moved. Ah! if science had only the means of conducting and reduplicating sounds, as it does the rays of light, what carols of happiness would then have entranced my ears! what jubilant hymns to Adonïs would have thrilled the illumined air!

I now comprehended how it was that the Count de Gabalis peopled his mystic world with sylphs,—beautiful beings whose breath of life was lambent fire, and who sported forever in regions of purest ether and purest light. The Rosicrucian had anticipated the wonder that I had practically realized.

How long this worship of my strange divinity went on thus I scarcely know. I lost all note of time. All day from early dawn, and far into the night, I was to be found peering through that wonderful lens. I saw no one, went nowhere, and scarce allowed myself sufficient time for my meals. My whole life was absorbed in contemplation as rapt as that of any of the Romish saints. Every hour that I gazed upon the divine form strengthened my passion,—a passion that was always overshadowed by the maddening conviction, that, although I could gaze on her at will, she never, never could behold me!

At length, I grew so pale and emaciated, from want of rest, and continual brooding over my insane love and its cruel conditions, that I determined to make some effort to wean myself from it. "Come," I said, "this is at best but a fantasy. Your imagination has bestowed on Animula charms which in reality she does not possess. Seclusion from female society has produced this morbid condition of mind. Compare her with the beautiful women of your own world, and this false enchantment will vanish."

I looked over the newspapers by chance. There I beheld the advertisement of a celebrated *danseuse* who appeared nightly at Niblo's. The Signorina Caradolce had the reputation of being the

most beautiful as well as the most graceful woman in the world. I instantly dressed and went to the theatre.

The curtain drew up. The usual semicircle of fairies in white muslin were standing on the right toe around the enamelled flower-bank, of green canvas, on which the belated prince was sleeping. Suddenly a flute is heard. The fairies start. The trees open, the fairies all stand on the left toe, and the queen enters. It was the Signorina. She bounded forward amid thunders of applause, and, lighting on one foot, remained poised in air. Heavens! was this the great enchantress that had drawn monarchs at her chariot-wheels? Those heavy muscular limbs, those thick ankles, those cavernous eyes, that stereotyped smile, those crudely painted cheeks! Where were the vermeil blooms, the liquid expressive eyes, the harmonious limbs of Animula?

The Signorina danced. What gross, discordant movements! The play of her limbs was all false and artificial. Her bounds were painful athletic efforts; her poses were angular and distressed the eye. I could bear it no longer; with an exclamation of disgust that drew every eye upon me, I rose from my seat in the very middle of the Signorina's *pas-de-fascination,* and abruptly quitted the house.

I hastened home to feast my eyes once more on the lovely form of my sylph. I felt that henceforth to combat this passion would be impossible. I applied my eye to the lens. Animula was there,—but what could have happened? Some terrible change seemed to have taken place during my absence. Some secret grief seemed to cloud the lovely features of her I gazed upon. Her face had grown thin and haggard; her limbs trailed heavily; the wondrous lustre of her golden hair had faded. She was ill!—ill, and I could not assist her! I believe at that moment I would have gladly forfeited all claims to my human birthright, if I could only have been dwarfed to the size of an animalcule, and permitted to console her from whom fate had forever divided me.

I racked my brain for the solution of this mystery. What was it that afflicted the sylph? She seemed to suffer intense pain. Her features contracted, and she even writhed, as if with some internal agony. The wondrous forests appeared also to have lost half their beauty. Their hues were dim and in some places faded away altogether. I watched Animula for hours with a breaking heart, and she seemed absolutely to wither away under my very eye. Suddenly I remembered that I had not looked at the water-drop for several

days. In fact, I hated to see it; for it reminded me of the natural
barrier between Animula and myself. I hurriedly looked down on
the stage of the microscope. The slide was still there,—but, great
heavens! the water-drop had vanished! The awful truth burst upon
me; it had evaporated, until it had become so minute as to be invisible to the naked eye; I had been gazing on its last atom, the one
that contained Animula,—and she was dying!

I rushed again to the front of the lens, and looked through. Alas!
the last agony had seized her. The rainbow-hued forests had all
melted away, and Animula lay struggling feebly in what seemed to
be a spot of dim light. Ah! the sight was horrible: the limbs once so
round and lovely shrivelling up into nothings; the eyes—those eyes
that shone like heaven—being quenched into black dust; the lustrous golden hair now lank and discolored. The last throe came. I
beheld that final struggle of the blackening form—and I fainted.

When I awoke out of a trance of many hours, I found myself
lying amid the wreck of my instrument, myself as shattered in mind
and body as it. I crawled feebly to my bed, from which I did not rise
for months.

They say now that I am mad; but they are mistaken. I am poor,
for I have neither the heart nor the will to work; all my money is
spent, and I live on charity. Young men's associations that love a
joke invite me to lecture on Optics before them, for which they pay
me, and laugh at me while I lecture. "Linley, the mad microscopist," is the name I go by. I suppose that I talk incoherently
while I lecture. Who could talk sense when his brain is haunted by
such ghastly memories, while ever and anon among the shapes of
death I behold the radiant form of my lost Animula!

Facts Concerning the Late Arthur Jermyn and His Family

H. P. Lovecraft

I

Life is a hideous thing, and from the background behind what we know of it peer daemoniacal hints of truth which make it sometimes a thousandfold more hideous. Science, already oppressive with its shocking revelations, will perhaps be the ultimate exterminator of our human species—if separate species we be—for its reserve of unguessed horrors could never be borne by mortal brains if loosed upon the world. If we knew what we are, we should do as Sir Arthur Jermyn did; and Arthur Jermyn soaked himself in oil and set fire to his clothing one night. No one placed the charred fragments in an urn or set a memorial to him who had been; for certain papers and a certain boxed *object* were found, which made men wish to forget. Some who knew him do not admit that he ever existed.

Arthur Jermyn went out on the moor and burned himself after seeing the boxed *object* which had come from Africa. It was this *object*, and not his peculiar personal appearance, which made him end his life. Many would have disliked to live if possessed of the peculiar features of Arthur Jermyn, but he had been a poet and scholar and had not minded. Learning was in his blood, for his great-grandfather, Sir Robert Jermyn, Bt., had been an anthropologist of note, whilst his great-great-great-grandfather, Sir Wade Jermyn, was one of the earliest explorers of the Congo region, and had written eruditely of its tribes, animals, and supposed antiquities. Indeed, old Sir Wade had possessed an intellectual zeal amounting almost to a mania; his bizarre conjectures on a prehistoric white Congolese civilisation earning him much ridicule when his book, *Observations on the Several Parts of Africa,* was published. In 1765 this fearless explorer had been placed in a madhouse at Huntingdon.

Madness was in all the Jermyns, and people were glad there were not many of them. The line put forth no branches, and Arthur was the last of it. If he had not been, one cannot say what he would have done when the *object* came. The Jermyns never seemed to look quite right—something was amiss, though Arthur was the worst, and the old family portraits in Jermyn House shewed fine faces enough before Sir Wade's time. Certainly, the madness began with Sir Wade, whose wild stories of Africa were at once the delight and terror of his few friends. It shewed in his collection of trophies and specimens, which were not such as a normal man would accumulate and preserve, and appeared strikingly in the Oriental seclusion in which he kept his wife. The latter, he had said, was the daughter of a Portuguese trader whom he had met in Africa; and did not like English ways. She, with an infant son born in Africa, had accompanied him back from the second and longest of his trips, and had gone with him on the third and last, never returning. No one had ever seen her closely, not even the servants; for her disposition had been violent and singular. During her brief stay at Jermyn House she occupied a remote wing, and was waited on by her husband alone. Sir Wade was, indeed, most peculiar in his solicitude for his family; for when he returned to Africa he would permit no one to care for his young son save a loathsome black woman from Guinea. Upon coming back, after the death of Lady Jermyn, he himself assumed complete care of the boy.

But it was the talk of Sir Wade, especially when in his cups, which chiefly led his friends to deem him mad. In a rational age like the eighteenth century it was unwise for a man of learning to talk about wild sights and strange scenes under a Congo moon; of the gigantic walls and pillars of a forgotten city, crumbling and vine-grown, and of damp, silent, stone steps leading interminably down into the darkness of abysmal treasure-vaults and inconceivable catacombs. Especially was it unwise to rave of the living things that might haunt such a place; of creatures half of the jungle and half of the impiously aged city—fabulous creatures which even a Pliny might describe with scepticism; things might have sprung up after the great apes had overrun the dying city with the walls and the pillars, the vaults and the weird carvings. Yet after he came home for the last time Sir Wade would speak of such matters with a shudderingly uncanny zest, mostly after his third glass at the Knight's Head; boasting of what he had found in the jungle and of how he had dwelt among terrible ruins known only to him. And finally he had spoken of the living things in such a manner that he was taken to the madhouse. He had shewn little regret when shut into the barred room at Huntingdon, for his mind moved curiously. Ever since his son had commenced to grow out of infancy he had liked his home less and less, till at last he had seemed to dread it. The Knight's Head had been his headquarters, and when he was confined he expressed some vague gratitude as if for protection. Three years later he died.

Wade Jermyn's son Philip was a highly peculiar person. Despite a strong physical resemblance to his father, his appearance and conduct were in many particulars so coarse that he was universally shunned. Though he did not inherit the madness which was feared by some, he was densely stupid and given to brief periods of uncontrollable violence. In frame he was small, but intensely powerful, and was of incredible agility. Twelve years after succeeding to his title he married the daughter of his gamekeeper, a person said to be of gypsy extraction, but before his son was born joined the navy as a common sailor, completing the general disgust which his habits and mesalliance had begun. After the close of the American war he was heard of as a sailor on a merchantman in the African trade, having a kind of reputation for feats of strength and climbing, but finally disappearing one night as his ship lay off the Congo coast.

In the son of Sir Philip Jermyn the now accepted family peculiarity took a strange and fatal turn. Tall and fairly handsome, with a sort of weird Eastern grace despite certain slight oddities of proportion, Robert Jermyn began life as a scholar and investigator. It was he who first studied scientifically the vast collection of relics which his mad grandfather had brought from Africa, and who made the family name as celebrated in ethnology as in exploration. In 1815 Sir Robert married a daughter of the seventh Viscount Brightholme and was subsequently blessed with three children, the eldest and youngest of whom were never publicly seen on account of deformities in mind and body. Saddened by these family misfortunes, the scientist sought relief in work, and made two long expeditions in the interior of

Africa. In 1849 his second son, Nevil, a singularly repellent person who seemed to combine the surliness of Philip Jermyn with the hauteur of the Brightholmes, ran away with a vulgar dancer, but was pardoned upon his return in the following year. He came back to Jermyn House a widower with an infant son, Alfred, who was one day to be the father of Arthur Jermyn.

Friends said that it was this series of griefs which unhinged the mind of Sir Robert Jermyn, yet it was probably merely a bit of African folklore which caused the disaster. The elderly scholar had been collecting legends of the Onga tribes near the field of his grandfather's and his own explorations, hoping in some way to account for Sir Wade's wild tales of a lost city peopled by strange hybrid creatures. A certain consistency in the strange papers of his ancestor suggested that the madman's imagination might have been stimulated by native myths. On October 19, 1852, the explorer Samuel Seaton called at Jermyn House with a manuscript of notes collected among the Ongas, believing that certain legends of a grey city of white apes ruled by a white god might prove valuable to the ethnologist. In his conversation he probably supplied many additional details; the nature of which will never be known, since a hideous series of tragedies suddenly burst into being. When Sir Robert Jermyn emerged from his library he left behind the strangled corpse of the explorer, and before he could be restrained, had put an end to all three of his children; the two who were never seen, and the son who had run away. Nevil Jermyn died in the successful defence of his own two-year-old son, who had apparently been included in the old man's madly murderous scheme. Sir Robert himself, after repeated attempts at suicide and a stubborn refusal to utter any articulate sound, died of apoplexy in the second year of his confinement.

Sir Alfred Jermyn was a baronet before his fourth birthday, but his tastes never matched his title. At twenty he had joined a band of music-hall performers, and at thirty-six had deserted his wife and child to travel with an itinerant American circus. His end was very revolting. Among the animals in the exhibition with which he travelled was a huge bull gorilla of lighter colour than the average; a surprisingly tractable beast of much popularity with the performers. With this gorilla Alfred Jermyn was singularly fascinated, and on many occasions the two would eye each other for long periods through the intervening bars. Eventually Jermyn asked and obtained permission to train the animal, astonishing audiences and fellow-performers alike with his success. One morning in Chicago, as the gorilla and Alfred Jermyn were rehearsing an exceedingly clever boxing match, the former delivered a blow of more than usual force, hurting both the body and the dignity of the amateur trainer. Of what followed, members of "The Greatest Show on Earth" do not like to speak. They did not expect to hear Sir Alfred Jermyn emit a shrill, inhuman scream, or to see him seize his clumsy antagonist with both hands, dash it to the floor of the cage, and bite fiendishly at its hairy throat. The gorilla was off its guard, but not for long, and before anything could be done by the regular trainer the body which had belonged to a baronet was past recognition.

II

Arthur Jermyn was the son of Sir Alfred Jermyn and a music-hall singer of unknown origin. When the husband and father deserted his family, the mother took the child to Jermyn House, where there was none left to object to her presence. She was not without notions of what a nobleman's dignity should be, and saw to it that her son received the best education which limited money could provide. The family resources were now sadly slender, and Jermyn House had fallen into woeful disrepair, but young Arthur loved the old edifice and all its contents. He was not like any other Jermyn who had ever lived, for he was a poet and a dreamer. Some of the neighbouring families who had heard tales of old Sir Wade Jermyn's unseen Portuguese wife declared that her Latin blood must be shewing itself; but most persons merely sneered at his sensitiveness to beauty, attributing it to his music-hall mother, who was socially unrecognised. The poetic delicacy of Arthur Jermyn was the more remarkable because of his uncouth personal appearance. Most of the Jermyns had possessed a subtly odd and repellent cast, but Arthur's case was very striking. It is hard to say just what he resembled, but his expression, his facial angle, and the length of his arms gave a thrill of repulsion to those who met him for the first time.

It was the mind and character of Arthur Jermyn which atoned for his aspect. Gifted and learned, he took highest honours at Oxford and seemed likely to redeem the intellectual fame of his family. Though of poetic rather than scientific temperament, he planned to continue the work of his forefathers in African ethnology and antiquities, utilising the truly wonderful though strange collection of Sir Wade. With his fanciful mind he thought often of the prehistoric civilisation in which the mad explorer had so implicitly believed, and would weave tale after tale about the silent jungle city mentioned in the latter's wilder notes and paragraphs. For the nebulous utterances concerning a nameless, unsuspected race of jungle hybrids he had a peculiar feeling of mingled terror and attraction; speculating on the possible basis of such a fancy, and seeking to obtain light among the more recent data gleaned by his great-grandfather and Samuel Seaton amongst the Ongas.

In 1911, after the death of his mother, Sir Arthur Jermyn determined to pursue his investigations to the utmost extent. Selling a portion of his estate to obtain the requisite money, he outfitted an expedition and sailed for the Congo. Arranging with the Belgian authorities for a party of guides, he spent a year in the Onga and Kaliri country, finding data beyond the highest of his expectations. Among the Kaliris was an aged chief called Mwanu, who possessed not only a highly retentive memory, but a singular degree of intelligence and interest in old legends. This ancient confirmed every tale which Jermyn had heard, adding his own account of the stone city and the white apes as it had been told to him.

According to Mwanu, the grey city and the hybrid creatures were no more, having been annihilated by the warlike N'bangus many years ago. This tribe, after destroying most of the edifices and killing the live beings, had carried off the stuffed goddess which had been the object of their quest; the white ape-goddess which the strange beings worshipped, and which was held by Congo tradition to be the form of one who had reigned as a princess among those beings. Just what the white ape-like creatures could have been, Mwanu had no idea, but he thought they were the builders of the ruined city. Jermyn could form no conjecture, but by close questioning obtained a very picturesque legend of the stuffed goddess.

The ape-princess, it was said, became the consort of a great white god who had come out of the West. For a long time they had reigned over the city together, but when they had a son all three went away. Later the god and the princess had returned, and upon the death of the princess her divine husband had mummified the body and enshrined it in a vast house of stone, where it was worshipped. Then he had departed alone. The legend here seemed to present three variants. According to one story nothing further happened save that the stuffed goddess became a symbol of supremacy for whatever tribe might possess it. It was for this reason that the N'bangus carried it off. A second story told of the god's return and death at the feet of his enshrined wife. A third told of the return of the son, grown to manhood—or apehood or godhood, as the case might be—yet unconscious of his identity. Surely the imaginative blacks had made the most of whatever events might lie behind the extravagant legendry.

Of the reality of the jungle city described by old Sir Wade, Arthur Jermyn had no further doubt; and was hardly astonished when early in 1912 he came upon what was left of it. Its size must have been exaggerated, yet the stones lying about proved that it was no mere negro village. Unfortunately no carvings could be found, and the small size of the expedition prevented operations toward clearing the one visible passageway that seemed to lead down into the system of vaults which Sir Wade had mentioned. The white apes and the stuffed goddess were discussed with all the native chiefs of the region, but it remained for a European to improve on the data offered by old Mwanu. M. Verhaeren, Belgian agent at a trading-post on the Congo, believed that he could not only locate but obtain the stuffed goddess, of which he had vaguely heard; since the once mighty N'bangus were now the submissive servants of King Albert's government, and with but little persuasion could be induced to part with the gruesome deity they had carried off. When Jermyn sailed for England, therefore, it was with the exultant probability that he would within a few months receive a priceless ethnological relic confirming the wildest of his great-great-great-grandfather's narratives—that is, the wildest which he had ever heard. Countrymen near Jermyn House had perhaps heard wilder tales handed down from ancestors who had listened to Sir Wade around the tables of the Knight's Head.

Arthur Jermyn waited very patiently for the expected box from M. Verhaeren, meanwhile studying with increased diligence the manuscripts left by his mad ancestor. He began to feel closely akin to Sir Wade, and to seek relics of the latter's personal life in England as well as of his African exploits. Oral accounts of the mysterious and secluded wife had been numerous, but no tangible relic of her stay at Jermyn House remained. Jermyn wondered what circumstance had prompted or permitted such an effacement, and decided that the husband's insanity was the prime cause. His great-great-great-grandmother, he recalled, was said to have been the daughter of a Portuguese trader in Africa. No doubt her practical heritage and superficial knowledge of the Dark Continent had caused her to flout Sir Wade's talk of the interior, a thing which such a man would not be likely to forgive. She had died in Africa, perhaps dragged thither by a husband determined to prove what he had told. But as Jermyn indulged in these reflections he could not but smile at their futility, a century and a half after the death of both of his strange progenitors.

In June 1913, a letter arrived from M. Verhaeren, telling of the finding of the stuffed goddess. It was, the Belgian averred, a most extraordinary object; an object quite beyond the power of a layman to classify. Whether it was human or simian only a scientist could determine, and the process of determination would be greatly hampered by its imperfect condition. Time and the Congo climate are not kind to mummies; especially when their preparation is as amateurish as seemed to be the case here. Around the creature's neck had been found a golden chain bearing an empty locket on which were armorial designs; no doubt some hapless traveller's keepsake, taken by the N'bangus and hung upon the goddess as a charm. In commenting on the contour of the mummy's face, M. Verhaeren suggested a whimsical comparison; or rather, expressed a humorous wonder just how it would strike his correspondent, but was too much interested scientifically to waste many words in levity. The stuffed goddess, he wrote, would arrive duly packed about a month after receipt of the letter.

The boxed object was delivered at Jermyn House on the afternoon of August 3, 1913, being conveyed immediately to the large chamber which housed the collection of African specimens as arranged by Sir Robert and Arthur. What ensued can best be gathered from the tales of servants and from things and papers later examined. Of the various tales that of aged Soames, the family butler, is most ample and coherent. According to this trustworthy man, Sir Arthur Jermyn dismissed everyone from the room before opening the box, though the instant sound of hammer and chisel shewed that he did not delay the operation. Nothing was heard for some time; just how long Soames cannot exactly estimate; but it was certainly less than a quarter of an hour later that the horrible scream, undoubtedly in Jermyn's voice, was heard. Immediately afterward

Jermyn emerged from the room, rushing frantically toward the front of the house as if pursued by some hideous enemy. The expression on his face, a face ghastly enough in repose, was beyond description. When near the front door he seemed to think of something, and turned back in his flight, finally disappearing down the stairs to the cellar. The servants were utterly dumbfounded, and watched at the head of the stairs, but their master did not return. A smell of oil was all that came up from the regions below. After dark a rattling was heard at the door leading from the cellar into the courtyard; and a stable-boy saw Arthur Jermyn, glistening from head to foot with oil and redolent of that fluid, steal furtively out and vanish on the black moor surrounding the house. Then, in an exaltation of supreme horror, everyone saw the end. A spark appeared on the moor, a flame arose, and a pillar of human fire reached to the heavens. The house of Jermyn no longer existed.

The reason why Arthur Jermyn's charred fragments were not collected and buried lies in what was found afterward, principally the thing in the box. The stuffed goddess was a nauseous sight, withered and eaten away, but it was clearly a mummified white ape of some unknown species, less hair than any recorded variety, and infinitely nearer mankind—quite shockingly so. Detailed description would be rather unpleasant, but two salient particulars must be told, for they fit in revoltingly with certain notes of Sir Wade Jermyn's African expeditions and with the Congolese legends of the white god and the ape-princess. The two particulars in question are these: the arms on the golden locket about the creature's neck were the Jermyn arms, and the jocose suggestion of M. Verhaeren about a certain resemblance as connected with the shrivelled face applied with vivid, ghastly, and unnatural horror to none other than the sensitive Arthur Jermyn, great-great-great-grandson of Sir Wade Jermyn and an unknown wife. Members of the Royal Anthropological Institute burned the thing and threw the locket into a well, and some of them do not admit that Arthur Jermyn ever existed.

Bibliography

Barlow, R. H. "A Dim-Remembered Story." *Californian* 4, No. 1 (Summer 1936): 72–87. Reprint, West Warwick, RI: Necronomicon Press, 1982.

Bierce, Ambrose. "My Favorite Murder." In Bierce's *Can Such Things Be?* (New York: Cassell, 1893).

Blackwood, Algernon. "The Man Whom the Trees Loved." *London Magazine* 28 (March 1912): 97–128. In Blackwood's *Pan's Garden: A Volume of Nature Stories* (London: Macmillan, 1912).

Cram, Ralph Adams. "The Dead Valley." In Cram's *Black Spirits and White* (Chicago: Stone & Kimball, 1895; reprint, West Warwick, RI: Necronomicon Press, 1993).

Crawford, F. Marion. "The King's Messenger." *Cosmopolitan* 44, No. 1 (November 1907): 89–93.

Dunsany, Lord. "The Unhappy Body." *Saturday Review* (London) No. 2843 (23 April 1910): 527–28. In Dunsany's *A Dreamer's Tales* (London: George Allen & Sons, 1910).

Hodgson, William Hope. "The Voice in the Night." *Blue Book Magazine* 6, No. 1 (November 1907): 136–42. In Hodgson's *Men of the Deep Waters* (London: Eveleigh Nash, 1914).

Long, Frank Belknap. "The Eye Above the Mantel." *United Amateur* 20, No. 4 (March 1921): 53–56. In Long's *The Eye Above the Mantel & Other Stories* (West Hills, CA: Tsathoggua Press, 1995).

Lovecraft, H. P. "Facts Concerning the Late Arthur Jermyn and His Family." *Wolverine* No. 9 (March 1921): 3–11; No. 10 (June 1921): 6–11. In Lovecraft's *Dagon and Other Macabre Tales* (Sauk City, WI: Arkham House, rev. ed., 1986).

Machen, Arthur. "The Inmost Light." In Machen's *The Great God Pan and The Inmost Light* (London: John Lane; Boston: Roberts Brothers, 1894).

Macleod, Fiona [pseud. of William Sharp]. "The Sin-Eater." In
    Macleod's *The Sin-Eater and Other Tales and Episodes*
    (Chicago: Stone & Kimball, 1895).

Morrow, W. C. "His Unconquerable Enemy." *Argonaut* (San
    Francisco), 11 March 1889. In Morrow's *The Ape, the Idiot and
    Other People* (Philadelphia: Lippincott, 1897).

O'Brien, Fitz-James. "The Diamond Lens." *Atlantic Monthly* 1,
    No. 3 (January 1858): 354–67. In O'Brien's *Poems and Stories*
    (New York: Scribner's, 1881).

Shiel, M. P. "Xélucha." In Shiel's *The Pale Ape and Other Pulses*
    (London: T. Werner Laurie, 1911). [Earlier version in Shiel's
    Shapes in the Fire (Boston: Roberts Brothers, 1896).]

A CATALOG OF SELECTED
DOVER BOOKS
IN ALL FIELDS OF INTEREST

A CATALOG OF SELECTED DOVER
BOOKS IN ALL FIELDS OF INTEREST

CONCERNING THE SPIRITUAL IN ART, Wassily Kandinsky. Pioneering work by father of abstract art. Thoughts on color theory, nature of art. Analysis of earlier masters. 12 illustrations. 80pp. of text. 5⅜ x 8½. 23411-8 Pa. $3.95

ANIMALS: 1,419 Copyright-Free Illustrations of Mammals, Birds, Fish, Insects, etc., Jim Harter (ed.). Clear wood engravings present, in extremely lifelike poses, over 1,000 species of animals. One of the most extensive pictorial sourcebooks of its kind. Captions. Index. 284pp. 9 x 12. 23766-4 Pa. $12.95

CELTIC ART: The Methods of Construction, George Bain. Simple geometric techniques for making Celtic interlacements, spirals, Kells-type initials, animals, humans, etc. Over 500 illustrations. 160pp. 9 x 12. (USO) 22923-8 Pa. $9.95

AN ATLAS OF ANATOMY FOR ARTISTS, Fritz Schider. Most thorough reference work on art anatomy in the world. Hundreds of illustrations, including selections from works by Vesalius, Leonardo, Goya, Ingres, Michelangelo, others. 593 illustrations. 192pp. 7⅛ x 10¼. 20241-0 Pa. $9.95

CELTIC HAND STROKE-BY-STROKE (Irish Half-Uncial from "The Book of Kells"): An Arthur Baker Calligraphy Manual, Arthur Baker. Complete guide to creating each letter of the alphabet in distinctive Celtic manner. Covers hand position, strokes, pens, inks, paper, more. Illustrated. 48pp. 8¼ x 11. 24336-2 Pa. $3.95

EASY ORIGAMI, John Montroll. Charming collection of 32 projects (hat, cup, pelican, piano, swan, many more) specially designed for the novice origami hobbyist. Clearly illustrated easy-to-follow instructions insure that even beginning papercrafters will achieve successful results. 48pp. 8¼ x 11. 27298-2 Pa. $3.50

THE COMPLETE BOOK OF BIRDHOUSE CONSTRUCTION FOR WOODWORKERS, Scott D. Campbell. Detailed instructions, illustrations, tables. Also data on bird habitat and instinct patterns. Bibliography. 3 tables. 63 illustrations in 15 figures. 48pp. 5¼ x 8½. 24407-5 Pa. $2.50

BLOOMINGDALE'S ILLUSTRATED 1886 CATALOG: Fashions, Dry Goods and Housewares, Bloomingdale Brothers. Famed merchants' extremely rare catalog depicting about 1,700 products: clothing, housewares, firearms, dry goods, jewelry, more. Invaluable for dating, identifying vintage items. Also, copyright-free graphics for artists, designers. Co-published with Henry Ford Museum & Greenfield Village. 160pp. 8¼ x 11. 25780-0 Pa. $10.95

HISTORIC COSTUME IN PICTURES, Braun & Schneider. Over 1,450 costumed figures in clearly detailed engravings–from dawn of civilization to end of 19th century. Captions. Many folk costumes. 256pp. 8⅜ x 11¾. 23150-X Pa. $12.95

THE INFLUENCE OF SEA POWER UPON HISTORY, 1660–1783, A. T. Mahan. Influential classic of naval history and tactics still used as text in war colleges. First paperback edition. 4 maps. 24 battle plans. 640pp. 5⅜ x 8½. 25509-3 Pa. $12.95

THE STORY OF THE TITANIC AS TOLD BY ITS SURVIVORS, Jack Winocour (ed.). What it was really like. Panic, despair, shocking inefficiency, and a little heroism. More thrilling than any fictional account. 26 illustrations. 320pp. 5⅜ x 8½. 20610-6 Pa. $8.95

FAIRY AND FOLK TALES OF THE IRISH PEASANTRY, William Butler Yeats (ed.). Treasury of 64 tales from the twilight world of Celtic myth and legend: "The Soul Cages," "The Kildare Pooka," "King O'Toole and his Goose," many more. Introduction and Notes by W. B. Yeats. 352pp. 5⅜ x 8½. 26941-8 Pa. $8.95

BUDDHIST MAHAYANA TEXTS, E. B. Cowell and Others (eds.). Superb, accurate translations of basic documents in Mahayana Buddhism, highly important in history of religions. The Buddha-karita of Asvaghosha, Larger Sukhavativyuha, more. 448pp. 5⅜ x 8½. 25552-2 Pa. $12.95

ONE TWO THREE . . . INFINITY: Facts and Speculations of Science, George Gamow. Great physicist's fascinating, readable overview of contemporary science: number theory, relativity, fourth dimension, entropy, genes, atomic structure, much more. 128 illustrations. Index. 352pp. 5⅜ x 8½. 25664-2 Pa. $8.95

ENGINEERING IN HISTORY, Richard Shelton Kirby, et al. Broad, nontechnical survey of history's major technological advances: birth of Greek science, industrial revolution, electricity and applied science, 20th-century automation, much more. 181 illustrations. ". . . excellent . . ."–*Isis*. Bibliography. vii + 530pp. 5⅜ x 8¼. 26412-2 Pa. $14.95

DALÍ ON MODERN ART: The Cuckolds of Antiquated Modern Art, Salvador Dalí. Influential painter skewers modern art and its practitioners. Outrageous evaluations of Picasso, Cézanne, Turner, more. 15 renderings of paintings discussed. 44 calligraphic decorations by Dalí. 96pp. 5⅜ x 8½. (USO) 29220-7 Pa. $4.95

ANTIQUE PLAYING CARDS: A Pictorial History, Henry René D'Allemagne. Over 900 elaborate, decorative images from rare playing cards (14th–20th centuries): Bacchus, death, dancing dogs, hunting scenes, royal coats of arms, players cheating, much more. 96pp. 9¼ x 12¼. 29265-7 Pa. $11.95

MAKING FURNITURE MASTERPIECES: 30 Projects with Measured Drawings, Franklin H. Gottshall. Step-by-step instructions, illustrations for constructing handsome, useful pieces, among them a Sheraton desk, Chippendale chair, Spanish desk, Queen Anne table and a William and Mary dressing mirror. 224pp. 8⅛ x 11¼. 29338-6 Pa. $13.95

THE FOSSIL BOOK: A Record of Prehistoric Life, Patricia V. Rich et al. Profusely illustrated definitive guide covers everything from single-celled organisms and dinosaurs to birds and mammals and the interplay between climate and man. Over 1,500 illustrations. 760pp. 7½ x 10⅛. 29371-8 Pa. $29.95

Prices subject to change without notice.

Available at your book dealer or write for free catalog to Dept. GI, Dover Publications, Inc., 31 East 2nd St., Mineola, N.Y. 11501. Dover publishes more than 500 books each year on science, elementary and advanced mathematics, biology, music, art, literary history, social sciences and other areas.